The Collected Supernatural and Weird Fiction of Sir Andrew Caldecott

The Collected Supernatural and Weird Fiction of Sir Andrew Caldecott

Twenty-Five Short Stories of the Strange and Unusual Including 'A Room in a Rectory,' 'The Pump in Thorp's Spinney,' 'Decastroland,' 'An Exchange of Notes,' 'What's in a Name?,' and 'Tall Tales but True'

Sir Andrew Caldecott

LEONAUR

The Collected
Supernatural and Weird
Fiction of
Sir Andrew Caldecott
Twenty-Five Short Stories of the Strange and Unusual Including 'A Room in a
Rectory,' 'The Pump in Thorp's Spinney,' 'Decastroland,' 'An Exchange of Notes,'
'What's in a Name?,' and 'Tall Tales but True'
by Sir Andrew Caldecott

First published under the titles
Not Exactly Ghosts
and
Fires Burn Blue

Leonaur is an imprint of Oakpast Ltd

Copyright in this form © 2025 Oakpast Ltd

ISBN: 978-1-917666-06-0 (hardcover)
ISBN: 978-1-917666-07-7 (softcover)

http://www.leonaur.com

Publisher's Notes

Contents

A Room in a Rectory

1

Narrow in bounds, but wide in variety, the garden of Tilchington Rectory was one of the most beautiful in the South Country. It lay in a hollow, some four to five chains broad, down the middle of which ran a small and clear brook marked on the ordnance map as R. Tilch, but beloved of its riparians as, simply, our stream. For half of its course through the rectory grounds the little river was impounded by successive dams to form three pools. The two upper of these provided easy watering for vegetables, while the third—into which a waterfall splashed between two clumps of bamboo under overhanging fronds of *Osmunda* fern—was the central and distinctive feature of the flower garden.

On either side were sloping lawns and to the north of it stood the rectory house, mainly in the Georgian architecture, but partly Victorianised by plate-glass windows. From the third pool, the stream cascaded down through a rock garden to the level of its natural bed, along which it dimpled and chattered by the side of the gravelled carriage drive, past rose-garden and orchard, until it slipped away from the rectory precincts, over a stone sill set in a small arch beneath the boundary wall. All this description has to be in the past tense, because the Ecclesiastical Commissioners have since sold both parsonage and glebe, and, for all that the writer knows, the fell hand of the improver may have fallen upon house, garden and rivulet.

That future rectors of Tilchington would need to live in humbler and less lovely environment never entered the mind of the present incumbent as, on the 17th June, 1900, from a deckchair on the further lawn, he gazed across ornamental water and flower beds towards a small shrubbery at the eastern end of the house where he had just finished clipping some too exuberant Portugal laurels.

He now surveyed the result of his labour with something of that satisfaction which the author of Genesis ascribes to the Creator, who, looking upon his creation, saw that it was good. The Reverend Nigel Tylethorpe was, and appeared, a fortunate and happy young man of thirty or so: happy in his ancestry, in his inheritance from a lately deceased great-uncle of a comfortable financial competency, in education, in mental endowment, in physical looks, in athletic prowess and (for the living of Tilchington was worth over eight hundred a year) in early ecclesiastical preferment. Nor was his parish less fortunate in him than he in Tilchington. Mr Bugles, sexton and verger, had given words to general opinion when he remarked to the People's Warden at the flower show that 't'new parson be the sort of man as'll do us good without us noticing.'

From the shrubbery the Reverend Nigel's eyes passed, with a foreboding of more clipping to be done on the morrow, to the climbers on the house itself. Of these there was a profuse variety: a japonica, wistaria, jasmine, roses and two kinds of ampelopsis. An intrusion into their midst, which he did not admire, was a rectangular patch of thickly-set ivy, which rather ostentatiously concealed a shuttered window on the ground floor. A slight frown flitted across the young man's face, and the pruning shears chattered impatiently in his hand as scissors do in a barber's. He would undoubtedly need to have a final battle with his housekeeper over that silly business of the disused room. Miss Roberta Pristin had served his predecessor for more years than the delicate conventions governing a woman's age would allow her to admit. At his death she had, with persuasive humour, asked Mr Tylethorpe to take her over with the rest of the rectory fixtures. Except for this one matter of the locked room, he did not regret having done so. A bachelor requires *quasi*-maternal attention, and Miss Pristin was *quasi*-maternal without being unduly familiar.

The young rector's thoughts were temporarily diverted from this matter of the empty room by the quarter chime of a clock in his dining-room, the french windows of which lay wide open. In another fifteen minutes, at half-past six, he would read the evening office in the chancel of his church, and so he must have a quick wash and brush up after his gardening. The next we see of him, therefore, is five minutes later as he passes across the narrow paddock separating rectory from churchyard. Mention may be found in more than one architectural handbook of the treasures and oddities of St Botolph's, Tilchington: the twelfth-century frescoes, the long tunnel-like hagioscope, the Early English colonnade set on Norman piers and capitals, the narrow

8

chancel arch with remains of screen and rood, *etcetera*.

Nineteenth-century restoration had been unusually discriminative and restrained; so much so that the west end of the building had been left just as it emerged from the demolition of a large and ugly gallery. To regulate the light at the turn of the staircase, now no more, to this gallery a narrow lancet window in the western wall of the south aisle had been walled up and replaced at a higher level by a wood-framed, square-paned window of domestic pattern. The retention by the restorers of a sacred edifice of so secular a feature may have been due to the fact that the glass, though not stained, had received superficial pigmentation and bore a spirited, if unusual, representation of St Michael vanquishing the Prince of Evil.

Mr Tylethorpe resented the survival of a window so completely out of period with the rest of the church and, having read the office and re-hung his surplice in the vestry, he walked down the south aisle with intent to visualise what would be the effect of walling it up and re-opening the lancet window, should the necessary money and faculty be forthcoming. From such general observation, he proceeded to particular examination of the offending feature. There were nine panes, each one foot square, in a main frame of three by three; and the artist had had to dispose his figures accordingly.

The top middle pane displayed the haloed head of Michael; the one below it his body; and the nethermost his feet planted firmly upon the prostrate form of Satan, whose proud and rather beautiful head projected from a scaly saurian body. By comparison the visage of the victorious archangel seemed commonplace and slightly bovine. The remaining panes on either side of the central three were taken up with Michael's wings above and with flames emanating from his trampled adversary below. In the two bottom corners, right and left, small oblong frames bore the legends '*Anno 1798*' and '*Rev. xii. 7*' respectively.

As Mr Tylethorpe glanced at these inscriptions a sudden bright beam from the westering sun flashed through the oblongs and disclosed to his view some very faint writing which a moment before had been invisible. The characters under '*Anno 1798*' looked like '*Nicolas Phayne Pinxit*', and those under the biblical citation as '*Ye Triumph of Authoritie over Intelligence*'. It took the rector but a moment to realise that they had been imprinted by a die or stamp held upside down; unless, indeed, the writing was intentionally antipodean.

'So, it really was him,' muttered the rector ungrammatically as, standing before the carved list of former incumbents on a panel in the porch, he picked out the name of Nicolas Fayne, 1796-1801. From the porch to a tiny triangle of ground between a large yew tree, the south wall of the graveyard and the swing-gate at its south-west corner took but a minute of his homeward walk. Here again on a flat, heavy, horizontal tomb-slab level with the surrounding grass stood out the name of Nicholas Phaine ('Why couldn't he stick to one spelling?' grumbled the rector); and, beneath it, the words: 'Found Dead January 27th *MDCCCI.*'

So, village tradition had been proved right about that window. Perhaps it might not be far wrong on one or two other points? The triumph of authority over intelligence, indeed! No wonder the inscription was all topsy-turvy: just as well that it had become illegible. Mental derangement was, of course, the most charitable, as it was the most rational, explanation.

The boom of his dinner gong reverberating across the paddock recalled the rector from speculative reconstuctions of parochial history to a pleasantly certain anticipation of the imminent repast. He had a good cook and a good cellar.

2

In conversation with his housekeeper after breakfast next morning Mr Tylethorpe declared an immediate intention to inspect the vacant room. Remembering previous parleys on this subject he felt some surprise that she expressed neither remonstrance nor apprehension.

'Very well, sir; and, of course, you'll need the key. I always keep it in this drawer; yes, here it be.'

On his way down the passage, he examined the wooden tab by which she had handed it to him. On it was neatly cut in capital letters::

SERMON CHAMBER
RE-OPENED 1858

. . . and underneath in his predecessor, Mr Hempstede's, handwriting appeared in faded ink the injunction: 'Keep Locked'. The key turned readily in the keyhole; for, so long as Miss Pristin had been in charge, the room had been subject to a weekly sweeping. 'An empty place'll always get dirt from somewhere,' she used to say; 'what with rats and all.' With no inlet or outlet for ventilation other than the chimney, the rector had expected the chamber to smell fusty and musty: he was relieved, therefore, to find its air not unduly oppressive, and proceeded to light the candle which he had brought with him for purposes of inspection. Only two thin streaks of daylight penetrated the shuttered and ivied window. The dimensions were commodious enough—some twenty foot square—for the library or study which he so badly required.

That all his reading and writing should be done in a dark corner of the dining-room, subject to the many interruptions inseparable from a punctual preparation and removal of meals, was fair neither to himself nor to the congregation that had to listen to discourses composed under such conditions. Carefully pacing the distance between the side walls and the central projection of fireplace and chimney in the southern wall he was gratified to find that his two glazed bookcases would exactly fit the recesses. The ceiling would require re-plastering; the walls, papering; and much of the floor, re-planking. The wainscot was rotten and must be replaced. A modern fireplace and mantelpiece were also desiderata, if he could afford them, as he thought he could. Gently locking the door behind him Mr Tylethorpe manifested his satisfaction with what he had seen by swinging the key wheel-wise by its tab and string as he returned, whistling, down the passage.

'I wonder, Miss Pristin,' he remarked as he gave it back to her, 'whether you would tell me all you know about that room. You've hinted at certain things, you know!'

'I can only tell, Sir, as I've already told; nor do I know no more. Him as was took in there, more nor a hundred year ago, is buried up by t' church yew, in that parcel of weeds as was never holied, they say. Nobody cared to bide where he were took, so they bricked up door and window and t' room had no hole to it for nigh sixty year. Then come old parson Witacre and set it open again; but for all he called it his "sermon chamber" no sermon did parson Witacre ever preach; for he had impeditations in his speech, and had to hire a guinea curate over from Frampton for to read service whenever unavoidable.

'My dear late master, 'e come next; and how long it was afore he give order to lock up t' room I don't rightly know: but locked it were what time I come to him and ever after. I mind, Sir, one of them early days asking him to let me use it for linen and what not; but "No," he says; and "Why not?" say I. "Roberta," he answers, that kind and solemn as were always his way with me, "It is wiser to learn from precept than by suffering. You leave that room alone." Them were his words; and leave it alone I ever have, and will; except, of course, for the cleaning which is next to godliness and therefore done regular. That's all I know, Sir, and make of it what you will: but he were a wise and good

11

man, were my late master; and "Leave it alone," he says, "for it be better to learn from precept than by suffering." Them were his words.'

The rector smiled upon his housekeeper with condescending benevolence: 'Thank you very much, Miss Pristin. I do not of course question for a moment Mr Hempstede's decision to keep the apartment locked and in permanent disuse. In such matters each must be governed by his or her conscience and discretion. I myself naturally mislike the idea of associating the performance of any work pertaining to my sacred office with the reputed scene of a mysterious and violent death. I have, however, analysed my distaste and discovered it to be rooted in sentiment rather than reason; and it would be clearly wrong in me to allow sentiment to acquire the appearance, if not indeed the nature, of superstition.

'I shall, therefore, take immediate steps to have the room restored and redecorated; and, although I shall certainly not allude to it by the name of sermon chamber, I intend to use it for writing my sermons and for reading. I have no doubt that your late master, if he were here with us today—and who shall say that he is not?—would appreciate my reasoning and applaud my decision. And by the way, Miss Pristin, don't forget to serve butter with the baked potatoes.'

On his way to the dining-room, the Reverend Nigel's conscience smote him for having been what he could not remember having ever been before: pompous and polysyllabic; quite eighteenth-century, in fact! Arrived at his desk he promptly penned a note to Messrs Burnidge & Hesselton, Builders and Decorators, of Minton Road, Trentchester, asking them to send a representative to advise regarding certain points of interior decoration contemplated by him at Tilchington Rectory. Within ten days the representative had come, inspected, advised, estimated, quoted, and eventually carried away in his pocket what he represented to his employers as 'quite a tidy little order'.

To the rector's keen disappointment, the repair and refurbishing of the room took no less than three months, although Burnidge & Hesselton's young man had indicated a maximum period of five weeks. There was not merely delay, but delay from unpleasant causes. Language used by the foreman plasterer, however interesting for a certain archaism and singularity, was nevertheless such as Mr Tylethorpe could not let pass without complaint. That the foreman regularly officiated as cross-bearer at the ritualistic church of St Terence, Trentchester (although pleaded in extenuation by its scandalised Vicar) seemed insufficiently explanatory of his vocabulary or of its unrestricted use in a country rectory. From this time forward there unhappily came about a distance and a coolness between Father Prodnose and Mr Tylethorpe.

The next untoward incident was the infliction of corporal chastisement by the paperhanger on his 'holiday apprentice', as he described a very youthful assistant. This in due course brought to Tilchington on investigatory visits an inspector of the Royal Society for Prevention of Cruelty to Children and a minor official' of the Paperhangers' Union. All such events wasted time; but what irritated the rector beyond endurance was Miss Pristin's attitude of obvious unconcern towards what might be going forward, or not going forward, in the room under repair.

If only she would quote his predecessor's injunction to 'leave the room alone', in reference to the present hindrances, he had his retort—and a very waspish one—ready for her. But she gave him no opening whatever for conversation in the matter, and it became annoyingly clear to him that the effect of Mr Hempstede's words on her simple but strong mind had been to place the room outside her range of thought or observation. It just did not exist for her; and Mr Tylethorpe felt as though he could have tolerated anything more easily than such total disinterest. It was perhaps well for both rector and housekeeper that, in mid-September, the former left for ten days holiday in Scotland, and did not return until the last week of that month when the room had been finished and the workmen gone.

He had left behind him a plan showing the disposition of furniture in his new study, and he was, therefore, able to ensconce himself in it on the very evening of his arrival, as soon as he had taken supper. A roaring fire of Welsh coal provided pleasant contrast to the equinoctially blusterous night without. Its reflection on ceiling, bookcases, armchairs, large writing-table, curtains and pictures suffused a general sense of cosiness and comfort. Mr Tylethorpe was specially pleased with the two pictures, the framing of which had been his last order before leaving for Scotland. They were not his own, but belonged to the church, being the largest of a series of water-colour drawings by an artist member of the Southshire Archaeological Society that had been kept rolled up in the iron chest which protected the parish registers. The one above the fireplace was a reproduction—one thirtieth the size of the original—of the Doom *fresco* above the chancel arch; while that on the opposite wall was a full-size replica of the picture painted on the square window, already described, in the south aisle.

As the firelight alternately flickered and faltered, the face of the

13

nether figure in the latter started into life and, as quickly, relapsed into a flat gloom. Its beauty in the original had not been lost in the copying, but the water-colour artist had introduced into its expression the vestige of a smile; faint, it was true, but sufficient to negative (what the subject so essentially demanded) an appearance of utter defeat and despair in the vanquished. The figure of the archangel, on the other hand, retained all the stolidity of its prototype in the window; and, from where the rector now viewed the picture, it appeared almost as though St Michael, in the repletion of victory, had allowed his eyes to close in sleep. Mr Tylethorpe felt much inclined to do likewise, for the grouse had been well hung and well-cooked and his uncle's port better than any he had drunk on holiday. 'Bother you, Mike,' he apostrophised the angel, somewhat irreverently; 'it's your beastly festival that keeps me from enjoying my armchair: but I simply must finish my Michaelmas sermon.'

Refilling his pipe, he sat down at the writing-table to the notes which he had jotted down in the train. 'Why, to be sure,' he looked again towards the figures on the wall, 'I've dealt with only one side of the picture. I must fill in the other.' For the next fifteen minutes his pen travelled over the paper rapidly and without pause: then, thrusting his notes into a drawer, he rose to have a look at his books. The older, calf-bound volumes of his uncle's collection made an odd miscellany: for instance, that set of *Annual Registers,* could there be anything still readable in them? He picked one out at random and sank sumptuously into an armchair. '*The Year's Poetick Review*' looked promising, but the laureate flatulence of Pye quickly disgusted him. Here, however, was something more crisp and terse; and, by Jove, the very thing to round off the end of his sermon!

He had read through the lines three times, admiring their relevance to the theme of his discourse, when the book slipped to the floor with a bang. What! Surely, he had not fallen asleep? No: obviously not, because he had memorised the verses perfectly and would now write them down. He resumed his seat at the table for that purpose and soon had them on paper. But did the first line of the last verse begin, 'So sleep not' or 'So be not'? He had better verify. This should have been easy enough, for he had not yet replaced the volume in the bookcase. Three times he went through '*The Poetick Review*', the third time page by page; but the verses eluded re-discovery. Never mind! He had noted them down with sufficient accuracy for a pulpit quotation, and it was now quite time for bed: no need to be meticulous.

He placed a guard against the grate, turned down the reading-lamp, and, carrying a candle, stayed at the door for a parting look at his new-found cosiness. The fire still glowed, and the room seemed loath for him to go. He quite envied the shadow cast by the fire-screen on the further armchair; it seemed so to enjoy the red leather upholstery. As a coal fell and flared, it appeared indeed to assume a momentary substantiality. 'Goodnight,' said the rector. If he had thought of it, that was the first time he had ever bidden goodnight to a shadow. But he was not thinking: long railway journeys are so dreadfully tiring.

3

Nigel Tylethorpe, though no orator, was by no means a bad preacher. This was because he took trouble to think of what he was going to say and to give his thoughts a clear and concise expression. Mr Bugles as usual was representative of majority opinion among the congregation when he remarked 'as how parson's sermons be well cooked and served up right-like, neither too warm nor too cold.' Many of his listeners however felt the peroration of his Michaelmas homily to have an unpleasant temperature: the sort of heat in fact that gives a chill. Having in the earlier stages of this discourse dilated upon the celestial ministry of angels (their service in heaven, errands upon earth, and vigil over mankind), the rector suddenly changed his tune to a minor key and gave to some of its chords a distinctly ugly modulation.

Just as all good was impersonated in the Deity, so was all evil impersonated in the Devil. Analogous to the Former's army of angels were the black cohorts of the latter. People had become accustomed to a comfortable and one-sided belief in guardian angels, but when the average man spoke of his evil genius did he realise that he was naming a companion equally constant and quite as personal? It was necessary that all should face facts; especially elemental facts. To deny or ignore the emissaries of the Evil One was to provoke their attentions. With the eye of the spirit, he felt that he could detect unbidden visitants among his congregation at that moment.

They were about to sing hymn No. 335. Why the compilers of *Hymns Ancient and Modern* had placed it among their selections 'For the Young' he did not know. Perhaps it was because the words presented only one side, of a picture whose other side Age, preferring to pretend blindness thereto itself, must logically hide from the eyes of Youth. Opportunely enough, continued the rector, he had recently come across in an old book certain verses which would serve to supplement the hymn and enable them to conceive the angelic and demonic ministries in a comparative and correct perspective. He thereupon recited the lines which he had memorised from his reading of the *Annual Register.* They ran as follows:

Around the mouth of Hell a band
Of fearful fiends for ever stand;
Their bat-like bodies tense and stark,
And on their heads the Beast's foul mark.
These, should some Holy One draw near
With store of love to give us cheer,
All-spoiling Satan with quick shout
Bids intercept and thrust him out.
On ev'ry Seraph in the sky
Keeps watch below a demon spy:
Doth angel guard thee overhead?
Two devils lurk beneath thy bed!
So, sleep not swordless, nor confide
Too much to them of Michael's side;
Lest, when the door of death is slammed,
Thou find thyself among the damned.

Mr Tylethorpe had read in novels of people undergoing the sensation of seeming to witness their own speech and behaviour from a detached and exterior angle. Such a strange psychological experience was his at this moment. In the concluding part of his sermon the feeling was unmistakable: he listened to himself with growing surprise and disapproval. He misliked the lines that he quoted and, now that the hymn was being played over, he realised with a shock that (although to appear in the *Annual Register* they must have been written more than a century ago) they sounded nevertheless like a Satanic parody of the more modern verses they were about to sing. Others perhaps felt similarly; for the choir seemed half-hearted and in the middle of the last verse the blower let all the wind out of the organ. It was altogether a dismal performance and, helping after service to count the collection in the vestry, Mr Bugles was not quite his natural self.

'Them was true words as you uttered just now, sir; and as Solomon said, there be nought nastier than truth.'

'But where did Solomon write that, Bugles?'

'I don't rightly know, sir, for I mind my grandfather's telling as how it were one of his unrecorded sayings. They were wonderful wise men, was Solomon and my grandfather.'

As he walked down the churchyard path on his way back to the rectory Mr Tylethorpe noted that such of his flock as he overtook, responded to his 'good evening' with a more than usual deference. Or was it apprehension?

The self-surprise which his Michaelmas sermon awoke in the young rector yielded before long to a growing interest in what had been its subject-matter. The fallen angels were seldom absent from his thoughts. Milton's *Paradise Lost* assumed a more goetic than poetic value for him, and he would sonorously declaim Tartarean passages from it in the pulpit.

There was only one conventicle of dissent in Tilchington, and this belonged to Mr Nehemiah Gattle, owner of a small market garden. It owned no allegiance or affiliation to any of the free churches, but had been started for the spiritual government of Mr Gattle by Mr Gattle for Mr Gattle. Nevertheless, it had attracted the more or less regular attendance of twenty or so free-lance religionists who, now that 'Hell was preached proper at the church', deserted Mr Gattle for Mr Tylethorpe.

In vain did the former expostulate that at 'The Unsectarian Mission Hall' he had always preached an honest Protestant devil, and that the rector's demons were dirty Romish impostors whom Satan would scorn to recognise. The names of Samael and Asmodai fell like magic music on the bucolic ear and, as the Reverend Nigel's library on his new pet subject increased in quantity and diversity, a growing congregation would listen open-mouthed and enraptured to the legend of Lilith and other apocryphal narrations.

A discourse on *Isaiah xxxiv,* 14, evoked an uneasy thrill; and another, upon the first six verses of Chapter ii of *Job*, was imaginative rather than exegetic. Even on Christmas Day the rector focused his remarks on the astromancy of the Magi instead of on the sublime purpose of their journey: the sorcery of Simon Magus was somehow dragged into this untimely disquisition.

It was unfortunate for Mr Tylethorpe that there was no big house in Tilchington. The admonitions of a plain-speaking squire might have pulled him up at the brink whereon he now stood. As it was, the only person of any social position in the parish besides himself was a Mr Adrian Gribden, a letter from whom to an old college friend, written in January 1901, will throw light upon our story.

17

My Dear Smith

I am so sorry you could not come for the New Year. There is little news to tell you, except that our worthy (?) incumbent intrigues me more and more. He is, believe me, surely and not slowly converting this countryside to a pseudo-mediaeval demonolatry. Those sermons I told you about in my last letter were in the nature of direct approaches to Manichaeism. Last Sunday he succeeded in being even more corruptive by prompting an undesirable reference to the Old Testament. You may remember that under a bequest of old Miss Hardham every seat in St Botolph's is provided with a copy of the Bible and Apocrypha. They are seldom opened, but there was an audible turning of leaves when Tylethorpe, preaching on the prodigal son, remarked that those of us who remembered the twenty-eighth chapter of the first book of Samuel, and especially the twenty-fourth verse, would realise that the return of the prodigal was not the only return associated in Holy Writ with a slaughter of the fatted calf.

The result of this reference was of course that every one of his listeners, from old Bugles down to the newest joined choir-boy, was quickly reading how the witch of Endor brought up the shade of Samuel from the grave. This continual harping upon the sinister and occult cannot be good for anybody and, if I mistake not, Tylethorpe himself begins to show nervous strain. For instance, he keeps turning to look behind him in an unpleasantly odd and furtive fashion and has taken to preaching not from the front of the pulpit but with his back to the wall at its side; just as though he feared that somebody might look or lean over his shoulder. This attitude so impressed me on Sunday that I found myself half expecting to see him suddenly propelled forward by some invisible and unwelcome agency! But enough of this nonsense. Do try to get down for a week-end soon. They have put on a good afternoon train leaving town at 4.23, if you cannot manage the 12.57.

Yours sincerely,

A. Gribden

The concluding sentences of this letter represent Mr Tylethorpe in transition from the first stage of his soul's malady to the second; from the active and enjoyed pursuance of a morbid interest to a passive and involuntary obsession by it. Before, however, we pass to the second phase, let us take a peep into his study towards the close of the first. He has again taken from his bookcase a volume of the *Annual Registers*, and it has again dropped from his hands during a perusal of the '*Poetick Review*'. Asleep?

No, hardly; because, as on a former occasion, he has memorised the lines he was reading. Can he find the page again? Bother it, no. Anyhow, he can jot them down from memory, and he does so. No authorship was subscribed, and he will send them tomorrow to the 'literary inquiry column' of the *Commentator* for identification. Here are the lines:

Down the chasms of the night
Flashed a comet, purple-bright,
Prone upon whose lambent tail
Clung an angel deathly pale.
All the heaven cried for shame
When was read the angel's name,
The dear sad name of Zadyra.
Fairest of all angels he
Had gazed upon the crystal sea;
Saw his image mirrored there
And cried, 'I am than God more fair!'
Which hearing, Uriel
Flung him from sky to hell.
The coward moon
Sank seaward in a swoon:
But the brave sun,
Seeing what deed was done,
Rode forth to shine on other worlds afar,
To us becoming no more than a star,
Because of what was wrought on Zadyra.
Nor was the Earth unchanged:
Great shapes arose and ranged
Along the mountain sides; but no man saw
What these forms were: for there was light no more.

Neither the literary staff of the *Commentator* nor any of its readers proved able to trace the authorship of these lines, nor even to elucidate the name Zadyra.

4

The second, some might call it the hallucinative, stage of Mr Ty-lethorpe's decline started with his suspicion, which rapidly ripened into conviction, that he was not in sole occupancy of his new study. A succession of dreams, each of which came to him while resting in one of the big armchairs, left him in no doubt as to who was sharing it. So vivid was the first dream that he would have mistaken it for reality but for two things. The first was that, though he was seated facing the fire, his view of the room was as though he were standing with his back to it. The second was that the furniture had become entirely different from that which he had so recently chosen and installed. In his dream the window was closely shuttered but not curtained, and the floor was uncarpeted.

Under the far wall was a long and deep chest, the size and shape of a church altar. On the door side of the room were two cases of shelves, the one filled with books and manuscripts and the other with what looked like laboratory equipment. At a large and untidy writing table in the bow window sat a black-habited figure, engaged apparently in limning some design on a pane of glass. Against one of the table legs leant a nine-light wooden window frame, whose shape and dimen-sions Mr Tylethorpe at once recognised as those of the window in the south aisle of St Botolph's. On the table in front of the artist was propped a looking-glass into which he appeared to keep peering, and at his side lay a sketch in charcoal of an angel. As the dreamer surveyed this scene its central figure turned slowly from the table and looked him full in the face.

The features were both beautiful and familiar. They were in fact those of Lucifer in the church window. 'So that was Phayne's self-portrait, was it?' ejaculated the rector aloud, and thereby woke himself from the dream. Thenceforward, however, he lived in two rooms in-stead of one and, in both the dream room and the real, Nicolas Phayne lived with him. He thought and thought upon this sinister predecessor of his. Had anybody ever before so identified himself with the Evil One as to impersonate him in a self-portrait? It seemed a dangerously wicked thing to have done, and still more wicked was it to have per-petuated this impersonation in the window of a consecrated building confided to his charge. These and similar reflections probably caused the dream to repeat itself; for repeat itself it did, three or four times, and except in one small particular without variation.

This one little change consisted in an appearance behind Phayne's back of visible disquiet in the air. It reminded the rector of that peculiar crinkling of a view seen through waves of intense heat. He remembered in particular having once looked up at the sky above the open flue of a brick-kiln and seeing just such a rippling or disquiet interposed between him and the clouds. The only distinction was that the focus of disquiet behind Phayne was not amorphous but took roughly the shape of a figure, though without differentiation of limbs and parts. The last time that this dream was repeated Phayne, or rather the appearance of him, seemed for the first time to be conscious of something astir behind him. At first, he made motions with his hands as though to brush away a gnat or moth, but finally he jerked round suddenly and saw. Mr Tylethorpe will never erase from his memory the horrible look that he then beheld. Surprise and fear were in it; but triumph also and never a trace of shame or remorse. After all, an offer had been made and accepted.

Mr Gribden's letter, reproduced some pages back, indicated the effect upon the rector of this new factor in his dream. He began, in fact, to look for and to expect appearances of visible disquiet in the atmosphere of his own daily environment; and very soon imagination began to usurp the place of sensory observation. Miss Pristin quickly saw that something was going seriously wrong with her young master. First there was that senseless fuss that he made over a flaw in the glass of the garden door. If one looks through such a flaw naturally there must appear whorls or twists in the view seen through it; so where was the cause for him to break the window with his walking stick?

Then came his sudden aversion to the pattern of the linoleum in the back passage. If he disliked a crinkly design, why had he himself chosen it barely five months ago? Well: she would have it rolled up and stored in the box room. Next occurred his complaints regarding the transparent shapes drawn by a night's frost on his bedroom window. Nothing could be done about those of course, except to keep the blinds drawn until they thawed out. Last and strangest whim of all, he forbade her ever again to wear on her bonnet her favourite big bow of black watered silk because (how could an educated man talk such nonsense?) 'it all went alive and crinkly when she moved.' This command Miss Pristin thought it wise to obey, but with the muttered reservation that she didn't hold with none such nasty fancies herself and hoped that somebody as she knew weren't forgetting to say his prayers regular.

'Forgetting?' Mr Tylethorpe rejoined, 'There is no forgetting for me, Miss Pristin, no forgetting at all!'

The second dream that came to the rector was not so distinct as the first; not because its verisimilitude was any the less, but because the scene presented was nocturnal and unilluminated except by a full moon shining through bare branches. At a block in front of a tree-trunk stood Nicolas Phayne with what looked like a black fowl fluttering in his left hand. With a downward sweep of his right arm there fell on the struggling animal an axe or other metal implement that glinted in the moonlight.

A moment later he appeared to be dismembering the victim, and then to be doing something to it with water and a dull fire. So Phayne had sunk to this! Mr Tylethorpe's recent readings had taught him enough of goetic ritual for him to realise that he had visionally witnessed a preparation of Admixtures for the Evil Sacrifice. He dreaded, and yet yearned with a hideous impatience, to witness its consummation. This impatience waxed to a madness when, after the fashion of its predecessor, the immediate dream repeated itself a second and a third time. Nor was this psychological state without its inevitable effect: it prevented the sleep that would enable the coming of a final dream to resolve the horrid yearning in experience.

With the onset of this insomnia the worsening of the rector's condition could no longer be hid from his parishioners. For several Sundays past he had been reduced to reading a distinguished ecclesiastical dignitary's printed sermons, and Mr Gattle's errant sheep had promptly returned to the 'unsectarian' fold. The rector's reading of the liturgy had also become lifeless and perfunctory. 'If t'poor parson,' said Mr Bugles, 'might be spoke of same as it might be one of my span'el pups, 'ud say as how he were sickening for distemper and p'raps ' get through and maybe not.' Mr Gribden took a less charitable view and gave up going to church. At this juncture, also, the rectory servants decided to give notice but, fearing to face the master in his present mood and failing to obtain the mediation of Miss Pristin, they postponed any action on their resolve.

Whether Dr Marlock was professionally correct in coming to see the rector on the summons of his housekeeper may be doubted, but that medical attention had become urgently necessary was obvious to everybody. The visit was not in itself a success, because the patient locked himself in his room and refused to see him. This, however, did not prevent Dr Marlock from leaving with Miss Pristin a small phial whose contents she undertook to pour into the after-dinner cup of coffee which Mr Tylethorpe, in spite of insomnia, still insisted on taking. It was indeed this surreptitious potion that induced sufficient sleep for the dreaming of his last dream.

Mr Tylethorpe had for some time given up trying to court sleep in his bed: having taken off his clothes and put on pyjamas and a dressing-gown he would return downstairs and settle himself down in an armchair before his study fire. The chair that he now chose was the one associated with his dreaming. On previous nights it had not been long before he was out of it again and pacing the room in an agony of sleeplessness. Tonight, however, thanks to the draught, he was sleeping soundly when Miss Pristin, who had taken upon herself a night's vigil at the doctor's request, looked in at half-past ten and again at eleven. The dream that now came to him was none the less terrible for being anticipated. The room appeared once more as in the first dream.

Phayne, robed in a black preaching gown, stood before the altar-like chest, on which stood an array of sacred vessels (pyx, flagon, paten and chalice) and by their side a box and a bottle which the dreamer recognised as those seen in his previous dream. The postures and gestures of the figure before the chest made plain that a shameful travesty of Christianity's supreme rite was being enacted. Most of the figure's manipulations were mercifully half-hidden by the sleeves of the black gown, but suddenly the head tilted back and the upturned chalice showed for an instant in a foul climax of sacrilege. For long minutes thereafter the figure continued to stand in erect rigidity, but with successive tremors suggestive of extreme emotion or, it might be, physical pain. Then all at once the knees sagged, the body lunged, and there lay on the floor a black and motionless heap. The rector started and awoke. The slight bleeding from his mouth was caused by his having bitten his lower lip.

The narration of this series of dreams will have taxed to breaking point the reader's capacity to bear with the obscene and macabre. Nevertheless, there remains, and must be told, their immediate and still worse sequel. Madmen, as distinct from mental defectives, have been said to fall into three categories: those who think senselessly from senseless premises, those who think sensibly from senseless premises and those who think senselessly from sensible premises. The man who now shuddered in his night attire on his armchair belonged to the middle category. His ratiocination was quick, clear and concise; its basis in religion, philosophy and ethics was temporarily destroyed; it was rooted only in his present terror.

He would never forget those dreams, even if they should not repeat themselves, which experience had taught him that they would. He could never rid himself of a consciousness of ghastly communion with the predecessor who had desecrated his priesthood in this room a century ago. Even if he should leave Tilchington, the spirit of Phayne, he felt certain, would accompany him, for were they not now fellow initiates in the Evil Mysteries? He could certainly no longer continue in his Ministry, and when the reason for his abandoning it became known he would be shunned by all as insane or unclean. In short, life would not be liveable; and a burden that cannot be borne must be laid down. He had heard suicides dubbed cowards by some and appraised as brave by others: but why prate of cowardice or bravery?

It was just a natural process that a man should take his life when he can no longer live it. The necessary act would be short and simple. This dressing-gown cord was both strong and smooth; there was no fear of the noose that he had just made in it not pulling tight or of its breaking. Yes: he could just reach the curtain rod across the bow window by standing on the writing table, and the other end of the dressing-gown cord was soon made fast to it. Now the table must be pushed away, and a chair substituted: for he would never manage to kick from under him a heavy table. What an ugly scrooping sound its castors made! But not loud enough, luckily, to wake the servants. Here was a chair of just the right height. There now! All was ship-shape and ready.

Miss Pristin also observed that all was ready. Attracted by the scrooping of the table she had entered noiselessly and now stood behind Mr Tylethorpe. Her next action she has never explained, for she has never told it to anybody. Neither to Mr Tylethorpe nor to herself did an explanation seem necessary. It was an effect probably of the strain under which she had mustered resolve to enter the, to her, unenterable room and of angry disgust at the scene on which she had intruded. Be this as it may, in a burst of violence and with all the strength at her command she first boxed the rector's ears and then, as he turned in his astonishment, slapped his face. Worn to extreme weakness by insomnia and mental misery the wretched man passively dissolved in a flood of tears and, powerless to resist her seizure of his left forearm, allowed himself to be meekly led by her to his bedroom.

There she locked him in and, having returned to the study, untied the dressing-gown cord from the curtain-rod and unknotted it. This was something which Dr Marlock need not see. Early next morning the physician found the patient still sleeping the sleep of exhaustion.

24

In three days' time he was strong enough to be taken by Dr Marlock and Miss Pristin in the midday train to Funtingham-on-Sea, where they left him in an efficient but not too fashionable Nursing Home.

5

Cyril Thundersley, by Divine Permission Bishop of Wintonbury, was entertaining a house-party at the palace. No misogynist, but himself unmarried, he preferred male company and was ever a little apprehensive of lady guests. His present company at breakfast was such as he thoroughly enjoyed. There was old Dean Burnfell from Penchester who, still young at eighty, had more than half a century before been a minor canon at Wintonbury and had kept up his connections with the place ever since. On the host's other side sat the Colonial Bishop of Kongea, home on leave from his tropical see. Not yet forty, he still bustled and hustled with the momentum of youth. Next to him, and the only layman of the party, was Leslie Trueson, Fellow of St Peter's, Oxbridge, who was pursuing some historical researches in the palace library. The fifth person at the table was Mr Lemmet, the Bishop of Wintonbury's chaplain. Quiet and untalkative but invariably attentive, he had been well chosen for his present position.

'Until yesterday,' remarked the Bishop of Wintonbury, 'I imagined myself to be living in the twentieth century.'

'You should never, my dear Cyril,' rejoined Dean Burnfell, 'pay too much attention to the almanacks. My life is nearing its close and it has been lived in many centuries. A man belongs to all the ages to which he is heir. I have found Plato more of a contemporary in many ways than most moderns. It is only births and deaths, not lives, that can be dated in *Time's Register*. Wordsworth, indeed, surmised that we come into the world trailing clouds of glory from an Ever Has Been. I don't know about that: but our religion assures us that we are destined for an Ever After and that we are in communion with departed saints.'

'Quite so.' Here the bishop helped himself to a second sausage. 'If it were a matter of communion with saints only, I should not have made my last remark. My reason for it was that, until faced yesterday by the fact, I would never have believed that a young priest of good family and excellent education, an athlete too, and a thoroughly manly fellow, whom I had specially selected for the best country living in the Diocesan gift, would have shamelessly taken to preaching sheer diabolism from his pulpit, and have ended by himself becoming demoniacally possessed; for such is my interpretation of the so-called breakdown

25

that has necessitated his removal to a home for neurotics. It sounds like seventeenth or at latest eighteenth century history to me!'

'Yes,' agreed Mr Trueson, 'it is certainly reminiscent of the Tilchington Trouble, as it was called, a hundred years or more ago.'

'What's that you say?'

'My dear bishop, please don't look so startled! There is a manuscript account of the matter in your library. It was a perfectly straightforward case of what you have termed diabolism and it ended in the rector's death.'

The man who has been received into a home for neurotics,' said the bishop impressively, 'is none other than the present incumbent of Tilchington: young Tylethorpe.'

'The deuce it is! Poor fellow, he may have found in his country cure something more than he bargained for. Lemmet, I wonder if you would be so good as to go across to the library, look up the index of manuscripts under T, and bring His Lordship the paper docketed "Tilchington Trouble". If I remember right, it's in one of the shelves under the oriel window.'

No one spoke until Lemmet returned. Sausages are better enjoyed and more expeditiously consumed in silence. It was not, however, more than five minutes before the manuscript had been found and produced.

'You read it to us, Trueson,' the bishop requested, 'as you are familiar with it.'

'Certainly; I'll do my best, but it's a trifle illegible in parts. The docket bears a note over the initials P.V.R. (that would have been Bishop Ranwell) that he had found his perusal of the file so unedifying and distasteful that he had destroyed all its contents except this one paper which, in his opinion, contained all that was necessary to leave on record in the matter.'

'I remember Ranwell,' interpolated the dean, 'as a kind and gentle old man. He once bought up all the Jacks-in-the-Box in a toy shop here, because as a small boy he had been frightened by one!'

'Ah! did he so?' resumed Trueson. 'That's what he may have intended to do in the present connection, if one may judge from what I shall now read to you. It is a letter dated the 3rd February, 1801, written by Archdeacon Howgall from his vicarage at Jedworth to Bishop Cumberley who, according to the panel in the Chapter House, was enthroned in 1794 and died in this palace in 1805. It was he who built the big block of stables and the extension to the palace wine cellars.

Now for the letter.

My Lord Bishop

The, I will not say lamented, death of Mr Phayne has relieved me of the pain and duty of adding to previous reports upon his malpractice and Your Lordship from the trouble and expense of processes necessary to his proposed deprivation.

In the final carriage of this matter, I have obeyed throughout Your Lordship's ordinance for the avoidance of all scandal; whereto I have been mightily assisted by the phlegm and incuriosity of the local physician, Dr Lammerton. From the fact that all three rectory servants were laid in bed with a sudden sharp colic after a meal of field puddocks picked in mistaking for mushrooms, whereof the dead man had also partaken, this learned doctor ascribed his death to none other cause and set his hand thereto in writing. The death chamber, as well as the body therein, were in fact unlooked upon until my arrival; but this not of intent or by discretion but by reason of general fear that there might be with the corpse such as were with him, as sundry assert, when alive.

On entering this room, I locked the door behind me and half-closed the shutters against the window, so that I could see sufficiently within nor be seen from without. I will not distress Your Lordship with a tale of all that I there found, but will state enough to show that the cause of our true religion hath suffered nought by this death save an extreme good riddance. That here had been, to say least, a mockery of the Sacrament was plain shewn by paten and cup set out upon a table-chest. Each of which contained a separate stuff; the ingredients whereof appeared from an open handwritten book beside them. The prescriptions were of a rank poisonous sort and were without doubt the certain cause of death.

Whether this Phayne was by law *felo de se* or no the physician has happily left us in no need to determine; and indeed, I doubt it, for the name of the evil rite in his book was such as may have had him think that damnation of soul would have fetch't him immunity of body from poisons and such like harms. This with other ten or eleven books of like blasphemy and mischief I did make a fire of in the grate, and when the whole had waxed hot and consuming did pour thereon the substances from the sacred vessels. These latter, having found them to be not those used in the church but the property of the dead man, I placed with him in the coffin. For as none in Tilchington would so much as touch the body it fell to me to compose it therein, which I did without removal of any of the habiliments wherein I had found it.

The carriage of the coffin to the churchyard was done in a garden barrow, as none would bear him on their shoulders, and the grave had been dug in a portion that was unconsecrate. None would attend the burying; but the Sexton, his two grown sons and myself did lower the coffin without breaking thereof, although it slipped from the forward ropes and fell end on. The help of these good men was on condition that I will say no prayers, nor did I so but to offer thanksgiving to Almighty God for deliverance of this parish from Satan's curse.

In regard to the points of my second and third letters, I caused the ash tree and that which was below to be hewn down and burned, as also the ivy bush and grotto. I also loosed such animals as remained. Conscience bids me dissent, but with humble deference, from Your Lordship's view that exorcisation is but a Romish vanity or superstition. Nevertheless, in obedience to Your Lordship's wishes I abstained from all motions there towards.

I have noted also Your Lordship's judgment that if only parsons would do more fox-hunting and less book-reading this See of Wintonbury would be in happier case. May I respectfully suggest that exhortations to this end would be more convincingly included in an episcopal charge than in archidiaconal admonitions?

Believe me to remain, My Lord Bishop,
Your most dutiful & obedient Servant,
T. Howgall
Archdeacon"

'So, you see, bishop,' added Mr Trueson, 'that what has been worrying you is only the latest chapter in a serial story, "The Tilchington Trouble".'

'It was a most reprehensible omission that should be remedied without delay,' said the Bishop of Kongea.

'What was?'

The omission to exorcise. We never dare run risks of that sort in Kongea. My sanctioned appendix to the *Book of Common Prayer* translated into Kongahili contains three occasional offices for the exorcisation of evil spirits. The first, relevant apparently to the rectory at Tilchington, is for their expulsion from buildings or places; the second for their ejection from infants and children; and the third for their removal from persons of riper years. All three Forms are in frequent use and of proved efficacy. We wouldn't be without them for anything. Even the *fauna* of Kongea teaches us to appreciate the Petrine warning that our adversary the Devil walketh about as a roaring lion seeking whom he may devour.'

The Bishop of Wintonbury walked to the window and for some minutes appeared wrapt in contemplation of a revolving cowl on one of his spare-room chimneys. He at length turned and addressed the Bishop of Kongea.

'You told me yesterday, Christopher, that you meant to spend a day in visiting Halmeston and Tilchington churches. I suppose from what you have just said that if you found yourself passing Tilchington rectory you would feel it a moral obligation, even in the rector's absence, to step inside and recite the office of which you have spoken?'

'I should certainly do so unless positively prevented. I have no English translation; but, as I would be alone, its recital in Kongahili would be all right.'

The Bishop of Wintonbury looked, as indeed he was, relieved. He did not wish to grant sanction as Diocesan to a ceremony that to his modern mind savoured of superstition. At the same time there were passages of scripture that could be quoted in justification of it, and many of the See's High Churchmen would certainly approve. Moreover, his personal scepticism in such matters had been severely strained that morning. He would not, therefore, expressly authorise the performance of the rite but, as his friend was minded to do it, he would not prevent it.

'Lemmet,' he said, 'I suggest you take a holiday from me tomorrow and accompany the Bishop of Kongea in the ten-thirty train to Tilchington. If you both carry sandwiches you can walk from there to Halmeston and lunch on the common. That is to say, Christopher, if weather permits. It's no use doing such expeditions in the wet.'

That night the wind rose to almost gale force and by morning had blown away the clouds and rain. The Bishop of Kongea and Mr Lemmet therefore set forth with the prospect of a bright if gusty day before them. All went according to plan for them except that Miss Pristin attended the service of exorcisation and, unable to follow the. Kongahili language, interspersed the rite at what appeared to her appropriate intervals with fervently ejaculated Amens. She had previously removed from their frames and now burnt in the kitchen fire, with full support from the Colonial Bishop, the two pictures that had hung on the walls. She also, after departure of the visitors and as her own particular contribution to a purification of the chamber, lit therein a sulphur candle of the sort used for medical disinfection.

The Bishop of Kongea was much interested in St Botolph's but one disappointment awaited him. The South aisle window, which was not protected by any wire grid on the outside, had been irreparably smashed that very morning, apparently only a few minutes before their entry into the church, by a small branch that had been snapped off one of the churchyard elms and hurled by the gale against the Western wall.

'I have always found exorcisation a very powerful rite!' the Colonial Bishop assured Mr Lemmet as they surveyed the debris.

6

A comfortable conclusion to this history would have been that Nigel Tylethorpe after a full recovery returned to Tilchington and lived there happily ever afterward. That, however, was impossible. Even if his health had permitted a return, his *amour pro pre* would have forbidden it. But in point of fact his condition, both physical and mental, remained critical for more than a year: and then, on medical advice, he sailed on a world tour which occupied a further eighteen months. He had submitted his resignation of the incumbency to the bishop within a fortnight of his first admission to the nursing home.

His successor, the Reverend Nathaniel Coltswood, brought with him to Tilchington a wife and seven children. He soon, of course, heard rumours about the room, but he made light of them. 'We have made it the nursery,' he declared, 'and if Old Nick is minded to make off with a couple or so of the brats, he's welcome to them. He can take his pick.' In actual fact there has been no unrest or discomfort associated with the apartment since his induction.

The Reverend Sir Nigel Tylethorpe, Bart (for thus he returned from his long cruise owing to the unexpected death of Sir Sylvester, his first cousin) soon settled down in the old family seat of Battlewick Hall. On Sundays he assists the Vicar of Cubley-cum-Battlewick by reading Service at the small church within his park gates. He is still unmarried, but house parties at the Hall invariably declare his establishment to be the best managed in Westshire. The name of his housekeeper is, as you may have guessed, Roberta Pristin.

Branch Line to Benceston

Although to know Adrian Frent was not necessarily to like him, he interested me from the very first. If his life contained much of the ordinary, the manner of his death was very far out of it; the biographical portion of these notes is therefore by way of preface to the mystery of his end.

I had lived at Brensham for two years before the Garden City Company showed any intention of extending Ruskin Road. So long as it remained a *cul-de-sac* the peace of my bachelor homestead would remain undisturbed, for beyond it lay only a wilderness of weed and bramble between the road's end and the Bren River. I watched therefore with misgiving a gradual clearing by the Company's roadmen of this barren strip and the construction by them of a gravel track down its centre. But I need not have worried, for a bridging of the Bren on a purely residential thoroughfare was quite beyond the Company's financial resources, and the sole purpose of the extension was to afford access to a vacant building lot on the side opposite to me and nearer to the river. On this quickly arose 'Brenside' and into it as first tenant moved Adrian Frent.

My first glimpse of him was during a reconnaissance made by me along the river bank for that very purpose. What would be the looks of a man whom I might have to live next to for long years naturally aroused my curiosity. Nor was my first impression unfavourable. I saw a man of nearly six feet, clean-shaven, oval-faced, dark-haired, well-knit and smartly tailored. Without hesitation I made up my mind to call as soon as he was comfortably settled in.

I did so some ten days later and found him very pleased to be doing host in his new house. Brenside had been wisely planned to provide one really large room, on the window side of which stood an Erard grand piano on glass castors. In front lay a large Persian rug, on whose beautiful and expensive expanse none of the surrounding leathered chairs were allowed to impinge. The pictures on the walls were all of religious subjects, though not pertaining to the same religion. They included a coloured print of the Sistine Madonna, a silver-point drawing of the Hermes of Praxiteles, a rather wishy-washy sketch in water colour of the Buddha, and an enlarged photograph of Hindu frescoes in the Ajanta Caves. There were two large bookcases, one containing books, whose titles I could not see from the chair into which Frent beckoned me, and the other largely filled by bound volumes of the *Railway Magazine*. Immediately above them was a scale model of a locomotive protected by an oblong glass frame.

This miniature engine and the magazines offended my aesthetic sensibility by their incongruity with the other furnishings, and made me curious to ascertain the nature of the books in the other case. Finding excuse in a draught from the window I soon transferred myself to a nearer seat whence my eye fell on a representative and well-bound collection of English classics, both in prose and poetry. The only exceptions were gathered on a shelf to themselves and might be categorised under the title borne by the largest of them, which was *Herbs, Simples, Drugs and Poisons.*

Frent caught my inquisitive glance. 'One of my many hobbies,' he explained. 'I grow them, you know. That's why I've chosen a place by the river. I lost a lot of valuable stuff last year at Tenford during the August drought. I'm going to make the garden here a herbalist's paradise; you must drop in occasionally and see how it's getting on. I've got my eye on the small greenhouse as a future laboratory. I not only grow the plants but I make them into medicines. I always make my own insecticides and the vermifuges for my dogs. They're in the kennel now, under treatment; come along and see them.' Leading me out by a side door he introduced me to two liver-coloured dachshunds in one of the outhouses. They were almost offensively affectionate, after the nature of their breed. 'I adore dogs,' he said. I was glad that he did not see me wince, but I hate men to use the word 'adore': it is woman's property.

Business men on their daily trek from Brensham to the City have a choice of three trains. The 8.47 runs you through to Cripplegate and is uncomfortably crowded. The 8.59 has a slightly superior *clientèle* but lands you at St Euston's Cross, midway between east and west, whence it is necessary to proceed by Underground. The 9.15, similarly bound, is patronised only by such as are in positions to determine for themselves their times of arrival and departure. It was in this third train that I met Frent next morning, and thereby placed him in the category of employer rather than of employee. Nor was my inference at fault, as I learned from his conversation on the way up. He was a partner in the firm of Frent, Frent & Saxon Limited, Music Publishers of 23 Great Penchester Street. His father, who had died last year, had left him in joint managership with Paul Saxon; whom indeed I remembered, somewhat indistinctly, as a fellow member of the Junior Camisis before its absorption by the older University Clubs.

It did not take me long, listening to Frent's talk, to realise that here was a case of a business house being very much divided against itself. To put the matter in a nutshell, Adrian was musically a severe classicist while Saxon was crazy on jazz. Each had, I gathered, in his own line brought grist to the common mill. Frent had at the unlimited expense of an aunt of the composer, who contributed also a frontispiece, published in album form Julian Grinley's 'Twelve Dream Pieces for Pianoforte'. Saxon undoubtedly struck a good bargain when he acquired publishing rights over a Jazz series which included such astonishing 'hits' as 'Gioconda' and 'Bendigo'. The pity of it was that each, while sharing in it, grudged the other his success.

Daily travelling in the same compartment Frent and I soon found ourselves on terms of acquaintance that bordered on intimacy. This was because I was glad to find him interesting and he glad to find someone whom he interested. I derived entertainment even from his knowledge of locomotives and running schedules and, acquiring the jargon of the initiate, was soon speaking of the permanent way as 'the road' and of signals being 'on' or 'off instead of up and down. His tales of railway history especially appealed to me, and (after he had pointed out the gas works siding which leaves the main line just north of Ponsden Priory as being all that now remains of an aborted London, Middlehampton and East Coast Railway) I often found my eyes straying from my evening paper, as we jerked over the junction points, towards the heavy gates that closed the siding against the main line of which it had been intended to form a most important branch. In moments of despondency the tale of this siding would appear to me as an allegory of what had happened to so many pet projects of my own scheming!

2

I forget the exact date of Frent's coming to Brenside, but it was at the beginning of March. On the 17th April poor old Miss Lurgashall of Rosedene, Hesseltine Road, was trapped in her bedroom and burned to death when the house took fire from defects in the electrical insulation. Rosedene and Brenside had been designed by the same architect and in both plans the front and back stairs occupied respectively the fore and rear of the middle section of the building. This arrangement, comparing it to a central flue, the coroner described as a death-trap. A criticism so characteristic of a Coroner's *obiter dicta* naturally passed unheeded by hundreds of people whose houses were on a similar plan: but not by Adrian Frent.

'What are you going to do about your stairs?' he asked me.

'Nothing,' I replied, 'and you?'

'I'm having a fire escape put in from the box room next to my bedroom.'

'That'll cost you something!'

'Oh! not much. All one needs is a trap-door and a length of rope. We used to have several of them at my prep. school. In case of emergency one lifts the trap, throws down the rope and swarms down it hand over hand. Cheap and easy! I'm a bit of a carpenter, as you know, and I cut the trap-door yesterday. Now all that remains to do is to get a rope.'

'You'll need a staple to fix it to,' I pointed out; 'and that means a hole through the wall and a plate.'

'Oh! I know of an odd job man who'll fix that up for me in no time and at very small charge. I strongly advise you to follow my example.'

I have recorded the above conversation for the reason (as well as for another which will appear later) that it well illustrates a basic defect in Frent's character. He was always starting things without consideration of their full implications and dropping them when he ran up against difficulties. In the present instance the example which he bade me follow was never set, for neither staple nor rope eventuated. He just forgot about them. It was the same story with his piano playing: he had excellent taste and touch, but I have seldom known him to play a piece right through. As soon as he came to a tricky passage he would break off with a 'sorry, I'm out of practice!' I suspected, however, that he had never been in practice, for he hated drudgery and all his activities lacked perseverance and system.

Take, for instance, the death of his dachshunds, the cause of which he never revealed to me. The vet., however, did. They had been poisoned by draughts out of a wrong bottle! How a man who prided himself on concocting his own insecticides and vermifuges could have been so careless passed my comprehension. Nor did the loss of these pets cause him any observable sorrow. I sometimes wondered in fact whether he did not derive a greater pleasure from the artistic little headstones that he had placed over their graves than any that the dogs ever afforded him while alive.

As these sentences flow from my pen, I am conscious that they become increasingly critical of Adrian Frent. This is not from any desire on my part to play the role of dissecting moralist, but because my portrait of the man cannot be rendered faithful or lifelike without painting in the shadows. He certainly suffered no qualms himself about personal criticisms, for his daily conversations with me became more and more charged with venom against 'the Klaxon' as he now insisted on calling his partner. His outbursts would indeed have been wearisome but for the many amusing turns of phrase and fancy with which he embellished them. Nevertheless, my conscience would sometimes accuse me of abetting slander; and by way of appeasing it I argued to myself that, by allowing Frent to blow off steam, I was preventing the accrual to his animosity of any explosive quality that might be generated by enforced repression.

As the summer wore on, we dropped in frequently at each other's houses, and I was privileged to see the burgeoning of the Herbalist's Paradise. These were his words, not mine; for a meaner collection of disreputable weeds could be hardly imagined: The only lasting memory of my inspection of it is of his telling me that what I still continue to call 'Deadly Nightshade' is neither Nightshade nor deadly. The so-called laboratory in the little greenhouse was equally unimpressive; indeed, it reminded me of nothing so much as the pitiful messes that children will make out of leaves and berries to serve as 'pretence food' in their toy dinner services. I could not but remember the sad end of those two dachshunds and found myself viewing the disarray of bottles, tins and saucers with mounting distaste. Frent perhaps discerned these thoughts. 'Come along indoors,' he said, 'and I will play you the *March Funèbre* out of that Beethoven *Sonata*.' The movement contains no really difficult passages and he did it justice. It little occurred to me that it was the last thing that I should hear him play.

3

September the fourteenth is my birthday, and I am able to set that date with certainty against the events that follow. I had lunched at his

37

club with my brother Gerald and, taking the afternoon off, made to catch the three-thirty at St Euston's Cross. I had hardly settled down in a corner seat before, to my surprise, in got Frent. I had never known him take so early a train before, and the fuss that he was in made me ask the reason.

'I'm through for good with Saxon,' he explained, 'and we shall have to dissolve partnership. I just hate him and all his works; and he knows it and trades on it. All our publications are now on his side of the show. I simply have to agree to everything he demands in order to get him out of my room. He knows how I loathe whistling and humming, but he hums or whistles his filthy jazz the whole working day, blast him! He rubs it in too about my daily bread being buttered with croon and swing. That *"Lulu on the Lilo"* tune is the rottenest stuff the house has ever published; and yet it's netted us some three hundred quid already. Tainted money I call it!'

At this point Frent thumped his despatch case into the luggage rack, and stood over me while he continued: 'and now this morning he comes and leans over my desk, breathing his beastly 'flu into my very nostrils. He knows well enough how prone I am to colds and how careful I have to be to avoid infection. And then to cap it all, he asks me to lend him my quack sniffle cure, as he thinks it funny to call it: Well, he asked for it and he's got it: I hope it chokes him!'

'As your worm mixture did the dachshunds,' I laughingly interposed.

Frent slowly sat down and scowled at me. It was the first time that I had made him angry. 'Can't you let me forget those damned dogs?' he snapped; and then added self-pityingly, 'what I need is a rest and a change of scene. Saxon's put all my nerves on edge.'

As the train glided out of the gloom of the roofed terminus into unimpeded daylight, I was shocked to see Frent's face. It was lined, drawn and grey: an ugly yellow-grey. The man was patently unwell.

'I'm sorry, old man,' I said sympathetically. 'If I were you, I would take a long weekend and run down to the seaside.'

'That's a good idea,' he muttered, and for the next quarter of an hour made a show of reading the evening paper, though his attention appeared far from concentrated on it.

The rolling-stock used on the three-thirty consists chiefly of old six-wheelers, and progress became bumpy as we gained speed. After rattling through Ponsden Priory station the carriage gave a bigger jolt than usual over the siding junction and something fell tinkling on to the floor. Frent's *pince-nez*, always precariously perched, had been jerked off his nose and I waited for him to pick them up. He remained however stock still with fingers outspread on his knees, staring down at the paper which had fallen over his feet. He looked so dazed and helpless that stooping forward myself I picked up the *pince-nez* and handed them up to him. After regarding them curiously for a few moments he lifted his eyes questioningly to mine and said, 'Thank you, sir: but are you sure they're mine'

'They were on your nose a moment ago!'

'Ah! Were they? I had forgotten. You must excuse me, but everything seems suddenly to have gone out of my head. It's quite extraordinary. For instance, your face seems familiar to me and I feel sure that we must have met each other before: but at the moment I've entirely forgotten your name. I'm so sorry.'

Not only Frent's face but the impersonal note in his voice, as though he were repeating a lesson, startled and distressed me. I felt relieved somehow that there was no third person in the compartment to overhear his conversation. He was undoubtedly seized by some sudden illness and consequent abnormality, and it must devolve on me to get him home to Brenside safely and without incident. It is strange how in emergency one sometimes finds the policeman element in one's character taking charge and directing operations. It was so now; for I heard myself addressing Frent in a calm and custodial manner that surprised me.

'My name is Johnson and yours is Frent,' I said. 'We live next to each other in Ruskin Road, Brensham, which is the next stop. You have been working too hard and worrying too much, and as a result your brain has gone temporarily on strike. But don't you bother about that. Go on reading your paper' (I picked it up for him) 'and when we reach Brensham I'll see you home and call in the doctor. He'll soon put you right again.'

Frent received my remarks with a passive and childlike acceptance and, save that I experienced an uncomfortable sensation of walking with a somnambulist, we reached Brenside without trouble. Having explained to the parlourmaid that her master had been taken ill I got him to lie down on a sofa and rang up Dr Jameson.

The latter was round within five minutes, and having looked at Frent and taken his pulse, he peremptorily and monosyllabically enjoined 'bed'. A telephone enquiry of the Brensham District Nursing Guild elicited that Nurse Margison was immediately available, and in less than half an hour she had Frent and Brenside in her charge.

'Let's drop in at your place, and I'll prescribe for you too,' said Jameson as we walked away. 'You must have had an anxious time getting that fellow home.'

He joined with me in taking his own prescription: it was 'a stiff one'.

4

Frent lay in bed five days before recovery. He was described by Miss Margison as an ideal patient; which meant that he slept most of the time, asked no questions and did whatever she told him.

It was on the second or third day that I read in my morning paper of Paul Saxon's death from influenza. The attack, a severe one, had been aggravated by acute gastric complications and had terminated, fatally, in pneumonia. Frent's fulminations against his partner had led me to envisage a Philistine of the Philistines. I was surprised therefore to read in the obituary notice of a distinguished academic career and of his identity with Publics' in the *Bi-monthly Review,* whose articles on art and literature I always enjoyed and admired.

I was permitted to visit Frent at the very outset of his recovery. His first request was indeed that he might see me. Considering that he might be said to have lost his self for several days I found him almost incongruously self-possessed. Before him lay a letter from Lyster, his Company's manager, reporting the circumstances of Saxon's death.

'How extremely annoying of him,' Frent complained, 'to die just when the doctor orders me a holiday. I simply must clear up the mess he will have left and it will take several weeks. All the same I shall have to run down to Benceston for a few days before long.'

'Benceston?' I queried.

Frent's face suddenly showed again (it may have been due to a reflection of sunset glow on the ceiling) the same deep lines and yellowgrey colour that had worried me in the train.

'I don't know what made me say Benceston,' he continued; 'any seaside resort would do; but I feel that I must get a whiff of the sea. By the way Saxon's funeral was this afternoon: I hope they didn't jazz the *Dead March*.'

The last words were those of a cad but, in consideration for Frent's state, I let them pass and the conversation slipped into generalities. For some reason, however, he gave me the impression of trying to drag our talk round to some subject from which, as soon as he had manoeuvred it into proximity, he veered away in distaste. It was an unpleasant sensation, and after half an hour or so I made as though to take my departure by asking whether I might send him over anything to read.

'Have you by any chance got a book called *The Bad Lands?*' he replied.

'I'm afraid not: but I remember reading a short story under that name: by John Metcalfe, I think.'

Frent seemed quite excited.

Was it about a fellow being in two places at the same time, and doing something criminal in one of them while he thought he was doing something good in the other?'

'I don't think,' I protested, 'that the author would appreciate such a crude summary! The tale was extraordinarily well and carefully written.'

'And, in the light of modern conceptions of space and time, very likely a true one!'

'What on earth do you mean, Frent?'

'I mean that space can get kinks and double back over and under itself. Of course, you know all that.'

'I most certainly do not, and I'm perfectly certain that you don't either. You must have been reading some such tosh as *Einstein Without Tears* or *Brainfood for the Brainless*. You had far better stick to your old *Railway Magazines*.'

'I know far more, Johnson, than you guess and than I wish. Someday, perhaps, I'll try to explain: but not now. *Au revoir!* and many thanks for coming round.'

I had recently purchased in five large volumes a series of maps of the counties of Great Britain with combined index. On reaching my house I went straight to the study and, taking down the index from its shelf, looked up 'Benceston'. My suspicions were not relieved. There was no such place.

5

I never met Frent again in the train after his recovery. This was because he changed his route and travelled from Wentlow, for East Brensham, to King's Pancras. This involved him in a mile and a half walk morning and evening; which, as being conducive to his good health, he gave as a reason for the change. His looks however belied the explanation. His condition indeed caused Dr Jameson and myself increasing anxiety; and my uneasiness was aggravated by his point-blank refusal to consult Jameson professionally or to call in any other doctor. It was reassuring therefore when he informed us that a cousin, Gilbert Frent-Sutton, was coming to live with him.

This cousin, he told us, was a Fellow of All Saints and a recognised authority on the Middle Ages. He did not tell us, but we soon found out, that his cousin was also to be identified with Frent-Sutton the old Camford rugger blue. From the moment he arrived we recognised in him a man who would stand no nonsense; and we therefore felt happier about Frent, who was already in visible danger of going all to pieces unless he had somebody to help to keep him together.

A week or so after Frent-Sutton's arrival the doctor and I were invited by telephone to drop in together at Brenside and have a drink. At the gate we were met by Frent-Sutton.

'Before we go in,' he said, 'I owe you both an explanation. Adrian refuses, doctor, to call you in professionally; but I got him to ask you round (using you, Johnson, as a sort of decoy) for a drink. The important thing is that, having attended him after his collapse, you should see him now and observe his present condition. It needs tackling at once. He has never told you yet about his delusions, though he suspects Johnson of having inferred their peculiar nature. Tonight, he has promised to make a clean breast of them, and I fancy that you will find them important from the medical standpoint.'

We went in and, sitting in a half-circle round the fire, began our drinks over the usual small talk. Frent-Sutton was, however, a believer in getting to grips with a job quickly and broke in early with a request that Adrian would tell us all about his Benceston business. 'Tell us everything, old man: right from the very beginning when your father and old Saxon held the stage.'

'I'll try,' responded Frent, not at all averse to becoming the centre of our interest, 'and I'll make it as short as I can. Our firm's name, you know, is Frent, Frent and Saxon; and that is because when my father turned the show into a limited liability company, he kept a third share for himself and reserved a second third for me (against the day when I should have grown up and proved my business capacity), while he allowed his manager, old Saxon, to take up the remaining third share.

'Old Saxon's boy and myself were unfortunately of the same age, and wherever my father sent me—to Heathcote, Winchingham and Oxbridge—old Saxon must needs send Paul. He dogged my footsteps everywhere and at both schools, and later at the Varsity, he excelled me both in games and work. My parents took shame from my inferiority and perpetually upbraided me with letting them down. As a result, I grew to hate Paul and detested him the more for a desire on his part to fraternise.

'Finally, we entered into the firm's business simultaneously; I to be my father's greatest disappointment and Paul to be his right-hand man and, at old Saxon's death, his energetic partner. Paul also inherited money from an aunt, and my father, in appreciation of his work, allowed him 'to purchase the share in the business which he had earmarked for me. On my father's death, therefore, I had only the one-third share in the business which I inherited from him against Paul's two. Frent, Frent and Saxon had become in reality Saxon, Saxon and Frent. I was permanently number two to my life's enemy; and during every day and hour of our partnership my hatred for him proliferated. It possessed my whole being.

'I don't very often go to church, but I had done so on the Sunday preceding my collapse in the train; and it was the parson's sermon that brought home to me the full significance of my hatred. He was preaching on sins of intention and quoted that text about a man committing fornication in his heart if he looks upon a woman lasciviously. The same logic, the parson pointed out, applies to the other commandments. Many people might regard themselves as pretty safe against a breach of the sixth; but we must remember that anybody who allowed his imagination to dwell on how much nicer things would be if only so-and-so were out of the way had already committed murder in his heart. I at once realised this to be true. I was murdering Paul daily: and, quite clearly, it was my duty both to him and myself that I should cut adrift from our partnership.

'Nevertheless, I delayed doing it, fearing the explanation which Saxon would demand and the loss of employment in which it must land me. This delay added further fuel to my hate. You will remember, Johnson, how, in the train that day, you joked about the possibility of the cold cure which I had lent to Saxon proving as deadly as the dose that killed my dogs. That jest of yours brought me, with a jerk, bang up against the actuality that I had, in passing the bottle to Saxon, thought how easy and pleasant it would have been to hand over some poisonous mixture, if any such had been to hand. I tried to keep my mind off this memory by reading the paper, but without success, and then endeavoured to concentrate on other thoughts.

Johnson knows my fondness for railway history and I had told him how an important railway project had ended ignominiously in a gasworks siding. I forced myself now to imagine what would have been the route of the abortive London, Middlehampton and East Coast Railway and what might have been the livery of its rolling stock. While my thoughts were being directed along these lines, we rattled through Ponsden Priory and, to my momentary surprise, I felt the train, instead of carrying straight on over the points, swing right-handed towards the siding. I say "momentary surprise" because, within a few seconds, it seemed perfectly right and natural to me that we should be travelling eastwards. I noticed the monogram, L.M. & E.C.R. on the antimacassars opposite and, above them, two pictures of Bencestonon-Sea and one of Bellringers Cliff. The scenery through which we were passing was also familiar, and I knew that before reaching Benceston the train would stop at Latteridge Junction to pick up passengers.

'I also had a certain foreboding that, among the passengers we should pick up, would be Paul Saxon. And so, it turned out. As the train glided in, I spotted him out of the corner of my eye and surreptitiously watched him enter a compartment three doors off from mine.

'At Benceston West he got out, and I heard him tell a uniformed porter from Fotheringham Hotel to take up his suitcase.

'That gave me my cue. I journeyed on to the East Station and took up my quarters at the Porchester. Paul and I, therefore, had a good three miles between us and ample space in which to avoid each other.

'This, however, was not to be. Walking, next day, along the summit of Bellringers Cliff, I suddenly heard a whistling of that filthy tune, "*Lulu on the Lilo*", followed by a loathesomely hearty "By Jove! How are we? Fancy meeting you up here! I say, what a magnificent view of the sea one gets!" He stood at the edge of the cliff, gazing seaward. I took a hurried look to right and left. We were alone. Striking him from behind, on both shoulder blades, I caused him to overbalance and fall forward. I was alone. My heart thumped with the joy of quick decision and prompt execution. Glancing at my wrist watch, I saw that it was a quarter to three. I started singing, and was just about to peer over the edge, in order to see if Saxon's body had fallen on the rocks above or below tide-level, when a a large hand grabbed me by the arm and swung me round so that I faced inshore. My aggressor was a man of over six feet and broad in proportion.

'"I will see you to the Police Station," he said, "and, mind you, no tricks! Give me your right hand." I suppose that I fainted, for everything seemed to go misty and black, and the next thing of which I became conscious was lying in bed, here in this house.

'Now you three persons listening to my story have doubtless relegated this Benceston part of it to the realm of dreamland; and that was my intention also. In order to prevent any recurrence of the stimuli that led to the nightmare I gave up travelling to London *via* Ponsden and used the other line to King's Pancras. In doing so I forgot that I had returned from Benceston not by train, but in a faint or swoon; and I soon learned to my horror that this process was reversable. During the past few weeks, I have re-visited Benceston many times in trance or swoon. I have stood my trial there for murder and heard sentence of death pronounced on me. The Governor of Benceston Prison has told me that my execution takes place tomorrow morning at eight. Give me a brandy, Gilbert.

'Thank you; that's better. Now I want all three of you to be here at that time tomorrow morning to protect me, and I will tell you why. I have noticed that things which happen at Benceston can simultaneously take place here, if in a different manner. For example, Saxon died from pneumonia at the same instant as I thrust him over Bell-ringers Cliff. The exact time of his death is one of the first things I ascertained after my return to work. Lyster had been at the deathbed. I have no doubt that punctually tomorrow morning, as the clock strikes eight, whatever it is that corresponds to me in Benceston will be hanged. Therefore, you must agree to be here with me at that hour. I can see that you think me mad: but if you will do what I ask, I promise you that at five minutes past eight tomorrow you will find me sane and sensible beyond all doubt. Whatever it be at Benceston that shares my identity and usurps my consciousness will have been killed by then and myself set free. Do promise, therefore, to come without fail.'

Frent directed a beseeching look at each of us in turn, and each nodded his assent.

On our way home Jameson was, for him, unusually communicative.

'I shall have to get Hasterton on to this case. Frent may think that tomorrow morning will see the end of his delusions; but he is wrong. I know these symptoms, and there cannot be a sudden end to them.'

Nevertheless, there was.

6

The doctor called for me next morning, and at ten minutes to eight we walked across to Brenside.

On entering the hall, I was surprised to see the hands of the large chiming clock registering seven fifty-five.

'That clock's fast,' I said to Frent-Sutton as he came out of the drawing-room, followed by his cousin, to meet us.

'Oh, no! it can't be. Adrian's been on to the Exchange twice this morning. That's Greenwich time all right.'

For a man who, in his own apprehension, stood in danger of imminent death, Frent struck me as unexpectedly calm and collected. He bade us take chairs facing the clock, and we must have looked a strange group as we sat watching the dial. The tick of the pendulum acquired unusual sonority owing to our silence: a silence dictated for three of us by our consciousness of the fatuity of the whole proceeding.

A click and a cluck, followed by a whirring of small wheels, heralded the chimes, and I saw Frent dig his fingers into the leathered arm of his chair. The interval between the chimes and the hour gong seemed interminable; but, at last, the eight strokes droned out—and, as we had foreseen, nothing whatever happened.

'And now you chaps must celebrate my release! Thanks ever so much for seeing me through. We can't very well have whisky at this hour though! Gilbert, tell Ada to bring coffee quickly, while I dash upstairs and get a handkerchief.'

Both cousins had thus left the room when Jameson exclaimed suddenly: 'What's that?'

'What's what?'

'Listen!'

The morning breeze made them faint; but we heard unmistakably the chimes of Brensham parish church; and then the distant boom of the great hour bell.

Simultaneously, there came from almost above our heads a noise of rending, a cry, a crash, and, nearer to us still, a dull, heavy thud.

We rushed down the back passage, where we ran into Frent-Sutton as he hurried out from the pantry. In the wooden ceiling above us gaped a yard-square hole, and immediately below lay the ruin of a trap-door, with hinges torn from the supporting joist. It was Frent's fire-escape. Over what was close beside it the doctor now leaned, and, having lifted one end, laid it gently back.

'Finish!' he said; 'broken neck.' And then, looking on the broken door beside him and up at the hole above, he added: 'Amateur carpentry and unseasoned wood! A fatal combination.'

'But why on earth,' I interjected, 'should he have gone into the *box* room?'

'And why,' murmured Frent-Sutton, 'should be have set that clock fast? He insisted on ringing up for the time and doing it himself!'

'Possibly,' Dr Jameson rose from his examination, 'they may know the answers to those questions in Benceston!' Possibly.

Sonata in D Minor

1

Mrs Tullivant rose from her seat and looked for her glasses everywhere but on the table where they very obviously lay.

'Here they are, my dear,' said her husband, with a thin smile that failed to hide his weariness of a good deed daily repeated.

'Thank you, Peter! Now I'm off to bed, and will leave you and Mr Morcambe to enjoy your music. I'm afraid that I'm a bit of a wet blanket where music is concerned.'

'My wife,' Mr Tullivant explained, 'has no use for composers whose names begin with B, H, M or S. That, of course, knocks out all the great masters!'

'What my husband says is quite true, Mr Morcambe. You can't imagine what a difference their names and initial letters make to my enjoyment of things and people! I just can't read the Bible, Milton or Shakespeare: and pictures by Holbein or Hogarth make me shiver. Although their styles and subjects are so different I feel a similar dislike for Millais, Morland and Murillo. And, by the way,' here she pointed an accusing knitting pin at her guest, 'your name begins with an M, you know!'

Before Morcambe had time to reply, the lady, with an ironical curtsey, had backed to the door and departed.

It may be said at this point that the mistress of Dulling Towers was known to her cottager neighbours and tenant as 'a proper caution'. Not that all she did was unacceptable but she was invariably and, sometimes it seemed, laboriously peculiar. This eccentricity she carried into all her activities, even into charitable works. Whether the latter category covered her annual distribution of two white mice apiece to the Sunday School children on Holy Innocents Day is doubtful; but, in order not to forfeit her largesse in other directions, the Vicar of East Dulling had to pretend that it did. On St. Valentine's Day she similarly presented a pair of white rabbits to every bachelor or spinster whose name appeared on the St. Stephen's Communicants' Roll; and on Michaelmas Eve a white goose was delivered from her farm to every married household among her tenantry.

Her attendance at Divine Service on Sundays and Holy Days was faithfully regular, except on festivals of saints whose names begin with B, H, M or S. The black-letter saints served this method of limitation quite as effectually and with greater frequency than the red-letter ones. Her noticeable absence from the Dulling Towers pew on the rare occasion of a Bishop of Wintonbury's visit made it necessary for the Vicar to explain to his Diocesan that the Sunday chosen for the Confirmation unfortunately coincided with the church's annual commemoration of the Venerable Bede.

In summer time she professed a strong faith in bare-footedness as a means to perfect health. Children's parties were accordingly given at the 'Towers' for which no footwear was permitted, and the Vicar sorely regretted the public exposure of corns and twisted toes entailed by his necessary attendance at the midsummer school-treat.

In her choice of clothes, hats, books, furniture and friends Mrs Tullivant was equally wayward and aggressive. Her vagaries must, in some directions, have proved expensive; but she intended them to be so. 'I value wealth,' she would say, 'only as the key to self-expression.' This key had passed to her, as only child and sole heiress, on the death of the late Sir Jeremy Andler, the proprietor of the well-known Andler's Nerve Tonic. Lady Andler had died long ago in an effort to provide her daughter with a little brother or sister; and the youth of Mrs Tullivant had been that of a pampered dictatress, whose every whim and fancy had met with paternal submission and encouragement.

'My wife'—Peter Tullivant turned his eyes from the closed door to meet those of his old friend—'probably appears to you to have perfected futility to a fine art. That unfortunately is not the case. There is a sinister method in her madness. Roger, old boy, I am an intensely unhappy man!'

Morcambe gazed at his host in sympathetic surprise at this confession, and waited for him to proceed further. To listen to a friend's complaints about his wife is forgivable, but not the prompting of them. Tullivant, moreover, quickly resumed.

'You did your best to save me from this marriage, Roger, and that is how I feel able to talk to you about it. I never really cared for Maud, much less loved her, but she amused me and I had no reason then to regard her oddities as anything but amiable and quaint. I anticipated that with the help of her large income we would live amicably together, and I enjoy the life of a leisured country gentleman. You know my tastes. I looked forward to a day or two a week with the hounds and to bridge or billiards of an evening; to motor tours on the Continent, and to some shooting here and in Scotland. That, of course, was what suggested to her her plan of campaign, or system of torture.'

'What on earth can you mean, Peter?'

'Bridge, billiards, hunting, motoring and shooting: B, H, M and S!'

'Good heavens! you don't mean to tell me. . .'

'I mean to tell you that in her apparently capricious and idiotic aversion to whatever begins with those four letters lies a cunning stratagem to thwart and frustrate me in everything and to make my life unbearable. I once told you my financial position as a bachelor: I had a meagre competence of some three hundred a year. Fifty of that I lost in a gramophone company, and what remains just about suffices to pay my club bills and keep me in clothes. For everything else I have to go to my wife, and she jots down in her account books every farthing I spend and determines on what I may, and on what I may not, spend it. It's nothing short of slavery, and if it weren't for one thing I'd pack up and quit.'

'What is it that keeps you?'

'My love for this dear old place and garden. Her pride in appearances prevents my wife blighting *them* with her ridiculous B, H, M, S taboo. She gets over it by pretending never to remember the names of trees or flowers; she realises that it is the spell of Dulling Towers that binds me to her, and is far too astute to give me my liberty by weakening that bond. On the contrary she encourages my passion for gardening because of the hold which it gives her over me.'

At this point Tullivant, in reality startled at the extent to which he had allowed himself to disclose his marital infelicity, made a show of self-possession by filling his pipe with much deliberation and apparent fixity of attention. This however did not deceive Morcambe, who at once effected the change of subject which he felt circumstances to require.

'Well, let's get on with the music! What are you going to play me?'

'There are four hundred gramophone records in that cabinet all arranged alphabetically under the composers' names. Make your choice. You'll find the contents listed on the cardboard schedule at the top of each drawer.'

Thus invited, Morcambe walked over to the cabinet and began his inspection.

'Hullo! this middle drawer is locked and there is no key. What do you keep in here?'

The pipe being by this time filled, Tullivant moved slowly over to the mantelpiece, picked a paper spill from a vase and stooped to light it at the fire. His back was therefore towards Morcambe when he made the unexpected reply: 'I wonder, Roger, whether you'd allow me to try a little experiment on you?'

2

'Experiment? What sort of experiment?'

'Oh! nothing difficult or troublesome,' Tullivant explained, rising from the fire and standing in front of it; 'only that I want you to put on the record which is in that locked drawer and play it to yourself while I go out of the room. The only other thing necessary to the experiment is that I should bolt the door on the outside after I've left you. The object of the experiment will be to ascertain your psychological reactions on an undisturbed hearing of the record which, as you will find out, is a very special and unusual one. That is why I keep it locked up.'

'But why bolt the door?'

'I'll tell you that afterwards, if you still want to know; but I think you'll soon find out. Ah! here's the key: I always keep it in my ticket pocket in order not to get it mixed up with those on my key-ring. There you are!'

Morcambe took the record and surveyed it with considerable curiosity. The colour of the disc was not the usual black but a dark chocolate brown, and it had a blank apple-green label on which was written in manuscript:

Siedel's Sonata in D Minor
Violin: Igor Vidal
Piano: Moritz Vidal

'I'll tell you all about that record when you've played it through,' Tullivant promised as he inserted a new needle in the pick-up, 'and till then I'm off. You know how to turn the thing on? I shouldn't have the loudspeaker quite full on if I were you. Now, please don't forget to register your sensations, for I shall want to know all of them: so, keep your mind on the music.'

Morcambe smiled a little wryly as his host closed the door and audibly slid the outside bolt. Really it all seemed rather ridiculous; but one mustn't blame the husband of so eccentric a wife for developing a few crazes of his own! The disc was now revolving, and with a firm but delicate touch Morcambe set the needle to its margin and, settling into his chair, awaited the music. Oh, *that* tune! He knew the piece well enough and associated it with D'Esterre's music at the Vallombrosa. But D'Esterre would never have murdered the violin like this! Whether the fault lay with player or instrument, the tone was indescribably horrible: it reminded Morcambe somehow of an animal moaning in pain, or was it rage? The piano, on the other hand, was being played exquisitely and, by contrast, made the violin all the more intolerable. Morcambe, indeed, rose from his chair to turn the radiophone off, but checked himself as he called to mind that this was an experiment and this his first reaction that he must remember to describe to Tullivant.

As he moved towards the fire the tone of the violin grew even more shrill and strident, and fiercer in its apparent enmity to the piano. Catching a sudden glimpse of his reflection in the mirror above the mantelpiece, Morcambe did not like what he saw and turned angrily round. *Sonata* indeed! Vendetta for violin and piano, that was what he was listening to. The violinist had now reached that pizzicato passage in the first movement, in which his brutal plucking of the strings moved Morcambe to fury. With a pounce at the grate, he seized the small poker from its tripod and brandished it towards the radiophone. No: there would be no relief in smashing that inanimate machine.

The music clamoured for violence to flesh and blood! In a nervous frenzy he sprang towards the door, and then as suddenly recoiled. That swine, Tullivant, in his dirty cunning had, he remembered, bolted it. But there was another way to get at him—through the french window! No, damn it! He had bolted that too. At this moment there rang out on the piano the lovely solo recapitulation of the second theme; but Morcambe shivered in anticipation of those piercing chords in which the two instruments would shortly wrestle in the tempestuous *coda*. If only he could get at Tullivant!

But before ever the chords sounded, there came in quick succession a thud, a scream, a choking and a moan; and then, save for the scratching of the needle on the record, silence. The sweat stood out on Morcambe's forehead and on the back of the hand in which the poker still hung limply clutched. Then with a clank it fell to the floor and he sank giddily into an armchair; nor did he hear the door unlocked before, looking up, he saw his host standing over him with a stiff brandy in his hand.

'Take this, old man; you'll soon come round. There's no delayed action about your nerves!' Here Tullivant picked up the poker. 'You'd have broken my skull if you could have got at me!'

Morcambe nodded and gulped down the brandy.

'And now perhaps you will be so good as to explain?' he suggested acidly.

'Certainly, Roger, I owe it you, and you shall have the whole story. You will remember my mentioning that I had lost money in a gramophone company. It was called Orpheophone Limited, and the idea was to begin business with the recording of a library of what our chairman chose to call "popular classics". Siedel's *Sonata* was among the first half-dozen, and we thought ourselves lucky when Ballister, our manager, told us that he had booked the Vidal Brothers to play it. We little knew, nobody in fact knew, that they were not brothers at all, but distant cousins locked in a deadly feud which was to have its fatal finale in our studio. Igor waited till Moritz was playing that solo passage on the piano and then stabbed him through the back with a stiletto which he had kept in his violin case. Some of our shareholders, I remember, were sanguine enough to fancy that the tragedy might prove an advertisement for Orpheophone records!

'Of this Vidal recording only two impressions were taken before the matrix was destroyed: one for the purpose of being put in as an exhibit in the murder trial that followed. It was never brought in evidence, however, and was accidentally dropped and broken by one of the Court attendants. The other was the one which you have just heard.

'How did I come by it? Well, as a matter of fact, I found it in a parcel awaiting me at a *Poste Restante* in the Riviera, where I was on a motor tour with my aunt, Lady Sulcock, the following spring. With it was a note from Baluster to the effect that, if I were to play through the record *by myself* (on no account was I to play it in company) I might perhaps understand the nature of his crime and think kindly of him. He dared to hope so, for he had always valued my friendship. This message completely mystified me, for I saw no English newspapers during our tour and had heard nothing of the second murder. Nor did I have a gramophone on which to play the record, which I therefore packed carefully in my trunk.

'On my return to England in late summer the tragedy was soon unfolded to me in a circular from the Orpheophone Company. By that time Ballister had already gone to the gallows for the unprovoked murder of one of the studio messenger boys. At the trial he had comported himself with great dignity and contrition; there was, he told the Judge, an explanation for his act which he would reserve for the judgment seat of the Almighty, as he could not expect any human judge or jury to accept it, true though it was. His bank balance he made over to the mother of the murdered boy.

'With Ballister's death Orpheophone Limited lost its best servant and, worse than that, mischievous rumours arose of the studio being haunted. The balance sheet for the second year presented the alternatives of winding the company up or of raising more capital. It seemed an unlucky enterprise, and the Board consequently decided not to risk throwing good money after bad: so the show was closed down.

'I never got an opportunity of playing the record, as I was living in hotels or staying with friends until after my marriage. I respected Ballister's memory too well to break his condition of solitary audience. Then I forgot about the thing entirely in my first enjoyment of Dulling, and it was not until my wife flew into one of her tantrums one evening and left me alone with the radiophone in this very room that I remembered the record and brought it downstairs. I shoved it into the machine forthwith, and with what psychological effects you can now yourself judge. I could not even wait for the end of the music, but grabbed a desk knife (which, by the way, I carefully stowed away before trying my experiment on you!) and rushed out into the hall and up the stairs. Well, that was when I first discovered that my wife always sleeps with her bedroom door locked!'

There was a moment or two of uncomfortable silence before Morcambe found his voice.

'Peter!'

'Yes, Roger?'

'That's a fine roaring fire behind you. What do you say to our consigning that record to the flames?'

'What! Burn it? Certainly not. I never chuck presents away, especially not those from friends that are dead. For everything comes its day of utility. There, now! It is safely locked up again in its solitary confinement. Many thanks, old fellow, for helping me to make sure that my previous experience wasn't just a matter of personal imagination. And now, I expect, you're about ready for bed?'

Morcambe was quick to agree, both because he had disliked the experiment and the ensuing conversation and also because he had to catch the 8.20 train at Brecklethorpe next morning. He slept not too badly, and had had breakfast and was already in the car when his host appeared on the doorstep in a dressing-gown to bid him goodbye.

'I wish,' said the departing guest, 'that we'd burnt that damned record.'

'I know exactly what you have been imagining, Roger,' Tullivant replied, 'but you completely misunderstood me. To put that old mind of yours at rest I'll give you this solemn assurance; that I will never lay violent hands on Maud. *Never.* You may take my word on that.'

The car was already in motion and Morcambe was not sure that he caught Tullivant's concluding words correctly, but they sounded to him like 'it won't be necessary'. That, however, didn't seem to make sense.

3

Four or five weeks later Roger Morcambe was having breakfast in his small house at Nether Foxbourne when his maid, coming in with the newspaper, asked if she might make bold to ask a question.

'Why, certainly, Bertha; and I hope I may be able to answer it; but I'm not an encyclopaedia, you know.'

'That's as may be, sir; but cook keeps asking the name of that place as you stays in down Penchester way?'

'Dulling—Dulling Towers, to be exact.'

'Ah! and the name of the lady and gentleman as it belongs to?'

'Mr and Mrs Tullivant. But why do you ask?'

'Because, sir, of what's been wrote in this morning's *Daily Scene.* Such a scandal, cook calls it, as never she knew; and if they be the master's friends, he'll sure be worried, she says.'

'Thank you, Bertha, for forewarning me. There's sure to be something about it in the *Morning Digest,* I expect; and I'll have a look after I've finished breakfast.'

No sooner had the door closed on Bertha than her master, yielding to the curiosity which he had felt it dignified to dissemble in her presence, tore open the paper. From its second page there stared at him these ugly headlines:

County Hostess Arrested
Alleged attempt to murder

From what followed, the reader was given to understand that the County Hostess in question was Mrs Tullivant of Dulling Towers, near Penchester, and that the intended victim of assassination was Miss Jane Cannot, her second housemaid. The lady had apparently been sitting at needlework in the drawing-room when the maid came in to clean the grate and lay the fire. The latter saw her mistress place a record on the gramophone and afterwards heard some music, but indistinctly as she was partially deaf. The next she knew was a dreadful pain in the back and her mistress bent over her, stabbing and stabbing again. At this she had fallen forward into the fireplace and fainted.

Mr Tullivant, it was next reported, was helping Mr Hopkins, the gardener, to prune and tie up the virginia creeper outside the french window. Hearing a scream, they dashed together into the room, where the former tripped over the carpet and falling against the gramophone overturned it onto the parquet floor, smashing the record which it had been playing and also the glass protecting the control dials. It was the gardener, therefore, who tore his mistress away from the prostrate maid and forced her into a chair. The latter had terrible wounds on neck and shoulder, and one on the left upper arm, the consequences of which might yet prove fatal. She had been removed by motor ambulance to the Penchester Infirmary. The attack had been made with a large pair of sharply-pointed scissors from Mrs Tullivant's work-basket.

Morcambe read this account with an apprehension that increased on a second perusal. Nor was his uneasiness allayed by the Court proceedings reported at intervals over the following weeks. The evidence of Tullivant, Hopkins and Cannot herself (whose recovery was happily speedier than the doctors dared to expect) tallied in every detail and was quite unshaken in cross examination. The accused woman, however, insisted on telling a story which inevitably raised the question of her sanity. The assault, she declared, had been engineered by her husband. He had left lying on the gramophone lid a record, with instructions that she must not play it while alone because of its depressing psychological effects.

He knew, therefore, that she would try playing it as soon as she had company, and he knew, too, that the first person to come in would be the deaf maid, Jane Cannot. He took up his position with Hopkins outside the french window in order to witness the success of his diabolical plan. It was the music that had compelled her to do the stabbing, and her husband had purposely fallen against the gramophone and smashed the record in order to deny her the proof of her statement. No: his purpose was not to injure the housemaid, though such injury was necessary to his plan. His object was to get herself, his wife, convicted and sent to prison so that he might have Dulling Towers all to himself.

This preposterous explanation of her act led the jury to suggest, and the judge to order, a remand of two weeks in order to enable a professional examination of her mental condition. For this purpose, she was removed to the St Dymphna's Home in Penchester, whither a very large number of reports concerning her past eccentricities were posted by shocked but mercifully inclined neighbours, including the Vicar of East Dulling.

The verdict of guilty but insane, found by the jury three weeks later, met with much approval. The feelings of all in East and West Dulling were expressed by the vicar's wife when she remarked at the Mothers' League, of which Mrs Tullivant had been patroness, that the poor thing could never have done it if only she'd been like other people. To which the assembled mothers added, 'Ah yes, indeed, poor thing!' It gave them naturally a thrill, after years of toadying to their cantankerous queen, to call her now a 'thing': poor thing!

Only for Morcambe did the lady's removal to a place of detention for the criminal insane raise unpleasant interrogations of conscience. Should he have volunteered his testimony in regard to that gramophone record? Would he not thereby have raised questions as to his own mental stability? He would, under cross-examination, have had to admit to very nearly a year's residence in Trantonhall for shell-shock; and they had told him, what indeed he knew, that his case had at one stage presented apparently mental symptoms. Then they would certainly unearth the tragedy of his uncle Edwin. Tullivant, of course, knew about all these things: and that was why, he now realised with shame and anger, Tullivant had chosen *him* to experiment upon that night!

'No,' he found himself muttering his conclusions out loud, 'my giving evidence would have been no manner of good to her but would have done all manner of harm to me. Moreover, from the standpoint of abstract Justice there is more perhaps to be said for locking up malignant eccentrics than unintentioned lunatics! But what a swine Peter has proved himself, he's worse than ever she can have been!'

Morcambe saw no reason to revise this opinion when in a sporting paper some weeks later he read that Mr Tullivant had obtained legal custody of his wife's estate and that frequent meets of the Haddenham

Hunt were being held at Dulling Towers in response to his hospitable invitation. He might at least have waited till the next season! Morcambe decided never to visit Dulling again.

4

Nevertheless, he did, and within the year too. It was to attend Tullivant's funeral.

The last months of Tullivant's life were of almost unadulterated happiness. Not the least of his gratifications was to be addressed as 'squire', a misnomer which evidenced his growing popularity throughout the countryside. The fame of the Dulling shoots, hunt breakfasts and card parties had indeed spread far and wide, and Tullivant took good care that they should reach the ears of his compulsorily cloistered spouse. His personal visits to her invariably so aggravated her condition that the asylum authorities had soon limited them to one a month.

Affecting still to humour her former fancies, and thereby to improve the conditions of her incarceration, he informed the doctors of her aversion to all things beginning with B, H, M or S and thus induced them to omit from her dietary and recreational curriculum many of the items which she liked best. This part of his revenge he found particularly sweet. He also extracted a sacrilegious enjoyment from the public prayers for his wife's recovery which the Vicar periodically offered at his hypocritical behest. With hands held over his eyes he would study through the chinks between his fingers the faces of choirboys and choirmen during such supplications. The lady had not been greatly missed, he inferred.

The only hobby in which Tullivant no longer cared to indulge was that of playing the radiophone. This had nothing to do with any defect in his sense of hearing but rather with some deterioration in that of sight. Whether he was developing colour blindness, or whether the illusion was due to some peculiarity in the room's illumination, he could never open a drawer of the record cabinet without seeming to find at its top a chocolate brown disc with an apple-green label. On each such occasion he found it necessary to steady his brain by repeating to himself the assurance that there had been only one such record and that he had most certainly smashed it to atoms. Nevertheless, the hallucination persisted, and so he had to give up the radiophone.

The death of Tullivant in the fullness of his new and ill-found bliss cannot be better or more exactly told than in the words used by Mrs Hallowby at the inquest.

'My house in West Dulling is flush with the main London–Oxbridge road, along which the motor traffic is incessant. The front door opens straight onto the pavement, my garden being at the back. Last Wednesday morning I was putting up flowers in the dining-room, and my son and daughter had just gone upstairs to the music room to practise the violin and piano together, when the front door bell rang. It was about eleven o'clock and my maid had gone down to the village shop. So, I answered the door myself and there found Mr Tullivant. He had walked over from the Towers by the footpath through Brereton's copse and had his black spaniel with him. He came in and I offered him a sherry after his walk but, as men often will, he preferred beer out of a pewter mug.

'While he was drinking we talked about our gardens, and he drew from his pocket a packet of hollyhock seed which he had promised me. After ten minutes or so he said that he must be getting back and, as I let him out of the front door, he pointed to an oncoming lorry and said, 'They ought to limit the size of these juggernauts, you know.' Then, with a wave of his hand, he walked across the road, and the dog was already on the other side. He had plenty of time to pass over and there was no need for the lorry-driver to slacken speed; but suddenly, right in the middle of the road he stopped dead with his head on one side as if listening to something. Then he turned completely round and shook his fist at the open window of my music room on the second floor. It was a mad act, for the lorry was on top of him in an instant.

'There was a crunching and squealing of brakes and I hurriedly put my fingers into my ears to keep out another sound that I knew must come. No; it was certainly not the driver's fault, and what suddenly possessed Mr Tullivant I cannot guess. He knew my son and daughter, but he certainly couldn't have seen them through the window for they had just that moment begun playing their piece for the village concert, and the piano is at the back of the room. I shall never hear that piece again without thinking of this tragedy; and it was a great favourite of my dead husband's too, and therefore very dear to me!'

'I sincerely sympathise with you, Mrs Hallowby,' said the coroner, 'for I am a musical man myself. Perhaps you would tell us the name of the piece?'

'Thank you, sir; most certainly. It was Siedel's *Sonata in D Minor* for violin and piano.'

Autoepitaphy

1

'You were right, Warden, beyond doubt in shutting the show down in such circumstances. The annoying thing is that they never let me know.'

'If they had, though, we shouldn't have had you with us tonight: so, you mustn't expect us to regret their omission!'

The scene is the Senior Common Room of Selham College, Oxbridge, and the preceding remarks have passed between Greville Tempest, the warden, and Cyril Hunslow, sometime resident fellow and history tutor, but now librarian and occasional master at distant Penchester.

'We've never really forgiven you for leaving us,' continued the warden; 'a man of your calibre's wasted on a public school.'

'Well, it's nice of you to miss me, but I've found more time for my writing and research there than ever I managed to get to myself here. I should never have got through the stuff for those two last books of mine outside the peace of Penchester! I owe more than I can say to the old aunt who left me Little Court and the money to live there. By the way, when are you coming down to stay with me again?'

'Very soon, I hope. I hear they've rebuilt your cathedral organ.'

'Now then, keep off music, please!' interposed Brisson, the sub-warden. 'We had quite enough talk of Bach and Beethoven and the rest of them last night. What I want to know is why should the closing down of the College Psychical Society, owing to the pranks of a pack of young fools, prevent *us* from hearing whatever Hunslow was going to tell 'em tonight?'

'An excellent idea! Yes, please do read us your paper, Hunslow. We got talking about ghosts here last week and nearly had a rough house.'

'Merely because,' explained old Harsleigh the chaplain, 'I endeavoured to suggest to certain of my more junior colleagues that a correct valuation of psychical data depends upon a nice discrimination between what is objective and what subjective.'

'And merely because,' exploded a young don with red hair and a freckled face, 'I pointed out that those terms connoted a distinction without a difference. To the idealist among philosophers the objective may be said to be subjective, and to the sensationalist in psychology the opposite is the case. If only Mr Harsleigh would stick to his theology and leave. . .'

'No more, Nicholls, please. We can't go ranging again over all that ground. Now, Hunslow, if you'll read us your paper I promise you a quiet audience in spite of these disputants.'

'Well, if you really want to hear it, I'll go upstairs and fetch it. It won't detain you for more than twenty minutes or so; and there's nothing in it that can't be explained in three or four different ways. So, everyone will be welcome to his own theory and solution!'

While Hunslow is away they stoke the fire, pull their seats into a semicircle in front of it, and set the big leather armchairs at either end for the warden and the reader. Except for the heavily shaded reading lamp on a small table at the latter's side all lights are extinguished. The reading then begins.

2

A Record of Certain Events Associated by the Writer with a Desk
by Cyril Hunslow

I have chosen the title of this paper carefully. It does not imply that the events which I shall narrate were of themselves connected with a writing desk, but only that I have associated them therewith. Whether the interconnection goes any further than that I must leave to your judgment. I only know that for myself the association will be permanent.

I will begin with four introductions.

First of myself. I am a historian and, as my books will bear witness, a critical historian. I have tried to apply the same critical standards to the preparation of this paper as to the compilation of my histories.

Secondly, of my paternal aunt, the late Mrs Agatha Telling, of Little Court, Penchester, my present home, which she left to me at her death. She was a Victorian lady of common sense and strong mind, and with no fads or fancies about her.

Thirdly, of Mildred Hudson, my aunt's parlour maid and after her decease my housekeeper. She was a gaunt, unimpressionable woman whom her mistress once not inaptly described as a footman in petticoats.

Fourth, and lastly, of the writing desk. It was of mahogany with inlays of patterned ivory on the slanting cover, which when opened and let down onto lateral draw-pins formed the writing board. Somebody, I forget who, once told me that the ivory inlays indicated the workmanship of French prisoners during the Napoleonic Wars. The catalogue of the Penchester Museum, however, to which I recently presented the desk, says nothing as to that; but classifies the piece as 'Miscellaneous: probably late Eighteenth Century'.

The first I remember of this desk was that it occupied a window corner of the almost disused morning room at Little Court. I only knew my aunt open it but once, and that was when on return from a walk with me she found on the hall table a telegram and a pre-paid reply form. Turning into the morning room and sitting at the desk she scribbled a quick reply. 'Here, Cyril,' she said, 'run along with this, will you, to the epitaph office?'

'Epitaph office?'

Did I say epitaph office?' My aunt seemed annoyed with herself. 'Of course I meant telegraph office. This wretched old desk always makes me talk and write nonsense!'

The inconsequence of this explanation of her mistake never occurred to me at the time. I was far too polite and politic a youngster ever to question the veracity or validity of an avuncular or auntly utterance. In point of fact, I completely forgot her remark until I caught myself in the act of making a very similar one almost twenty years later: when the old lady had recently died and I was making a first entry on my inheritance. Nothing relevant to the subject of this paper happened, at least to my knowledge, in the intervening period.

I was, at the time to which we have now jumped, making a preliminary stay of two nights at Little Court before moving in my few bits of personal furniture. I wanted to see where they would fit in. It was an evening in early July and the daylight still strong enough after supper for me to try which of the four sitting-rooms on the ground floor would best suit my research work and writing. I wished to leave the drawing-room as Aunt Agatha had left it, I felt sure that she would have preferred it so. The dining-room was too dark and the hall too open to interruption. There remained, therefore, only the morning-room, which (with substitution of my large writing-table for the too small old desk) would suit admirably. With a view to testing the light, which I like having over my left shoulder, I sat down at the desk, opened it and looked for paper whereon to write. There were no loose sheets, but there was one of those Victorian 'commonplace albums' with pages of different coloured papers, of which some twenty or so had been torn out and the remainder left blank.

Taking up a pen, with my thoughts focused on a future rearrangement of the furniture, I jotted down a few unpremeditated words on the top leaf. The light was quite satisfactory, and I decided to give instructions for my table to be sited exactly where the desk now stood. Before shutting it up again I glanced down at what I had written in the album, and what I saw gave me a little jerk of surprise. This is what I had written:

Autoepitaphy
being a Miscellany of
Messages from the Beyond
selected as suitable for engraving upon the
senders' tombs and for edification of the
passing reader: complete with appropriate
titles in superscript, carefully chosen
by The Editor

My first instinct was to ejaculate 'What rubbish!' when those long-forgotten words of my aunt suddenly rushed back on me: 'This wretched old desk always makes me talk and write nonsense.' And then, of course, she too had said something about epitaphs. Ah, yes! now I remembered: 'the epitaph office', that was it! Well, it was getting too dark now in the morning-room; so, having closed the album and shut up the desk, I returned to the cosiness of the drawing room, where curtains were already drawn and the lights lit. Having read the daily papers and two or three chapters of a novel I went to bed well satisfied with my new home.

I always keep on a table at my bedside a number of books and a writing pad; not because I am slow in going to sleep but because I wake early, especially on a bright summer's morning. I did so on the morrow of the events just recorded and, taking up the writing pad, amused myself between six and half-past seven o'clock by trying to compose a few epitaphs and titles for them on the lines of the nonsensical entry which I had made in the old album the night before. I managed with some racking of the brain, and certainly without any inspirational afflatus, to hammer out two; and these, for a reason that I shall shortly explain, I will now read out to you. The first is a message from 'Everyman' and its title 'Ex Nihilo Nihil'.

Producer, actor, audience, in one
I played 'My Life', and lived the parts I played:
The curtain's down; my piece has had its run;
Nothing remains: a shadow leaves no shade.

The second was from 'A Horticulturist' and its title 'In Heaven as it is in Earth'.

Too garish are these bright Elysian fields
Of endless summer and unfading flowers!
Must I then pine while Recollection yields
Solace of cloud and sunset, wind and showers?
No! I have found a corner of the sky
Where soil is heaped, and ash and mulch and mould;
Where leaves still fall, buds burst and blossoms die;
Where the First Gardener gardens as of old!

My reason for reciting these verses is that you will have at once noticed their entire difference in matter and manner from the stuff and style of my writing in the album the previous evening; which must have struck you, as it did me, as redolent of the eighteenth century. Those of you who have read my published metrical efforts—I dare not call them poems—will recognise my two epitaphs as quite of a piece with them. I was, indeed, gratified to find myself so normal on a slightly abnormal theme; and, by the time I had had breakfast and kept an appointment with the headmaster of Penchester regarding my acceptance of the post of School Librarian, I had forgotten all about the old desk and the album within.

Such forgetfulness was not, however, to last for long. On my return to lunch, Hudson (as Mildred desired me to address her in her new dignity of housekeeper) begged my pardon but had I expected any visitor that morning? My negative reply appeared to puzzle her and elicited the comment that in that case it was a most peculiar thing.

'What is peculiar, Hudson?' I enquired.

'Well, sir; you know of them fainting fits as I were telling you of yesterday? While I were in the morning-room and you was out, and I bent my head over the writing-desk to see as whether there weren't no ink in the inkpot which Mrs Telling always said it was my duty for to see to properly, I suddenly come over that giddy and strange that I lay down longways on the sofa and shut my eyes, and whether I goes into a faint or a doze or what not I don't rightly know, but when I opens them again I see a gentleman sitting at the writing-desk and looking hard at that book as is inside of it. He was dressed queer too, just as though he step out of one of them fancy balls; in fact, he looked like a bishop, only worse.'

'What do you mean by "worse", Hudson?' I enquired.

'Well, he had little spindly legs same as a bishop, but were all un-tucked about the neck and no proper collar to him either. So, he sits there laughing at what you had wrote in the book; and it was lucky, I thought to myself, as my dear dead mistress had tore out all her drawings of gravestones with rhymes on 'em as I could never make sense on, nor she neither I reckon, poor lady, for 'tweren't her as done it but the old desk, she would say. Well, sir, as I were a watching the old gentleman what should I do but tumble off the sofa, and when I pulls myself up again there weren't no old gentleman there at all and I minded that I must have been in a dream. But it were peculiar all the same, for my digestion weren't bad this morning and I ain't one to dream on a calm stomach nor in the daytime neither.'

'Don't worry yourself, Hudson,' I replied. 'Most of us have night-mares, and all that you have had is a daymare! There's nothing to be upset about: it's all perfectly natural.'

It is significant, is it not, that a majority of men and women seem to derive comfort from being told that a thing is natural. It is difficult not to infer that most of us tacitly accept the existence of phenomena classifiable in the opposite category!

At this stage of my experience and information in regard to the writing-desk I was no longer sceptical, though I remained acutely critical, of its association with some stimulus or urge towards sepul-chral inscriptions. Indeed, it wounded my self-esteem to have to con-fess that through lack of adequate mental concentration I had allowed my pen to write words of which I could not consider myself the author. Nor was my discomfiture in any way relieved by Hudson's dis-closure that a woman of my late aunt's strength of mind and character had suffered a similar subjection to an uninvited influence. I was glad in fact not to have to broach the subject to Hudson again, as I had already ordered the desk's removal to a big spare bedroom in order to make way for my writing-table downstairs.

In its new venue the desk was quite forgotten by me for some six months after my entry into permanent residence at Little Court. During that time, I had no guests to stay, and it was not until after a succession of four visitors had been incommoded by it in the ensuing year that I offered the piece to the Penchester museum and paid for its removal thither. It is not necessary for the purposes of this paper that I should give the names of my four friends, nor have I their permission to do so. It will suffice to call them A, B, C and D.

A is a member of the Indian Civil Service, whose most marked traits are a profound pride—his enemies would call it conceit—in his profession; and a bigoted and militant atheism. He would suffer no criticism, serious or jocular, of either. I therefore studiously avoided both subjects and, as we found plenty to talk about outside of them, did not find their avoidance difficult. I was sorry therefore when on the third day he told me that he must leave on the morrow. He struck me as oddly fidgety and ill at ease in saying goodbye and, as his cab drove off, put his head out of the window to say, 'I'm afraid you'll find I've written some nonsense in your album: please forgive me.' Curiosity carried me quickly upstairs, and opening the album I read as follows:

Gloria in Excelsis
(from an Indian Civil Servant)
We sons of heaven here agree
Not to appear too fervent;
Each has the honour just to be
God's most obedient Servant.

Good Form
(from an Atheist)
On earth I would mutter a curse on all
Fools who believe in God's essence:
But here it seems rather too personal
To pass such remarks in His presence.

The writing was indubitably in A's firm and readily legible hand; but just as certainly what was written constituted a plain negation of his authorship. It was, to use. Hudson's expression, 'a most peculiar thing'.

B came to stay a month or so after A, and in not removing the album from the desk but leaving it available to subsequent visitors I yielded to my curiosity to see what, if anything, they would write in it. At the time of his visit, B was Bishop's chaplain in a North Country

See. He had previously been a country parson in East Anglia and has since become a much-respected Archdeacon in the Midlands. I always found him tolerant of criticism of the clergy by the laity and frank but restrained in his reciprocation. The lines which he wrote (and for which unlike A he did not apologise, though he expressed surprise at having produced them) were incongruous in form rather than in substance with his ordinary writings. In the three weeks of his visit, he wrote more than a dozen verses, of which I will read out three.

Except as a Little Child
(from a Lord Bishop)
Complete with mitre, cope and staff
I knock at Heaven's gate:
Why this should make the angels laugh
I cannot explicate.

Nor Thy Judgments My Judgments
(from a Minister of Religion)
That God is colour-blind in love
I from the grave forthtell:
My flock's black sheep are penned above,
My white lambs bleat in hell!

Immortality (from an Undertaker)
I, who with coffin, hearse and bier
Folk to their long rest laid,
Find in this dull and corpseless sphere
An insult to the trade.

I now come to verses written in the hand of C, but so aggressively naive and anachronistic that they at once appeared to me, and still appear, to leap at one straight out of the eighteenth, or very early nineteenth, century. C himself regarded them quite impersonally and apathetically as 'rum stuff'. A person of considerable inherited wealth and of consequent leisure, he was, nevertheless, devoid of any literary accomplishment or discrimination. With the remark that he doubted whether his old aunt (who had left him his money) would have approved of them, he was, apparently, able to dismiss the verses he had written from mind and memory, although he had contributed no fewer than nineteen additions to the album, of which I have selected eight as typical. Here they are:

Re-Union

(from an Uxoricide)
Who, hanged by neck till I was dead,
Had paid for my wife-murder
Now find the bitch arrived ahead!
Pray, what could be absurder?

Reductio Ad Absurdum
(from a Recidivist)
Did I not sin sans fear or tear
Great sins of rape and arson?
Then why am I detailed to hear
Confessions from a parson?

Unemployment
(from a Courtesan)
For harlotry my soul I sold
On men's desire reliant,
But now must walk the streets of gold
Nor ever find a client.

Continuity'
(from a Politician)
The shams of party strife
Bred falsehood in my breath:
So did I lie through life
Who now lie still in death.

The Mighty from Their Seats
(from a Parish Clerk)
When the Duchess was churched, I intoned the response,
'Who putteth Her Ladyship's trust in Thee';
But her faith in the Lord must have suffered mischance
For Her Grace fills no castle in Sion's citie.

Redemption at Par
(from a Company Promoter)
Unwanted? I? So good at schemes
To make thrice two look seven!
In need of no prospectus seems
The Company of Heaven!

Sadism
(from an Usher)
The bad boys made me sad; the worse
Sadder (thou rightly addest);

But daily flogging his obverse,
The worst boy made me saddest.

Cynolatry
(from a Dog Fancier)
No dogs allowed? No room for 'Squaw',
My friend I loved so well?
Too well,' St Peter said, 'and more
Than God: so Heaven's your Hell!'

The final entry to be made in the album before the desk's removal to the museum brought me face to face with tragedy. D had for many years been my greatest friend; and, as soon as I heard that his doctor had ordered him a complete rest and change of scene, I telegraphed an invitation to stay at Little Court. His rapid success at the Bar had led to overwork of both brain and nerve, and he had never been of really strong physique. Nevertheless, on meeting him at the station, I noticed none of the pallor or decline that I had expected in one sent for a rest-cure.

On the contrary, D's complexion was florid and he appeared to walk and talk at full steam. It was unfortunate that I was reassured thereby into letting him sit up late in discussion and argument. I need not blame myself, however, for I heard later that his condition had puzzled even the specialists and that he was far from being what *medicos* call a straightforward case. It was a long way past one o'clock when we bade each other 'goodnight' in the upstairs corridor; and his last words to me were: 'Well, I feel a different man after our talk! Quite like old times, eh?'

At seven-thirty next morning I was awakened by Hudson knocking at my door to say that she was afraid that poor Mr D had been took very queer, and would I ring up for the doctor? To cut this sad story short, severe cardiac symptoms were diagnosed and my dear friend entered upon what could only be described as four months of protracted death before his final release. Two days after this collapse, he was removed, at his own request, to a nursing home run by a cousin of his at Davenham-on-Sea.

On my return from seeing him into the train—in which the doctor had arranged for him to be accompanied by a trained nurse—I found Mildred Hudson in tears. She hadn't meant to pry into what weren't nohow her concern; but would I go upstairs and see what the poor gentleman had written in that book? I of course did so and, from a shaky scrawl, deciphered the following:

Sham epitaphs I will not dare to write
In vein jocose: for I may die tonight.
This pain that stabs me through from chest to back
Must be precursor of a heart attack.
All I can offer is this sage advice,
'Cling hard to life: for dying is not nice!'

The grief caused me by these lines was not without remorse that I had not removed the album or locked the desk before D came. I sat down straightway and wrote a letter offering the desk to the Museum Committee. Pending their reply, I had it carried down and placed in the dark cupboard under the stairs. I had come suddenly to hate the sight of it.

It was six months or more after D's death, by which time I had succeeded in forgetting about the old desk and its associations, that, in my rearrangement of the School Library, I came across a portfolio docketed: 'Some materials for a history of Penchester'. Inside was a large number of unindexed and unarranged papers in print and manuscript; most of them belonging to the first half of the nineteenth century. On a cursory inspection they seemed of very unequal interest; but everything is grist to the mill of the historian, and I began placing them in chronological order as a first step towards a more thorough examination.

A folio to which my attention was drawn by its unusual calligraphy, was headed: '*An Appreciation of our Cathedral Clergy, with a Short Note on Doctor Ermytage*'. The clerical appreciations were nauseating examples of polysyllabic flattery; so that I turned with relief to the curt and crisp note on Dr Ermytage, which proved very far from appreciative. It is important to my purpose, and I will therefore read it to you in full:

Anselm Ermytage came to our organ *anno* 1795 and *obiit* 1806. Upon that instrument he would discourse sweet harmonies, but proved himself an organ of great discord in our midst. His quarrel with the Dean arose in the matter of music for *Magnificat,* whereof he set the whole to soft and sad melodies save only the sentences 'He shall put down the mighty from their seat' and 'the rich He shall send empty away'; the which he put to a great shouting by the quire with much noise upon the organ.

Now the dean's prohibition of this music lay upon the ground that singing after such sort made of the holy canticle of the Virgin nought but a dangerous song of revolution and contempt for the nobility. Wherein, Doctor Beven had the support of all persons of decent birth and superior understanding, but Dr Ermytage took his discipline so ill that he spread abroad an epitaph against the dean's death, which he hoped might be soon, and vented therein his spleen upon the whole people of Penchester. The words of his lampoon, which few accounted wit, ran thus:

Such as knew Dean Beven well
Doubt not he has gone to hell.
Do not pity Doctor Beven,
After Penchester 'tis Heaven.

Whereafter, he wrote many and diverse false epitaphs to the scandal of our city and to the sad annoyance of the dean and chapter. Moreover, upon his death, it was discovered in his testament that these and many more wicked verses had been set apart by him in his desk for posthumous printing, to which end he charged upon his estate the sum of one hundred guineas.

But, upon the advice of his attorney, Mr William Telling of Little Court in this City (who became sole executor under this will after the death of the other, which had been Mr Mathew Bilney) did destroy these verses by fire and paid the whole amount aforesaid into the bishop's chest for the sick and needy.

And this he did notwithstanding a solemn caution in the said testament contained that, failing due and faithful execution thereof, the testator reserved the right of personal enactment. Of this solemn caution the attorney made light, holding that it was vain and beyond the law and impatient of a wise interpretation: but in late life Mr Telling was wont to confess that he doubted his action had been right and that he did not care to sit at the desk wherein the verses had been left by Dr Ermytage.

'That, gentlemen,' said Hunslow, 'concludes my paper. I will gladly answer, to the best of my ability, any question that you may wish to put to me. But any attempt at explanation I must leave to your more experienced judgment in such matters. As an historian I have endeavoured to present as true and full account of a series of events as my sources of information and experience permit. Beyond that I cannot go. I thank you for your patient hearing of what has been a longer paper than I anticipated when I accepted your invitation to write and read it.'

3

There was silence for a minute or so after the reading of the paper, during which its author leant forward and self-consciously poked the fire.

'I speak for us all, Hunslow,' said the warden, 'when I say that we've thoroughly enjoyed your paper. For myself, I confess that its literary transcends its psychical interest.'

'I'm not so sure about that!' exclaimed Nicholls, getting up and moving towards the electric-light switches. 'Hunslow's story needs examination in the cold bright light of reason. This spooky glimmer of the fire and huddling of shadows on the ceiling make for imagination and credulity. Let us, therefore, indulge in the symbolism of turning on the lights!'

There was a clicking of switches, a momentary flash, the splutter of a blown fuse, and a sudden relapse into gloom.

'As none of you have any questions,' Hunslow said, 'I think, if the warden will allow me, I'll be turning in now. Goodnight!'

The Pump in Thorp's Spinney

1

The present that pleased Philip Falmer most on his fourth birthday was the wooden working model of a garden pump sent to him by his Aunt Sarah. The accompanying letter informed him that it was the handiwork of young Simon Tubbins, the gardener's boy at Sockstead Hall, where Aunt Sarah's husband, Sir James Redlaw, reigned as Squire over the two parishes of Upper and Nether Sockstead. The model stood on a tripod, which could be placed and held firm by Philip's left hand in a basin of water, while his right worked the handle up and down and brought the water pulsing from the spout. Philip felt that he was now one up on his one-year-older brother, to whom, three months earlier, the same aunt had sent a model of a stationary steam engine.

Edgar was not allowed methylated spirit for this engine, except when Miss Williamson, the nursery governess, was there to superintend its operation: for Mrs Falmer had declared it a dangerous gift for a child. Edgar disliked being called a child, and could not view as a gift to him anything of which he was forbidden sole and unrestricted use. The pump, on the other hand, was rated by the mother as 'most sensible and suitable', and, for a week or so, Philip and his pump were in reciprocating, and almost perpetual, motion. It was only when he tried pumping brilliantine taken from the bottle on his father's dressing table as a variant from water that some few parental restrictions had to be enacted and enforced.

It may be doubted whether the generality of aunts, uncles, godfathers, godmothers, parents and other customary donors of presents to children sufficiently realise the dangers of unintelligent generosity. If your godson asks for a pump, by all means give him one; for his request shows that he is already pump-minded. But to walk into a toy shop and there order a steam engine for Edgar, a pump for Philip, and a pistol for Arthur without knowing whether Edgar wants an engine, Philip a pump or Arthur a pistol, involves a terrible responsibility. Just as a twig thrown into a mud bank may in time deflect the channel of a river, so may a chance-chosen toy determine the course of a child's psychology.

Thus, it came about that Philip, who had never previously paid any attention to pumps, soon began to search them out as objects of prime interest in the houses and gardens of his parents' neighbours and friends.

One afternoon indeed he made bold to work the handle of the large and ancient pump in Tarrington Churchyard. The Sexton must have been cleaning up the vestry when he heard its sonorous clanking, for, to Philip's consternation, he came fiercely running out of the door in the south aisle. The boy need not however have been frightened, for the old man, seeing who he was, seemed vastly amused and bade him go home and tell his father, 'as he had found where to draw white wine with plenty of body in it'. Philip, though not understanding the message, disliked the rather sinister cackle with which it had been confided; and, because of this dislike, he did not repeat it to his father, but suppressed it. He could not however forget the incident, which caused him thenceforward to classify pumps in two categories, nice and nasty, and to suspect all pumps in lonely or unusual places as likely to belong to the latter.

Philip's new interest soon extended to other items of hydraulic apparatus besides pumps. Although his parents never traced the disaster to his agency, the overflowing one morning of their main cistern and the consequent fall of plaster from the ceiling of the bedroom beneath, resulted from Philip's first self-introduction to a ball-cock. For many months he could never resist the thrill to be derived from pressing the copper float under water and then allowing it to spring up again—a sudden, jerky movement for which the mechanism was not designed.

Then there were taps. Here, again, a dual classification suggested itself. There was the honest straightforward tap with a spout which, if you turned it, showed clearly what it was doing; but there was also the mysterious and secretive tap (to be found in dark cupboards, long passages, or under iron flaps in the outside pavements), whose purposes were hidden. Experiment in regard to the latter was hazardous. When the bottom of the kitchen boiler was burnt out for lack of water, Philip, overhearing cook's loud complaint to his mother, rushed speedily upstairs to readjust the tap in the wainscot of the housemaid's closet with which he had previously meddled, thereby flooding the kitchen range, putting the fire out, and spoiling the dinner.

Luckily Mr Falmer, on the data before him, decided that there must have been a temporary blockage in the supply pipe, and his son went unsuspected. Strangely enough, it was a tap of the straightforward variety that shortly afterwards led to his temporary undoing. It was the First Sunday in Advent, and he had greatly enjoyed joining in the singing of hymns about 'Rejoice! Rejoice!' and 'dee-he-heeply wailing', when he noticed a dribbling and a bubbling, and heard a slight sizzling, from the escape-cock of the radiator at the side of the family pew. The temptation was too great and he gave the little tap a smart twist. There was a merely momentary interruption to the vicar's recital of the Litany, but permanent injury to Miss Williamson's smartest hat, damage which clearly necessitated a beating from his father, even though it was Sunday.

Once a week Mrs Falmer would drive over in the pony trap to do shopping in Bludborough, and it was there that Philip caught his first rapturous glimpse of that apotheosis of a pump, a fire engine in action. It was in Bludborough, too, that, at the invitation of the Waterworks Superintendent (who was Miss Williamson's brother-in-law), Edgar and he were allowed to inspect the huge beam-engined pumps that lifted water from the marsh meadows up to the town reservoir above the railway station.

The hydraulic ram which supplied the large tank at Tarrington Hall Philip found not altogether pleasant. The nature of the apparatus at the intake on the bank of Tarrington mill-pond was explained to him by his father, with the aid of the letter scales on the library writing-table. The slow, rhythmic click-clack which was audible above the iron plate protecting the intake reminded him somewhat of the tick-tock of the grandfather clock on the stairs. The din coming from the ram itself in its shed below the mill dam (a *clang* and a *scroosh*, as Edgar described it) was a very different sort of noise and, Philip felt, rather alarming. Nor was his apprehension lessened when, finding the shed door open one day, he ventured to peep inside.

The man who was doing repairs or making adjustments undoubtedly meant to be kind; but, accustomed to preach in a neighbouring chapel, he proceeded, 'after explaining to Philip the principle of the ram, to point a religious moral. 'You'll have took heed, young sir, as how precious little of the water that comes down from the pond gets into this small pipe as leads to the 'all on the 'ill. Most on it spills out, as you see, and runs down the drain: which be a true parable of the Lord's working; for it's only His elect as may be squirted through the valve of grace up the narrer pipe to 'eaven, while most on 'em goes splashing down the sewer of sin to 'ell.'

The half-light, half-gloom of the shed; the alternate thump, squelch and gurgle of the dimly discerned ram, and the awful admonitions of its guardian, put poor Philip in a sudden fear of he knew not what. Precipitately he rushed from the shed, banging the door behind him, and made off home as fast as his legs would carry him. As he ran, his fear became gradually submerged in a sense of shame at having been a coward; but, before reaching the front gate of Gorse Lodge, he had regained his self-possession sufficiently to try to dismiss both fear and shame from his mind. When, therefore, his mother asked where he had been (it was Miss Williamson's afternoon off and both boys were left to their own devices), he replied that he had walked down along the fields by Highbarrow to have a look at the cows and pigs. So, indeed, he had—on his way to Tarrington mill-pond. But he couldn't forget that ram; or its noise, or its keeper!

2

During the next year and a half nothing much occurred of relevance to our tale. The model pump lasted only a matter of months, Philip having soon become tired of it. Its final breakdown was due not to fair wear and tear, but to use as a missile against a too vocal cat. Philip's interest in hydraulic paraphernalia, which the model had aroused, nevertheless persisted and expanded. In spite of parental, and even fraternal discouragement, he paid surreptitious visits to the Bludborough sewage farm. But, beyond this, there is nothing else to be told of the period which intervenes between the events already recorded and those about to occupy our attention.

The scene now is Sockstead Hall, where the Falmers are paying a spring visit to the Redlaws. The reader will remember that Lady Redlaw, donor of the model pump to Philip, is Mrs Falmer's sister. The two boys, now nearly six and seven-and-a-half respectively, are on their best behaviour; being slightly overawed by the grandeur and dignity of ancient Sockstead as compared with the modest modernity of their own home at Gorse Lodge.

It is the third afternoon of the visit, and the whole party, except Philip, have driven off in the wagonette to Penchester to see the reconstructed retrochoir of the cathedral and the new reredos. Philip was considered too young for such an architectural treat; and, moreover, there was no room for him in the wagonette. Having ascertained that the cathedral was, apart from its font and an antiquated system of hot-water pipes, barren of hydromechanical devices, Philip did not at all mind being left out of the party. He had in fact been waiting for an opportunity of having an uninterrupted yarn with Simon Tubbins, the artist of the model pump. Simon was in due course found in the big potting-shed between the greenhouses in the walled garden. Although still called 'gardener's boy' Simon seemed to Philip to have grown to full-size manhood since they last met two years ago.

He was, consequently, shy in starting conversation; but, at the first mention of the model pump, all reserve melted away and they were soon jabbering together as old friends. Yes: Simon still made models in his spare time, if he could find any. He was now at work on one of a windmill pump. What! never seen a windmill pump? Well, Squire had had one put up by the home farm, and it was well worth looking at. It would certainly be working today, with this spanking wind. No: the model Her Ladyship had bought two years ago for a Christmas present wasn't a copy of the pump in the kitchen garden, but of the one in Thorp's Spinney. Where was Thorp's Spinney? Well, if the bull weren't out, you could take the short-cut and it was only two fields away beyond the home farm. The pump had been put there to water the cattle, but the well ran dry most seasons; so, there were no cattle kept there now, and nobody used the pump.

No, unfortunately; Simon couldn't possibly go there with Philip that morning, because he must get these three-dozen flower-pots ready filled for Mr Lewkin to put the cuttings in at twelve o'clock. But if Master Philip would like to go by himself, he couldn't possibly miss the way. You walked straight as far as the home farm gate, where you would see the windmill pump in the field on your left and the stile leading to Thorp's Spinney on your right. If the bull were out there was always a notice by the stile, and then you walked on down the lane and followed it round instead of cutting across the fields. There wasn't more than five minutes difference really.

With these directions Philip found his way easily enough. As Simon had foretold, the windmill was spinning round merrily in the strong wind and the water spurted resonantly into the cistern below. After a brief inspection Philip walked on towards the stile and saw, propped against it, a board on which 'Ware Bull' had been crudely daubed in tar. So, he continued down the lane and, after a quarter-mile or so of its meanderings, found himself in Thorp's Spinney and in sight of the object of his exploration.

The pump stood just outside the spinney fence; and that neither it nor the trough below it had been in recent use was shown by the riot of nettles and burdock that surrounded both. Slipping under the fence Philip found, as he rose on the other side, something to engage his attention besides the pump. His steps had till now been directed westward, but he was now facing east and what he saw there did not please him. The sky above Thorp's Rise was inky black, and as he gazed on it in surprise there was a glint of distant lightning. He also became suddenly aware that the westerly wind had dropped and that the scene before him lay wrapt in a stillness of expectancy.

Snugly abed, with sheets to cover his eyes and pillow-ends to smother his ears, Philip did not bother about thunderstorms; but out-doors and all alone he found himself in fear of one. His first impulse was to bolt home and leave the pump uninspected; but his second thought, prompted by self-respect, was to pay it hastened attention before he ran. His nerves were, therefore, in a state of high tension and apprehension when he grabbed hold of the handle and worked it jerkily up and down. This was not easy, for the bearings had rusted, and at the fourth or fifth downstroke the plunger came out with a rattle and the shaft jammed.

At this moment there grated on Philip's ear a most horrible and unearthly sound. Frozen in stark fright he was unable even to lift his hands to his ears to keep out the awful moaning that seemed to pro-ceed now from the spout of the pump and now from the very ground beneath his feet. It was a hideous ululation, expressive of abysmal pain and despair, and how long it continued Philip was never able to tell. It might have been a matter of seconds or of minutes; to him it was a timeless agony. What released him from its spell was a clap of not very distant thunder. With a quick dive beneath the rail of the fence he dashed back into the lane. Two things only impinged themselves on his numbed senses as he raced along. One was that the bull, after the manner of cattle, kept pace with him on its side of the dividing hedge; and the other was that the windmill had ceased to turn for lack of wind. He noticed these irrelevancies as in a dream.

But although insensitive to other external impressions Philip was already turning a problem in his mind. What should he tell, if any-thing, of his horrible experience? The truth was plainly incredible.

Edgar would not merely disbelieve but laugh. He must either keep silence altogether about his afternoon's expedition or pretend that it had passed off without incident. Before he had arrived at a conclusion he had reached the potting-shed and heard himself hailed by Simon from within.

'What? Back already! Why, good gracious, Master Philip, what be the matter? You're as white as chalk. Don't tell me as you forgot what I said and have been chased by the bull?'

Philip jumped at the explanation thus suggested. Invention was always pleasanter than suppression, and Edgar would envy the fictitious adventure.

'Why, yes!' he answered. 'I stupidly forgot on the way back, and had to run for it. Luckily, I found a hole in the hedge.'

Simon's manifest admiration of this brevity showed Philip that a laconic touch would serve also in imparting the lie to Edgar. As he left the walled garden a crash of thunder made him run towards the short-cut to the Hall which lay across a footbridge over the river. Rain had already begun to fall in large ominous drops when he discovered that the bridge gate was locked and that he must needs go round by the drive; a detour which resulted in his being soaked to the skin before he arrived at the porch. There was no shelter *en route* against a shower of tropical heaviness. It had hailstones in it too, and was shiveringly cold.

Edgar found his brother very poor company at supper that evening. He evinced no interest whatever in descriptions of Penchester Cathedral, and very little more in the mysterious disappearance of Lenny Gurscall, the village idiot, about which all sorts of strange tales and rumours were current in the servants' hall. Nor was Philip's account of his escape from the bull such as to excite or amuse. The fact was that the hideous reality of the experience which he was suppressing prevented him from giving to the fictitious taurine encounter any sufficient veneer of verisimilitude. Beginning the meal with mere lack of appetite he ended it with a positive feeling of nausea.

Coming in with Lady Redlaw to bid both boys goodnight his mother quickly saw that all was not well with the younger. A clinical thermometer confirmed her apprehensions by recording a temperature of a-hundred-and-two. Philip was therefore put promptly to bed and Edgar removed to a separate room.

'Not,' Mrs Falmer explained, 'that I suspect anything infectious, but one can't be too careful. Running away from that bull must have made the boy hot, and then on top of it he got caught in that icy downpour. He's probably got a chill.'

So, indeed, it appeared; for, in spite of a hot-water bottle, Philip was taken with shivers and passed a night far from peaceful either for himself or for those in the adjoining bedrooms. The reader may be left to guess for himself the nature of the dreams that caused him to wake up, screaming, not less than three times in twice as many hours.

3

It is not the purpose of this tale to curdle the reader's blood or make his flesh creep by presenting Philip's dreams in horrific detail. For a proper understanding of the trouble that temporarily over-whelmed him after his shell-shock in 1918 it is, however, necessary to sketch the development of what might be called the pump motif in his subconsciousness. The trouble indubitably arose from the fact that neither of his parents, excellently kind as both were, was sufficiently sympathetic or appreciative of childish fears and imaginings to en-courage confidences between him and them on such subjects.

In conversation with his brother, moreover, Philip was studious to avoid any appearance of juniority such as might lead Edgar to patronise him. The consequences were that he kept the unpleasant episodes of Tarrington churchyard, the mill-pond ram and Thorp's Spinney religiously to himself; that his secretive repression bred recur-rent remembrances of the incidents in his dreams; and finally, after his shell-shock, a critical condition of neurosis.

At his preparatory school he was nicknamed 'Screamer', and often awoke from his nightmare with a cake of soap in his mouth. This treatment proved successful in putting a stop to his habit of actual yelling and saved him from later persecution in the big dormitories of Winchingham where a tooth-jug of cold water was accepted as the only remedy for even loud snoring.

The common source of all his dreams lay in the three episodes already recounted, and especially in that of Thorp's Spinney; though they differed and divagated in detail. Sometimes, for instance, the pump usurped the fictitious role of the bull as pursuer and came lung-ing, lurching, and clanking along behind him with its handle swinging viciously up and down in an effort to reach and strike him. Another night the pump would wear a foul bestial face, of which the spout formed a trunk that trumpeted at him. There were nights, too, when it was robed in a silk academic gown like that of the headmaster, and its handle became an arm brandishing a cane.

There were hundreds more of such variations but each of them augmented rather than diminished the offensiveness of the nightmare. There appeared no rhyme or reason about its periodicity. Sometimes Philip would be without it for as long as three months at a stretch, and then suffer it for two or even three nights in succession.

He grew up into a man of strong character who was not going to let himself be beaten by a dream. He disciplined his sleeping self so well, in fact, that he would often succeed in waking himself up at the very outset of the familiar vision. It was not until shell-shock deprived him of his self-control that the nightmare proliferated and reproduced itself so incessantly as to threaten his sanity. In this tragic plight he was wisely counselled by a friend to consult Dr Hasterton, whose success with such cases was beginning at that time to become well known.

Philip took to this specialist at once, and in the course of general conversation at their first meeting it transpired that Hasterton had just returned from Sockstead, where the Hall and surrounding property had been acquired by his brother after Sir James Redlaw's death in 1913. The conversation then turned naturally to shooting and the doctor mentioned how he had brought down two high birds with a marvellous right and left just above Thorp's Spinney.

To his own immense surprise Philip heard himself enquiring whether the pump were still there. Such an unusual question gave the doctor a cue, which he discreetly and cleverly followed up; with the result that in less than half an hour Philip had made a clean breast of all his silly pump, ram and ball-cock secrets. Finally, Hasterton suggested that, as he was running down to Sockstead again the next weekend but one, Philip might accompany him. If so, they could ramble round the old place together and possibly shoot a rabbit or two. To this suggestion Philip gladly agreed.

Arrived at Sockstead Hall, Philip found Hasterton's brother as companionable and easy to get to know as the doctor himself. After Mrs Hasterton and her daughter had gone to bed, the three men sat up late over the big log-fire in the smoking-room. Their talk turned on sport, and the doctor couldn't resist mention once more of his prowess at Thorp's Spinney.

'Talking of Thorp's Spinney,' said his brother, 'we made a rather gruesome discovery there the week before last. It landed us in a coroner's inquest too! No; it wasn't murder or anything of that sort. 'Death by Misadventure' was what they brought it in; but the odd thing is that the accident must have happened some twenty years ago. But perhaps this bores you?'

'Far from it! Please go on.'

'Well, about a fortnight ago my bailiff, Horton, suggested that we put the three fields on Thorp's Rise under roots, but Gumwell (the new man at Home Farm) wouldn't hear of it. They were such excellent pasture, he said, and he wanted to use the old cowsheds below the rise if only water could somehow be led to them. Only a few days ago he had come across the remains of an old pump by the spinney. Its suction pipe had been broken away and he could find no signs of a well. But there couldn't very well have been a pump there without one and he suggested that I should send a man down to dig about and see. So, I sent old Comper, and it wasn't long before he came back to report the discovery of a large flat stone that rang hollow and looked a likely well-cover. The same afternoon Horton, Gumwell and I with two farm hands, in addition to old Comper, took down two crowbars and a rope, and sure enough we found a large pit under the stone.

'It wasn't a well though, but a large underground tank some fifteen feet in diameter. About seven feet from the top there opened into it a large circular brick culvert, large enough for a man to crawl through, and within five minutes or so we had traced its other end. It led from the big ditch above the Spinney, but the opening was so blocked with brambles and weeds that I had never noticed it when rabbiting. The downhill side of the ditch had scoured out a hundred yards higher up, and any water it brings down nowadays runs away on the other side of the wood. Consequently, the tank was dry and I gave instructions for a ladder and lanterns to be brought down after breakfast next morning, so that we could inspect the condition of the brickwork. I was delayed on the morrow by the arrival of some important letters, and by the time I got to the Spinney they had already made their discovery of human remains at the bottom of the tank. I was there, however, when old Comper brought up the clue to their identity. It had once been a silver hunter watch, but now looked like a black pebble. On the inside lid at its back were engraved the words '*Jude Gurscall*, 1859'.

'Well, to cut this long story short, Jude Gurscall's widow is still alive, and the remains were undoubtedly those of an idiot son. The unfortunate fellow is still well remembered in the village, for on reaching puberty he had shown signs of becoming dangerous and the question of getting him locked up had begun to be raised by neighbours when he unaccountably vanished and was seen no more. One of his madnesses had been to crawl down holes, and platelayers once had great difficulty in extricating him from the culvert under the railway embankment at Bemsford. He had undoubtedly met his end by creeping along the Thorp Spinney drain and falling down into the underground tank at its end, a good twenty-foot drop. If there was more than his own height of water in it, he must have been drowned; if it was dry he probably broke his bones and perished of starvation. However loudly he called for help his cries could never have reached human ears.'

'That,' Philip interrupted, 'is where I'm sorry to say you're wrong: because they happened to reach mine!'

<h2 style="text-align:center">4</h2>

Dr Hasterton's concern as to the likely effect of his brother's narrative upon his patient had waxed greater as the tale unfolded. If he could have anticipated such a sinister *dénouement*, he would certainly never have brought Philip to Sockstead. There was indeed a grave risk that what had just been told might cause a recrudescence of the young man's dreaming and re-establishment of subconscious obsessions. The doctor was therefore relieved to note that Philip's face, which he kept under constant but unaggressive attention, indicated neither distaste nor apprehension but only intense interest as the story proceeded. Philip's sudden interruption of it provided the opportunity for preventing the development of any tendency to self-reproach on his part for having, though unwittingly, left a man to his death. This opportunity the specialist promptly seized.

'And now, Falmer, please explain to my brother how a kind providence used your childish fears, and your disinclination to relate your experience in the spinney, to prevent discovery of the lunatic and the lifelong misery for him of incarceration in an asylum.'

Thus encouraged Philip gave a full and unrestrained account of that terrible episode in his boyhood. In doing so he showed neither repression nor self-criticism. His two auditors listened sympathetically and made it clear that Philip's conduct had been perfectly natural in a small boy and that they would have behaved similarly.

'As my brother remarked,' said his host at the conclusion of Philip's confession, 'your silence was providential. A return of the lunatic after his merciful disappearance would have been a tragedy. The first words that his old mother uttered when they told her of our discovery were 'Lord help us, but don't let him back here!' Only when she realised that he had been dead these twenty years past did she become maternal and proprietary. Then her imagination ran quickly to a fine funeral, and in this the whole of both Socksteads were with her. Her better-off neighbours contributed to the cost of an interment which could be fully enjoyed without necessity for any pretence of sorrow. A large crowd turned up for the ceremony and the *Penchester Pioneer* sent over a special reporter to take pictures.

Favourite hymns were sung vociferously at the graveside and, as the country saying goes, a good time was had by all. Only the parson objected to the levity of the coffin being matched by that of its bearers. To cap all, they sent round a subscription list for 'a tombstone. It's in that desk now, together with a drawing of the design. Horton tells me that the inscription is to be partly in Latin. We'll have a look at it!'

The drawing was duly unrolled, and the proposed epitaph ran as follows:

In Memory of
Leonard Job Gurscall
Born November 16, 1876
Died *circa* May 9, 1894
'*Thou hast in love to my soul delivered it from the pit of corruption.*'—*Is. xxxviii*, 17

'What can Horton have meant about the inscription being partly in Latin?' the doctor enquired.

'Well,' laughed Philip, 'one would hardly call "*circa*" English!'

Hasterton noted the laugh with satisfaction. It looked as though the cure might prove permanent and complete. So indeed, it proved: but the specialist was slightly chagrined some weeks later to learn that his patient in no way ascribed it to his professional ministrations. 'Of course,' Philip declared, 'the nightmares were bound to stop as soon as they discovered and removed the presence in the well.'

·

Whiffs of the Sea

1

In front of the thatched summer-house on a lawn over-looking rockery and water garden at Telbury Grange sat Rupert Madgeby and the two old college friends whom he had invited for the weekend. Of these, Richard Penham was a don at Oxbridge and Derek Singleton a literary and art critic on the staff of the *Evening Review*. Madgeby himself after being called to the Bar had come in for money on the death of an uncle in the steel trade, and now seasoned his limitless leisure with honorary secretarial work for a number of philanthropic causes. None of the three men was much over thirty, Singleton being the eldest at thirty-three and a half.

'It's the jasmine at the back of the summer-house,' Madgeby was saying; 'I've never known it so sweet as this year. It is a strange thing that so little trouble has been taken by horticulturists to develop or even to preserve the scent of flowers. I hear that, after sacrificing the scent of sweet peas to magnifications of size and accentuations of colour, they have been driven to the absurdity of introducing a special class at flower-shows for sweet Sweet Peas! Nor is it always the fault of the florist. Musk in recent years appears to have deodorised itself of its own initiative. No musk smells nowadays.'

At this point Penham interpolated the suggestion that gardeners and garden owners did not as a general rule care about the smell of flowers; otherwise, the seedsman would cater for them quickly enough. There was, he said, no literature of scent as there was of colour and sound. Smell was the Cinderella of the senses.

'It isn't correct,' Singleton complained, 'to represent that there is no literature of scent. Oddly enough, I happen to be compiling an anthology on this very subject, and my citations are already so voluminous as to need pruning. Surely, Penham, you can't have forgotten that lovely passage in Bacon's essay, *Of Gardens*? I can quote you the first sentence: "*And because the breath of flowers is far sweeter in the air* (where it comes and goes, like the warbling of music) *than in the hand, therefore nothing is more fit for that delight than to know what be the flowers and plants that do best perfume the air.*"

'Then there is that delightful bit about flower scents in *A Hind in Richmond Park*. I can't repeat the words from memory but Hudson's argument was that the odour of blossoms, although charged with memories, never lost the freshness and charm of novelty.'

'You wouldn't, I suppose, suggest,' Madgeby enquired, 'that memories ever created a scent?'

'No; but Alphonse Karr came very near to such a proposition in his *Tour of my Garden*. His statement was so unusual that it has stuck in my mind; this is what he wrote:

'"There often exhales from certain flowers something more and even better than perfume—I mean certain circumstances of life with which they are associated and with which they inseparably dwell in the mind, or rather in the heart, even as the *hamadryads* were not able to quit their oaks."'

'Is your anthology limited to what has been written about the scent of flowers?'

'Oh, no! The longest section will in fact be about smells of the sea. There's some very fine poetry, and prose too, about them.'

'Ugh!'

The exclamation seemed to have been jerked from Madgeby's mouth involuntarily, but he temporarily avoided interrogation by addressing the butler who had just arrived with the tea things.

'Parkins, when you fetch the hot toast will you be so good as to bring me the red notebook lying on top of the small bookcase in the morning-room? The red one, remember; there are several of them there but only one is red.'

'Very good, sir.'

'You were about to ask me, I think'—Madgeby turned-to his two friends—'why I said "Ugh!": so, I've told Parkins to bring you the explanation. I never like being called a liar to my face though I've no objection to people disbelieving me behind my back. That's why I've written down a short account of an experience the actuality of which I can't very well expect anyone else to accept. To put it crudely, I was once haunted by a smell and the memory is not so pleasant as to make me want to talk about it. So, you two can read my notes after tea, while I walk down to Merriman's to remind him about Mrs Gibson's geranium cuttings. Thank you, Parkins: yes, that's the right one. Sugar,

Dick? Nor you either? What commendably economical guests!'

As soon as tea was finished and Madgeby had disappeared down the shrubbery path, Penham took up the notebook and, at a nod from Singleton, began to read aloud.

2

(From the Red Notebook: First Part)

I bought the water-colour drawing at Herbertson's in Redford Row for two guineas. It was the picture of some harbour or estuary; sea lavender, shingle, samphire and mud in the foreground; two rowing boats moored to a buoy in the middle distance, and a third boat with two oarsmen approaching from a ketch in midstream; beyond the channel a line of more mud, fields and hedges; and above them, between two clumps of elms, a distant spire; more distant still a glimpse of wooded downs. I had never heard the name of the artist (the picture was signed 'C. Withentake, 1841'), nor had old Herbertson. He had thought the drawing and colouring good, as did I, and had bought it on its own merits at a sale for two pounds. He had subsequently developed a dislike for it and would let me have it for that sum. 'Nonsense,' I replied, 'you would die of remorse when you tot up your accounts! I'll give you three guineas for it. In my opinion it's good.'

I was confirmed in this opinion when I saw the picture hanging in my rooms at Stanners Court, and Hollingdon, who dropped in for tea, congratulated me on the buy. 'It's got quite as much atmosphere in it,' he said, 'in spite of its accuracy of detail, as any of our modern impressionist stuff. The scene is almost unpleasantly alive.'

I am never a sound sleeper and in the early hours of next morning I went into my sitting-room for a book. The moment I opened the door my breath was caught by a strong, very strong, smell of the sea; not merely a fishy, shrimpy, muddy, weedy or salty smell, all of which odours can be sensed in isolation, but that unmistakable concentrated amalgam of them all that one inhales on the shore at low tide. I do not like this smell at any time, and always avoid a seaside holiday. I thought little of it now, however, as the window was open and I postulated a high tide in the Thames and a wind from the south-east.

It struck me as strange to read in the newspaper next morning that tides were neap and the wind in the north, but I dismissed the matter from my mind as negligible, and would have forgotten all about it but for a repetition of the smell that very next night and during many succeeding nights. A professional writer might find words adequately to describe the cumulative nastiness of these experiences. I will only say that I loathed the smell more and more and began to dread its recurrence. I understood now the full significance of the common phrase which predicates of a hateful thing that it stinks in one's nostrils. This filthy sea smell stayed and stank in mine.

I disliked it none the less for a nightmare that would often synchronise with it. In this dream I would find myself cabined in a very small metal compartment and seem to hear all around me the swishing and gurgling of water. A complete airlessness foreboded early suffocation. In a frenzy of despair, I would try to beat my hands against the sides of my prison, only to find that they as well as my legs were securely tied with ropes. At this point, with a horrid jump of the heart, I would wake up in a cold sweat, and with the smell of the sea pungently around me.

I was beginning to mistrust my sanity, or at any rate, my ability to retain it, when my trouble was brought into perspective with the humdrum and commonplace by Mrs Durren. This lady is employed by Stanners Court Flats Limited under the impressive designation of Lady Supervisor of the Company's Residential Premises; but to all of us tenants she has always been just 'Mrs D'.

'Ferguson has been telling me of the smell that hangs about your sitting-room when he takes the coals up of a morning.'

'So, he's noticed it too?'

'Yes, and I went this morning to see, or perhaps I should say, to smell, for myself. Mr Madgeby, there must be seaweed in the back of that new picture. That's where the smell comes from. Please have it opened up and the stuff taken out. My husband used to keep seaweed nailed onto a board and called it his barometer. He was seldom far out in his forecasts either, but I couldn't a-bear the smell it gave off, and this one's exactly the same.'

'But nobody would place seaweed behind a painting!'

'And why not? Quite likely it was the artist's keepsake from the beach where he drawed it. Anyway, there's no mistaking the smell, and if the seaweed isn't there, we shall have to look somewhere else. But my nose, which is a sharp one, has traced it to that picture!'

3

(From the Red Notebook: Second Part)

As I anticipated, Mrs Durren was proved wrong. There was no seaweed nor anything else found at the back of the picture. Its unframing, however, disclosed some faint writing on the reverse of the drawing, which had been imperfectly erased and could without great difficulty be read as follows:

Who toils for us is our toilerman
And his lad our toiler boy;
If he boil not who is boilerman
Hie to our boiler boy:
So, hey, sing hey, for our boilerman
And hey for the boiler boy.

These lines struck me not merely as meaningless but as positively idiotic but, such is the perversity of the human brain, I could not get them out of my head.

At the time of which I am writing the comic operetta, *Sailors Seven,* was having its record run at the Golconda, and every guttersnipe in town was whistling the tune of that song which begins:

The bosun yelled at the cabin boy;
Young son of a dog, roared he.

To this wretched tune the words on the back of the picture attached themselves in my involuntary imagination: it was a maddening combination! Nevertheless, it had an interesting development.

I was in the library of my club, where I thought myself alone, when, stepping down from a ladder with a book on Tudor Monuments in my left hand, I sang to myself softly and absentmindedly, to the comic opera tune, the words:

So hey, sing hey, for our boilerman
And hey for the boiler boy!

'Good heavens! who's that?'

Dropping the book in my surprise and turning round, I saw Aubrey Lenville staring at me from the writing-desk in the alcove.

'I'm sorry, Madgeby, to have startled you,' he said, 'but you gave me such a shock. Where on earth did you pick up that song you were singing; I mean the words?'

When I told him that I had found them at the back of a painting he grew more excited than ever.

'Do you know what they mean?'

'Certainly not,' I replied. 'They can't mean anything! The whole verse runs like this' (I repeated all six lines) 'and it's obviously tosh.'

'It may seem so to you, Madgeby, but by Jove I'm glad to have overheard you! There's history in it.'

'History in what?'

'In that verse! Let's get into these comfortable chairs and I'll explain. That's better. I wonder if you've yet seen any books in that "*Sidelines of History*" series that Goldenshaw's are publishing?'

'No; but I've read the *Decade's* review of the one on Lepers and Lunatics. It sounded interesting and I jotted it down on my library list.'

'Well, I've been commissioned to write the volume on *Smugglers,* and that's how I'm able to place your song and give it a meaning. It's part of an old smugglers' shanty, and I'll tell you all about it so far as my researches have gone so far.'

Lenville walked over to the desk where he had been writing, and came back with a large number of notes written on blue foolscap. After a minute or two's search he found the sheet he wanted.

'Here we are. This is my note, and I'll read it as it isn't too long: "In Thornychurch harbour the smugglers for some undiscovered reason called their leader 'the boiler-man' and the following verse is still known at Itchenham as the Smugglers' song:

Who coils our rope is coilerman
And his son our coiler boy;
If he boil who is our boilerman,
Beware his boiler boy:
Once ho! twice ho! for our boilerman;
Thrice ho! for our boiler boy.

'(A different version from yours, Madgeby, or maybe a second verse to it?)

"Most of the *gang* lived on the Itchenham side but tradition has it that they landed their stuff across the water at Bosnor, where the Emstead and Thornychurch channels meet. A spit of shingle near their junction is still known as Boilerman's Hard. The trade appears to have prospered well into the Queen's reign when the leader, one Charles Wapentake—"

'Withentake, not Wapentake,' I found myself interrupting.

'What on earth—'

'Never mind, go on reading. I'll explain afterwards.'

"One Charles Wapentake, agreed with the Customs House man at Itchenham to betray the whole business for a consideration but, before the bargain could be kept, Wapentake disappeared entirely from the vicinity, nor was he ever heard of again either there or anywhere else. The rest of the gang are believed to have transferred their activities to Graylingsea, where in the face of increased wariness on the part of the Customs the trade soon petered out. It became known after his mysterious disappearance that Wapentake had entered into an agreement with the Dean of Thornychurch to make certain drawings of the cathedral before commencement of its restoration."

'That finishes my note. It's only half the story of course, but it gives the meaning of the lines you were singing. I don't suppose that I shall ever succeed in finding out anything more about the Bosnor gang; I pumped my local sources dry.'

'You've certainly provided a context for my song, but hardly a meaning! Now, if you can find time to come round with me to my rooms in Stanners Court I would like to show you the picture on which the verse was scribbled. The painter signed himself as C. Withentake: that's why I interrupted you just now.

'You *can* come? Well, that's splendid. Let's be getting along.'

Twenty minutes later we both stood opposite the picture in my room. A twitching of Lenville's facial muscles belied the apparently calm deliberation with which he proceeded to examine it through my magnifying glass.

'You're right about the name; it's certainly Withentake, and the drawing is just as certainly a view of Thornychurch harbour. There's no mistaking Thornychurch spire. It must, I think, have been sketched from Bosnor beach. What, by the way, is that thing which the boats are moored to?'

'Isn't it a buoy?'

'Perhaps so; but it's such a strange shape, more cylindrical than conical.'

'Yes,' I politely agreed, 'more like a boiler than a buoy.'

Lenville suddenly gripped my arm, so violently that it hurt.

'You've got it, Madgeby; you've got it, by Jove.'

'Got what?'

'Why, the boiler buoy, of course! *Sing, hey, for the boiler boy!* It's all as clear as a pikestaff. This was the smuggler's buoy, and the receiver who kept rendezvous by it and landed their smugglings they must have called their boiler-man. The fire which he lit on the shore would be a signal of safety only if it were without a cauldron or kettle; or, in the words of your song, if he boiled not who was boilerman. Nor were signals given at Bosnor only. There's other stuff very typical of known smugglers' codes in the rest of the verse. A man and a boy at work in the fields by Dittering Gap or coiling, ropes on Bulver Quay, would have indicated some item of intelligence. There may, too, have been some significance in the number of Heys! or Ho's! to be shouted. One can't hope to establish the exact details now, of course; but, thanks to you, Madgeby, the main puzzle is solved.'

'Possibly,' I replied. 'But I'm now going to tell you something which has been worrying me and which, I fear, will prove unexplainable.'

Lenville listened critically but not incredulously to my narration of the recurrent smell and nightmare. He felt sure, he said, that both must bear some relation to the picture, and thereupon fell silent and pensive over a whisky-and-soda which I had poured out for him.

'What are you doing next weekend?' he at length enquired.

'Nothing particular; why?'

'Because I want you to run down with me to Thornychurch on Friday evening, and we can get back on Monday morning. That will give us two whole days to have a look round Bosnor. The farmhouse there has been derelict for a long time and there's nobody living on the headland, but I can get two men to row us over from Itchenham and lend a hand.'

'Lend a hand at what?'

'Investigation.'

'But what do you expect to find there?'

'What you've been dreaming about: a narrow metal chamber, airless and dark, surrounded by a gurgling and swishing of water. In other words, the boiler buoy. There's no port authority in Thornychurch, and where the buoy once floated there, it must have since sunk. You can still see the one that used to mark the Stocker Shoal if you look over a boat's edge there at low water in spring tides. If we should succeed in fording it, it might be possible to have it opened. From the words of those two verses, I guess that the inside may well have been used as the Smugglers' *cache*. Anyhow, the clue's worth following up. Will you come?'

I promised to do so.

'By the way,' Lenville concluded, 'we shall need to have this picture with us in order to get our bearings. So, take it out of its frame, will you, and pack it at the bottom of your suitcase where it won't get crumpled.'

4

(From the Red Notebook: Third Part)

When we landed in our boat from Itchenham on the spit of muddy shingle off Bosnor known as Boilerman's Hard the tide was still on the ebb and there was an hour or so to go before low water. Lenville walked straight up the pebbly strip towards the foreshore, carrying in his hand the portfolio in which I had placed the Withentake picture. On reaching the line of sea lavender and dried seaweed that marked the season's high water-mark he took the drawing out and compared it with the actual scene before him. A puzzled look quickly crept into his face. In the picture Thornychurch spire was exactly over the water end of the hard, where the boats lay moored to the buoy.

Our own boat, now occupying an identical position, was completely out of line with the spire! Lenville was explaining this discrepancy to me when one of our boatmen came up: a man named Burdenshaw, who, having served as a yacht-hand in his younger days, now made a comfortable living by looking after many of the small craft at Itchenham, which their owners found time to sail only at weekends.

'It's plain to me, sir,' he politely struck in, 'that this here droring were done afore the Yardle Creek came to be shifted after the storm of seventy-two, when the spring tides spilled over Tilsea Bank and flooded all the Brinsley flats. The old sluice, way back there where you see them gulls, were washed away when the water as had got in had to make its way out again at change of tide; and the creek as it now lays follows the straight cut as was then made. The water cut through the old hard, it did; and that's the old hard all right what we sees in that picture.'

'But you told me over at Itchenham,' Lenville objected, 'that *this* was Boilerman's Hard.'

'Well, sir, so it be and so it bean't. After the Bosnor levels were reclaimed (and a mort of money was lost when the sea broke in again) farmer Betterman started grazing his cattle off them, and it were he as made the present hard with shingle from Haylesworth bar. Betterman's Hard it should rightly be called, but the name of the old got stuck onto the new and Boilerman's Hard is what it is called by.'

'So that's how it is!' Lenville said with a recovered cheerfulness. 'Well, now we've got to find the end of the old hard, and it shouldn't be difficult. You two must now go back to the boat, while I walk along the shore till I get Thornychurch spire exactly half-way between those two clumps of elms, as it is in the picture. Then I want you to row slowly along at the edge of the muds till I give you a shout. That shout will mean that you've reached a spot on the direct line between me and the spire, and that's where you'll want those poles, we've brought. Just go on prodding the bottom till you hit on something hard; then stake it with a pole and shout for me. While you're prodding don't forget to keep an eye on me, or you'll soon drift off the line. As long as I keep my arms down you can take it that you're all right, but if I hold out either arm you must pole the boat towards that side until I drop it again. Is that quite clear?'

It was; so Burdenshaw and I rejoined the other man in the boat and, as soon as Lenville shouted, commenced our prodding. We had prodded for a long half-hour and the stench of the mud, which reminded me unpleasantly of the smell in my nightmare, had begun to make me feel sick when Burdenshaw asked what it might be as the other gentleman expected for to find?'

'An old buoy, I believe.'

'Then it ain't no good us prodding here in the water for what's been high and dry five miles away for more nor thirty year! The old buoy be up at Appleham under the sea wall; as I would have told the other gentleman if he had asked after it: but he never did, did he, Bill?'

'He sure didn't.'

I bade them row to the new hard and had soon explained the position to Lenville, who bitterly cursed old Dingleby, the landlord of the Crown and Sceptre at Itchenham, for not having told him all he might have done. We must now, he added, go straight to Appleham.

This as it happened was easy enough, for the wind was blowing strongly up the harbour from the south-west, and under a small lugsail we were soon running before it at a good speed and, on passing Itchenham, saw that the yachts at their moorings were already swinging to the flood tide. This was also in our favour for, by the time we had reached Never Point, we found sufficient water for us to row right up the channel to Birdquay, whence a walk of little more than ten minutes brought us to Appleham sea wall.

When I caught sight of the object of our search, I felt sure that the boatmen must adjudge us lunatics. In this, however I was wrong, for I soon realised that their sense of local importance vested everything in Thornychurch harbour, or near it, with an interest that needed no explanation, much less apology. The object might once have been an actual boiler: if so, the inspection plate had been removed many years ago, and I found what might perhaps be the remains of it quite nearby.

The resultant hole in the cylinder, into which the plate would once have fitted, had been worn and widened by corrosion and rust into a large and irregular aperture. Inside there lay a drift of sand, dried sea-weed, crab-shells and other wind-borne rubbish; for the boiler lay above the level of ordinary tides. With the help of a spade, Lenville satisfied himself that it contained nought else, and we then started on a long and laborious row back to Itchenham against both wind and tide. Having at length arrived there, I noticed that Lenville paid both boatmen much more than the amount agreed upon, presumably by way of compensation for the bad temper which he had exhibited on the way back.

After a polite 'thank you!' the younger of the two (Bill, whose sur-name I never got) mumbled something about old Dingleby's father having been sexton up at Appleham before they built the new church, and about an uncle having kept the 'Crab and Lobster' at Birdquay. With this parting intimation the two made off and, turning to Len-ville, I suggested that we might turn into the 'Crown and Sceptre' for some food and drink as well as for a questioning of old Dingleby.

'If he knows more than he's already told me, he's a damned old scoundrel,' Lenville assented, 'but we'll make sure.'

5

(From the Red Notebook: Fourth Part and Postscript)

'We didn't never expect to see you back here so soon, Mr Lenville,' Old Dingleby remarked, as he set before us the beer, bread and cheese which we had ordered, 'for there hasn't been none of your history-making here since you went away, and you sucked us as dry as an orange, you did, over them smuggler stories.'

'I'm not too sure about that,' rejoined Lenville, 'though you swore that you'd told all you know about the Bosnor *gang.*'

'Aye, sure!'

'But you said nothing at all about the buoy which lies under Ap-pleham sea wall, did you?'

'Ah! then I didn't tell you about that, didn't I? Well now, if that isn't strange! But some days I remember and some days I forget, though most days and most ways I mind well what were told me by my fa-ther. He never told me nothing that weren't worth minding, didn't my father.'

'And what did he tell you about that buoy?'

'That it were broke away from its mooring off Bosnor in the big tides before Jubilee and were drifted up under Appleham wall, where it now lays.'

'Anything else?'

'Nothing, except that it were opened up by Squire Marcroft and Parson Hayden and nothing found but mud and bones.'

'What did they expect to find?'

'Something maybe as might be more comfortably stowed in their own insides! It were a smugglers' buoy, you mind.'

'Ah, yes; I see: and what then?'

'Well, my father said as the Chief Constable come down one day out of Thornychurch; and bodies be one thing, he says to the Squire, and bones be another. What is took out as bones may have been put in as bones, he says; and them as finds can lose. So, Squire Marcroft was for chucking them into the creek; but Parson said as they must be given benefit of the doubt, and buried them as you come to the old churchyard stile; and if ever they belonged to a Christian body, he said, they could climb over easy at the doom.'

At this point, Lenville called for two more mugs of beer and some more cheese.

'I wish, Landlord, you'd told me all this before. It would have saved my friend and me a long journey and a wasted morning. I suppose that your father never told you of any suspicion he may have had about those bones?'

'Not exactly suspicions, but he and my uncle, as had the "Crab and Lobster", this side of Birdquay, used to argue as how they might have belonged to Smuggler Withentake. It's in the Dean's books that Withentake took an order to make drawings of the cathedral, and afore he could do that he must need get out of his old trade. But, asks my uncle, would his mates over at Bosnor make him free? No, answers my father; that they wouldn't: for why, he knew their secrets. Therefore, my father and uncle agreed, he must have gone to the Customs and offered to do what would at the same time rid him of his bad company and fetch him money for his paints and what not.

'Then, hearing as he were about to play Judas on them, his mates would have set on him and shut his body, alive or dead, into the old buoy. That was what my father would say, and my uncle too; and my father used to add that it were his honest hope as they killed their man first, for to be shut up in that boiler without light or drink or food, and to hear the water gurgling and licking the outside—'

'That's enough!' I interrupted, and hurried outside, leaving Lenville to explain that I was of a somewhat nervous disposition and to settle the account. Lenville, very considerately, talked of other subjects all the way back to London; but as we parted at the railway terminus and were shaking hands, he smilingly, instead of 'Goodbye', said 'Q.E.D.'

R. Madgeby

17th September, 1899

Postcript.—Since writing the above notes, I have not once been incommoded by the smell or by the nightmare therein described. Mrs Durren, to her great satisfaction, traced the former to the use of seaweed in his bath by the tenant of the rooms immediately below mine. He had it sent up twice a week by rail from the south coast and found that it relieved his rheumatism.

R.M. 13.XII.99

6

Penham and Singleton were still discussing scents and dreams—both generally and with particular reference to what they had just read in the notebook—when they saw their host returning by the grass path between the herbaceous borders and carrying under his arm a picture-frame.

'I thought,' Madgeby explained, 'that you might like to see the actual painting about which I wrote in those notes. I keep it locked up in a cupboard nowadays, because of its associations; although, here at Telbury, we're seventy miles from the coast and unlikely to catch any whiffs from the sea! I think that you'll agree as to its being a good piece of work.'

After a careful and critical examination, for which purpose Madgeby propped the frame against the back of a garden seat, both guests assented, Singleton enthusiastically. All three men thereafter reclined once more in the comfortable deck-chairs and lazily accepted the drinks and smokes which Parkins brought round on a tray. The evening was warm and windless and conducive to reverie rather than to argument. The night-scented stocks in the bed round the summerhouse began to add their fragrance to that of the jasmine—a blend which would have been sickly but for the admixture of tobacco smoke.

Suddenly however the closeness of the atmosphere seemed to be lifted, and a rustle in the silver poplar on the lawn was followed by a whispering in the maple above the summer-house. A number of yellowish leaves fell fluttering down and, so nearly inaudible as to be felt rather than heard, came the rumble of distant thunder. The three friends raised their eyes simultaneously to the sky overhead, which, however, gave no hint of rain or storm. Something nevertheless began to impinge on a sense other than those of sight and hearing. Faint, but definite and unmistakable, and as though it came from an infinite distance, there was wafted into their nostrils the smell of the sea. Penham and Singleton glanced at each other as if for mutual verification, then at the picture on the seat, and, lastly, at their host.

For a few moments, Madgeby continued to sip his whisky-and-soda in silence. Then, setting down the glass carefully on a stool by his side, he turned to his friends with a smile of enquiry. 'I wonder,' he said, 'whether either of you have ever had personal experience of auto-suggestion?'

In Due Course

Fate, poaching as ever on preserves of human enterprise, had fired two barrels at young Alec Judeson. Malaria first got him down; dysentery prevented recovery. The board of doctors that yesterday examined him would, as they had warned him, in due course certify not merely that he must go home forthwith, but also that he must never return to the tropics. The days of his rubber planting in Malaya were numbered.

The medical examination had been at Penyabong, the chief town of Senantan, and Alec was now on his way back to the estate at Sungei Liat to pack up and to say goodbye. Tonight, he would stay at the little resthouse on the summit of Bukit Kotak Pass, and leave the remaining forty-one miles to be driven in the cool of the early morning. Backing his two-seater car into the resthouse stable he suddenly realised how bitterly he would miss the touch of its steering-wheel and the feel of that patch on the driving seat where the stump of a fallen cheroot had burned through the leather. Nevertheless, he must get out a quick advertisement for its sale if he was to scrape together enough dollars for his passage.

A zig-zag of earthen steps led from the stable up to the small plateau on which the resthouse was perched. Empty beer bottles, sunk neck-downward into the soil for half their length, formed the vertical front of each step and so protected the stair from scour or detrition. On either side, amid the knee-deep Lalang grass, sprawled straggly bushes of red shoe-flower or hibiscus. How weak he had become was brought home to Alec by painful inability to mount the steps without several stops and waits. 'Those damned doctors were just about right!' he muttered crossly, slashing with his cane at a stem of hibiscus that slanted across the path.

The action dislodged, and brought rustling and fluttering to the ground at his feet, a large green mantis. Uncannily swivelling its triangular head, the insect fixed him with protuberant black eyes and challengingly crooked its long forelegs in the posture that has earned for the species the epithet of 'praying'. He flicked it distastefully with his stick into the gutter, climbed the few remaining steps to the resthouse verandah, and there sank heavily into one of the long rattan chairs.

A whisky-and-soda helped him regain his breath before, taking a packet of letters from his pocket, he drew out one from a blueish, crested envelope, unfolded it, and began to scan its contents attentively. The embossed address was: 'Saintsend, Dedmans Reach, Tillingford', and the manuscript below it ran as follows:

> "My Dear Alec—I am greatly distressed by the news of your breakdown in health. You will remember my dubiety as to your physical fitness for work in a tropical climate and my unavailing attempts to dissuade you therefrom. This letter, however, is written in no spirit of 'I told you so', but repeats my former invitation to come and live with me here at Tillingford. Your father (and I state this with certainty, as he told me so only ten days before he died) would have approved. It is indeed obviously right that you should get to know, and to regard as 'home', the property that you will come into sooner rather than later; for I am now 67 and do not need a *medico* to tell me that I've got a dicky heart. So do come along, and if you want to bring with you any of your oriental paraphernalia, there's plenty of room here for its exposition or stowage.
>
> Yours avuncularly—
>
> Matthew Judeson
>
> P.S.—You will find several improvements at Saintsend. The Conservancy people refused to let me root out those pollarded willows from the river bank; so I have blotted out all view of them by continuing the garden wall round to where the boathouse used to be. This I have pulled down, filled in the dyke, and built instead a decent-sized studio, music-room and library—my 'Athenaeum', I call it."

'Yours avuncularly!' 'Exposition or stowage of oriental paraphernalia!' 'Athenaeum', indeed! Alec winced as these phrases stung him into remembrance of Uncle Matthew's pomposity and humourless affectation. And why, in heaven's name, wall off the old willows and thereby lose those lovely glimpses of river? Well, in due course (a half-conscious euphemism, this, on Alec's part for after his uncle's death), in due course the wall could be pulled down again; and a temporary circumvallation would only in small degree detract from the amenities of an exceedingly comfortable and commodious residence. Amused that his thoughts should thus run in terms of a house agent's advertisement Alec mentally registered acceptance of his uncle's offer. He would telegraph to the old man as soon as his sailing date was fixed; but, for the moment, he felt it sufficient to clinch his decision with another whisky-and-soda.

As he lay in the long chair, sipping it, there clumsily alighted on the verandah rail beside him another mantis; or, maybe, the same one as before, for the beady stare and aggressive genuflexion were identical. Making a trigger of right forefinger and thumb, he flipped the creature off its perch into the garden and, in doing so, turned his eyes towards the sunset. This was of that jaundiced kind for which. Malays have the ugly word *mambang*. Not merely the western sky but the whole vault was dyed an ugly stagnant yellow. Hills and jungle seemed to soak in it, and Alec remembered that, on such an evening, Malay children would be kept indoors: an understandable, albeit superstitious, precaution.

Five minutes or so later, the yellow glare having dimmed with a suddenness reminiscent of opera, the resthouse-keeper lit the lamp which hung above the dry-rotten table whereon he would shortly lay supper. Numerous patches of iron-mould gave the badly laundered cloth a resemblance to maps of an archipelago, and so turned Alec's thoughts to Java and to the set of shadow-show silhouettes which he had bought on holiday there eighteen months ago. He had, indeed, already been twice reminded of them this evening by the praying mantis, the disproportion of whose neck and arms to the rest of its body was as great as in the case of the shadow puppets. In their case this disproportion was of course necessary in order that the jointed arms should be long enough for the showman to jerk them by their slender rods into the attitudes and gesticulations demanded by his miniature drama.

A marionette is manipulated by strings from above, a shadow silhouette by spindles from below; the one being pulled and the other pushed much in the same way, Alec cynically reflected, as weak or obstinate characters need pulling or pushing in real life. He would certainly take these shadow figures home with him, as being the only 'oriental paraphernalia', to use his uncle's expression, that he possessed. They had been cut in thick buffalo hide and elaborately painted in gold, silver, crimson, saffron, brown and indigo; but on one side alone, the other being left polished but bare: for a shadow drama is watched from both sides of a stretched sheet—on one side, spectators see the painted surfaces of the figures against the white cloth and in the full glare of footlights;' on the other, the clear-cut shadows of them projected through the cloth. From neither side is the showman visible, for he operates between two parallel screens of palm-leaf immediately beneath the sheet.

The meal, over which Alec Judeson indulged in these Javan memories, was not, for dietetic reasons, that prepared for him by the rest-house-keeper, whose menus depended for edibility on liberal libations of Worcestershire sauce. His hostess at Penyabong had prudently provided him with a hamper of more palatable, and less dangerous, fare. Nevertheless, he was too tired to eat more than a few mouthfuls of each dish; and, before many minutes passed, he gave up the effort and went straight from table to bed.

As he undressed a slight movement of the mosquito-net aroused his curiosity; so, before taking off his shoes, he got up from the chair to investigate. To his annoyance he discovered, for the third time that evening, a mantis. So strong was the grip of its hind legs on the curtain that its head and neck were thrust toward him, at right-angles to the body. Neglectful of their sharp spurs Alec seized the waving forelegs and was sharply pricked for his rashness.

This angered him. Savagely grabbing it by its back and wing-cases, he tore the creature roughly from the net and held its head over the smoking chimney of the lamp. As the black, starting eyes became incinerated into opaque grey, he heard a sizzle and a crackle before he threw the still-wriggling insect to the floor and crushed it under foot. Next moment he was hating himself for this cruelty. Walking to the window he stood for some seconds listening to the stridulation of cicadas in the jungle; then spat into the darkness and returned to his undressing. A few minutes later he parted the mosquito curtains and crept into bed.

Out of weakness and exhaustion he was soon in the indeterminate borderland between waking and sleeping. Pictures passed before his closed eyes of Saintsend garden and he found himself wondering whether, after all, Uncle Matthew had not been right about those pollarded willows at the river edge. Were they not, perhaps, a little too like those gruesomely vitalised trees in Arthur Rackham's illustrations to *Peter Pan?* There certainly seemed to be a group of shadow-show figures in the tree to the left of the sundial, and there appeared, too, to be something waving at him from among the spindly boughs of the one on the right.

Then of a sudden they parted, and the thing looked out at him 'O hell! That bloody mantis again!' He had cried this aloud and thereby woken himself out of his half-sleep. Was the wretched fever on him again? Having lit the bedside candle and rummaged in a suitcase for his thermometer, he took his temperature. Normal. Nerves, then, must have caused his dream, and small wonder after that episode of the mantis! To guard against further nightmare by forcing all nonsensical fancies out of his brain, he now set it to visualise Saintsend with all the accuracy and detail of which his memory was capable. This stern mental exercise, which within half an hour induced a sound sleep, enabled him also to contemplate, with pleasurable anticipation, various improvements to house and garden which it would be possible to make—in due course.

2

Nine weeks later a taxi from Tillingford pulled up at the steps of Saintsend. Young Judeson had scarcely opened its door before he heard the voice of his uncle raised in ponderous salutation.

'Alec, my dear boy, how splendid to see you again! You must excuse a rising septuagenarian for not coming down the steps to greet you. The legs are willing but the heart is weak! Come along up and let Larkin attend to your impedimenta. What? only two cabin trunks? I thought you Eastern *nabobs* travelled with more than that!'

'*Nabobs* may do so, but not a broken-down planter!' frowned the nephew as he paid off the taxi-man and turned to mount the steps. 'Why, uncle, how fit and young you're looking!'

'Looks are liars, I'm afraid, my dear boy. *Soon falls the rotting leaf that autumn gilds*: that's from one of my own poems. Now, if you hand over your keys to Larkin, he'll show you upstairs and help you unpack. They're putting you in the south wing, where you'll enjoy a safe refuge from avuncular intrusion. No more going up and down stairs for the victim of myocarditis! Come and see the Athenaeum as soon as you've tidied yourself up, and don't take too long about it, because our new neighbour at Sennetts, Miss Scettall, has promised to drop in to tea, and you will like to have a look round before she comes.'

Alec highly approved the bedroom and adjoining sitting-room assigned to him. The windows of both gave on to the riverside, and he could look over the new wall and the willow-tops on to the marsh-land and wood beyond. In the right foreground rose a whitewashed gable of the new studio or music-room, which looked far too nice and unpretentious to be dubbed an Athenaeum. In order that it might be above flood-level, it had been built on a raised terrace and was approached by a ramp of masonry leading from a french window in the library. Steps had thus been avoided at either end, and the rough stonework was already ornamentally studded with patches of saxifrage and wall-rue. It would be a dangerous passage to fall from, and Alec found himself considering whether the addition of a rail or low parapet might not be an improvement—in due course.

A deferential cough woke him from this reverie, and, turning round, he saw Larkin standing in the doorway.

'Pardon me asking, sir, but would you be wanting them two parcels as is atop of the brown trunk to be undone? Both of 'em seems to be stuck up with sealing-wax, like.'

'Oh no, thank you, Larkin; just put them, as they are, into that big drawer below the cupboard. Be careful not to shake the square cardboard box: it's got some rather rare and valuable insects inside it.'

Larkin seemed greatly interested at this. 'Then who'll be attending to their feeding, sir, if I may ask it? My young Tom, now, 'e's fair nuts on caterpillars. Hentomolology, the master names it in 'is school report; but, "Tom," I says, "don't you never be putting them bug 'utches again in my pantry, for they ain't 'ealthy; not about the 'ouse."'

'No; but mine aren't alive, Larkin! They're stuffed specimens, like you see in a museum. The fellow in the dispensary on our rubber estate gave them to me when I was saying goodbye. I had been telling him about an experience with what they call a praying mantis. You tell young Tom, next time he has a half-holiday, to pop in here, and I'll show him all sorts of queer things—scorpions, centipedes, mantises, and what not. A bit of a surprise for him after butterflies and moths!'

Having dismissed Larkin with this invitation for Tom, Alec brushed his hair with unusual attention, for the benefit of Miss Scettall, and started to go downstairs. He walked slowly and musingly. His uncle's appearance had very greatly shocked him by its promise of longevity. The cheeks were fuller than he remembered them and positively ruddy. The hair too was but little greyer, if at all, and the eyes gave no hint of weakening. Matthew, in short, looked good for another ten years at least; whereas during the voyage home from Malaya Alec had been nursing the prospect of a brief spell of nepotal attention being speedily rewarded by grateful benedictions from an early deathbed.

After all, had not his uncle indicated as much in his letter of invitation? But not only did he now appear in deplorably rude health, but in five minutes of conversation had paraded all those exasperating affectations that would render any long companionship with him intolerable. Those bleats of 'my dear boy' and 'your poor old uncle'! That periphrastic avoidance of the first person singular; a maddening habit copied, perhaps, from those among the Anglican hierarchy who address their children in God as 'Your Bishop'!

Alec was by now at the foot of the staircase and in the long corridor leading to the library. On either side hung paintings in oils of his grandfather's hunters and dogs, heavily and gaudily framed. The names were on plaques beneath: Caesar, Hornet, Buster, Ponto, and the rest. Alec made a mental note for their removal in due course; and then he suddenly frowned. With his uncle in such good trim, how could his promised inheritance be expected any longer to eventuate in due course. It was bound to be overdue: damnably overdue!

As if to corroborate this anticipation, Matthew Judeson emerged at this moment from the library door, and in full bleat. 'What, down again already? Good on you, my boy; quick work! Now be careful of this rug; it's apt to slip on the marble floor and have you over. Now one goes out through the french window and here we are, you see, on a ramp or isthmus; no steps to negotiate, just a gradual incline. And this is the door of the *Sanctum Sanctorum!* Open it, Alec; and please not to say that you are disappointed!'

Alec certainly was not. He was wondering in fact how so fussy and finical a man could have evolved so restful a room. The plain large open fireplace, the unstained panelling, unceiled barrel roof, grand piano in unpolished oak, red Dutch tiles and rough cord carpets, deep broad leathered chairs—all were right and pleasing.

'One tries,' his uncle resumed, 'to do a good turn to friends whenever occasion offers. The Scettalls are poorly off, so I called in young Alfred for a fee to help with the designs and furnishing. He would already have set up as an architect by now, but for his having got mixed up in a business of which his sister is best left in ignorance. He can rely on his present benefactor, of course, not to tell her.'

'What do you mean by his present benefactor?'

'Why, this old uncle of yours: who else?'

'Well, this unfortunate young nephew of yours. . .' Alec had thus begun in bantering imitation of the old man's circumlocution when

Larkin appeared, not obtrusively but withal importantly, in the doorway and announced: 'Miss Scettall'.

At her finishing school the lady who now entered had been known among the other girls as 'Mona Lisa'. Her likeness to Leonardo's famous picture had grown rather than lessened with her years, and renders any detailed description of her appearance unnecessary. It need only be said that she was fully conscious of the likeness, dressed to the part, and expected all the attention that it demanded. During the conversation that followed her introduction to Alec, although politeness required her to address her remarks mainly to her host, she held the younger man's interest and attention by beck or smile and was gratified to find him all eyes and ears. The tea talk was suitably trivial, but two bits of it must be recounted as bearing upon later developments. The first related to a review in the *Tillingford Gazette* of Matthew Judeson's locally printed *Second Posy of Poesy,* wherein it was opined that the best compliment payable to the second posy was that nobody could have suspected its authorship to be identical with that of the first.

'Now tell us, Mr Judeson,' Mona Lisa commanded with a shake of the forefinger, 'just how you feel about that criticism. Are you conscious of having changed, or shall we say "developed", so greatly? Does your old self know your new self? Or *vice versa?*'

The question was clearly distasteful to Uncle Matthew; for he answered with a certain acidity that he would ask his nephew to read the books, of which Larkin had already been instructed to place author's presentation copies by his bedside, and to pass judgment. He could not help feeling that his first 'posy' had been much underrated. Only forty-three copies had in fact been sold.

That ended discussion on this topic; but after desultory talk of weather, crops and the new vicar at Fenfield the conversation took its second turn of relevance to our story.

'By the way, Mr Judeson,' said Miss Scettall in low confidential tones, 'your friend spoke to us again last night.'

'Which? Saint or the corpse?'

'Well—both or either; you see, our saint *was* the corpse!'

After this enigmatic utterance Miss Scettall turned to Alec and, raising her voice, continued: 'Now let me warn you before it is too late, Mr Alec, not to allow your uncle to interest you too much in his spiritualism. It isn't always quite comfortable, and I'm glad that he's got your company now in this old house. Good gracious, six o'clock!

I must be off at once or Alfred will go without his supper, for we've no cook these days.'

As they escorted her to the front door, Alec wondered how earlier in the day he could have thought his uncle looking well. Perhaps it was the gloom of the corridor, but his face now appeared drawn and grey.

'Alec, my dear boy,' he said as soon as the guest was gone, 'the excitement of your arrival has quite knocked me over.' (Alec noted this first allusion to himself as 'me'.) 'I shall need to take dinner in bed if you will excuse me. Please make yourself thoroughly at home. You can't think how eagerly I have awaited your coming. Tomorrow we'll inspect the gardens together and the fields. There's lots to show you. Goodnight, my dear boy, and God bless you!'

Alec, too, was tired and went early to bed. He woke but once in the night when he heard the stable clock strike four. A patch of light which he had vaguely noticed before falling asleep still showed on the ceiling. One of the curtains, he now saw, had been only half drawn and, going to the window to adjust it, he found that the light came from a chink in the shutters of his uncle's downstair bedroom. Was the old fellow then afraid to sleep in the dark?

3

Of Alec's first days at Saintsend it is necessary only to record his growing affection for the place and increasing dislike of his uncle. This dislike was only slightly relieved by curiosity in regard to his character and behaviour. The two books of verse, which Alec found duly placed by Larkin at his bedside, certainly presented an enigma. *A Posy of Poesy*, published six years ago, was a collection of what might be described as period pieces; metrical exercises of classical artificiality. The first to catch Alec's eye as he opened the volume ran as follows:

Time was when I with heart intact
Would mock the poet's fancy
Whose heart, he quoth, was well nigh crackt
For love of pretty Nancy.
But, now I know, be stated truth:
Of me the same were spoken
Save that my dearling's name is Ruth,
My heart completely broken!

And so on, page after page, until Alec, nauseated by the banality of:

My heart is locked and, woe is me,
Cressida doth keep the key
And will not unlock it!

. . . .closed the book with a vicious snap and picked up its newly published successor. In order not to waste time over it he would read the first poem, then the last, and then one taken at random from the middle.

The first was headed '*Red Idyll*' and, as it seemed rather long, he looked at the last two verses only:

He smelt the hot blood spurting; then
Pressed the red blade to his own heart:
Oh throbbing wild embrace! Next morn
They two were difficult to part.

The dayspring crimsoned overhead,
But grey and cold they lay beneath;
Starkly protesting to the skies
Swift tragedy of love and death.

Good heavens! Uncle Matthew trying to be passionate and modern! What about the end piece? Here it was, written in a loose hexametrical form and entitled '*On My Portrait by N. . .*'

How can you bid me, sir, accept the ME of this portrait?
Does it not lie by its truth, a truth that is irreligious?
Secrets are blabbed by those lips that my will had sealed for ever,
While from the eye peeps hunger for things that I live to dissemble:
The nose, too, is tendentious, sniffing up self-approval,
And a smug ear sits tuned for flattering insincerities.
Take it away, I beg: I cannot conspire betrayal
Of the poor Jekyll who gives to Hyde, out of decency, biding.

Uncle Matthew turning auto-psychoanalytic! Good gracious me! And now for a piece from the middle. Here we are—'*Firewatching*'.

What seest thou in the caves of fire?
I see red avenues of desire
Slope to a fen of molten mire.
What hearest thou in the caves of fire?
I hear the hiss of a hellish quire,
The knell of a bell in a falling spire.
What smellest thou in the caves of fire?

I smell the reek of a funeral pyre,
Foul incense raised to Moloch's ire.
What tastest thou in the caves of fire?
The gust of rouge when cheeks perspire,
The acrid lips of a wench on hire.
What touchest thou in the caves of fire?
The dead grey ash of lust's empire
Cold or ever the red flames tire.

'Really, Uncle Matthew!' murmured Alec, and then hastily corrected himself. 'No, *not* really, Uncle Matthew. It just can't be; it's the sort of stuff he won't allow himself even to read. It's quite beyond or, he would say, below him.'

The next poem, in three *cantos* headed '*addenda*', '*corrigenda*' and '*delenda*', repudiated his authorship even more loudly; but Alec was prevented from trying to guess any solution to the puzzle by a knock at the door and the entry of Larkin. Young Tom was going to be at home that morning and would Mr Alec be so good as to show him them insects? Yes, Mr Alec would, and at half-past eleven if convenient. At that hour consequently we find young Tom in a transport of delight and his father performing the role of commentator.

'Coo! Weren't that stinging crab a fair caution? Beg pardon, sir, did you say scorpion or scorpicle? And 'ooever seed the likes of this 'ere? A prying mantis? What, sir, prying like what they pries in church? Well, fancy that! 'E don't look much of a church-goer to me. But now, Mr Alec, if I may make so bold, please don't let Tom 'ere waste any more of your time. If you'll let me take the box downstairs 'e can make some drorins of the creeturs in the pantry for 'is Natural 'Istory master and I'll mind 'e keeps it careful as gold.'

'Very well, take it by all means: and when Tom has finished his drawings you can place it on the hall table where you put the letters.'

Who could have foretold that this simple and reasonable request was a first link in the chain of destiny that was to drag two masters of Saintsend to their deaths? Yet so it was to prove; and with speed.

On return from a walk down-river that afternoon Alec found a car at the front door and a sadly worried Larkin to greet him. His uncle, so Larkin said, had been took very poorly, not to speak of a fit, and the doctor was with him now. It had all happened along of them insects, for Mr Judeson must have seen the box on the hall table and had opened it. Talk of a shock, why in all his life Larkin had never seen anyone took worse. Matthew Judeson was indeed in serious case. Not a stroke, luckily, said the doctor, but nevertheless a cardiac upset of grave omen for the future. Of his surviving the present collapse the doctor was very hopeful, but he must lie in bed until further notice and receive no outside visitors. With the aid of a draught sent post-haste from the Tillingford dispensary the patient fell into a restful sleep and it was Alec, not he, who lay awake into the early hours of the morrow, thinking of the many things which he would venture upon in due course and congratulating himself on a probable acceleration in the time schedule.

His uncle's salutation when he went to see him next morning was unusual. 'I suppose, Alec,' he said, 'you don't believe in witches? No, I thought not. Nor had your old sceptic of an uncle ever done so until he met Miss Scettall. Now, however, he has his doubts, and perhaps you would be interested to hear the reason.'

'Look here, uncle,' Alec interrupted at this point, 'the doctor says that you're not to tire yourself. So please cut out all this roundabout talk of "your old uncle" and try to speak of yourself as "me" or "I". Yes, I would like to hear about that Mona Lisa woman if only you will speak naturally.'

Matthew contrived to turn a wince into a smile with some diffi-culty, because his conversion of first into third person was a trick that enabled him, as it were, to sit with the audience and admire his own play-acting. However, he affected to take the request in good part and continued, 'Anything to please you, my dear Alec! Well, when Miss Scettall came to Sennetts last year she somehow took to me and I to her. We were excellent neighbours. But as the months passed by, I noticed her becoming increasingly possessive, and on New Year's Day I got a card from her with the message, 'May this Leap Year bring you happiness!' That put me on my guard, and when she suggested a walk on the afternoon of 29th February, I was ready for her. After ef-fervescing about her love for the river country, she began to enthuse over Saintsend and said that all the dear old house needed was an understanding chatelaine. It was then that I quoted two lines from my first book:

Ah! hapless nymph, what boots it him to harry
If Strephon is resolvèd not to marry?

She gave a laugh, but the sound of it was unpleasant. 'Surely,' she said, 'you don't imagine that I'm the sort to angle for superannuated fish? Come along to Sennetts and I'll give you a cup of tea.' I had to go, of course, and when tea was over and Alfred had joined us, she began the *séance* business that has been the curse of my life ever since.'

The doctor's arrival at this point gave his patient a respite from completing the story. This was just as well perhaps, for he was becoming exhausted.

4

Three or four days were to pass before, at Alec's prompting, his uncle took up the unfinished tale. Once again, he started with a question.

'You know perhaps the origin of the name Saintsend?'

'Why, yes: I've read it in Bennet's *Tillingford*.'

'And what does Bennet say?'

'That before the big house at Sennetts was burned down in 1747 and the estate broken up, the farm we now call Santry was known as Sennett's Entry and Saintsend as Sennett's End. The present names are just contractions.'

'Then what does he say of Dedman's Reach?'

'Oh, that's a much more modern name. The land belonged not so long ago to a Sir Ulric Dedman.'

'I wish, my dear boy, that what Bennet wrote were true. Unfortunately, I know better, or perhaps I should say, worse. I learned the real truth during those *séances* I have told you of. The first spirit we got into touch with gave his name as Saynt; Lemuel Saynt. He said that he wanted to warn me about evil existences in the riverside willows that had brought about his drowning (Saintsend, you see, means Saynt's end) in 1703. That he was right about the willows I found out soon after, for I very nearly fell into the stream myself. I distinctly felt a push from behind, and there was a sort of gurgling grunt as my left leg slipped in. It was a horribly near thing. I have seen them too sometimes—or rather their arms and legs. That was why your mantis and stick-insects gave me such a shock last Friday. Luckily, I cannot see the willows any more now that the wall is finished and I sleep downstairs.

'You can still see them from your room of course, and I advise you to keep the curtains drawn on moonlit nights. We never managed to get a clear account from Saynt of the dead man in the reach. You heard Miss Scettall say the other afternoon that it was Saynt himself. I suspect her and Alfred, however, of inventing things when I am not there, and I've caught Alfred trying to guide the planchette. I'm certain, too, that both of them try to incite the willow Things against me. On quite windless nights I sometimes hear them scraping and scratching at my new wall. Who was it, Alec, who said that Hell holds no fury like a woman scorned? It's true enough of Adeline Scettall. She's playing the witch on me night and day. Your coming here, my dear boy, made me feel safer until I opened that box of yours. Magnify that mantis a dozen times and you'll have some idea of what's in the willows. You believe me, don't you? It's all perfectly true, and I simply had to tell you.'

Alec sat thinking for some moments, and then he drew his bow at a venture. 'Uncle,' he said, 'you spoke just now of Alfred guiding the planchette. Does that by any chance account for your second posy of poesy?'

'It certainly came from the planchette,' was the answer, 'and there was a spirit's order to publish it in my name I hope that it was not Alfred: if so, he's as bad as his sister. All my nice friends are offended by the verses, and the vicar at Fenfield has even asked me to give up taking round the bag. From being a sidesman I've become an untouchable! I can't blame him either.'

Unable to repress a slight smile at this ecclesiastical deprivation, Alec told his uncle not to take such things too seriously. Everything would be right and normal again so soon as the *séances* were stopped. Then, bidding the old man calm himself and take a nap, the nephew went out into the garden to think things over. For an hour or more he paced slowly to and fro, his eyes upon the ground. Finally, with the air of one who has laid his plan, he walked briskly across the stable-yard, through the coach-house (now used as a garage) and into the little harness-room.

On a shelf stood two old acetylene car-lamps, one of which he took down and filled with carbide. He had promised, to show Larkin how the shadow puppets worked and now he needed only a dust-sheet, which was soon got, for a practical demonstration. This he gave in his bedroom after dark and, when Larkin left to lay the table for dinner, he switched the beam of the lamp for a brief moment onto the white gable of the Athenaeum. *Jadi!*' he said; which is Malay for 'It'll do'.

Next morning, as though to assure his uncle that he had seen nothing incredible in the previous day's narration, he remarked that, having had to get up just after midnight to open the window, he had made the mistake of looking at the willows. There was certainly something there which he could not associate with the vegetable or animal creation. He felt that his uncle must shake himself and Saint-send free from this ugly tangle of spiritualism without a day's delay. It was getting on his own nerves too.

This speech had the desired effect. 'I'll write at once,' the uncle replied, 'to Miss Scettall and tell her to arrange a final *séance* at Sennetts tonight. A final *séance* is necessary because Saynt has hinted before now of other and more direct methods of approach to me and I must avoid that at all costs. We must pension him off decently, so to speak. The doctor won't like my going out to dinner, but to be quit of this wretched business will be better medicine than any he has ever pre-scribed. Anyhow, I have made up my mind to go.'

After lunch Alec heard Larkin being told that his master would be out to dinner at Sennetts and that brandy, whisky and two glasses were to be put on the small table in the Athenaeum against his return. Larkin need not sit up; he would close the house himself.

'If the whisky and the second glass are meant for me,' interposed Alec, 'I must ask to be excused. I feel a bout of malaria coming on and shall go early to bed with a couple of quinine tablets. You can tell me all about your evening at Sennetts after breakfast tomorrow.'

'Very well, Larkin; the brandy and one glass only. Be careful not to forget, for after my recent collapse I may need it.'

Thus, came it about that, when at nearly midnight he heard the sound of his uncle's car returning down the drive from Sennetts, Alec was in his bedroom. But not in bed. He sat on a stool by the window. On a small table behind him stood an acetylene car-lamp with a sheet of heavy cardboard pressed against the glass to block its rays. In his right hand he held a shadow puppet ready for manipulation. Through the window he could now see the figure of his uncle moving up the ramp towards the Athenaeum. Just as the figure reached the highest point Alec suddenly whipped away the sheet of cardboard and ma-nipulated his puppet. Simultaneously, on the white gable above his uncle, loomed a long-armed, narrow-bodied, spindly shadow, beckon-ing and waving.

There was no cry nor sound of any sort save a dull dead thud on the gravel path beneath the ramp. Within five seconds the acetylene lamp was in a cupboard, the puppet back in its box, and Alec's head on its pillow. Nothing occurred to disturb the remaining hours of night, but early next morning Larkin found the lights in the Athenaeum still burning. A moment later he knew the cause. Another light, and one that could not be relit, had been extinguished.

5

The interval between the inquests on uncle and nephew was almost exactly four months. Certain events during this period are worthy of brief record for the purposes of rounding off our tale.

Nobody knows whether Leonardo da Vinci liked or disliked the smile on his Mona Lisa. Worn by Miss Scettall on a call of condolence it infuriated the new master of Saintsend. So also did her remark that all of us must come to the grave *in due course*. What the hell did she mean by that? Had she any suspicions? Anyhow, he wasn't going to have her poking her nose into his affairs: so, he told her bluntly that he attributed his uncle's death to her spook-raising and that she would not be welcomed at Saintsend again so long as he was there. 'No doubt you'll have company enough without me,' she had replied: and what exactly did she mean by that?

Larkin always said that his new young master's heavy drinking began on the night of the old one's funeral. A tile had been blown off the bedroom roof and while dressing for dinner Alec heard the drip-drip of a leak from the ceiling. The drops were falling on the puppet box, and removing the top ones he carefully wiped each before putting the box into a drier place. He did not trouble to wash his hands thereafter and Larkin said to him as he sat at table, 'Why, sir, your fingers is all bloody!' The crimson veneer from a damp puppet had in fact come off on them, but there seemed no sufficient reason in this for Alec's extreme concern and annoyance. His face turned scarlet and then suddenly white; he swore at Larkin and bade him bring a neat brandy.

On the following morning, he threw the whole collection of shadow figures, box and all, into the river. Revisiting the place that evening he cursed himself for not having corded the box. As a result of the omission one of the figures suddenly protruded itself at him from the swirl of an eddy. It seemed to him to have expanded in the water and to be now nearly life-size. That, of course, must have been an optical illusion; but Alec never cared to walk on the riverbank again and when the masons arrived by his order to pull down the garden wall, he abruptly told them to leave it alone and get out. The same day he had his bed moved downstairs to a room at the opposite end of the corridor to where his uncle had slept. He was suffering, he said, from insomnia. A week or so later he ordered all windows on the river side of the house to be kept closed and shuttered by day as well as night.

The effects of heavy drinking had indeed begun to exact a heavy toll on mind and body. Larkin was accused of allowing young Tom to put scorpions and centipedes into Alec's boots and shoes and a scarlet mantis into his bed. All patterned carpets and rugs had soon to be taken up and stowed in the box-room, for Alec felt that in some strange way insects and shadow figures had got woven into the designs. Curtains were next taken down because of what he believed to lurk in their folds, and pictures because of what might hide behind them. No window might now be opened, even on the landward side, and bath plugs must be kept firmly in their sockets for fear of what might otherwise crawl out on him.

The faithful Larkin at last gave notice. Before its term was up, however, the end had come, and from a trivial causation. The Tillingford Grammar School was about to stage a speech-day pageant, of which one item would be a 'grasshopper parade' performed by the smaller boys. Their costumes, cheap but effective, were of green-dyed sacking with long thin osier shoots for antennae and legs. After rehearsal one evening Tom, thus clad, ran up to Saintsend to show his father. In an end-of-term exuberance he jumped the little clipped yew hedge below the rose garden and landed nimbly on the lower lawn. Alec at this moment, perhaps in maudlin remorse, was gazing down from the stone ramp on to the spot in the gravel path below where his uncle had fallen to his death. Out of the corner of a bloodshot eye he caught a sudden glimpse of the boy-grasshopper. With a hysterical cry of 'Good God! that mantis again!' he stumbled, pitched forward and fell.

Larkin, who was tidying up inside the Athenaeum, heard both cry and thudding crunch. Quick though he ran to his master's assistance, it was to no use; for the neck was broken.

6

Saintsend thus passed into possession of a distant and wealthy cousin, John Fenderby-Judeson. Within a year or so he had made many improvements, including the removal of Matthew Judeson's wall. Later he married a neighbouring lady whose Christian name was seldom spoken, for he chose to call her 'Mona Lisa'. The most recent accounts from Tillingford and Fenfield suggest that the riverine air of Saintsend is not suiting her too well and that she would like the dividing wall to be rebuilt. She complains, too, of bad nights, but her husband assures her that, if only she will exercise patience, an end will surely come to them in due course.

Light in the Darkness

1

It is over ten years since Martin Lorimer's death, and there is no-body now living to whom the publication of these notes could, as far as I can see, cause pain or offence. However, in order to make safety on this point safer, I have falsified all personal and place-names through-out the narrative; and the first fact, therefore, to be recorded about the man of whom I write is that in real life he answered neither to the name of Martin nor to that of Lorimer.

Few of his old school or college friends kept up with him in after life. This was because Lorimer entered upon an educational career under the Colonial Office and was posted to distant Kongea, where he eventually became principal of a Teachers' Training College and the author of several works on and in the Kongahili language. What bound him and me in the ties of fairly regular correspondence over two decades was a mutual interest in philately. He stayed with me more than once while on furlough and I must say that, had it not been for our common hobby, my initial invitation to him would not have been repeated.

The fault in Lorimer's make-up was a strain of militant and out-moded free thinking. Successive Directors of Education in Kongea had found in this quality of his, a counterweight to the predominantly missionary element in Kongean scholastic circles. His appointment as head of Takeokuta College came indeed as a thunderbolt to the local leaders of all religious denominations, and it was followed in the very next issue of the *College Chronicle* by an article from his pen entitled 'Creeds and Crudities'. To this the still youthful and pugnacious Bish-op of Kongea retorted in the *Kongean Catechist* with an editorial on 'Rot in Rationalism'. This, however, only had the effect of provoking the *College Chronicle* into a further dissertation on 'Mind versus Mitre'.

Lorimer would send me (and I still have them in my cuttings

book) copies of his articles in various newspapers and one of them, in the *Takeokuta College Chronicle,* is of special relevance to subsequent events. I will, therefore, reproduce it in full. It ran as follows:

Murk-Made Mystery

"The scandal of the Sadilena pilgrimage shows no abatement. This year in fact there are more pilgrims than ever before, owing to a report that the effulgence from the so-called sacred cave-wall is of unprecedented brightness. It will be remembered that the Sadilena cave was not discovered until the Boundary Commission of 1873 and that it did not become the focus of superstition until 1889, when Ubusda (self-styled hermit, but known to the police as a professional cheat and gambler) discovered the luminosity of the inner cavern and, at the small cost of a plaster statue of the goddess Vahrunda which he set up in its middle, invented all the lying propaganda about miraculous cures and fulfilments of petitions that later achieved his fortune and fame as self-inducted cave-priest.

"When he died in 1899 many hoped that the government would seize the opportunity of sealing up the cave and thereby save the ignorant masses from further pseudo-religious exploitation. Unfortunately, it did not do so, and within a year or two an ambitious priest from the temple below Nikoduna migrated to Sadilena and there turned troglodyte. Under his astute management the pilgrimage soon became a profitable business enterprise wherefrom only an infinitesimal part of the profits accrued to the cult of the goddess Vahrunda. The stock-in-trade of this giant hoax is nothing more than a patch of phosphorescent fungus or lichen growing on a cave wall. The pretension of its miraculous nature is maintained only by a sacerdotal injunction against introduction into the cavern of lamps, candles, matches, or any other means of illumination. Thus, simply but effectually, does murk make mystery and darkness dower deceit. We warn our readers against allowing themselves to be made dupes of such deception!"

Some eighteen months after receipt of this cutting I got a letter from Lorimer, posted from a hotel at Bournepool, to say that he had been invalided from Kongea and was home on pension. Could he come and stay with me for a night or two and bring some stamps with him for possible exchange? Having replied in the affirmative I met him a fortnight later at Boscote station, which is three miles from my Westshire cottage.

His first remark on alighting from the train was that he was feeling rotten. His face confirmed it too; though it would be truer to say that he looked rotting rather than rotten. He wore an appearance of active, not static, decay.

'I suppose, Robinson,' he enquired with some agitation, 'that you wouldn't mind my opening that cabin trunk a moment before it's put into the car? I have an idea that I've gone and left something very important behind.'

'But why open it here?' I replied. 'If you wish to wire for anything the telegraph office is only two minutes' walk from my cottage. You won't get anything sent down today, though, for the last train left London half an hour ago.'

'Very well, I'll wait. Do you think that we could have the hood down? After that dingy railway carriage, I feel like getting a spot of sun and a breath of fresh air.'

To this I readily agreed, for he seemed to me to have used a too heavily perfumed hair oil or else to have given his handkerchief an overdose of scent. I could not call to mind having noticed such a failing in Lorimer on his previous visits, although I am particularly sensitive to an over scented atmosphere.

During the short drive from the station, I saw him look several times inside his coat-sleeves and, by twisting and bending each leg in turn, inside his trousers too. 'Fleas,' he explained, catching my inquisitive glance, 'or possibly something larger! That's the worst of railway travel.' I had never myself found our railway verminous, but I refrained from saying so. Incidentally, this was the first time I had known Lorimer travel first-class.

No sooner had we arrived at the house and his trunk been carried to his room than Lorimer went upstairs to unpack. In my study below I could hear him throwing things out on to the floor, and then suddenly I heard hurried footsteps on the staircase and he burst in on me, white and trembling.

'For God's sake, Robinson,' he said in a strained voice, 'lend me an electric torch. As I feared, I have left mine behind.'

'You won't need one,' I replied. 'There's an electric-light switch under the pillow and a bed-lamp besides.'

'That'll be no use. You see, Robinson, I must have light under the bedclothes. The lamp will never shine through the blankets and eiderdown.'

I looked at him in amazement. He must, I thought, have become what is vulgarly termed 'dippy' and the only thing for me to do was to humour him. Fortunately, I did happen to possess an electric torch which I used when locking up the greenhouse and garage each night. I therefore promised to lend it him provided that he would come out with his full reasons and treat me as an old friend anxious to help him. This is what he then told me.

2

'You may remember,' Lorimer began, 'a newspaper cutting which I sent you some eighteen months ago about the Sadilena pilgrimage? Well, last year three of my senior pupils at Takeokuta asked leave of absence in order, as they put it, that they might go and worship the Holy Gleam. I was, as you may imagine, very angry. I replied that a condition of their going would be that I should accompany them, and that I should duly demonstrate to them and to any pilgrims present the material nature of the phosphorescence. It was as absurd to call it a holy gleam as to deify a glowworm or a firefly.

'So, in a few days' time we set out together, but as soon as we had left the train and started walking along the ten-mile footpath I could see that my company was distasteful to them. For the whole length of our progress, they sought to dissuade me from exposing and exploding the bogus mystery. The more they argued and entreated the angrier and more resolute I became, and my annoyance reached its climax when on arrival at the outer cave all three prostrated themselves before its hairy and unwashen custodian: a most disgusting sight! Here, too, I found the pilgrimage to have been commercialised to the extent of our having to buy tickets before entering the inner cavern.

'The passage to it though short was crooked, with the result that no daylight could penetrate the interior. Once inside, the glow from the walls became rapidly visible. I must confess that the luminescence exceeded my anticipation and I realised that less imposing phenomena have in the course of history been hailed as miraculous. So much greater the need, I reflected, for nipping the present superstition in the bud. The moment for action had arrived. With the fingers of both hands, I vigorously scraped the shining rock surface and sure enough there fell into my palms a luminous mildew or lichen, slightly cold and damp to the touch. It shone a blueish-green and, heaping it all into my left hand, I held it aloft for all to see. With my right hand I whipped out from my trouser pocket a small electric torch. "Look now," I cried, "at your wonderful mystery. Nothing but a handful of dirty fungus or mould!"

'Before I could switch on the light, however, the torch was struck from my hand in the dark and fell with a clanking thud at my feet. Although I could not see them, somehow, I felt my three pupils leave my side and soon heard their steps retreating down the passage. Nevertheless, I knew myself not to be left alone; indeed, I have seldom had so vivid a sense of company. Of its nature there now came audible indication; for there fell in my ears a succession of versicles and responses intoned antiphonally by what I surmised to be a company of priests. The words that I heard were Kongahili but, although I have never consciously translated them, it is in an English version that they have become engraved on my memory. This is how they ran:

V. Whom name ye guilty of the sin of sins?
R. Him who lays band upon the Holy Gleam.
V. A man may touch by hap, not of intent.
R. Vahrunda pities: he shall be forgiven.
V. Another in youth's folly, or in wine.
R. Him she will burn with fevers, but let live.
V. But if the act be purposive and planned?
R. Who sinneth thus shall die within the year.
V. But first a hundred days of witless fear,
R. And sixty in half-knowledge of his doom:
V. Two hundred more beneath Vahrunda's curse
R. Of shining plague, whose reek be must inhale
V. Until the year be up and he may die.
R. Thrice six score days of misery; then death.

'The chanting ceased and I groped my way towards the passage. Somebody must have followed me for, just as I emerged blindly into the outer cave, I heard a repetition of the final response croaked in a cracked voice from the gloom behind me:

Thrice six score days of misery; then death.

'There was no sign outside of my three pupils. The whole place seemed deserted. I started, therefore, on the homeward trek alone. Whomever I passed on the footpath gazed at me so oddly that I supposed my clothes to have become badly soiled in the cave. Inspection, however, showed that this was not the case. Perhaps it was that my fingers were bleeding round the nails. It was foolish to have scraped so hard. Three times I tried to buy fruit at wayside stalls, but they refused me on the ground that they sold only to pilgrims. The news of my deed had obviously preceded me.

'The more I thought of my three pupils the angrier I felt towards them My mission in the cause of truth had not been a success. The cave priests clearly had been forewarned and thereby enabled to stage a scene of melodrama. I had been made a fool of: perhaps something worse than a fool. The only sensible course would be to dismiss the whole wretched episode from my mind and think of it no more.

'This, however, proved impossible. Within two days I was summoned by the Director of Education and, from the moment that I saw him, I realised that I had lost a friend. He was amazed, so he said, by my disregard for Kongean religious susceptibilities. The chieftains were demanding my dismissal from the College, and the governor had called for an immediate report. Thirty-seven influential parents had already withdrawn their sons from attendance at my lectures, and it had, therefore, been his duty to order my transfer to the Central Education Office, where I should find useful employment in translating some recently-arrived primers into Kongahili.

'Mr Cadgeby (a cousin of the bishop's, whom I despised more than any other of my colleagues) had been instructed to succeed me as Head of the College. There need be no handing-over; and, indeed, it would be inadvisable in all the circumstances for me to enter the College premises again. To be quite explicit, he had no option but to forbid my doing so. That, for the present, was all: but I should probably be required, in the near future, to reply to a formal disciplinary charge of having conducted myself in a manner unbecoming a public servant.

'From this unpleasant interview I returned to my house, to find it deserted by the whole staff of Kongean servants. Until I succeeded in inducing three rascally half-breeds to take, their places, I had to go to the European Club for all my meals. Here, too, I found myself an object of disapproval, being asked by several heads of business firms why the devil I couldn't leave other people's religions alone. The bank manager accused me stoutly of stirring up anti-British prejudice, and a pioneer planter of having let down the white man. The majority of members avoided me. It was my first taste of ostracism.

'I could have borne it better, perhaps, if I had felt well. But unfortunately, I had begun to sleep badly of nights, owing to a severe itching at my finger-tips. There had been no water near the Sadilena cave in which to wash my hands after scraping the wall, and some infectious matter must have got in under the nails. The doctor gave me some ointment; but, in spite of its curing the irritation, the insomnia to which it had given rise persisted. I became a prey to all sorts of fears and fancies about my health. With the aid of a handbook entitled *Every Man His Own Doctor* I diagnosed my disorder successively as diabetic, tubercular and cancerous. I could not say which was the greater at this time: my loathing of life or my fear of death. Both gripped me simultaneously. The doctors grew worried and I was ordered up to Bendosari, our only hill station. It was there that I had the first inkling of my real trouble.

'While suffering from insomnia I used to imagine that nothing could be worse. The kind of sleep or torpor into which I now fell night after night at Bendosari proved how wrong I had been. Repeated nightmares can be infinitely more wearing and alarming than mere sleeplessness. Shortly before dawn each morning I woke up drenched by a cold sweat of horror at what I had dreamed. I had been in the Sadilena cavern again. Again, I had scraped its luminous wall, and again heard that chanting in the dark. The words began to take on a frightening significance. A hundred days of witless fear! Was not that exactly what I had recently suffered? And could I hide from myself any longer that I was daily suppressing an intuition of what was in store for me? I knew that it was not diabetes; not phthisis, nor cancer. None of those would account for a certain anaesthesia, a lumpiness and sense of corrugation whenever I stroked my legs, arms or face.

'The moment that I allowed my lips to frame the fatal word, I felt as though a dam had burst inside me, and I rushed through the hotel crying "Leprosy! leprosy! leprosy!" The other guests, not unnaturally, complained; and I was quickly recalled to Takeokuta for examination by a medical board. None of the three doctors who composed it can have any experience of leprosy, for they stupidly assured me that I showed no signs of it. What they invalided me for, I have never had the curiosity to ask. I knew the truth, and was thankful to get out of Kongea on pension, whatever label they might choose to set on my condition.

'On the voyage home the full foulness of my fate was finally revealed to me. One hot and windless night I woke to find myself gazing at my bare feet as they rested against the end of the berth. It struck me as odd that they alone, of all objects in the cabin, should be in the moonlight. I moved them, and the moonlight seemed to follow. I looked at the porthole. There was no moon! My heart thudded with sudden realisation. My leprosy was luminous. Vahrunda's curse, the shining plague!'

'Shaking all over, I switched on the lights to hide it; and every night I kept them switched on until we were off the coast of Spain, when cold compelled the use of a blanket. If only I could have drilled myself not to look under it, I might have been spared much. But I could not. Curiosity kept me constantly peeping under the bedclothes to see how far the luminosity had crept above my ankles; for I felt that it would surely, if slowly, invade my whole body. That, Robinson, is why I cannot sleep now without an electric torch between the sheets. The batteries run out every now and then. Every time this happens, I find the disease to have crept higher. It is already half-way up my thighs. Eventually, of course, it will reach my face and hands. That is why I frequently treat them with antiseptic soaps and lotions.

'I have begun, too, to be conscious of the emanation from my skin of a faintly civet-like odour, which I daily disguise by a liberal use of oils and scents, as you have probably noticed.

'Well, that's the whole story. So please hand over that torch, and don't, for God's sake, start telling me that it's all imagination, as the damned doctors do. If it's their way of saying that there is no cure, I agree with them: but they might have the decency to be honest about it!'

3

I was not sorry when, two days later, Lorimer left me. Somehow or other, I missed the announcement of his death (which occurred some weeks later) in the daily papers. I read of it, however, in the 'Weekly Summary' of the *Westshire Review,* which gave, also, some account of the inquest. The body had been found in Thanwell tunnel, on the main line to Wolmingham, and a Mr Algernon Cutley, of 11 Almington Crescent in that city, gave evidence as follows:

"We were alone in the compartment. The main switch for the whole carriage must have fused since we ran through the tunnels outside King's Pancras, when all the lights were on as usual. At Thanwell, we plunged into pitch blackness. After a minute or so, I heard my fellow-traveller ask whether I could see anything luminous on him. I smiled at the oddity of the question and answered: "Nothing, except the dial of your wrist-watch." Then I heard him get up and slide open the corridor door, muttering something about washing his hands. When the train ran out of the tunnel, I got up and walked along the corridor to the luncheon-car. I noticed that the exit door at the side of the lavatory door was ajar, but thought nothing of it at the time. When I came back from lunch, somebody had slammed it too probably the ticket-collector. My compartment was now empty and I supposed that my fellow-traveller had got out at Trentchester, while I was eating lunch. No, sir, I noticed nothing unusual about the gentleman, except for his odd question and for his smelling very strongly of scent."

In thanking Mr Cutley for having come forward with his valuable evidence, the coroner remarked that, in one single respect only—and that an unimportant one—had his account not tallied with the circumstantial details of the case, so far as these had proved ascertainable. The slight difference lay in the fact that the body, as found, carried no wrist-watch.

Decastroland

1

In Kongea it is ever hot of an afternoon, but the annual meeting of the Kongean Art Club seemed always to engender a special warmth. Perhaps it was a mistake to hold it so early as four o'clock, but members wanted to be at the Swimming Club by seven; and who could foretell how long old Jenderby, the president, might meander on in his comments on the annual report or how many protests would need to be listened to on the subject of hangings, rejections and awards at the last August show? On one point only were all the older members agreed: that Mr Lorenzo de Castro's pictures must never be refused; because they invariably attracted buyers, the Club reaping a commission of ten *per centum* on all sales. Mr Eckington of the *Kongean Courier,* knowing what his editor (a keen collector of 'de Castro's') expected of him, would begin accounts of each successive exhibition with some such words as:

'This year, no fewer than a score of Mr de Castro's striking canvases will be found on the walls of the Main Gallery.'

To disregard or criticise the public taste for de Castros would have been to throw doubt upon the financial acumen of the colony's merchant princes and leading bankers, most of whom had been wheedled by their wives into, buying examples and were wont to excuse the purchase by pronouncing it 'a good spec'. Mr Eckington signed his articles, not as 'Art Critic', but as 'Art Correspondent': wherein lay a distinction; for Mr Eckington was not unconscientious.

Of de Castro's own origin and history there were many and divergent rumours. The only established fact was that he had entered the colony some eleven years ago, on a Spanish passport. Thereafter, he had found employment as superintendent of decorations at the Austral Restaurant and, enthusiastically vouched for by its directors, had recently been granted letters of British naturalisation. Whatever might have been his Iberian past, his Kongean present was thus entirely satisfactory and acceptable. Under the magic of his brush, the dingy old 'Austral' had blossomed into an ornate cheerfulness that was handsomely reflected in bookings and bar-takings. Indeed, the long and short of it is that de Castro was a clever scene-painter; and if only he had rested content with such achievement, what is about to be narrated could never have happened. Kongea, however, supposed him—and he, himself—to be an artist.

'And now, ladies and gentlemen,' boomed Mr Jenderby, 'we have to determine the date of our next exhibition. Hitherto, it has always been held in early August; but this year we are confronted with a serious difficulty.'

Here, Mr Jenderby paused to clear his throat, and so afforded Miss Cavilege the opportunity to snap in with: 'What difficulty? We know of none.' Miss Cavilege, recently appointed Art and Music Preceptress at the Takeokuta College, had already won the esteem of its alumni by painting a portrait of the principal as ugly and unpleasant as the likeness was unmistakable.

Mr Jenderby, with an air of not having heard the interruption, continued sonorously: 'Any of us who has the welfare of this Club at heart will be aware of what that difficulty is; for it is common knowledge that Mr de Castro is sailing for England by the *Rutlandshire* and will not, therefore, be here for an August show. To hold it in his absence and without any exhibits from him would be to forgo the Club's principal item of revenue and main attraction to the public. There appears, therefore, every ground for making some sort of special arrangement.'

'What do you mean by special arrangement?' again interposed Miss Cavilege with a hostile sniff; 'the organisation of the Club shows is governed by Rule 23, I believe.'

The glare which the President now fixed upon Miss Cavilege being met by a counter-glare no less fierce, the Honorary Secretary tactfully tipped over the vase of alamanders abutting his minute-book and so diverted the attention of the meeting to a clearing up of the mess.

'I was about to say,' Mr Jenderby resumed when the mopping was complete, 'that Mr de Castro has submitted a sensible and generous suggestion. Provided that we agree to hang two dozen of his as yet unexhibited and unsold pictures in the sky-lighted portion of our premises, and not to mix them up with the work of other contributors, Mr de Castro will leave that number with us for exhibition in his absence. He will choose the canvases himself and thereby relieve the

Selection Committee from unnecessary trouble.'

Miss Cavilege's reaction to this announcement graduated from a sniff into a snort. 'I oppose it,' she said, with an ominous restraint of voice. 'I have learnt not to expect consideration for art from this society; but this proposal isn't even cricket. It would be monstrous to degrade our gallery into a saleroom for Mr de Castro, especially at this juncture, when a real artist is about to come amongst us.'

'A real artist?'

'Yes, a real artist, if such a phrase conveys anything to members of this Club. The Principal of the College got a cable this morning to say that John Mainbarrow was on his way out for a three months painting tour in Kongea and the archipelago. Possibly, however, you may never have heard of him. It wouldn't surprise me.'

From this sally, Mr Jenderby took cover in a look of unctuous incomprehension. 'If Mr Mainbarrow,' he said, 'should honour our Club with his attention, I have no doubt that we shall accord him a fitting welcome. If he should condescend to contribute to our exhibition, space for his pictures could certainly be found; if necessary, we might temporarily displace the Bugson Bequest. But I am quite unable to see the relevance of his approaching visit to a consideration of our old friend Mr de Castro's proposal, which I now put to the meeting for grateful acceptance.'

The right hands of all present, except Miss Cavilege, shot upward and, muttering the one word 'typical', she picked up her portfolio and strode from the room. Her exit, however, caused no comment, for members of the Club were well used to such ebullitions. Later, at the Swimming Club, over a very acid lime squash, Miss Cavilege expressed her frank opinion of Mr Jenderby and, over a stiff whisky-and-soda, Mr Jenderby his of Miss Cavilege. The afternoon heat survived the sunset.

2

John Mainbarrow's one-man show at the Grangeby Galleries had been a distinct success. He had sold some fifteen pictures, netted two hundred pounds or more, and won favourable notice in *The Easel*, from the pen of Professor Sedley. According to the professor, his pictures, surprisingly various in subject, displayed a homogeneity of conception, expression and technique such as to justify his admirers in their talk of Mainbarrow style.

Such praise, from such a quarter, would in any young artist of

131

John's sensibility have induced an excusable measure of conceit. In his case, however, it also instigated three months of overwork, resulting in a bad bout of nerves and insomnia. When, therefore, he received an invitation from his old Oxbridge friend, Cadgeby (now acting Head of Takeokuta College), to come and stay for two or three months in Kongea, his doctor advised telegraphic acceptance of the invitation and as early a sailing as could be arranged.

The advice had been taken and Mainbarrow was now nearing the end of his outward voyage. He already knew how and wherewith to replace the dews that tropical temperatures wring from the human body and had made many acquaintances at the smoking-room bar. Among these was old Sir Joseph Pagworth, for thirty years resident manager of Kongean Cinchona Limited, and, in his present retirement, chairman of its London board of directors.

'I am always glad,' Sir Joseph was saying, 'to visit the old colony again; though, in these days, it's in a hell of a muck. Too many mixed faces in the Council and too much red tape in the secretariat. One can't propose anything, now, without their passing some law or other against doing it. However, none of 'em dare meddle with fundamentals. Whisky and gin, I mean: have another?'

Both did.

'They tell me, by the way, that you're one of these painter chaps. Well, you'll get colour all right in Kongea, plenty of it. I mind one evening, when our Mickey's nose bled all over my wife's yellow-satin frock. "Why, there's a Kongean sunset for you," I told her. But my wife never could appreciate poetry. Used to sing, though. I almost seem to hear her now. "*Every morn I bring thee violets*"—that was her favourite. Sang it in German, though. Yes, you'll get colour all right. I hear that a young man called Castrato, or some such name, is making quite a good thing out of his sketches in Takeokuta.

'Doesn't stint his paints, either: more than two dollars' worth of 'em on every picture, they say. I guess you two'll be no end of pals when he's given you a tip or two. Then there's a frosty old virgin on the College staff, name of Sacrilege, I believe. Dabbles in water-colour stuff; you know the sort, I expect. Used to be barmy on the bishop, till he told her over a pineapple ice at the governor's garden party that he had a stern vocation to celibacy. So, you be wary of her, or she'll be queering your palette for you. Have another?'

It was not only from Sir Joseph that Mainbarrow heard of de Castro. Most of the planters and miners on board also spoke of him and of how he had recently raised his prices from twenty-five to sixty dollars a canvas. Some, whose wives had made them buy at the earlier price, now took credit for having known a good thing when they saw it. According to them, de Castro was going to England to book space for his pictures in next year's Academy. His stuff would make some of the Old Masters look a bit dowdy, they guessed.

John's ears, still pleasantly tingling with echoes of Professor Sedley's encomium, were ill-attuned to this jargon of Philistia. He quickly came to loathe the very name of de Castro. The fellow must be a vulgar mass-producer, a shameless pot-boiler. How lucky that they would never meet, journeying, as they were, in opposite directions! The nearest that they would come to each other would be when the *Rutlandshire* passed the *Tirynthian*. This happened to take place at night; but not at too late an hour for jocular exchange of marconigrams between homeward- and outward-bound Kongeans. To Mainbarrow's surprise, one such missive was for him. Tearing it open, he read:

"Sorry Miss You Welcome to Cradle of My Art De Castro."

Well; of all damnable impertinences! Cradle of his art, indeed! For an hour or so John lay awake drafting withering replies, each of which he tore up in turn as hopelessly inadequate. Finally, reflecting that silence is the sharpest sword of contempt, he turned over and courted sleep.

But was this sleep that came? Yes, he reasoned afterwards; for without sleep there is no dreaming, and what he now saw could only be a dream. In the middle of the cabin sat a man feverishly painting at an easel. His head moved neither upward, downward, nor aside. There was something sinister, even malevolent, about its fixity. Then, with a shudder, he saw the explanation. Beneath the eyebrows were no eyes, nor eyelids: only a flat, blank ledge of flabby, ashen skin. Its obscenity wrung from Mainbarrow a groan that mercifully woke him into action. Hastily switching on the light, he snatched from the berth-rack a detective novel lent him by Sir Joseph and grimly set himself to banish from his mind the foulness he had dreamed. In this, however, he was only temporarily successful, for he found to his vexation next day, that any mention of de Castro by a fellow-passenger revivified the memory of his nightmare.

'Come along now,' called Sir Joseph, 'and let me introduce you to a gin-swizzle, the proper nectar for an artist. Oh! by the way, I got a wireless message last night from that Castrato chap, asking me to look after you. I suppose you painter fellows practise a sort of freemasonry, don't you? Anyhow, I wirelessed back, ordering three of his latest daubs at a hundred dollars apiece. That was what he may have been after, of course. Well, I don't expect to be too badly down on it when the time comes to sell off my tropical junk. Hullo! Why, that must be the outer-shoal buoy to starboard there: we ought to be alongside and tied up by lunch-time. Another?'

Sir Joseph's anticipation of a lunch-time arrival proved correct. On the wharf stood Cadgeby, with two servants and a car, ready to receive and transport his guest. On their way from the docks, he expressed regret that John's visit should coincide with the absence from the colony of their premier artist, one de Castro, a dozen or so of whose landscapes he proudly pointed out on the walls of his bungalow immediately after their arrival. John's inspection of them was, he hoped, marked by such appearance of interest as common courtesy required; inwardly, he damned them as slick and meretricious, as indeed they were.

'I suppose,' he said, by way of making polite conversation, 'that de Castro has to repeat his subjects pretty often.'

'He is far too conscientious to paint duplicates,' Cadgeby replied; 'but, naturally, in the course of his long residence here he has often painted the same thing more than once. Which reminds me; the bishop will be dropping in after tea to show us de Castro's design for a central panel in the cathedral reredos. I understand that he has introduced Kongean scenery as background for a Madonna in the style of Bouguereau.'

Mainbarrow winced: then, turning from the pictures and directing a puzzled glance at his host, 'Cadgeby,' he said, 'what is the real name of this colony?'

'What on earth do you mean? Kongea, of course!'

'Sorry, old man! It's stupid of me, but I thought it might be Decastroland.'

3

Mainbarrow's first month in Kongea was productive of some of his best pictures. Three of them ('Sadilena Falls', 'Vahrunda's Altar', and 'Portrait of a Pioneer') were placed on the line in next year's Royal Academy. The model for the 'Pioneer' was none other than old Sir Joseph, got up, somewhat disreputably, for a fishing picnic; and John's first thought for a title had been: 'Have Another?'

Takeokuta College being in vacation, Cadgeby was able to motor his guest round the cool highland districts, and the time so spent, though very pleasurable and full of opportunity for painting, was uneventful for purposes of this record. It was on his return to Takeokuta that John first came under Miss Cavilege's assiduous and unsolicited attention. So many questions, she said, arose in the teaching of art at the college that could only be answered after reference to a real artist. Opinions, or *obiter dicta,* of Mr de Castro were continually being quoted at her by students; most of which, she felt, called for correction, if not denial. During his tour upcountry Mainbarrow had managed, without much difficulty, to banish de Castro from his thoughts, and it irked him greatly that he should now be inveigled into criticism and controversy concerning him. The Cavilege woman, however, was importunate, and his annoyance with her became a stimulus rather than a counterirritant to his distaste for de Castro.

It was under such provocation that Mainbarrow set himself, after early tea of a morning, to an unwholesome and unworthy piece of painting. His consciousness of its unworthiness was evidenced by the care which he took to hide it away under his travelling rug and in a cupboard whenever he left his bedroom. He worked at it, moreover, not in the room itself (which servants were wont to enter, after knocking), but with locked doors in the adjoining bathroom. It was the picture of a man painting at an easel. The landscape on which he was working recalled unmistakably de Castro's 'Mountains at Morn' which hung in the college hall. The face of this painter had neither eyes nor eyelids. Where these should have been, there was indicated only a flat, blank ledge of flabby, ashen skin. John was, in fact, giving substance on canvas to his nightmare on the voyage. 'I'll send it in for the local show,' he chuckled; 'I wonder what the Selection Committee will make of it!'

He found difficulty, however, in finishing the picture to his satisfaction. Whenever he uncovered it, after laying it by, the figure seemed to invite compassion rather than the contempt—which he intended. He would, thereupon, set brush to it again ill-temperedly and, by the time that it was ready for framing, he was heartily sick of the thing. Heaving a sigh of relief, he tacked it into a gilt surround, locked it in the bathroom cupboard, and went out for a breath of fresh air in the public gardens. Here, from a passing car that nearly knocked him down, Miss Cavilege waved and kissed her hand at him. He meant what he muttered.

On his return to the bungalow Cadgeby met him on the steps with a copy of the *Kongean Courier* in his hand, and, pointing to a front-page paragraph, said: 'Bad news for us and you, I'm *afraid;* read that.'

Mainbarrow took the paper and did so. This was the paragraph:

Art-lovers will learn with distress of our receipt of disquieting news concerning Mr Lorenzo de Castro. On arrival in London, he is reported to have complained of pain in the eye sockets and to have consulted leading specialists. The case is understood to present unusual symptoms and to have so far defied definite diagnosis. His last engagement before leaving for treatment and complete rest at Southgate-on-Sea was to see the three pictures by Mr John Mainbarrow (now on a visit to Takeokuta) which were recently purchased by the Bournepool Municipal Gallery. His many friends and admirers in Kongea will join with us in wishing Mr de Castro early and complete recovery.

Handing the paper back to Cadgeby, Mainbarrow yielded to a sudden desire to have another look at the picture he had just finished. As in other tropical countries, a bathroom in Kongea has two doors: one into the bedroom whereto it belongs, and the other giving directly onto the garden, whence water for the bath is carried in by the waterman. Finding the light from the windows too dim, John swung open the garden door and, standing with his back to it, surveyed his clandestine work. He regarded it with intense disapproval for five minutes or more. It was, he saw, intrinsically wrong and ugly; displaying strength without virtue. Its exhibition, even if there had not come this news about de Castro, would have been indecent. He felt a sudden rage, and, striding into the bedroom, took from the dressing-table drawer a Kongean dagger which he had bought as a curio.

Back in the bathroom, he pounced on the canvas and stabbed it into small strips. Then, as he stood contemplating the wreck of several hours' work, it struck him as strange that, amid tropical heat, his sweat should feel cold. Damn de Castro! Shivering slightly, he turned suddenly round at a hint of rustling in the bamboo hedge outside the open door. Nobody was there, so far as he could see, and a waving of a casuarina bush behind the hedge was, he persuaded himself, caused by a wind off the sea. The bonfire of weeds and clippings that was burning beyond the canna bed determined his next movement. He carried out the ruin of his canvas and poked it under the glowing embers.

After dinner that evening Cadgeby was called to the telephone. The editor of the *Courier* had rung him up to say that, according to a press cable just received, de Castro had committed suicide; presumably under fear of complete blindness.

<h1 style="text-align:center">4</h1>

If Miss Cavilege had, as the saying goes, been throwing herself at John Mainbarrow, she now indulged in a reverse process of throwing herself away from him. Nor was her method of doing so one of mere avoidance. She would attend functions at which they were bound to meet and then pointedly disregard him. Perhaps, he surmised, conscience was smiting her for a thousand uncharitable things she had said to him about de Castro. Such a probability, indeed, seemed indicated by the lip-service she now paid to the dead man's work. At a special meeting of the Art Club, convened to pass a vote of condolence with the bereaved family, Miss Cavilege astonished her fellow-members by reading a carefully composed essay on his talent. In it she made a veiled reference to somebody who might, in his own estimation, be a better artist; from which not a few of her hearers inferred that her infatuation for Mainbarrow must have ended as infructuously as her earlier pursuit of the bishop.

The full reason for her change of front was, however, revealed to John Mainbarrow at a small dinner given by Cadgeby in the last week of his stay. Conversation having veered fitfully from art and literature to philosophy and religion, Miss Cavilege was heard to ask the bishop whether his lordship believed in witchcraft. Sir Joseph Pagworth's remark that, in his experience, all women were witches, more or less, elicited only a contemptuous glance and a repetition of her question, with an added special reference to the Kongean practice of sticking pins into the effigy of an enemy.

'The superstition to which Miss Cavilege alludes,' the bishop responded, 'is agelong and far from being peculiar to Kongea. In Europe, it could be traced back, I believe, to the Mycenaean Age, and a still longer history be found for it in Asia and Africa. From the records of their trials, it is clear that witches sincerely believed in their craft; and it has ever been a weakness of the human mind to translate coincidence and imprecation into causality and agency. The insertion of pins into a material object is an action physically complete in itself; but as to whether accompanying mental or psychic states may or may not have telepathic consequences, I prefer not to speculate. Our Faith bids us to live in charity with all men; and to stick pins into one's neighbour, however vicariously, is certainly not charity. For the Christian,

137

therefore, such practices, whether effective or not, are clearly taboo. The angels are not on the side of the witches.'

'Thank you, Bishop; I am sorry to have bothered you with such an unusual question. What put it into my head was a silly dream that I had the other day of an artist painting the portrait of a rival, but without any eyes, and then stabbing the picture to bits with a knife. It must have been poor Mr de Castro's eye-trouble and suicide that put such nonsense into my brain. What added to the dream's absurdity was that the artist was painting in his bathroom!'

'Why ever not?' grunted Sir Joseph; 'that's where I sing opera.'

Mainbarrow was grateful to the old Philistine for thus switching the conversation away from Miss Cavilege's gambit into comicalities. So, the quivering of the bamboos and casuarina had been due to something more substantial than a breeze! It would, of course, be useless to tell Miss Cavilege about his dream on the voyage out. She had put her own melodramatic construction on what she had seen and would doubtless stick to it. Indeed, she pointedly avoided saying good-night to him, and he saw her on only one occasion more. This was at a farewell tea given in his honour by the Art Club. At its close, Mr Jenderby presented to him, as a memento from the members, a small canvas by the late de Castro, entitled 'Kongean Nightpiece'. The scowl which Miss Cavilege directed at him while he was returning thanks left him in no doubt that, whatever picture or figure she might have chosen to represent him, it must already resemble a porcupine.

5

Lying in a long deck-chair on the *Lacedaemonian,* John Mainbarrow reflected that, much as he had otherwise enjoyed his Kongean visit, the whole de Castro business had been nasty and discomfiting. He must, at any rate, get straight with himself about it: so, fetching pencil and paper, he jotted down the following notes:

1 Bad attack of nerves owing to overwork and insomnia Trip to Kongea taken for recuperation.

2 Plagued by fellow-passengers with eulogies of hack painter de Castro.

3 This got on already sore nerves and induced nightmare of eyeless artist. Dream image resurrected whenever heard name of de Castro.

4 On arrival in Kongea, found his daubs everywhere and heard

them extolled as highest art.

5 Miss C. added fuel to fire of my aversion by daily quotation of opinions alleged to be de Castro's.

6 Discovered her intentions towards me were matrimonial. She talked of a union of minds based on a common hatred.

7 As safety-valve for my feelings, started work secretly on picture of my eyeless dream-image.

8 When inspecting it before destruction, realised that nose, mouth and chin were those of Miss Cavilege. I had never set eyes on de Castro.

9 Common sense tells me that I had no hand in de Castro tragedy, but dislike having painted secret malicious picture, even though destroyed.

This ninefold apologia Mainbarrow showed to Dr Hasterton, whom he found it necessary to consult some four months later after reading in the *Sunday Post* an article headed 'Telekinetic Homicide'. This famous psychiatrist, having told John to come back in ten days, found occasion in the meantime to look up their mutual acquaintance, Professor Sedley.

'I remember,' said Hasterton, 'reading an article of yours not so very long ago on the work of John Mainbarrow. Do you happen to have seen any of the things he did in Kongea or since his return?'

'Oh, yes! I was round at his studio last Tuesday afternoon.'

'Any change in style? Deterioration, perhaps?'

'I shouldn't say so, though it may take him some time to get the tropical sun out of his eyes. Personally, I liked what I saw very much. But why do you ask?'

'Because—this between our two selves—he's under an illusion that all his recent output is in the spirit, even by the spirit, of a dead man called de Castro. I can deal with the case all right—there's nothing very novel about it—but before starting to do so I needed an authoritative judgment as to whether there has or has not been any real change in his work. Many thanks, professor, for giving it me.'

A fortnight later, Mainbarrow stood with Hasterton in front of a reconstruction of the Kongean bathroom picture, executed by him at the latter's order.

'That's excellent,' the psychiatrist commented, 'but before I purchase it (which I insist on your allowing me to do) I want you to put in eyes—*unseeing* eyes. Not blind eyes, mind you, but the eyes of a man who has no intellectual or aesthetic outlook or mental vision.'

'Oh! but de Castro mayn't have been as bad as all that!'

'What's it got to do with de Castro? Now do as I tell you, please, and finish your picture to the text, "They have eyes but see not".'

The new title, John found, necessitated a new picture with a fresh conception not associable with de Castro or any other individual. In his painting of it he thus found a way out of what he later used to call his 'de Castro complex'. The canvas was favourably noticed by critics of his next show and its associations for him became entirely gratifying. He has, indeed, been known to laugh and joke about his 'de Castro period'.

Recent letters from Kongea tell of the arrival there of an extremely good-looking and well-to-do Chief Justice. He is unmarried as yet, but Miss Cavilege is reported as hot on his scent.

A Victim of Medusa

I am no student of aetiology, but lying in my hot bath of a wintry morning and watching the steam precipitate on the window-panes I am struck by the fact that the resultant rivulets seldom if ever follow the same courses today as they did yesterday. It is remarkable how often a down-speeding globule of water will unforeseeably take an abrupt turn to right or left, as does the electric fluid in a discharge of lightning. There must, of course, be cause for each twist and turn, though unperceivable, and similarly there must be cause for every twist and turn of human experience. Such causes can seldom be sensed with certainty even by the human agent, or patient, whose behaviour is determined by them: their recognition by an outside observer is still more problematical. Nevertheless, I believe myself to have stumbled on connected links in a chain of events that culminated in the sudden and violent death of my bachelor cousin, Herbert Sidden, at the age of forty-three.

The coroner's verdict was death by misadventure. Herbert had been knocked down and killed where the footpath from Haddenham Green used to cross the railway on the level. The present footbridge was erected after (possibly because of) the accident. On rounding the curve by the tile factory, the driver of a down excursion train saw him stooping right in the middle of the track. Though he blew his whistle, Herbert never moved and a few seconds later a broken bleeding body lay in the six-foot way. Nobody else witnessed the fatality and the only object found by the police on the sleepers of the crossing was, irrelevantly enough it seemed, a jellyfish. This, it was ascertained, had dropped from the toy bucket of a small boy on his way home from paddling. Possibly, the coroner remarked, the deceased had slipped on it; but there was no evidence to support the conjecture.

There was certainly no ground for suspicion of suicide. My cousin had inherited a comfortable income, and his enjoyment of it as a leisured *litterateur* was without ill health or other detraction. Of his numerous acquaintances many would have welcomed a greater intimacy, but he inclined towards seclusion rather than society. In myself he seemed to take a mild cousinly interest suggestive more of curiosity than of liking. It was, therefore, a surprise to find that he had left me five thousand pounds, free of duty, together with the whole of his not inconsiderable library. During my inspection of its contents, I came across the two manuscript volumes and a scrapbook which, if I am not mistaken, afford clues to the problem of the testator's end.

The older manuscript book, much smudged and dog-eared, bears in an unformed hand the endorsement 'prayrs and pomes'; the second is headed in firm well-written capital letters 'JUVENILIA'. Between their respective contents there is great difference both in matter and style. Verses in the earlier have an authentic ring of childhood and the sentiments which they express are neither affected nor precocious. They are devoid of punctuation, as the following five examples will show:

Example (1)
PRAYR
plese help me god
to be quite good
and never rude
or cross or odd
so when i die
or the werld ends
we may be friends
up in the sky ⋆

⋆ *Note.* At first reading I thought the order of the rhyming strange for a small boy, but I afterwards remembered that he must have sat through many sermons in the family pew at Haddenham confronted by a mural tablet whose inscription ended with:

There lyeth here
But dust and bone:
The soul is flown
To Heaven's sphere.

Example (2)
DETH
I felt sad and Mary cried

when the poor canarry died
we berried him in the chiken run
and hated god for what he'd done

Example (3)
MUSIC PRACTIS
in saxling church on Saturday
we herd aunt madge the organ play
she did the hyms a trifle sadly
the sarms and other peices badly

Example (4)
RAILWAY JURNEY
the railway carrage keeps quite still
but things outside it fly
mile on mile pole after pole
the telygraff wires streak by
up and down, down and up
scratching along the sky
a bush comes sliding down the hedge
the fence dives into a pond
green woods like catapillers crorl
eating the hills beyond

Example (5)
FUNAREL
yesterday we found a jellifsh
nanny said it were a smelly fish
so we berried it in sand
the funarel was grand
nanny says she does not know
where good jellifishes go
but she thort the chances are
that jellifsh is now a star

In contrast to the foregoing, the verses in 'Juvenilia' are patently not the work of a child, even if a moiety of them may perhaps have been written in revision of earlier efforts or have reflected memories of childhood.

They leave the impression that their author must have taken pains to trick them out for grown-up recital or even perhaps for publication. Two specimens of such fake-stuff will suffice.

MR BROWN UNDER EXAMINATION
As we went walking down the town
Whom should we meet but Mr Brown?
Auntie says that she has never
Met a person half as clever,
So we thought that he'd know what
She and Uncle Tom do not:
Why God allows good men to die
And how do babies come and why.
But Mr Brown behaved so queerly;
He made a face and said 'O really!'

TO A JELLYFISH
Out of proper respect for you, Sir,
I shall call you Mr Medusa
(A name that I took
From our animal book);
Gentlemen in Debrett or Kelly
Don't have names like Fish, A. Jelly—

The sophistication of this last piece is in strong contrast to the *naïveté* of 'funarel'. I have selected these two verses for special citation and reference because no less than four of the 'pomes' and nine of the 'Juvenilia' contain allusions to jellyfish or *medusae*. They appear, indeed, to have become an obsession. In the Juvenilia, for instance, there is a painful parody of Shelley's 'Skylark' beginning, 'Hail to thee, blithe jelly, Fish thou never wert'; and, even worse, a travesty of an Easter hymn in which the terminal Hallelujahs are replaced by 'Jellyhoohahs'.

Pastings in the scrap-book show a similarly large proportion of newspaper and magazine cuttings on the same subject and even excerpts from books. For example, there is an account taken from the *Southshire Daily News* of the 17th September, 1902, of an experimental tank for sea anemones and jellyfish in the Bournepool aquarium, and a letter from a correspondent to the *Borehaven Gazette* recording measurements of a giant jellyfish found on the beach below Corley Head. Its diameter was exactly the length of the correspondent's umbrella stick.

In another cutting a 'Lover of Nature' reported having seen a weasel emerge from a tamarisk hedge, dash down the muddy bank of a creek and return with a jellyfish in its mouth. It is indeed amazing that a man of my cousin's intelligence and education should have accumulated such a litter of nonsense and misinformation. His childhood's prayer against becoming 'odd' had clearly been unanswered.

Oddities of taste and interest seldom conduce to mental or psychological well-being. In Herbert's case the jellyfish motif appears to have become queerly associated with his tendency to dabble in clairvoyance and mysticism, as the following typewritten entry in the scrap-book will illustrate. It is headed in his handwriting: 'Copied from Captain Philip Smythe's *Geographical and Historical Relation of a Hitherto Undescribed Island in the South Seas,* London, MDCCIV.'

The natives on this coast are adept soothsayers and tellers of fortune, to which end they employ divers ingenious devices; whereof I deem this peculiar to them that whenever there be high winds and sea, they will diligently search the beaches for jellyfishes of which (there being in that region no diurnal rise nor fall of tides) none will be stranded in fair weathers. The same being found they will in no wise move or touch lest it lose virtue thereby but will bring to it a Seer or *magus* for his divination. If the number of coloured rings within the transparency be fewer or greater than four, which is the common order, it is held of excellent augury for a revelation.

The *magus* will regard the fish without nictitation until the coloured rings appear to him to turn in a revolution contrary to that of the sun, when he will cry in the native tongue '*camphui*', that is, 'I descend!' Any that be with him shall then keep silence until he say '*timphui*', that is, 'I ascend!'; whereafter he will recite to them the revelation, if one there be. In the mean space he will have fallen into a dream or trance, the manner of which was thus explained to me. The apparent rotation of the rings will by slow degrees become a gyration of the whole substance, waxing faster and yet more fast, until the *magus* is as a man gazing into a vortex wherein, he soon feels sucked down into utter darkness.

If a prophecy be vouchsafed, he will now hear it as if chanted from afar; but if there be no prophecy, he will hear but a hissing and seething of waters whereat he shall not tempt the oracle beyond its sufferance but cry forthwith '*timphui*' and declare that there is no revelation. If any should tempt the oracle unduly or misstate the message given, he will haply suffer the fate that befell the arch-*magus* Rangitapha as described on page 57 of this Relation.

Beneath this excerpt my cousin had written a note as follows:

'N.B. I have not troubled to copy the account of Rangitapha's death as it was clearly brought about by quite ordinary misadventure.'

My last selection from the scrap-book will be of a final entry in my cousin's handwriting, initialled by him over a date some two months prior to his end. It runs thus:

I fancy that my experiments in divination by *medusae* would strike most people as folly and waste of time. I find them, however, of absorbing interest and am deeply grateful to old Willerton for lending me Smythe's *South Seas Relation*. I suppose the process to be akin to crystal-gazing but for me the results have so far been more encouraging. I have twice now heard the hissing of waters in the vortex and yesterday afternoon a *medusa*, dropped by some child on the old barge wharf, yielded an even more promising reward for my mental and ocular concentration. This probably indicates that I now achieve a more complete and effective abstraction than when I first started my experiments.

Be that as it may, I yesterday distinctly and unmistakably heard, above the hiss and gurgle of waters, the screech of a locomotive whistle and roar of a train. Unfortunately, the hissing and gurgling caused me to call '*timphui*' before there was any further development and I must now possess my soul in patience until another marooned *medusa* turns up to tell me what the engine whistle and roar of a train can have portended. I shall not allow myself to be cheated of a prophecy again by 'noises off'.

Since reading the above I have had little doubt as to the causation of my cousin's death. I am thankful to believe that it must have been instantaneous and painless. The shadow cast before it by a coming event is mercifully not always recognisable.

Fits of the Blues

1

David Crispwood and Dudley Lenbury sat in deckchairs on the lawn of the Residency at Kokupatta. Schoolfellows at Ruggenham, they had not met again until today. Both had in the meantime done well, David in the Kongean Civil Service and Dudley in the family business of Scrutton and Lenbury, jewellers and silversmiths. The two were far from alike: David fair, short and stocky; Dudley thin, tall and dark. In character also they were dissimilar: David communicative and congenial, Dudley introspective and reserved. Nevertheless, they had been inseparable at school and their present chatter in the Kongean twilight reflected a renewal of mutual liking and understanding.

'A District Commissioner's job,' Crispwood was saying, 'is full of snags and surprises. Take my own case. I counted myself lucky to be posted to Kokupatta but within a month of my arrival here we've had first a flood and then a cyclone—all our crops ruined and the fishing fleet smashed up. As a result, we're short of food and are having to get supplies down from Sadilena. The main problem, however, is their distribution, and I find both the headman and his people most uncooperative.'

'Uncooperative? But surely, they don't want to starve?'

'Not exactly want to,' resumed Crispwood, 'but they're suffering from a sort of fatalism or superstitious apathy. By the way, Dudley, hasn't your business something to do with precious stones?'

'Everything to do with them. But what's the connection between my family business and your people's fatalism or apathy?'

A servant appearing at this moment with a tray of bottles and glasses, Crispwood poured out two tumblers of whisky-and-soda before replying.

'No connection,' he said, 'except that it won't bore you too much perhaps if I tell you about a local ceremony that has to do both with jewels and with fatalism.'

'Go ahead then, I could bear with anything over whisky like this. Mawson's blue label, isn't it?'

'Yes, good stuff. Well, the Kongeans, as you may have heard, are polytheistic and their pantheon reflects human society to the extent that its lady members are the danger spots. Up country they worship a truculent goddess named Vahrunda but here on the Coast all our troubles are ascribed to a she-God of the waters, Situwohela, who manages or mismanages the tides, the waves, the rivers and the rain, so that she requires propitiation by cultivator and fisherman alike. At the moment this good lady is said to be in high dudgeon at having been cheated by her votaries. Every year on the night of full moon in the month Kashti of the Kongean Kalendar a sapphire is sacrificed to her by being thrown ceremoniously into the lagoon.

'This year, according to my secret information, a bead of blue glass was substituted and the real sapphire traded to a gem-merchant from Takeokuta. The local priest was taken by a crocodile on Tuesday while bathing, so Situwohela's got even with him all right. But she's still without her sapphire and the offering of a specially fine one is timed for eleven minutes past eleven tomorrow night, the next full moon after Kashti. In the meanwhile, the natives won't do anything to avert or mitigate the results of her punishment of them by storm and flood; that's what I meant by their fatalism or superstitious apathy. I can hope for some measure of co-operation from them perhaps after tomorrow night.'

'I should be interested to see that ceremony,' Lenbury remarked. 'Is there by any chance a rest-house where I could put up tomorrow night after you've gone on circuit?'

'No, but you're welcome to stay on here, as I shall be leaving cooky and the house-boy behind. They'll look after you all right and I'll tell old Punchaya the headman to let you stand by him at the lagoon. Provided that you don't ask to examine the sapphire—for I expect that they'll be more than usually touchy about that after the recent swindle—the people will be honoured by a white man's presence. I should like to be there myself, but I can't alter my circuit programme at short notice. Don't expect too much of a show, though, for these country people are no ritualists and the whole ceremony will be got through in less than ten minutes. Hullo! That's the dinner gong.'

As they strolled from lawn to verandah the nearly full moon rose between the coconut stems. Its light, slightly obscured by curls of smoke from a pile of burning fronds beneath the palms, looked curiously blue in contrast with the red glow of the embers.

'I have often wondered,' mused Lenbury, 'what can have been the origin of the phrase "*once in a blue moon*". Anyhow, that moon seems blue enough.'

'A good omen perhaps, for it happens to be Situwohela's liturgical colour. That's why they offer her sapphires. Mind that broken doorstep!'

2

The offering of the sapphire was not, as Crispwood had forewarned, much of a show; but Lenbury had been impressed by three things. First and foremost, by the size and beauty of the stone. What wouldn't his firm have given for it, and how his fingers had itched to touch and turn it over! Secondly, there was the actual tenderer of the oblation: a youth barely in the twenties and reminding Lenbury by his charm and sensuousness of expression of the Bacchus in Velasquez' '*Los Borrachos*'.

Completely nude except for a light blue loin-cloth, the moonlight revealed his body and limbs in all their Grecian symmetry. The pale bronzeness of his skin, not over-oiled in the manner of most Kongeans, showed him to be of higher caste than the peasants and fishermen who stood by. The mere throwing of a jewel into the water would of itself have been neither graceful nor impressive, but enacted by this youth it partook of both these qualities.

The third thing that struck Lenbury, and irked him exceedingly, was the, to him, wanton waste of a stone beyond price. It was, indeed, this last consideration that was keeping him awake and restless in the hot Kongean night after return to the Residency. Finding that he could not lie still for heat of mind and body he strolled out in his pyjamas onto the lawn and on beyond it to the spit of sand and coral that separated sea and lagoon. There was no one in sight and, having taken off his pyjamas, he waded nakedly into the cool brackish water on the landward side. The bottom was smooth and sandy but here and there he trod on a pebble or mussel and, each time that he did so, bent down to pull the object out for inspection. Perhaps this reflected memories of paddling as a boy for cowries and fan-shells; or were his dippings motivated by something less distant in time and not so innocent? He was now in deeper water and soon found himself swimming, a favourite exercise.

To cool his brain, perhaps, he swam largely under water and continued to grab pebbles from the sand, bringing them to the surface for inspection. How repetitive habits ingrained in childhood can be! This one didn't look like a pebble, though. Good heavens! Surely it couldn't be Situwohela's sapphire? Why yes, it certainly was; how extraordinary that his swim should have brought him to the Beach of Offering and that his pyjamas should be lying on the shore not thirty yards away. He dried himself before putting them on again for, oddly enough, he had brought a towel with him on his stroll. He felt cooler now after that bathe, even somewhat chilly, and went back to the Residency at a brisk run, clutching every now and again at the pyjama pocket as if to make sure that something was there. It was.

Before getting back to bed he had satisfied himself that his make-believe of a chance swim and a chance find was very credible indeed. Indeed, if he had not caught his satisfied look of achievement in the dressing-table mirror he might have convinced himself of its truth. As it was, he felt it an adequate sop to his conscience to murmur contentedly to himself, 'Well, I've prevented a damned waste anyway.'

His dreams were pleasant enough. One was that the Kongean youth looked in on him from the verandah window and smiled. It was not until he was shaving next morning that he doubted whether the smile had been altogether kindly. However, on the train journey from Kokupatta to Takeokuta he dismissed the whole night's happenings from his mind and read the English newspapers that had reached him by yesterday's mail. Only once or twice did he feel for his wallet to make certain that an important new bulge in it was there.

Next day he embarked on the *Northumbria* for England, and we take leave of him sitting in his cabin, the door of which he has bolted, sorting and inspecting the various stones bought by him for the firm during his tour. The best of them is a large sapphire which he is examining intensely under a magnifying glass.

3

It is not the purpose of this narrative to relate the history of what was later to become known to the law courts as the Lettiswood Sapphire. Its association with the firm of Scrutton and Lenbury terminated on its sale by them to a Colonel Barwell, from whom it subsequently passed to its Lettiswood owners. All that need concern us is that the success of his son's tour prompted Mr Lenbury Senior to retire from partnership in the firm, which by common consent of the

Scruttons devolved on young Dudley. He was thus at the early age of twenty-nine comfortably established and in a position, had he had the inclination, to marry. That, indeed, was his father's desire, but Dudley's thoughts were differently occupied. He had been brought up to a high sense of personal honour, and it worried him, therefore, that he had prevaricated to the firm about his acquisition of the sapphire. To have told the truth would have lost him the esteem of the Scruttons and of his father. They would quite likely have insisted upon a return of the stone to Kokupatta for re-immersion in the lagoon and have written him off as an unprincipled and untrustworthy agent.

He had represented himself, therefore, as having struck a marvellously good bargain with a Kongean gem-merchant and was now reaping a golden harvest from the lie. Nor was an unquiet conscience his sole trouble. He had begun to have doubts about his eyesight, a matter of crucial importance to his work. Had he perhaps tried it too much by his repeated examinations of the sapphire on the voyage home? These had been made not merely daily but almost hourly, by lamplight as well as daylight, for the reason that the stone seemed to him to exhibit strange variations in colour: always of course blue but sometimes darker and sometimes lighter. Once or twice after locking the stone away he had seemed to see things as through a mist, so that the white paint of the cabin and the enamel of the wash-hand-basin looked faintly bluish.

This illusion had had recurrences since his disembarkation and quite ordinary pieces of crystal sometimes appeared to him to have a blueish iridescence about them, such as a tot of gin will give to a glass of tonic water. This, he quickly realised, was a grave impediment to the work of a dealer in jewels, and one afternoon, when a lady wanted to exchange some aquamarines for other stones, he had felt obliged to call in an assistant for fear of taking over worthless trash. He had managed to seek this advice without raising suspicions of his own inability; but he told himself, this sort of thing must not be allowed to go on indefinitely.

And then, to make bad worse, there arrived a letter from David Crispwood with the following postscript:

"Since writing this letter, I've heard that poor old Situwohela has had another dirty trick played on her. That sapphire which you saw chucked into the lagoon is reputed to have been what the natives call a *teshta dahima* or 'spilling stone'. It's all nonsense, of course, but certain rubies and sapphires are credited here with spilling their colour on the eyes of their owners, so that they see everything red or blue. What tripe! Still, it remains to be seen what Situwohela makes of it. As she is described in Kongean poetry as the 'Blue Water Queen', she may take it as a compliment. Let's hope so, at any rate. I have reopened the envelope to add this piece of news, as I'm sure it will amuse you."

Lenbury was not at all amused: far from it. It was nonsense, of course, as Crispwood had written, but uncomfortable nonsense. The oculist whom he had consulted a week ago had categorically assured him that there was no vestige of glaucoma or other eye trouble, and had merely advised him to take a rest from his work so far as it involved examination of stones or, better still, to take a complete holiday for a fortnight or so. He had decided on the latter and would run down on Friday to Hugh Blessingworth's place on the Southshire coast. Meanwhile, today (Wednesday), he was to lunch with Hugh at the Anchusa Restaurant, with the prospect of a real curry. Before leaving the office, he tore Crispwood's letter into small pieces and burned them in the ashtray. Fancy David's having time to write such twaddle!

The Anchusa's curry was excellent, and its service by oriental waiters unobtrusively attentive. Old Easterners were wont to pronounce the Anchusa the only place where they could recapture the pleasures of a Sunday tiffin in the tropics. Lenbury, with a comfortable sense of repletion, was enjoying his black coffee and green chartreuse when his host enquired whether he still indulged his taste for good pictures. Replying in the affirmative, Lenbury regretted that he had little time nowadays for visiting the Galleries, but that he was thoroughly enjoying the volumes of reproductions from the great masters issued by the *Parnassus Press*. He had placed a running order for them. Blessingworth agreed as to their excellence and mentioned as particularly good the Velasquez volume. 'I wonder,' he continued, 'if you remember his picture of "The Drinkers". I've forgotten its Spanish title. You do? Well, if you turn round now, you'll see the dead spit of young Bacchus waiting at the table behind you. He struck me, just now, as trying to attract your attention; but you don't ordinarily lunch here, do you? Good God, man, what's up?'

Lenbury had upset his coffee cup and was noticeably shaking. Within a few seconds however he had composed himself and muttered something about the after-effects of malaria. Perhaps he had better be getting along in case he were taken again that way. He was more sorry than he could say that he had spoiled the end of a perfect lunch, but—At this point, Blessingworth cut in with a sympathetic 'That's all right, old chap. I'll see you into a taxi. Come along.'

Alone in the taxi Lenbury cursed himself for a neurotic. How lucky that nobody but his old friend Blessingworth had witnessed his foolishness! Or was it altogether foolishness? He had become used to seeing the Kongean youth in occasional dreams; but Blessingworth was no dreamer. There might, of course, be some Kongeans on the Anchusa staff, which would be one solution. No, it wouldn't, though, because what had struck him most about the youth at the lagoon that night had been his utter dissimilarity to other Kongeans. 'A queer business,' he muttered to himself, 'and beastly, too; damned beastly.'

His murmurings in this strain continued as he crossed the pavement to the entrance of Stonegate Mansions, where he rented a flat on the third floor, and must have been audible, or half-audible, to passers-by. Otherwise, there was no reason why the taxi-man should put a forefinger to his cranium and wink knowingly at the hall-porter.

4

Lenbury spent Thursday in bed, feeling in no mood to do anything or see anybody. When Blessingworth rang up to ask how he was, he replied that he felt better than he usually did after a malarial attack and would certainly be able to make the train journey to Blaybury on the morrow. In point of fact, Lenbury had never had malaria; but Blessingworth would have no means of discovering this, and a safe lie is an easy one. Replacing the telephone receiver (the instrument was on a table at his bedside), Lenbury noticed that his sheets and pillow-case had been given too much blue in the washing. He would have to register a complaint in the laundry book; or better, perhaps, see the oculist again before doing so, for the sheets were now looking not so blue after all.

Lying on his back he spent the rest of the morning in a series of self-imposed experiments, shutting his eyes and then opening them suddenly or gradually; staring now at the window, now at the ceiling, and now at the walls; winking, blinking, half-closing his eyelids or squinting through the finger-chinks of an upheld hand. Sometimes he detected a blueness in his vision, sometimes not: there appeared to be no law or order about it, and the only result of his trials was a splitting headache.

This, however, did not deter him from a protracted experiment of a different kind in the afternoon and evening. The idea had occurred to him that, in any assemblage of people, quite a number might bear some resemblance to the Velasquez 'Bacchus'. He therefore went laboriously through whole piles of illustrated papers and photograph albums with the aid of a magnifying glass; and, by nightfall, was seeing Bacchuses everywhere, a *reductio ad absurdum*. Such sleep as came to him that night was the dull torpor of exhaustion.

Rising at eight o'clock next morning, he decided to brace himself for a brisk holiday by taking a cold bath. On second thoughts however he turned on the hot tap full-cock before getting in. While dressing he whistled a jaunty air from some old comic opera and picked out a cheerful claret-coloured tie. Down at the breakfast-table however he was very soon at his experiments again. Were the egg-cups really a delicate shade of blue or were they a pale cream, as he seemed to remember them? The waiter, to whom he referred the point, appeared to take the question as a joke, for he replied with: 'You're all right there, sir; everything looks a bit blue the night after, don't it?'

At the railway terminus he kept his eye steadily on the ticket counter, in case some Bacchus of a booking clerk should leer at him through the pigeon-hole. Seated, however, in the corner of a first-class carriage, he reverted to yesterday's experiment and began to stare at the faces of all who passed him on the platform or in the corridor. A plain-clothes policeman on duty at the station put him down as an amateur detective. Nobody appeared to want to be his fellow-passenger and, having the compartment to himself, he was able to concentrate his thoughts introspectively. First, he silently reviewed the whole of his experiences since his meeting with Crispwood at Kokupatta, reconstructing every detail. Then, as the train flashed through Ormington Junction, he suddenly straightened himself and sat stiffly erect, speaking out loud to the empty carriage.

'These occurrences,' he said, 'must be either hallucinations or real happenings. If the former, then I'm going mad. I'm nervy, I admit; but I've never felt saner in my life. Anyhow, it was Blessingworth, not I, who saw young Bacchus at the Anchusa; and Blessingworth is certainly not mad. So, hallucinations are out of it and I'm up against real happenings. I've never believed in the supernatural up till now, but I'm quite ready to accept the verdict of my senses. The oculist can't explain why I'm seeing things blue; Crispwood's letter does explain it. Well, nobody has ever died of wearing blue goggles and I'm not going to worry. As for that Kongean youth, he may have come to England for all I know or care. If he or Situwohela are on my tracks they can jolly well do their damnedest; I can't undo what I did, and I'm not going to let myself be disturbed by their pranks. So there!'

Lenbury had been thumping the floor with his stick as he spoke and now matched his thumps to the rhythm of the wheels. Looking up at the notice below the communication cord, he began singing the words to a tune very like '*Nuts in May*':

To stop the train pull down the chain,
Pull down the chain, pull down the chain,
To stop the train pull down the chain

and then, mimicking an intonation of the Litany:

Penalty for improper use; five pounds.

An observer, had he had one, would have guessed him slightly and cheerfully drunk.

Such a diagnosis was actually formed by Blessingworth as they drove in the car from Chindley station to Blaybury, for Lenbury enthused the whole way over the blueness of the hills and of the sea although the former appeared that morning to Blessingworth particularly green, and the latter unattractively grey. Anyhow, he had beside him a far livelier and easier guest than the one whom he had seen into the taxi on Wednesday; and his wife, Margaret, wouldn't need to bother overmuch about entertaining him.

It was mid-July; the weather windless and hot. Tea, therefore, was served on the terrace and, during it, Blessingworth explained that he and Margaret would have to leave Lenbury to his own devices for an hour or so after dinner as they had to attend a Flower Show committee meeting at a quarter to nine.

'A guest left alone finds joys of his own,' said Lenbury. 'Isn't that a proverb or something?'

Blessingworth hadn't heard it before and went on to talk of the new swimming pool he was having constructed beyond the rose garden. 'It'll be ready for use tomorrow afternoon or Sunday morning,' he said; 'they were fiddling about with the pump and filter all this morning, Tomkins tells me. It's twelve feet deep below the springboard; so, you'll be able, Dudley, to practise your dives. Did you get any bathing in Kongea?'

'Lots!' Lenbury replied, and added facetiously: 'You should have seen me diving for jewels. They grow on the bottom there, you know, whole bunches of 'em. You ought to sow some in your pool and ask me down for the harvest.'

Before coming down to dinner Margaret looked in at her husband's dressing-room. 'What on earth's the matter with Dudley?' she said. 'He's just like a boy back from a prep. school. It isn't like him at all.'

'Holiday spirit, I suppose,' returned her husband; 'but I agree that it's damned silly. Due to his malaria, perhaps.'

Lenbury's facetiousness and exuberance persisted throughout dinner, so much so that host and hostess were relieved to get away to the Flower Show meeting, leaving their guest to take a stroll 'in the cool of the evening'.

The evening, in fact, was not cool, but oppressively warm; and Lenbury, standing on the springboard of the new swimming-pool, which he had not been slow to discover, thought the blue coolness below him most inviting. There was a waist-high rockery wall round the pool, securing its privacy; and it was supper-time, he reflected, in the servants' hall. He need fear no intrusion, therefore, and decided to be the first to enjoy a swim in the new bath. Having stripped himself bare, he gave a little jump or two on the springboard and then dived in.

5

'Yes, sir, it were a nasty mess and no mistake,' Tomkins deponed to the coroner; 'head all bursted in, like as if 'e'd dived in. There wouldn't be no sense in that though, seeing as 'ow the bath was empty. He was took giddy, I guess. No, sir: not a drop of water, nor 'adn't been neither; for the cement were still a-drying. They practised the pump straight into the overflow. No, again, sir: there ain't no blue or green tiles, only white ones, same as you sees in the railway lavat'ry. There weren't nought on top of 'em, neither, 'cept a chip of blue glass, might be the size of an 'azel-nut, as my young lad picked up in the rose bed and throwed in for play. I mind fetching 'im a clip on the ear for it, too.'

Death by misadventure.

Christmas Re-union

1

'I cannot explain what exactly it is about him; but I don't like your Mr Clarence Love, and I'm sorry that you ever asked him to stay.'

Thus, Richard Dreyton to his wife Elinor on the morning of Christmas Eve.

'But one must remember the children, Richard. You know what marvellous presents he gives them.'

'Much too marvellous. He spoils them. Yet you'll have noticed that none of them likes him. Children have a wonderful intuition in regard to the character of grown-ups.'

'What on earth are you hinting about his character? He's a very nice man.'

Dreyton shuffled off his slippers in front of the study fire and began putting on his boots.

'I wonder, darling, whether you noticed his face just now at breakfast, when he opened that letter with the Australian stamps on?'

'Yes; he did seem a bit upset: but not more so than you when you get my dressmaker's bill!'

Mrs Dreyton accompanied this sally with a playful pat on her husband's back as he leant forward to do up his laces.

'Well, Elinor, all that I can say is that there's something very fishy about his antipodean history. At five-and-twenty, he left England a penniless young man and, heigh presto! he returns a stinking plutocrat at twenty-eight. And how? What he's told you doesn't altogether tally with what he's told me; but, cutting out the differences, his main story is that he duly contacted old Nelson Joy, his maternal uncle, whom he went out to join, and that they went off together, prospecting for gold. They struck it handsomely; and then the poor old uncle gets a heart-stroke or paralysis, or something, in the bush, and bids Clarence leave him there to die and get out himself before the food gives out.

Arrived back in Sydney, Clarence produces a will under which he is the sole beneficiary, gets the Court to presume old Joy's death, and bunks back here with the loot.'

Mrs Dreyton frowned. 'I can see nothing wrong or suspicious about the story,' she said, 'but only in your telling of it.'

'No! No! In *his* telling of it. He never gets the details quite the same twice running, and I'm certain that he gave a different topography to their prospecting expedition this year from what he did last. It's my belief that he did the uncle in, poor old chap!'

'Don't be so absurd, Richard; and please remember that he's our guest, and that we must be hospitable: especially at Christmas. Which reminds me: on your way to office, would you mind looking in at Harridge's and making sure that they haven't forgotten our order for their Santa Claus tomorrow? He's to be here at seven; then to go on to the Simpsons at seven-thirty, and to end up at the Joneses at eight. It's lucky our getting three households to share the expenses: Harridge's charge each of us only half their catalogued fee. If they could possibly send us the same Father Christmas as last year it would be splendid. The children adored him. Don't forget to say, too, that he will find all the crackers, hats, musical toys and presents inside the big chest in the hall. Just the same as last year. What should we do nowadays without the big stores? One goes to them for everything.'

'We certainly do,' Dreyton agreed; 'and I can't see the modern child putting up with the amateur Father Christmas we used to suffer from. I shall never forget the annual exhibition Uncle Bertie used to make of himself, or the slippering I got when I stuck a darning-needle into his behind under pretence that I wanted to see if he was real! Well, so long, old girl: no, I won't forget to call in at Harridge's.'

2

By the time the festive Christmas supper had reached the dessert stage, Mrs Dreyton fully shared her husband's regret that she had ever asked Clarence Love to be of the party. The sinister change that had come over him on receipt of the letter from Australia became accentuated on the later arrival of a telegram which, he said, would necessitate his leaving towards the end of the evening to catch the eight-fifteen northbound express from King's Pancras. His valet had already gone ahead with the luggage and, as it had turned so foggy, he had announced his intention of following later by Underground, in order to avoid the possibility of being caught in a traffic-jam.

158

It is strange how sometimes the human mind can harbour simultaneously two entirely contradictory emotions. Mrs Dreyton was consumed with annoyance that any guest of hers should be so inconsiderate as to terminate his stay in the middle of a Christmas party; but was, at the same time, impatient to be rid of such a skeleton at the feast. One of the things that she had found attractive in Clarence Love had been an unfailing fund of small talk, which, if not brilliant, was at any rate bright and breezy.

He possessed, also, a pleasant and frequent smile and, till now, had always been assiduous in his attention to her conversation. Since yesterday, however, he had turned silent, inattentive, and dour in expression. His presentation to her of a lovely emerald brooch had been unaccompanied by any greeting beyond an unflattering and perfunctory 'Happy Christmas!' He had also proved unforgivably oblivious of the mistletoe, beneath which, with a careful carelessness, she stationed herself when she heard him coming down to breakfast. It was, indeed, quite mortifying; and, when her husband described the guest as a busted balloon, she had neither the mind nor the heart to gainsay him.

Happily, for the mirth and merriment of the party Dreyton seemed to derive much exhilaration from the dumb discomfiture of his wife's friend, and Elinor had never seen or heard her husband in better form. He managed, too, to infect the children with his own ebullience; and even Miss Potterby (the governess) reciprocated his fun. Even before the entry of Father Christmas it had thus become a noisy, and almost rowdy, company.

Father Christmas's salutation, on arrival, was in rhymed verse and delivered in the manner appropriate to pantomime. His lines ran thus:

To Sons of Peace
Yule brings release
From worry at this tide;
But men of crime
This holy time
Their guilty heads need hide.
So never fear,
Ye children dear,
But innocent sing 'Nowell';
For the Holy Rood
Shall save the good,
And the bad be burned in hell.

This is my carol
And Nowell my parole.

There was clapping of hands at this, for there is nothing children enjoy so much as mummery; especially if it be slightly mysterious. The only person who appeared to dislike the recitation was Love, who was seen to stop both ears with his fingers at the end of the first verse and to look ill. As soon as he had made an end of the prologue, Santa Claus went ahead with his distribution of gifts, and made many a merry quip and pun. He was quick in the uptake, too; for the children put to him many a poser, to which a witty reply was always ready. The minutes indeed slipped by all too quickly for all of them, except Love, who kept glancing uncomfortably at his wrist-watch and was plainly in a hurry to go.

Hearing him mutter that it was time for him to be off, Father Christmas walked to his side and bade him pull a farewell cracker. Having done so, resentfully it seemed, he was asked to pull out the motto and read it. His hands were now visibly shaking, and his voice seemed to have caught their infection. Very falteringly, he managed to stammer out the two lines of doggerel:

Re-united heart to heart
Love and joy shall never part.

'And now,' said Father Christmas, 'I must be making for the next chimney; and, on my way, sir, I will see you into the Underground.'

So saying he took Clarence Love by the left arm and led him with mock ceremony to the door, where he turned and delivered this epilogue:

Ladies and Gentlemen, goodnight!
Let not darkness you affright.
Aught of evil here today
Santa Claus now bears away.

At this point, with sudden dramatic effect, he clicked off the electric light switch by the door; and, by the time Dreyton had groped his way to it in the darkness and turned it on again, the parlour-maid (who was awaiting Love's departure in the hall) had let both him and Father Christmas out into the street.

'Excellent!' Mrs Dreyton exclaimed, 'quite excellent! One can always depend on Harridge's. It wasn't the same man as they sent last year; but quite as good, and more original, perhaps.'

'I'm glad he's taken Mr Love away,' said young Harold.

'Yes,' Dorothy chipped in; 'he's been beastly all day, and yesterday, too: and his presents aren't nearly as expensive as last year.'

'Shut up, you spoilt children!' the father interrupted. 'I must admit, though, that the fellow was a wet blanket this evening. What was that nonsense he read out about reunion?'

Miss Potterby had developed a pedagogic habit of clearing her throat audibly, as a signal demanding her pupils' attention to some impending announcement. She did it now, and parents as well as children looked expectantly towards her.

'The motto as read by Mr Love,' she declared, 'was so palpably inconsequent that I took the liberty of appropriating it when he laid the slip of paper back on the table. Here it is, and this is how it actually reads:

Be united heart to heart,
Love and joy shall never part.

That makes sense, if it doesn't make poetry. Mr Love committed the error of reading 'be united' as 'reunited' and of not observing the comma between the two lines.'

'Thank you, Miss Potterby; that, of course, explains it. How clever of you to have spotted the mistake and tracked it down!'

Thus encouraged, Miss Potterby proceeded to further corrective edification.

'You remarked just now, Mrs Dreyton, that the gentleman impersonating Father Christmas had displayed originality. His prologue and epilogue, however, were neither of them original, but corrupted versions of passages which you will find in Professor Borleigh's *Synopsis of Nativity, Miracle and Morality Plays*, published two years ago. I happen to be familiar with the subject, as the author is a first cousin of mine, once removed.'

'How interesting!' Dreyton here broke in; 'and now, Miss Potterby, if you will most kindly preside at the piano, we will dance Sir Roger de Coverley. Come on, children, into the drawing-room.'

3

On Boxing Day there was no post and no paper. Meeting Mrs Simpson in the Park that afternoon, Mrs Dreyton was surprised to hear that Father Christmas had kept neither of his two other engagements. 'It must have been that horrid fog,' she suggested; 'but what a

161

shame! He was even better than last year:' by which intelligence Mrs Simpson seemed little comforted.

Next morning—the second after Christmas—there were two letters on the Dreytons' breakfast-table, and both were from Harridge's.

The first conveyed that firm's deep regret that their representative should have been prevented from carrying out his engagements in Pentland Square on Christmas night owing to dislocation of traffic caused by the prevailing fog.

'But he kept ours all right,' Mrs Dreyton commented. 'I feel so sorry for the Simpsons and the Joneses.'

The second letter cancelled the first, 'which had been written in unfortunate oversight of the cancellation of the order'.

'What on earth does that mean?' Mrs Dreyton ejaculated.

'Ask me another!' returned her husband. 'Got their correspondence mixed up, I suppose.',

In contrast to the paucity of letters, the morning newspapers seemed unusually voluminous and full of pictures. Mrs Dreyton's choice of what to read in them was not that of a highbrow. The headline that attracted her first attention ran '*Xmas on Underground*', and, among other choice items, she learned how, at Pentland Street Station (their own nearest), a man dressed as Santa Claus had been seen to guide and support an invalid, or possibly tipsy, companion down the long escalator. The red coat, mask and beard were afterwards found discarded in a passage leading to the emergency staircase, so that even Santa's sobriety might be called into question. She was just about to retail this interesting intelligence to her husband when, laying down his own paper, he stared curiously at her and muttered 'Good God!'

'What on earth's the matter, dear?'

'A very horrible thing, Elinor. Clarence Love has been killed! Listen;' here he resumed his paper and began to read aloud: "The body of the man who fell from the Pentland Street platform on Christmas night in front of an incoming train has been identified as that of Mr Clarence Love, of 11 Playfair Mansions. There was a large crowd of passengers on the platform at the time, and it is conjectured that he fell backwards off it while turning to expostulate with persons exerting pressure at his back. Nobody, however, in the crush, could have seen the exact circumstances of the said fatality.'"

'Hush, dear! Here come the children. They mustn't know, of course. We can talk about it afterwards.'

Dreyton, however, could not wait to talk about it afterwards. The whole of the amateur detective within him had been aroused, and, rising early from the breakfast-table, he journeyed by tube to Harridge's, where he was soon interviewing a departmental sub-manager. No: there was no possibility of one of their representatives having visited Pentland Square on Christmas evening. Our Mr Droper had got hung up in the Shenton Street traffic-block until it was too late to keep his engagements there. He had come straight back to his rooms. In any case, he would not have called at Mr Dreyton's residence in view of the cancellation of the order the previous day. Not cancelled? But he took down the telephone message himself. Yes: here was the entry in the register. Then it must have been the work of some mischief-maker; it was certainly a gentleman's, and not a lady's voice. Nobody except he and Mr Droper knew of the engagement at their end, so the practical joker must have derived his knowledge of it from somebody in Mr Dreyton's household.

This was obviously sound reasoning and, on his return home, Dreyton questioned Mrs Timmins, the cook, in the matter. She was immediately helpful and forthcoming. One of them insurance gents had called on the morning before Christmas and had been told that none of us wanted no policies or such like. He had then turned conversational and asked what sort of goings-on there would be here for Christmas. Nothing, he was told, except old Father Christmas, as usual, out of Harridge's shop. Then he asked about visitors in the house, and was told as there were none except Mr Love, who, judging by the tip what he had given Martha when he stayed last in the house, was a wealthy and openhanded gentleman. Little did she think when she spoke those words as Mr Love would forget to give any tips or boxes at Christmas, when they were most natural and proper. But perhaps he would think better on it by the New Year and send a postal order. Dreyton thought it unlikely, but deemed it unnecessary at this juncture to inform Mrs Timmins of the tragedy reported in the newspaper.

At luncheon Mrs Dreyton found her husband unusually taciturn and preoccupied; but, by the time they had come to the cheese, he announced importantly that he had made up his mind to report immediately to the police certain information that had come into his possession. Miss Potterby and the children looked suitably impressed, but knew better than to court a snub by asking questions. Mrs Dreyton took the cue admirably by replying: 'Of course, Richard, you must do your duty!'

4

The inspector listened intently and jotted down occasional notes. At the end of the narration, he complimented the informant by asking whether he had formed any theory regarding the facts he reported. Dreyton most certainly had. That was why he had been so silent and absent-minded at lunch. His solution, put much more briefly than he expounded it to the inspector, was as follows.

Clarence Love had abandoned his uncle and partner in the Australian bush. Having returned to civilisation, got the Courts to presume the uncle's death, and taken probate of the will under which he was sole inheritor, Love returned to England a wealthy and still youngish man. The uncle, however (this was Dreyton's theory), did not die after his nephew's desertion, but was found and tended by bushmen. Having regained his power of locomotion, he trekked back to Sydney, where he discovered himself legally dead and his property appropriated by Love and removed to England. Believing his nephew to have compassed his death, he resolved to take revenge into his own hands. Having despatched a cryptic letter to Love containing dark hints of impending doom, he sailed for the Old Country and ultimately tracked Love down to the Dreytons' abode.

Then, having in the guise of a travelling insurance agent ascertained the family's programme for Christmas Day, he planned his impersonation of Santa Claus. That his true identity, revealed by voice and accent, did not escape his victim was evidenced by the latter's nervous misreading of the motto in the cracker. Whether Love's death in the Underground was due to actual murder or to suicide enforced by despair and remorse, Dreyton hazarded no guess: either was possible under his theory.

The inspector's reception of Dreyton's hypothesis was less enthusiastic than his wife's.

'If you'll excuse me, Mr Dreyton,' said the former, 'you've built a mighty lot on dam' little. Still, it's ingenious and no mistake. I'll follow your ideas up and, if you'll call in a week's time, I may have something to tell you and one or two things, perhaps, to ask.'

'Why darling, how wonderful!' Mrs Dreyton applauded. 'Now that you've pieced the bits together so cleverly the thing's quite obvious, isn't it? What a horrible thing to have left poor old Mr Joy to die all alone in the jungle! I never really liked Clarence, and am quite glad now that he's dead. But of course, we mustn't tell the children!'

Inquiries of the Australian Police elicited the intelligence that the presumption of Mr Joy's death had been long since confirmed by the discovery of his remains in an old prospecting pit. There were ugly rumours and suspicions against his nephew but no evidence on which to support them. On being thus informed by the inspector Dreyton amended his theory to the extent that the impersonator of Father Christmas must have been not Mr Joy himself, as he was dead, but a bosom friend determined to avenge him. This substitution deprived the cracker episode, on which Dreyton had imagined his whole story, of all relevance; and the inspector was quite frank about his disinterest in the revised version.

Mrs Dreyton also rejected it. Her husband's original theory seemed to her more obviously right and conclusive even than before. The only amendment required, and that on a mere matter of detail, was to substitute Mr Joy's ghost for Mr Joy: though of course one mustn't tell the children.

'But,' her husband remonstrated, 'you know that I don't believe in ghosts.'

'No, but your aunt Cecilia *does;* and she is such a clever woman. By the way, she called in this morning and left you a book to look at.'

'A book?'

'Yes, the collected ghost stories of M. R. James.'

'But the stupid old dear knows that I have them all in the original editions.'

'So, she said: but she wants you to read the author's epilogue to the collection which, she says, is most entertaining. It's entitled "Stories I have tried to write". She said that she'd side-lined a passage that might interest you. The book's on that table by you. No, not that: the one with the black cover.'

Dreyton picked it up, found the marked passage and read it aloud.

There may be possibilities too in the Christmas cracker if the right people pull it and if the motto which they find inside has the right message on it. They will probably leave the party early, pleading indisposition; but very likely a previous engagement of long standing would be the more truthful excuse.

'There is certainly,' Dreyton commented, 'some resemblance between James's idea and our recent experience. But he could have made a perfectly good yarn out of that theme without introducing ghosts.'

His wife's mood at that moment was for compromise rather than controversy.

'Well, darling,' she temporised, 'perhaps not exactly ghosts.'

An Exchange of Notes

1

It is doubtful whether you would call Telmington a village or a small country town. Until 1849 it had boasted a weekly cattle market; but after completion of the Daven Valley railway this was transferred to Shallowford, some four miles distant. An annual Hilary Fair survived until its site was usurped by the Jubilee clock-tower, the gift (as a marble tablet bears record) of Edmund Giles Touchwood, J. P., of Telming Hall in this Parish. Shorn thus of its market and fair Telmington attracted but few visitors; its seven shops and two inns catering almost solely for its thousand or so inhabitants. In this stagnancy it remained until the inauguration, in 1907, of a motor-bus service to and from Shallowford station twice daily.

Edmund Touchwood having died a widower and without male issue, Telming Hall in the autumn of 1910 was the home of his only daughter, Mrs Parlington. Her Christian name, Letitia, she ascribed to an apocryphal sneeze by a godmother at her baptism. She much disliked it; but, as such names will, it stuck to her like a burr; and Letitia she was called, though not to her face, by all and sundry in the neighbourhood. An energetic, capable and kindly, if rather managing woman, she gardened, beagled, cycled, served on the Rural District Council and Board of Guardians, sketched in water-colour, and played the organ in church.

Dr Holmbush described her intellectual interests as middle-brow. Although of general good temper she could on certain subjects, music for instance, be argumentative and touchy. Indeed, her seat at the church organ was occupied on the express understanding that, while the choice of hymns lay with the rector, it was for her to determine the tunes. Her language on this point had been blunt. 'The words of half your hymns, rector, are tosh. That's your lookout, of course; but I refuse to play toshy tunes.' In a matter of months, she had the choir on her side, and within a year or two the congregation also; the rector being left in lonely lament for rejected 'old favourites'.

Another subject on which Letitia could speak harshly and hotly was spiritualism. Her aversion to it was not from disbelief in spirits but from belief in them. She ever maintained that her husband, who had been killed in the Boer War, appeared to her before her receipt of the War Office telegram. She saw him standing in uniform at the foot of her bed. He looked at her, smiled sadly and was gone. In that moment, she averred, was established complete and eternal understanding between them. His smile showed that he had no cause for fear; its sadness that he was sorry at the ending of their earthly companionship. There was no reason for him to reappear; nor did he. Her theory was that if a departing spirit (she emphasised the present participle) had a message to give, he or she would give it.

Once departed (again an emphasis on the tense of the participle) he or she would be quit of earthly connections and worries. If table-rappers and so-called mediums ever really managed to put a call through, it would be an unwarranted and generally unheeded interruption; like a telephone call after one is snugly abed. Small wonder, she said, that the answers they got, if genuine, were such tosh. *Séances* were, more often than not, charged with fraud on the quick; and always with insult to the dead.

These views, thus trenchantly expressed, gave offence to Miss Godwinstowe, founder of the *Telmington Psychic Circle,* without commending themselves to out-and-out sceptics. The rector, however, fancied that he found in them a reflection of his own.

'I'm so glad, Mrs Parlington,' he confided, 'that you share my conviction that apparitions of the dying are just simulacra without power of speech.'

'I've never said that; or thought it. My husband had no need to talk, nor I to hear. Our converse was total and complete without it.'

'Ah! Exactly so, exactly so!' nervously assented the rector, anxious to avoid any disagreement.

'But if,' continued Letitia, 'he had felt speech necessary, he would certainly have spoken. And don't you forget, rector, that if you were to choose toshy hymns for my funeral you would certainly find me a talkative ghost.'

The rector deprecated this sudden turn towards levity. 'You are more likely to be at my obsequies than I at yours, Mrs Parlington; but really, we oughtn't to speak lightly of grave matters, ought we? Dear me, how the days draw in to be sure! I must be getting home, for I forgot to put any oil in my bicycle lamp.'

'You were a bit hard on the foolish virgins in your sermon last Sunday, I thought. Well, goodbye, and look out for those loose stones by the lodge; they're dangerous.'

She watched him free-wheeling down the drive.

'How difficult it must be to be a parson,' she mused half-aloud. 'The little man means well.'

2

The Reverend Septimus Tardell did mean well. Nor, as too often is the case, was well-meaning mated with ill-reasoning or tactless scheming. His main present problem was how to remedy a division of his parishioners into two camps. Division perhaps was a wrong term to apply to two groups which, although Telmington was geographically their common ground, and its church should have been so spiritually, had never really come together. An improved bus time-table and the incipient vogue of private cars had led to speculative building on the fringes of the village and to an invasion not only of regular week-enders, but even of daily-breaders who went up to London by the nine-three from Shallowford and returned by the six-eighteen.

Such households had no roots in the countryside; they professed a liking for rural scenery and quiet, but their mental landscape remained essentially urban. As a result, there was no neighbourliness, worth the word, between what the postmistress called 'our old people' and 'that new set'. Polite calls paid by the former on the latter were as politely returned; but at that it ended. The gulf of mutual disinterest was unbridged. In church such newcomers as attended slunk shyly to seats at the extreme west end, rather than incur inquisitive glances from pew-holders of long standing. In vain did the rector periodically proclaim that all seats were free, and exhort his congregation to sit as near as conveniently possible to the pulpit. He might as well have bade water mix with oil. Things could not be put right by a homily.

Nevertheless, he felt in duty and conscience bound to do something to prevent permanent cleavage. The age was yet to come when a parson's job would connote an intensive specialism in church services with occasional sick-calls in the wake of the district nurse. Mr Tardell felt and knew himself still to be an influential personage. Though he had but two maids and a bicycle, did he not reside in a twelve-bed-roomed rectory with stabling for six horses? The popular estimate of the importance of an office, as banks and business houses have long found out, is often in proportion to the size of its premises. In 1910 rector and rectory, vicar and vicarage, still counted for much in the rural social fabric. The parish looked to the parson not merely for ministry but for leadership.

Mr Tardell was a systematic man. He kept, for instance, a notebook docketed '*Parish Memoranda & Agenda*', which we find him perusing, pencil in hand, on the morning after his call on Mrs Parlington. The two pages open before him contain notes upon the various village societies and clubs. He is going to place a tick against any that might be made use of for the breaking down of social and cultural barriers. *Telmington Cricket Club.* A promising field, no doubt—but wait a bit though; weren't they talking of playing on Sundays? Well, Charles Dickens had approved of it (a strong Dickensian, Mr Tardell) and it was bound to come, anyway. So, a tick. *Query.* Why no football club? Play on the rectory field was unorganised and spasmodic. *Mem:* get hold of young Towling and suggest that he start one. Hockey too, perhaps. *Telmington Horticultural Society.*

Their annual flower show was excellent and some of the new people were already exhibitors. A tick. *Query:* why not two or three shows a year—spring, summer and Michaelmas? *Mem:* suggest this to Colonel Bratton. *Working Men's Club.* Useful, but not for the present purpose; no newcomers in this category. *Telmington Psychic Circle.* The rector reddened and frowned. Just as Miss Godwinstowe's *séances* had ceased to attract the curious in such matters, some village wag had given the circle a new lease of notoriety by painting 'Licensed to Retail Spirits' above her front door in Church Street. Worse still, Miss Tisdale (easily his best Sunday-school teacher) was reported to be attending its meetings. No tick against this item! *Philharmonic Club.* Moribund, alas, since the Gurdstones left Telmington.

A chorus and orchestra would be the very thing to rope in quite a lot of people, new and old. *Two* ticks! The difficulty was how to go about it. Mrs Parlington had quite enough to do already, running the church choir. Besides, a choral society would need tact rather than tyranny! He mustn't hurt her feelings, though; and there would be no harm in asking her to be patroness, in view of her position as the Lady of Telming Hall. Patronesses are ornamental, not executive. The right person to resuscitate the club would undoubtedly be Dr Wrenshall, retired organist of Wintonbury Cathedral, who had just come to live at Fretfield Grange. The Mus.Doc. and F.R.C.O. after his name would look well on the club's programmes—if only he would take the job on. Anyhow, he couldn't object to being asked.

The rector called at Fretfield Grange, and later at Telming Hall, that very afternoon. Dr Wrenshall agreed to serve, subject to reconsideration, should there emerge an insufficiency of singers or instrumentalists; and to the stipulation that he alone should choose all works to be practised or performed. Mrs Parlington also consented to be patroness, with a promise (that the rector thought it prudent to extract) that, if ever she had suggestions or criticisms to make about the music or its rendering, they should be tendered privately to Dr Wrenshall and not bruited in the course of practice or rehearsal. Dr Wrenshall, the rector pointed out, was accustomed to a highly disciplined choir; so, care must be taken not to upset him. 'Naturally,' Mrs Parlington rejoined, 'and, from what I've heard from friends at Wintonbury, one thing that he won't stand at any price is toshy tunes. So, you'd better be careful yourself, rector!'

A public meeting to promote the revival of the *Telmington Philharmonic Club* was largely and enthusiastically attended, both by old inhabitants and by newcomers. Dr Wrenshall was elected President and Conductor; Mrs Parlington, by acclamation, as patroness. Next Sunday morning Mr Tardell preached on '*Music in the Bible*'. Mrs Trimshaw, wife of the people's churchwarden and an ex-governess, remarked that the dear rector's learning seemed quite cyclopaedic. So indeed, it was, in the sense that the sermon had been lifted straight out of an encyclopaedia.

3

In the course of the next two years the *Telmington Philharmonic Club* increased both in membership and in competency. Dr Wrenshall told the orchestra that they had begun by playing with scores, and were now learning to play them. He refused all requests for a concert during the first formative eighteen months; but agreed to conduct a public performance in celebration of the club's second birthday. In the meanwhile, Mr Tardell had made the acquaintance of Sir Cuthbert Kewbridge, the composer, and had obtained for the club the privilege of being the first to render his Poem for Chorus and Orchestra entitled *Northern Lights*. The music was still in manuscript; for Sir Cuthbert wished to hear the effect of certain passages before authorising their publication. A good deal of copying of the voice parts had to be done; and Mrs Parlington, with her usual helpfulness and energy, produced most of the copies.

As a result, she claimed to know the whole thing backwards, and to have discovered what she characterised as weak spots. Her criticisms receiving no encouragement from Dr Wrenshall, she finally focused her faultfinding on one particular note in the *soprano* part.

'The treble F in the third bar of line five on page twenty-three should certainly be A,' she protested. 'I feel it in my bones that Sir Cuthbert couldn't have meant F; it makes tosh of the whole passage. You simply must write to him, Dr Wrenshall, and get his permission to alter it.'

'What do you say, rector?' asked Dr Wrenshall, after scrutinising the note and bar in question. 'I think there's something in what Mrs Parlington says; but you know the composer, and I don't; so, if anybody's going to write to him, it should obviously be you.'

'I fancy, Wrenshall, that he might feel it almost an impertinence. After all, he's coming down to hear our little concert with the express purpose of detecting any imperfections in his composition. Personally, I would not dream of trespassing on the field of his artistic creation or musical judgment.'

Mr Tardell's voice, and face, reflected considerable satisfaction at having been able thus obliquely to squash Letitia—had she not dubbed his favourite hymn-tunes tosh?—and she was quick to perceive it.

'Very well,' she retorted, 'he shall hear what he undoubtedly meant to write, and not what he has miswritten. I shall sing A *fortissimo*; and you know, rector, what my *fortissimo* can be.'

'But, my dear lady, you could not do that, you know, without injustice to Dr Wrenshall, who is taking such pains to secure an exact rendition.'

'I shall merely make a mistake, and Dr Wrenshall can apologise for me afterwards to Sir Cuthbert if he thinks it necessary. But I bet you half a crown, rector, that Sir Cuthbert won't think it a mistake.'

'As you are aware,' Mr Tardell spoke in a tone of reproval, 'I do not bet, even in joke. If I did, I would certainly take yours. But if you are set on such an improper course, Mrs Parlington, I sincerely trust that you will say nothing of it to the other singers.'

'Of course not,' she replied tartly; 'I've already given you my word on that. Well, I must be off now to catch the post; these new collection times are most inconvenient.'

As she left the room Dr Wrenshall smiled and shrugged his shoulders. 'Temperamental,' he said, turning to the still ruffled rector, 'very much so. Yet she has been of tremendous assistance in copying out all these parts; and an intentional mistake will be a change from the unintentional ones of other singers. I doubt, too, whether Kewbridge will notice just a single voice on the A, whatever her *fortissimo*. So don't let it worry you unduly.'

'No; but I hate indiscipline. She won't stand it herself from the church choir.'

Dr Wrenshall smiled again. 'Quite right too,' he murmured, sitting down to the piano.

4

The evening of the concert arrived. Seated in the front row, next to Sir Cuthbert Kewbridge, Mr Tardell viewed the packed hall with a full sense of satisfaction. The new and old strata of his parishioners were pleasantly intermingled both on the platform and in the auditorium. The Philharmonic Club had indeed attracted all who were musically inclined; many acquaintances had been made, and not a few friendships formed. Dr Wrenshall moreover informed him that both choir and orchestra had developed a team spirit, and that he anticipated a highly creditable performance. The rector's sole cause for anxiety had been removed by Mrs Parlington's departure for Wolmingham some days previously, to help look after an old school-friend who had been taken suddenly and seriously ill.

She expected to be away for ten days at least, and had asked Miss Tisdale to deputise for her at the church organ. Mr Tardell intended during the interval to ask the latter to play some of his old favourites; but, looking round the hall, he could see no sign of her. Then with a frown he remembered that it was Thursday, and that she was probably at the Psychic Circle. Miss Godwinstowe, he had been told, refused to put off their weekly *séance*, holding that the Philharmonic Club should have chosen some other day for its concert. How typical of her!

In the first half of the programme choir and orchestra amply justified Dr Wrenshall's expectations of them. The items were unambitious, and their execution such as to give the performers confidence in their ability later on to render *Northern Lights* not unworthily of the composer's presence.

The rector had just begun to inform Sir Cuthbert that the resuscitation of the Philharmonic Club had been his own idea, when he was annoyingly interrupted by a message to the effect that Miss Tisdale particularly wanted a word with him at the outer door. Excusing himself to Sir Cuthbert he made his way down the gangway and, without the usual courtesy of bidding her good evening, asked abruptly what it was she wanted.

'I supposed that you would have been at the Psychic Circle,' he added sarcastically.

'Well, yes, rector,' she replied, 'and that's why I've run up here to see you.'

'What do you mean by "that's why"?'

'Well, Miss Godwinstowe thought it only fair that somebody should tell you: before it's too late!'

'Tell me what?'

'That there's some spirit trying to get through to you. We don't know who it is; but it's someone.'

The wind blew icily in at the doorway, but it was not so cutting as Mr Tardell's reply.

'You can tell Miss Godwinstowe that you have delivered her message. She knows what I think of such things. I must now be hurrying back to Sir Cuthbert. He will be wondering where I've gone. Goodnight, Miss Tisdale.'

Back inside the vestibule he muttered an angry 'Preposterous!' and on regaining his seat was disappointed to find Sir Cuthbert no longer there but in conversation with the leader of the orchestra. He was also perturbed by the dimness of the footlights. The village gasworks were notorious for reducing pressure without warning. If it went any lower, the singers and instrumentalists would hardly see their notes. He was just about to say so to the returning Sir Cuthbert when a rap of the conductor's baton transformed the buzz of conversation into a tense silence of expectancy.

The rector had reproved churchwarden Trimshaw, at the dress rehearsal, for describing the music of the short overture to *Northern Lights* as 'snaky'. Snakiness, he had observed, was not a word in the vocabulary of musical criticism. Now, as he listened to it this evening, he admitted to himself that certain passages, in the violin parts particularly, had a reptilian quality. It gave him a vague feeling of discomfort, which was aggravated by a draught of cold air that began to chill the back of his neck and the bald patch on his head. Somebody must have opened the east window, which he had given orders to keep closed. He hoped he would not catch cold. It might be his imagination, but the gas jets seemed to him to burn lower than ever; and, as the singers rose for the opening chorus, he began scanning their faces to see whether any of them had difficulty in seeing their music.

Apparently not; but, he reflected, probably they knew it all by heart after so much practice and rehearsal. Then all of a sudden, his gaze became riveted on the vacant row which separated trebles from altos. Mrs Parlington was standing there; and, he thought, looking not at the conductor or her music but pointedly at him. Drat the woman! She must have rushed down for the concert and caught the three-eighteen from London. Now, of course, she would sing that threatened A! She appeared to be saving up for it, too, for her mouth was closely shut and her lips motionless. It seemed to him an age before the crucial passage came. But come at last it did. A brief half-second before the conductor's beat the closed lips opened, but only narrowly. From them he seemed to hear momentarily a faint note as of a pitch-pipe or tuning-fork; and then, to his consternation, the whole three rows of *sopranos* burst out on A, *fortissimo*.

Horrified, he glanced anxiously at Sir Cuthbert. The composer's head was thrown back; his eyes were closed; and his lips bore the suggestion of a smile. Had he noticed? It seemed not; but surely, he must have? Much puzzled, Mr Tardell turned his eyes nervously back to the platform, and again found it hard to believe them. Mrs Parlington had gone! He looked carefully at each row of singers, but there was no sign of her. How cold that draught was! He dug his hands deep into his trousers pockets for warmth, bringing his finger-nails into sharp contact with coins and a bunch of keys. The lights were burning more brightly now, but his feeling of anxiety persisted. He was not enjoying the music or attempting to follow it. He was, indeed, hardly conscious of the ending of the final chorus or of the burst of applause that followed. It was Sir Cuthbert's movement towards the platform steps, in answer to cries of 'Composer', that brought him back to full alertness.

'I have been delighted,' Sir Cuthbert was saying, 'by this performance of my most recent work. I most gratefully felicitate both choir and orchestra on its excellent interpretation, and I congratulate them—and not only them, but all music-lovers in this neighbourhood—on having in Dr Wrenshall a trainer and conductor who will lead this Philharmonic Club ever further along the never-ending road to musical perfection. You, Ladies and Gentlemen of the audience, will be interested to hear that we have had an example of his superlative musicianship this very evening. In making my final manuscript of *Northern Lights* I made a careless mistake, when copying the treble part from my rough draft. I wrote an F instead of an A.

'I noticed the error only this morning, while refreshing my memory of certain passages which I particularly wanted to hear in actual performance; and I felt most unhappy, as the mistake entirely ruined a climax in the second chorus. I felt that it would be unfair to mention the matter to Dr Wrenshall at the eleventh hour, when there was no possibility of further rehearsal, and decided to grin and bear the result of my own carelessness. Imagine, therefore, my relief and delight when that A rang out so triumphantly from the trebles. He had rehearsed right, though I had written wrong. I am grateful beyond words. In conclusion I must thank you all very warmly for the kind reception that you've given to my little work, which I shall always associate with Telmington and its kind people. Thank you all again.'

Sir Cuthbert stepped down from the platform amid loud clapping and, on his way to resume his seat before the singing of the National Anthem, stooped to pick up something from the floor at Mr Tardell's feet.

'You've lost half a crown, I think, rector? A hole in a trousers' pocket perhaps.'

Mr Tardell's thoughts were apparently elsewhere; for his reply was most inconsequent.

'Oh! no, I never take bets,' he said.

5

The news of Mrs Parlington's death in the Eldonhall train smash was in the newspapers next morning. She was travelling back to Wolmingham from a day's visit to her lawyer in London and was in the carriage next behind the engine that was completely telescoped. Her neck was broken and death must have been instantaneous. Shortly after breakfast Dr Wrenshall called on three of his leading *sopranos*, to enquire why they had sung A instead of F and so won him unmerited commendation from Sir Cuthbert. The first replied that she didn't know that she had sung A; the second that she supposed that she had just followed the others; and the third that the higher note seemed somehow to be in the air and she simply had to sing it.

He then walked up to the rectory, where he saw the doctor's dog-cart standing outside the gate.

'You can go in for a minute or so,' Dr Holmbush said, 'but the rector's running a high temperature and has passed a sleepless night. He wants to see you though, about something to do with last night's concert; and he'd better get it off his chest, if he doesn't take too long about it.'

Dr Wrenshall listened sympathetically, but incredulously, to the rector's account of what he had seen and heard in the village hall. The fever had probably already been on him, Dr Wrenshall surmised, and given rise to delirious fancies. The silly message from the Psychic Circle might have suggested them perhaps. Back in his own house, despite such scepticism, Dr Wrenshall took the trouble to look in his newspaper again for the exact time of the Eldonhall accident, and to compare it with that of the interval in last evening's concert.

'Not that it signifies anything,' he muttered to himself on finding that they more or less tallied, 'but I'm very sorry that we've lost Letitia. They'll miss her a lot here.'

They did. No previous Telmington funeral had been so largely attended. Among very many wreaths the most noteworthy was one from Dr Wrenshall. It was in the shape of a capital A. The rector re-covered in time to officiate, but still looked poorly. The prefatory sentences and a psalm were sung; but there were no hymns.

Cheap and Nasty

1

Moonlight, and curtains not back yet from the cleaners! That was why Tom Cromley was still awake at one o'clock of this cold November night; and how he was able to see his wife, Kathleen, rise suddenly in her bed and sit rigidly upright. Tired, and in no mood for conversation, he continued to lie still and pretended sleep. He watched her nevertheless until, again suddenly, she thrust an arm across the narrow space between their beds and clutched his eiderdown. It slipped across him and a corner of it brushed his face.

'Hullo, Kitty, what's up?' he asked in cross surprise.

'Hush, Tom! Can't you hear it?'

'Hear what?'

'That moaning, groaning noise. Listen—there!'

'Oh that? Why, it's only the hot-water pipes. They're bound to grunt and growl a bit at first. We started the stove going only a few hours ago, and there are probably air locks. One can't expect perfection on a trial run. All the same, the radiators are piping hot; which is the main thing. You did a fine stroke of business, Kitty, in getting the stove so cheap; and this house too. We couldn't have found a nicer one at double the price. Now lie down and go to sleep again, darling, and don't keep your ears waiting for noises, or you'll begin imagining them.'

'I'll try, Tom, and I'm so thankful you like our new home. It has been great fun, really, getting it all fixed up; but I wish—' The sentence was left unfinished, and merged into a little sigh.

'You wish what? Look here, Kitty, I hope you're not worrying about all that rubbishy talk of Aubrey Roddeck's.'

'No, not exactly; but I wish I'd never listened to him. There! I've taken another of my tablets, and ought to get to sleep quickly. You'd better do the same, darling. Thank Heaven, that horrid noise has stopped.'

Cromley did not like his wife's taking sleeping tablets; especially as she had no idea what they contained, and had been given them not by a doctor but by her artist friend, Miss Bevisham. What could be the cause of her insomnia? She had no physical weakness, he was sure, being of a strong athletic type and able to give him points at golf or tennis. Her nerve, too, was good at both games; even in matches and tournaments. Nor had she been nervy in other things until quite lately. On the contrary, lawyers and brokers, employed by her in the management of her inheritance from a godfather-uncle, had spoken to him of her business grip and quick brain. Of the rightness of their judgment, he himself found proof in her running of household affairs; he had in fact added garage and garden to her domestic domain after his discovery that she could get much more out of the two men than he, and they less out of her than of him. He thus had nothing now to interfere with his work, which (as that of a regular writer for a leading daily, two weeklies and several monthlies) had become voluminous and exacting.

He was just as deeply in love with Kathleen as when he married her six years ago; and to the bonds of affection had been added those of gratitude. One grievous disappointment they equally shared. They had no children. Was it brooding over this, perhaps, that made Kathleen nervy and sleepless? The thought so worried him that he began fidgeting with quilt and pillows; but a moment later, as though symbolising the lifting of a load from his mind, he extracted his now lukewarm hot-water bottle from between the sheets and laid it on the bedside table. No: it definitely couldn't be that; for her insomnia had started suddenly, and he could put a date to it. It was the night following Roddeck's visit.

He cursed himself now for ever having asked Aubrey to stay with them. One might have guessed from his novels that he would introduce unusual, if not sinister, topics of conversation. But what was it that Aubrey had actually said? Kitty, he remembered, had been boasting about the bargain she had struck in getting house and land for five thousand five hundred. 'Cheap,' she had said, 'and the opposite of nasty.' It was then that Aubrey butted in with 'cheapness is never without cause: the vendor must have had good reason to get it off his hands.' 'What on earth do you mean,' Kitty had challenged, 'the place isn't haunted, you know, or anything of that sort.' 'Not haunted perhaps, but waiting', were, Cromley remembered quite clearly, the exact words of Aubrey's reply; but of the explanation that followed his recollection was less distinct. He must make an effort therefore to reconstruct it if, as he felt sure, it had been the root cause of Kathleen's trouble.

At this point he slipped out of bed, and crept silently on tiptoe to see whether she was yet asleep. Yes—and peacefully. Reassured, he climbed back again and braced himself for an inquisition of his memory. Present perception, Aubrey had said, is a sense-stream trickling between the sludge of the past and the sands of the future; ever eating away the latter and depositing it on the former. On this stream fall many reflections, sometimes of things upon its alluvial bank and sometimes, though less often, of things that loom upon the other. Most often of all, the rippling of the stream over pebbles and shells prevents its reflecting anything. Of Roddeck's explanation of this simile Cromley found it impossible to recollect anything intelligible, except that Aubrey had gone on to claim for himself an ability to sense in the atmosphere of a house (such was his jargon) reflections of its past, in which case he classified it as 'haunted', or of its future, in which case he categorised it as 'waiting'. He himself, he had concluded, would prefer the former sort of house to the latter.

Kathleen, Tom remembered with a grin, had paid Aubrey back in his own coin by asking him whether he did not feel that *her* house might be waiting for his early departure. They had all three laughed at this retort, but rather a stagy sort of laugh; and the thought of play-acting reminded Tom that Roddeck had said that 'waiting' houses always gave him the feeling of an empty scene on the stage before the entrance of actors.

'Damn Aubrey,' muttered Cromley; 'that's three o'clock striking, and not a wink of sleep so far. I must get all this business off my mind till the morning: so now for counting sheep.'

Sleep did come to him at last; but with a foolish dream, in which he and his wife were paddling in a little stream between two banks. He was picking from it little stones and shells, while Kathleen looked as though she were trying to skim off from its surface some dark reflections from either bank.

2

Mrs Cromley's insomnia grew no better. Her pride in Thurbourne Manor was unabated; but her enjoyment of it marred by recurrent fits of depression. For the first time in their married life Tom found her not always quite sure of herself. Until now she had been in the habit of looking through the advertisement columns of newspapers in search of bargains. That was how she had picked up the central-heating stove so cheaply. A notice in the *Stokehampton Mercury* had invited offers for it to be sent to a post-box number; and their surprise had been great when a small lorry drove up the back drive three days later, with the stove aboard, and its owner prepared to deliver it on payment of the modest sum she had offered. Tom, with previous experience of such stoves (it was a No. 3 Keepalite), had inspected and approved; and the stove was fixed up for them next day by old Fennings, a retired plumber, in place of the old-fashioned and worn-out fuel-eater that they had found in the house.

In her present changed mood Mrs Cromley was no longer on the look-out for bargains, and even began to consult her husband before placing the most ordinary orders for household goods on well-established firms. She would also examine such purchases on delivery with a strange air of suspicion. One day, for instance, he found her gazing intently at a new meat-saw, which she had unwrapped on the hall table.

'I suppose,' she said, avoiding his glance of inquiry, 'that surgeons have to use something of this sort?'

'For amputations, yes: but I've never been in an operating theatre, nor want to for that matter.'

'No; it's a horrid-looking thing; but cook insisted on our having one, though I can't imagine what she wants it for. I always order small joints. I shall hide it in the tool cupboard.'

'Very well, but it may be wanted if Sir Matthew sends us venison again next year.'

'I detest venison,' Mrs Cromley muttered crossly, very far from her usual self.

Little outbursts of this kind were becoming of daily occurrence; so much so that her husband began to think of seeking medical advice. They and her insomnia must be interconnected; but which was cause and which effect? Or were both the result of some third trouble? It would be interesting to see what, if any, effect Christmas with the Bridleys at Hartlingsea would have on her condition. He would not, Tom decided, consult any doctors until the new year.

Sir Matthew and Lady Bridley were excellent as host and hostess and the house party was convivial. In such surroundings Mrs Cromley soon regained sleep and normality. But on return to Thurbourne the former symptoms began to reappear, and her husband's work to suffer from his anxiety. Then, in mid January, she went down with influenza; but to his surprise and relief physical illness seemed to improve rather than aggravate her mental malaise. It was not until she was convalescing that fits of irritability and depression again set in. A possible clue to their causation was soon to be furnished by a trivial accident.

Although she was no longer in bed, the doctor would still not allow her downstairs. As he sat with her in the bedroom one evening she asked Tom to bring up her writing portfolio from the library, and on the way back there fell from it a thin notebook. He had unconsciously swung it against the banisters. Stooping to pick the book up he noticed, on the page at which it had fallen open, a newspaper cutting. The headline was '*Will Murder Out?*' Hurriedly putting the book back in the portfolio Cromley decided to take an early opportunity of a further look at it; for why had his wife taken and kept a cutting of that sort?

He had not to wait long. The same evening, after supper, Kathleen asked him to read aloud to her; and he had not droned more than three or four pages before he saw that she was asleep. That was good, for she had slept little the night before. He soon had the notebook out of the portfolio, and looked first for the newspaper cutting. It was not too long for reproduction here.

Will Murder Out?

"It is credibly reported that the incoming tenant of a house in this vicinity has found in his vegetable plot certain remains; which may afford some explanation of the sudden departure, without address given, of his predecessor; also perhaps of the previous disappearance of the latter's housekeeper. Complaints made by neighbours of disagreeable odours from a stove chimney may or may not prove to be of relevance to police investigations now understood to be in hand."

The name of the newspaper was not on the cutting, but the greenish paper and the wording of the report were suggestive beyond doubt of the *Stokehampton Mercury*. Ever since its proprietor, old Mr Catchwater, had been mulcted in heavy damages for an article about hauntings at Tresswell Court, the editor had been under strict orders not to insert any local news that could be represented as likely to cause depreciation of the value of any specified premises or property. But fancy printing such stuff; and fancy (Cromley frowned at the thought) cutting it out and pasting it in a notebook!

Puzzled and discomfited he turned to the other pages. Many were

183

blank; others contained addresses, recipes, prescriptions, names of books, new stitches for knitting, a list of insecticides for the garden, and so on, uninterestingly, to the last page. At the top of this was written 'Quotations' and the entries, only two, were in manuscript. The first was from the Bible:

Until a time and times and the dividing of time. Dan. vii, 25.

Under this was a note in pencil: 'But see Revised Version and Rev. xii, 14.' Odd, thought Cromley, for his wife was no Bible reader. The second quotation was from Aubrey Roddeck's last published novel, *Arrival Platform,* and ran as follows:

"We are prisoners set to quarry in a crevice between the cliff-face of the future and the slag-heap of the past. At any moment either may cave in and fall on us."

Having put the notebook into the portfolio Cromley lit a cigarette and sat down to think things out. His wife slept on.

3

Tom Cromley's meeting next day with Colonel Honeywood, the Chief Constable, in the Stokehampton Club was not, so far as the former was concerned, accidental. He knew the colonel to be in the habit of lunching there on Tuesdays, and this was not the first time that they had sat down together at the same table. They had been contemporaries at Winchingham and Oxbridge.

'Anything behind that rubbish in the *Mercury,* some weeks ago, about human remains being found in somebody's garden, colonel?'

'More than I like, I'm afraid; bits of a body buried in the fowl run, and the rest of it, probably, burnt in a stove. The *Mercury* made a boss shot about the housekeeper, though. She left to take up another job, and is alive and kicking somewhere near Penchester.'

'Any clue yet as to murderer or victim?'

'No, but one or two pointers. We're pretty sure now that no killing was done down our way; only disposal of a body, and not necessarily a murdered one. That's all I can say at present.'

'What sort of stove was it?' asked Cromley; aware, as he put the question, of its oddity.

The colonel slowly helped himself to salt and mustard before reply. 'I rather think, Cromley,' he said, 'that I know the real question at the back of your mind; and it may save you further beating about the bush if I answer it at once. The new tenant of the house, when reporting the unpleasant find in his garden, asked whether we had any objection to his removing the stove forthwith. He didn't fancy its associations. We agreed; on condition that he gave us details of its disposal for our future reference, should need arise. He advertised it in the *Mercury*; and, as I believe you to have already guessed, the purchaser was Mrs Cromley. Well, you've got a first-rate stove, but I wouldn't let your wife get any inkling of its past history, if I were you: women are so imaginative. I've a Keepalite No. 3 myself, by the way, and wouldn't mind feeding it with little bits off more than one person I could name!'

This little joke, as the colonel intended, enabled them to drop the subject with a feeble laugh; and their talk shifted to vagaries of the weather and prophecies about the coming bye-election.

On the drive home Cromley decided that he must tell Kathleen of his verification of what, he was sure, had been her suspicions. He knew now why she had been so upset by moanings and fizzlings in the hot-water pipes. His sharing with her the facts about the stove would, he told himself, reassure her. What a pity she had kept her suspicion to herself! Or would he, perhaps, if she had told him, have merely exhorted her to put foolish fancies out of her pretty head? Anyhow, it was for him to do the telling now. Better wait though, he reflected, till she was quite recovered from the 'flu. In the meantime, he would drop a line to Roddeck and warn him not to make trouble for his friends in future by his insane mystifications. Back, therefore, at Thurbourne he went to his desk and wrote as follows.

My Dear Aubrey

I feel it right to let you know that ever since your stay with us Kathleen has suffered considerably from nerve trouble. Some of your quaint theories and metaphors about the past, present and future have stuck in her mind and made it most uneasy. I know you well enough to be sure that you would be the last man wittingly to cause anxiety to a lady friend and that is why I write this letter. You have probably never had cause to consider the effect of your fantasies (is this the right word?) on an unsophisticated mind. Even such a remark as yours about cheapness never being without cause may lead to sinister speculation. Indeed, to be quite frank, I do not think that my wife has been quite happy about this house since you said that to her. I am sorry to have to write this but, as I said at the beginning of this letter, I feel in conscience bound to let you know. With all good wishes.

Yours ever,   Tom

The letter was posted that evening.

4

The scene now is Lestwick House, in Northshire, where Aubrey Roddeck was staying the night with Lord Henry Hoverly. Lady Henry being on a visit to friends in Ireland, the two men sat alone in the library after dinner. They were second cousins, Aubrey's mother having been a Crimley-Hoverly; but their acquaintance had arisen not out of their family connection but from Lord Henry's partnership in the firm which published Roddeck's novels.

'I don't much care,' Lord Henry was saying, 'for modern tendencies in art, literature or music. There seems to be in all three a spirit of revolt from rhyme or reason, a sort of constitutionalising of anarchy. I noticed in last week's *Cosmos* that even that sane chap Cromley is catching the infection. By the way, do you remember telling me that his wife had bought Thurbourne Manor, the house that I've always had an eye on? It used once to belong to the Hoverly family; in Stuart times I think.'

'I remember your saying that you'd give me a thousand guineas if I could induce her to sell it to you.'

'Not guineas, Aubrey, pounds.'

'Well, make it guineas and I believe that I could do the trick for you.'

'We'll make it guineas then; but no tricks, mind you. You said before that nothing would induce her to part with it, but I'd willingly give ten thousand; a good deal more than it would fetch in the market.'

'Not inclusive of my commission of a thousand guineas, I hope?'

'No, that would be by way of charity to an indigent cousin or undeserving author. But seriously, Aubrey, you seem to possess unusual powers of persuasion. You got that house at Badwood for the Frannocks, and the old churchyard cottage at Mistlebury for—I've forgotten whom. How do you manage to do it?'

'Oh! I just put wanted houses on my waiting list; throw out a hint or two perhaps, if occasion offers, and bide my time. For instance, when I stayed at Thurbourne, Mrs Cromley struck me as not finding the house as comfortable as she had expected; and I expressed a sympathetic understanding of her disappointment. To my mind the Cromleys and Thurbourne Manor somehow just don't fit; and the thought occurred to me that the next time I stayed there it might be as guest of a noble cousin and with a thousand guineas in my pocket!'

'Well, you seem to make money easily,' grunted Lord Henry, 'and to my taste rather nastily. You haven't, I suppose, got your eye on *this* place for anybody, should I get Thurbourne?'

'No, my bent is to get houses at the lowest possible price; and I can't see you parting with Lestwick for a song, unless—'

'Unless what?'

'Oh, nothing! I was stupidly thinking of somewhere else. Sorry. By the way, I notice that you've had the archway into the old north wing built up. Hardly an architectural improvement is it?'

'No, but my wife was always complaining of draughts.'

One feels them quite unaccountably in old buildings, doesn't one? You'll both be more comfortable at Thurbourne, if only I can induce the Cromleys to sell.'

It would be an hour nearer to London, that's its main attraction for me. But look here, Aubrey, don't you go spreading it abroad that this house is draughty.'

'Ah! Lady Henry imagined it, did she? That's another drawback to old houses. People begin imagining things, especially women when they're left alone.'

Lord Henry was plainly annoyed by the turn which their conversation had taken. 'I wish, Aubrey,' he said, 'that you wouldn't talk like a character in your books. I know nothing about people's imaginations, and have no truck with spooks or anything of that sort.'

'But I said nothing about spooks.'

'No, but I could see that you were leading up to it. Well, I'm off to bed. Switch the light off on the landing, will you, when you come up.'

'Certainly, and it won't be long before I turn in too. I've only got one letter to write. Goodnight.'

Ruddick's one letter ran as follows:

My Dear Tom

Thank you so much for writing to me about poor Kathleen's neurosis. There is certainly no call for any but plain words between old friends. I should feel happier about her than I do if I could share your belief that my idle talk had any causal connection with what you report. I am however certain that her trouble had begun before my short stay with you. As you know I am critically observant of people's psychology. The modern novelist has to be. Very soon after my arrival at Thurbourne her too enthusiastic references to the bargain which she had made in her purchase of the house indicated to me beyond doubt her actual disappointment in, even dislike of it. This however did not surprise me because nature has endowed me with the faculty of sensing the past and future associations of a building, an unpleasant sort of intuition that I would much rather not possess.

On stepping inside your hall, I was at once affected by a presentiment of not far distant tragedy. I hate writing this, but as you have been frank with me I must be equally so with you. Should you and your wife (as I much hope may be the case, in your own interest) think of moving elsewhere I believe that I could prevail on my host here, Lord Henry Hoverly, to offer almost twice as much for Thurbourne Manor as she gave for it. It used, as you probably know, to belong to the Hoverly family and a return to ancestral proprietorship might perhaps mitigate, if not dispel, the ominous atmosphere that I so vividly sensed. Be that as it may I shall not of course breathe a word to Lord Henry about my apprehensions. *Caveat emptor!*

Yours ever,

Aubrey

Having inscribed, stamped and sealed the envelope Roddeck looked at the clock as it struck eleven, smiled, and murmured purringly to himself 'a thousand guineas!' And so, to bed.

5

'Why of course, darling, we'll sell at that price,' Mrs Cromley exclaimed, 'and there's no need to bother about replacing the stove. It seems quite providential, doesn't it, for we can now store the furniture and make our promised visit to your brother in New Zealand. It'll do your writing good to have a change of scene, and you can send your stuff to the papers by this new air mail. So that's that.'

That was that. Tom, overjoyed at his wife's recovery, fell in at once with her eager plans; and the lawyers were instructed to put through the transfer of Thurbourne Manor to Lord Henry Hoverly for a consideration of ten thousand pounds. By midsummer the ownership had passed to him.

Aubrey Roddeck saw the Cromleys off by the boat train from London. He rather overplayed, Tom thought, the role of benefactor; but of course, they had good reason to be grateful to him. The voyage out was entirely enjoyable; calm seas, a pleasant lot of fellow passengers, and a well-found and well-run ship. At the journey's end they found New Zealand so much to their liking that they accepted the invitation of Tom's brother to stay over Christmas.

It was two mornings or so after Christmas that their host tossed a newspaper across the breakfast table with the words 'Column five on the second page will interest you both.' It was a telegram from a *London Correspondent*, reporting the death of the novelist Aubrey Roddeck. He was spending Christmas, they read, with Lord Henry Hoverly at Thurbourne Manor, when a fire broke out in the furnace room as a result of logs and firewood being stacked too near the stove. Mr Roddeck, who was sleeping in the room above, jumped from its window in ignorance, presumably, of there being a paved terrace between house and lawn. The Stokehampton Fire Brigade got the fire under quickly and prevented its spreading to the rest of the mansion. Had only Mr Roddeck preserved presence of mind, he could have made his escape by a door leading into a back passage. But it was surmised, he was too stupefied by the fumes.

Mrs Cromley sat staring out of the window. Then, turning to her husband, 'Poor Aubrey!' she said, 'So his premonition was true. He must have felt the walls about to cave in on him!'

Grey Brothers

1

Collinson's *Kongea,* published in 1883, stated the highlands of that Colony to be 'well suited for coffee or spice gardens: excepting the Nywedda valley, which is rendered unfit for human habitation by the miasma exhaled from its marshland.' Present-day passengers, who watch their ship being loaded at Takeokuta wharves with case after case, and crate after crate, all stencilled '*Nywedda Produce*', might guess Collinson to have been misinformed. He was right, however, according to the terminology and medical science of his day; the habitability of the valley began only with the completion of a great drainage scheme round about 1908. Until then it was devoid of population, save for one solitary individual, of whom and whose fate the pages that follow will give some account.

Of Hilary Hillbarn's origin and history before his arrival in Kongea, at the end of 1895, there is no record. The papers dealing with his appointment as Assistant Entomologist to the Takeokuta Museum must have been lost in the fire that later destroyed the curator's office. He was not a Colonial Office recruit, or there would have been despatches about him in the Secretariat record room. His contemporaries in the museum remember him as reticent, secretive, unsocial and pedantic. The incoming mails brought no letters for him, and he made no friends in Kongea.

The work which he was set to do was that of a field collector, many of the museum specimens standing at that time in need of amplification or replacement. The consequent expeditions into the jungle proved most congenial to Hillbarn. His brief periodical returns to Takeokuta and civilisation were dictated by the necessity of replenishing provisions and handing over his collections. He never stayed long. As a collector he had great success. His specimens included not only some much-needed *lepidoptera*, but also a number of interesting *arachnids* hitherto unrepresented. The only cause of concern to the Director of Museums lay in a growing unwillingness on the part of Kongean assistant collectors and camp carriers to accompany Hillbarn on his explorations. This unwillingness culminated in point-blank refusal after the death in mid-jungle of an assistant collector. A formal departmental enquiry had to be instituted.

Complaint against Hillbarn at this enquiry was on two main grounds. First that all his collections were being made in the Nywedda valley, notoriously the home of devils and disease; secondly that all the work of collection was being done by Hillbarn himself, his assistants and subordinates being forced by him to spend their whole time in felling trees, and in building a large timber hut in the middle of the forest. To these charges Hillbarn replied that the Nywedda valley was of all Kongean regions the richest in insect life, hence his choice of it for his expeditions; and that a weatherproof hut was necessary for the treatment and conservation of his specimens.

The Kongeans being a not unreasonable folk, the director was disinclined to accept these quite plausible replies without some degree of verification. He decided, therefore, wet season though it was, to go and see for himself. It was not a journey that he was to remember with pleasure. His party had to spend two nights in rain-sodden, leech-ridden scrub; was bogged twice; and had to make circuitous detours, hacking their way through dense and spiny undergrowth. This effort and labour was, however, rewarded on the second morning by the disclosure, in a small clearing on rising ground, not of a small hut but of a commodious two-roomed timber shed, walled with bamboo wattles and thatched with palm-leaf.

'What else did you expect?' Hillbarn replied to the director's expostulations, 'it's no use doing anything by halves: I shall need every inch of this space when I get the big specimens.'

'*Big* specimens?' asked the director angrily. 'What the devil do you mean? Specimens of what.'

'*Arachnids*, you old fool,' Hillbarn barked back. 'You're blind if you didn't see them against the sunrise this morning. Just you wait till I bag one.'

The homeward journey was less physically arduous, for they followed the trail that they had hacked on the way up. It was, however, rendered even more uncomfortable for the director by a growing conviction that he had to deal, not merely with an insubordinate officer, but with a mental case. He had been called an old fool in the hearing of English-speaking Kongean staff: well, he felt himself big enough to forget that; for Hillbarn was the best collector that he'd had. But this talk of *arachnids* against the sunrise and sunset (for Hillbarn affected to see them again that evening before they made camp) he could not bring himself to forget. Perhaps the young man, who boasted of being malaria-proof, had contracted it in some unusual form detrimental to mental stability. He would send him for medical examination as soon as they got back to Takeokuta.

It was not Hillbarn, however, but the director who shortly under-went medical examination. He, with three others of the party, suc-cumbed to a severe attack of malaria within a few days of their return, and before he had completed his notes of enquiry or recorded the findings. He lay in hospital a whole fortnight. On his return to duty, the director found among the letters awaiting his personal attention a short memorandum from Hillbarn.

Director of Museums
I return herewith my salary cheque for April, having decided to terminate my service on forfeit of a month's pay as provided by clause 12 of my agreement.

H. Hillbarn

May 5th, 1897

Nobody in Takeokuta could tell the director where the signatory had gone. He had indeed become known to very few. Enquiry at shipping offices made it certain that he had not left the Colony: The director therefore concluded that he must have taken up some job on an upcountry plantation. A month or more later, however, he was reported by a headman to have been seen buying provisions in the little shop near Kechoba, which lies at the foot of the Nywedda valley. There were no plantations in the vicinity at that time, so the director knew at once that he must have returned to that jungle shed. Well; he was no longer a government servant, and the department bore no responsibility for his movements. All that need or could be done was to inform the commissioner of police of his recent behaviour and of his present whereabouts. This the director duly did.

2

The Nywedda valley is incorrectly so called. It is not a depression between two ranges of hills but an oval marshy basin, some three thousand feet above sea level, and roughly fifty square miles in area.

There are high hills along seven-eighths of its circumference; the remaining eighth consists of a narrow ridge or saddle-back, at the western foot of which lies the small hamlet of Kechoba. This ridge is of granite, and unbroken by any watercourse. Were the rainfall more than it is, the basin would soon become a mountain lake instead of damp jungle interspersed with bogs and shallow meres.

More than one authority claimed parentage of a scheme to drain it by tunnelling through the ridge. The idea was, indeed, likely to occur to any engineer who inspected the terrain, or studied a contour map of the district. To finance such a project was a more difficult problem. Its cost was finally allocated, in equal shares, between the Colonial Government and a newly formed plantation company, to which the basin was appropriated under a ninety-nine-year concession. This concession was instrumented and promulgated by special ordinance in 1900; an incidental effect of which was to alter the status of the region's solitary inhabitant from squatter to trespasser. He no longer camped on Crown land but on private property.

The necessity for Hillbarn's eviction might not have arisen, at any rate in the initial stages of the tunnel scheme, had it not been for his reputation among the local Kongeans. To them he had become the familiar, if not an impersonation, of evil spirits of the mountains. He was seen only when he emerged to obtain provisions at the Kechoba shop. These appearances became fewer as he gradually accustomed his digestion to a diet of jungle herbs and berries. His clothing diminished with each visit, and was finally standardised in a loincloth. His hair grew long and shaggy, covering not only his head and chin but also his legs, chest, arms and backs of the hands. It was a rusty grey. He walked barefoot; and the surface of his skin, where it was not covered by hair, was blotched with sores. The steel-blue eyes seemed set in a challenging stare; he answered neither greeting nor question.

When his stock of currency notes and coin had run out, Hillbarn traded upon the Kechoba shopkeeper's fear of him by taking goods without payment. The second time that he did so the shopman had summoned up courage to ask for it; but Hillbarn pointed menacingly to the hills, crooked his arms, moved them backwards and forwards like a crab, and blew a thin grey froth of saliva through tightly closed lips. This, to the Kongeans, was a sure sign of demoniacal possession. Hillbarn indeed may have intended such an interpretation.

The upshot was that, when the Survey and Public Works Departments received instructions to take levels and measurements for the tunnel scheme, not a single native could be induced to set foot in the valley so long as Hillbarn was at large.

The surveyor-general appealed to the Commissioner of Police; but the latter professed powerlessness in the matter until Hillbarn should have received and acknowledged a formal notice to evacuate. But how serve such a notice on a man hiding in thick jungle? Both officers sought escape from this quandary by explaining their predicament to the attorney-general.

'Well, well!' was his reply, 'it's a lucky thing that, in drafting the special ordinance, I had in mind that there might be nomad aborigines on whom notices could not be served. So, I inserted a provision that notice can be given by proclamation. I'll draft one right away, and have it sent up for the governor's signature. It'll have to be gazetted, of course, and posted conspicuously at Kechoba. When that's been done, your man will have ten days' grace in which to clear out.'

'But suppose he doesn't?'

'Ah! That's quite another matter. I never advise on hypothetical cases. We must first wait and see.'

The proclamation was duly issued. Its posting attracted quite a crowd of villagers outside the Kechoba shop. None of them could read it, being in English, but the Royal Arms at its top evoked their curiosity and admiration. It was, they supposed, some potent hieroglyphic that would strike terror into the man-devil. But of such comfortable doctrine they were rudely disillusioned next morning, when Hillbarn appeared at the shop-front, bent as usual on loot. He read the proclamation; slashed it into shreds with his jungle knife and, dashing into the shop, seized on one of the ledgers and tore from it some two dozen pages. These he set on the counter, and began writing on them with the shopman's pen and ink. He scribbled fiercely for more than an hour, every now and again savagely tearing into small scraps what he had just written. The shopman, in fear for his life, joined the gaping crowd outside.

Having at last produced a manifesto to his satisfaction he strode with it to where the proclamation had been posted, and pinned it up. Then, having made a larger rape of goods than usual from the shop, he made off into the jungle. Again, nobody could read what was written; but a Kongean sub-magistrate, passing by on his return from circuit, declared it to be a bad sort of writing, unpinned it, and took it away with him to Takeokuta.

To the commissioner of police next morning, it appeared a very bad sort of writing. This is how it ran:

We
Hilary Hillbarn, of Nywedda *King*
By conquest, *Lord Protector* of the Hills,
Defender of the Forests,
Emperor of all that lives or lies within this vale,
Give by these presents to Our subjects *Greeting.*
Whereas by proclamation of a recent date
A governor of Kongea has presumed
That *We* shall quit Our rightful Realm and Throne:
Now Know Ye that the said presumption *We*
Do utterly contemn and set at nought.
We shall continue here to reign and rule,
And peradventure he attempt by force
Our Person to evict, let him *Beware*:
For *We* upon his emissaries
With unrelenting hand will quick unleash
The Hounds of Death, high-kennelled in the hills.
Hilary R.I.

The commissioner of police grunted and frowned. He would have to show this disloyal nonsense to the chief secretary; perhaps to the governor himself. At noon, therefore, we find him in the former's office, and at a quarter past the hour both officers are walking together towards Government House.

Sir Wilfrid Narrowgate prided himself on being able to see a thing quickly and state it shortly. 'Madman, rebel, or both,' he said, 'the fellow has got to be got out. We won't bring the attorney-general in on it at this stage: it's easier to act in charity than in law. You've satisfied me that there's a sick man in the jungle; so, I shall send a search party to bring him safely out. Here's my specification for the party; you two must settle its personnel. First, a Civil Servant of magisterial rank; second, a young medical officer; third, a gazetted police officer; fourth, a government surveyor who knows the lie of the land.

'All four must be good men in the jungle: we can't send natives with them if they are as scared as you say of Hillbarn. So, the party must travel light: sandwiches and flasks in their haversacks; enough for two days. They must be prepared for violence, but not use it unless forced to. They must get the fellow out without injury to him or to themselves. We needn't prescribe methods now, or probe too curiously into them afterwards. Arrange for a wagonette to meet them at Kechoba on the return journey; and tell the P.M.O. to have accommodation ready at the Tenekka Asylum. That's all for the present; but let me know as soon as they've got their man and handed him over. That's when we may have to call in the attorney-general.'

The chief secretary and commissioner of police discussed personnel for the expedition as they walked down from Government House. 'What I like about the governor,' the commissioner remarked, 'is the way he relieves one of responsibility.'

'Yes,' dryly assented the chief secretary, 'but not of work.'

3

The next day but one the search party set out for Kechoba. Its senior member, Hugh Milversom, Assistant District Officer of Karatta, was well known as a hunter of pig and big game: he knew his jungle well. Medical Officer Leonard Hatley, also from Karatta, and Frank Nearwell, Assistant Commissioner of Police, were next in age and official standing. The youngest was Tasman Copworth, a surveyor on agreement from Australia. All four were as physically fit and mentally spry as the purpose of their present expedition demanded.

They had discussed strategy over whiskies and soda the night before. If Hillbarn had any inkling of their search for him he would, Milversom thought, make off into the jungle and elude discovery. Their only hope of speedy contact lay in finding him at his hut. On this point they all agreed; and Nearwell, arguing from police experience, declared that it would be necessary for them to separate a mile downstream of the hut, and later converge on it simultaneously from the four points of the compass. This plan, Copworth objected, postulated the possibility of four men making an efficient cordon, which he felt to be absurd. They must keep together, and manage somehow to surprise their quarry.

At this Dr Hatley, who was making patterns with his forefinger on the marble-top table out of a splash of spilled soda water, began speaking in a low meditative tone. 'This fellow Hillbarn,' he said, 'has long been an enigma to us doctors. He ought to have died years ago. Malaria completely blotted out the local aborigines; so how has he, a soft-bred European, managed to survive? From all accounts he suffers from emaciation and scurvy; but just think of his dietary! In this hothouse climate, of course, nudity is not injurious, except. . .'

Hatley here making a premonitory pause, the others impatiently cut in with 'Except what?'

'Except that he can't possibly wander about naked at night at that altitude. As you know, the wind blows hard for eight out of the twelve months; and for an hour or so before dawn it is positively icy. It gets unpleasantly cool soon after sundown. Wait and see for yourselves tomorrow. It's particularly bad this season. We've a score of pneumonia cases in the Karatta hospital. Take my word for it, Hillbarn must keep to his hut of a night, and use blankets too. That's where we shall find him, if we time our arrival after dusk: a hundred to one on that.' The bet was not taken; for the others, though they had not thought of it before, agreed. So, they planned their timetable accordingly. They could take things easily on the way up, clearing a path, wherever necessary, in order to facilitate their journey back with Hillbarn.

Their progress up the valley proved uneventful. It was dry underfoot, the weather fine and, owing to the wind, not oppressively hot. At about half-past five in the afternoon, they found themselves on rising ground, from which Copworth's trained eyes were able to descry a small clearing, not more than a quarter of a mile away, and in its middle a brown patch which could be nothing but a hut or shed. The scrub round about them was now only breast-high, its branches and twigs bearded with tufts of a grey-green lichen. They decided, therefore, to sit down for a smoke and rest; for Hillbarn might not repair to his hut before sunset. They had not, however, sat long before there broke on their ears the clang of a pan or tin being struck six times.

'Six o'clock,' Nearwell laughed, 'Fancy the fellow beating the hours in deserted jungle!'

'I might do it myself,' mused Hatley. 'His mind may be travelling back to some old church clock striking across a village green. Even lunatics occasionally escape into the past.'

Milversom, who on hearing the clangs had made his way further up the rise, returned at this point to suggest that they might use what remained of daylight to get as near to the clearing as they could without being seen. This they proceeded to do; walking half-bent, and speaking only in undertones. Creeping, thus silently forward they came before very long up against the prostrate trunk of a felled tree, on the edge of the clearing. Peeping from behind it they could see the hut, a few chains distant, and its surround of half-grown coconuts, bread-fruit trees, plantains and chillies. From a slanting bamboo pole there hung by a piece of cord an inverted kerosene tin. A stick, lying on the ground below, evidenced its use as a gong. East and west of the pole two large stones had been set into the ground, each as big as a man could carry unaided.

Milversom was considering whether his party had better wait for complete darkness to veil their approach, or go forthwith to the hut, when they beheld Hillbarn hobbling feebly towards them. He had clearly injured his right leg; for he dragged it laboriously, using a stick. There was no chance, Milversom realised with relief, of his bolting into the jungle. As usual he wore a kind of loin-cloth, but supplemented this evening by a blanket hung down his back from the shoulders like an academic hood. Behind him slunk a very lean black cat, which, on reaching the bamboo pole, he hit at with his stick and drove away. Muttering something which his watchers could not overhear he then began to beat the tin, as though in imitation of the ringing of a bell for church. Indeed, when the tolling had ceased it was plain to the four who spied on him that they were witnessing some sort of religious ritual; for he advanced to the large stone on the west side, made signs of beckoning towards the hills, and began to chant words which Milversom afterwards thus reconstructed from memory:

Creep down, creep down, grey spiders of the sky
And leave the cobweb clouds that ye have spun
Across the face of day;
For day now dies.
Creep down, creep down the brazen chain of rays
Flung by the sun aslant the western hills;
It shall not burn you,
For the sun now dies.
Creep down, creep down to weave a pall of mist
From hill to hill; so, hide me from the stars,
Until the morrow dawn
And they too die.
Creep down, creep down; there is no moon to thwart
The workings of the night; and I have called
All shapes of Hell
To keep me company.
But none so dear to me, O spiders grey,
As beady belly slung from eight lean legs
Poised for a pounce
Or crouching low to spin.
What if you be invisible to such

As see not what I see, live not my life,
Have other thoughts than mine,
Act otherwise?
This makes you the more mine, me yours;
So do I bide the promised time when I
Grey spider shall become,
My manhood shed.
Creep down, Creep down, entoil the trespasser
In grey cocoon of death; so, keep me free,
My dark soliloquy
Inviolate.

At the close of this incantation Hillbarn limped back to the pole; gave the tin a loud bang and, peering this way and that, cried out 'I smell white men!'

'Your nose doesn't deceive you,' Milversom said, climbing over the tree trunk and signalling the others to follow. 'There are four of us here. How do you do?'

Hillbarn glared angrily at the extended hand. 'I do not know you,' he said, 'or what brings you here.'

'We've come to take you home with us tomorrow. The governor's sent for you. He can't allow you to die here in the jungle, you know. You already look half-dead.'

'You must be brave men to venture here; but bravery kills more people than it saves. If you are alive, I will come with you tomorrow; but you will not be. They have already marked you.'

'Who have?'

'My grey brothers. Come inside the hut. The sun is down.'

The inside of the hut was bare of furniture; but in a corner on top of a pile of leaves and rushes lay a heap of discoloured blankets. The floor was of trampled earth. In the middle of it a few logs smouldered, yielding little heat or light but emitting an acrid smoke, for which the palm-thatched roof offered no vent. It was consequently sooted over, and the fumes hung in layers below it.

The party had brought candles in their haversacks and now proceeded to light them, as the last of the twilight faded from the doorway. The resultant glimmer revealed only one thing of interest. There was a closed door in the wall or partition on the right-hand side of the entrance; presumably therefore a second room beyond. In front of it Hillbarn stood shivering, for the evening was already cold. Or was it from excitement? His eyes, now burning with defiance, were certainly those of a madman, and perhaps of a dangerous one.

'They are hungry,' he snarled, 'and will leap on you swiftly, but softly and silently. There may be worse deaths than yours, but none more noiseless. I bid you goodbye.'

At this he wrenched the shut door open.

Milversom afterwards confessed that his heart was in his mouth. Nearwell whipped out his service revolver, and Copworth had a hand on his jungle knife. Only Dr Hatley kept his eyes away from the opened door. They were focused keenly on Hillbarn.

Nothing emerged from the door, and they could see nothing but blackness beyond it.

'They invite you to see them first,' Hillbarn said; 'take your candles and look inside.'

They did so. In various positions crouched a large number of huge spiders; the body of each about the size of a coconut, the legs covered with a grey-green inch-long hairiness. They were not grouped on one level; some were on the floor, others clung to racks against the walls, yet others hung from the rafters. All were motionless.

Again, Milversom's heart was in his mouth, and Copworth's fear broke out chokingly with 'God help us! Just look at the bloody things!' Nearwell pointed his revolver at the nearest of them. The doctor's gaze, however, was still riveted on Hillbarn, as though that were the quarter from which danger might come. He had in fact noticed, what the others had not, that since their entry into the hut Hillbarn had picked up from somewhere, and now held in his hand, a heavy chopper.

This atmosphere of apprehension and suspense was all of a sudden dispelled by a happening that in the recollection, but not at the time, appeared ludicrous. The lean black cat must have passed unnoticed through the door when Hillbarn opened it. It now sprang across the floor at some mouse or rat, and in doing so knocked over three or four of the spiders. The bodies, that had looked the size of coconuts, were now revealed *as* coconuts; the legs as twigs with lichen on them. Hillbarn had modelled them into spiders so realistically that they would have deceived in a stronger light than that of the candles. Dr Hatley, on a considered review of the case, had no doubt that the wretched man believed himself to have endowed them with life.

There was no time for thought at the moment, for a horrible scene ensued. Hillbarn lurched savagely forward; his injured leg gave way beneath him, and he crashed headlong to the floor, knocking over

201

more of the spiders and pinning the cat under his left elbow. With the chopper in his right hand, he hacked at its protruding forelegs; and then, grabbing its tail with his left, half-decapitated it. Twistily struggling to a kneeling posture he held the shuddering animal above his head, its blood dripping on to his hair and forehead, and hurled it against the wall. With a circular swing of the chopper, he next smashed a couple of the spiders that lay nearest to him, and then giddily attempted to regain his feet.

'Get that chopper from him,' shouted Hatley; and Milversom, with a kick at his right wrist, sent it clattering to the ground. In an instant Nearwell and Copworth had closed with him, hauled him erect and propped him against the wall. It needed their full strength to hold him upright, for he seemed suddenly to have gone limp and inarticulate.

'Lay him down on the blankets, please,' the doctor ordered in a professional tone, 'I rather fancy he's finished.'

He was. Whatever store of vitality there may have been in his underfed, underclothed body, it had been squandered in that final paroxysm of rage and violence. As Hatley examined it now upon the bed of leaves and rushes there was neither breath nor heartbeat. Hilary Hillbarn was dead.

There was nothing more that they could do that night; so, having pulled palm fronds from the roof and laid them as mats before the fire, they lay down, ate some sandwiches, drank from their flasks, and talked themselves into such sleep as they managed to get.

4

The presence at Hillbarn's passing of a magistrate, doctor and senior officer of police would, without doubt or question under Kongean law, have enabled immediate interment. Milversom, however, reminded his colleagues of the Kongean proverb that '*every planting makes a haunting*'. To leave the corpse in that valley would be to make an evil reputation worse. They slung it, therefore, in a blanket from a long bamboo and, shouldering it, marvelled at the lightness of their burden. It was little heavier than a child.

Starting at dawn they reached the Kechoba shop by three o'clock. The wagonette was there; and the body was duly taken to the Takeokuta mortuary.

Next day the four members of the search party were summoned to the Secreta.

'The governor wishes me to thank you for your services,' the chief secretary told them, 'having heard the main gist of your report from the commissioner of police. His Excellency was greatly distressed about the cat. He has come across a passage in an old *Museum Journal* which he thinks might interest you. You will find it on the writing-table in the waiting-room, in case any of you would like to take a note. His Excellency has marked the passage in pencil on page thirty-seven.'

The *Museum Journal* was that of the third quarter of 1893, and the marked passage read as follows:

. . .but the Kongean *araneae* have been insufficiently collected, and many of the museum specimens are not in a condition to ensure correct identification. One of the *avicularia* appears to be of a size hitherto unreported from any tropical region; but the specimen is too disintegrated to admit of exact measurement. It may have been this species that gave rise to the legend, current within living memory among the aborigines, of man-hunting spiders. The legend is no longer heard, but there survives in some districts a superstition of mountain spirits that assume a visible but impalpable *arachnid* form. Medicine men and war-locks are still alluded to in such districts as 'those who behold the eight-legged ones', and a popular but fanciful derivation of the name Nywedda is from *nyiva* (leg) and *edda* (eight). For its true derivation the reader is referred to the Rev Josiah Hugh-son's monograph on *Some Place Names in Western Kongea*.

Milverson, who had been holding the book, suddenly dropped it. There had crept out on to his hand, from the hollow back-cloth, a small but seemingly vicious grey spider.

203

Quintet

1. Introduzione

A small party sat up in the parlour of Brindlestone Manor to see in the new year. There were five of them, three men and two women. The stillness of a windless frosty night and the warm glow of a log fire made them sleepy; yet it was only a quarter past ten.

'I vote we each tell a ghost story to keep ourselves awake,' said the youngest of the men. 'I want to practise my shorthand and I'll try jotting them down.'

The speaker was Vernon Ruthwell, recently appointed to the Colonial Service and due to sail for Kongea in six weeks' time. His idea was to spice the routine of an administrative career with attempts at authorship. Had he not edited a college magazine and taken English and French literature in the schools? That was why he had during his last three vacations attended a course in typewriting and shorthand. He felt that he had it in him to observe, describe and characterise. The other members of the party were Vernon's paternal uncle, Philip; Aunt Susan, his wife; Miss Clara Godwinstowe, on a Christmas and new year visit from Telmington; and a Mr Felworth who, having lately rented the manor cottage, had been asked out of neighbourliness to drop in for the evening.

These four persons require but little introduction. Philip Ruthwell typified the moderately successful business man, with just a tinge of pomposity; Mrs Ruthwell the comfortable not over-brainy wife. Miss Godwinstowe was an elderly and somewhat assertive spinster, proudly possessed of a 'psychic ego', whatever she meant by that. Readers of an earlier story may remember her as foundress of the *Telmington Psychic Circle*. Of Mr Felworth his present companions knew little or nothing. His past history, if at all reflected in his present conversation, might have been dull. His contributions to the evening's entertainment had so far been an occasional 'yes', 'no', 'exactly' or 'quite'; a question as to when the church bells would be likely to start ringing; and his opinion that it was more cheerful to hear them in company than alone.

Vernon's proposal of ghost stories, however, moved him to one further remark. 'You will excuse my being only a listener, I hope,' he said, 'for I always feel the telling of ghost stories to be a trifle incautious.'

'By Jove, that's a splendid introduction!' laughed Vernon. 'You've certainly made your contribution, Mr Felworth. The telling of ghost stories incautious! One couldn't improve on that. Now I'm going to sit at the desk with my notebook and the reading-lamp. We'll have the other lights off. There! Why the fire's burning a bit blue already, isn't it? Well now; ladies first, I think; you must start off, Aunt Susan.'

2. ANDANTE

'I wish that you hadn't left your chair, Vernon,' complained Mrs Ruthwell; 'having this empty place beside me makes me feel quite creepy.'

'Ah! that's the atmosphere we want. Now go ahead, Aunt Susan, and trot us out a real grisly.'

'Well, I can't very well do that, I'm afraid, for I've never really seen a ghost or anything of that sort: unless—'

'Unless what; Susan?' said her husband. 'You're not going to tell us about that bedside companion, I hope.'

'Don't be foolish, Philip. Companion indeed! Why I've not seen him more than twice. Anyhow he's the only thing in the ghost line that I ever came across, and if you want a story from me it's got to be him or nothing.'

'That's right, Aunt Susan,' interposed Vernon, 'go straight ahead and don't mind Uncle Philip. His turn'll come next.'

'Well, it's difficult to know exactly where to begin, but looking back now I think that it all started with a whisky advertisement. You probably all remember that picture of a man in green velvet coat, chocolate breeches, top-boots and an eyeglass. Well, the picture caught my fancy as a little girl, and I used to try to copy it in my exercise book with pencil and paint. Awful splodges I made, too, and I used to feel that the man in the advertisement was laughing at them. Quite kindly, though. Then one day I cut him out from the cover of a Christmas number, put him into a frame and hung him on my bedroom wall. From there he seemed to smile at me more than ever.

'At Christmas time I would put a tuft of mistletoe or sprig of holly

206

over him; sometimes too a daisy-chain in spring, or a rose in summer. Then, when my room was repapered, the frame got taken down and somehow mislaid and lost. My parents told me that anyhow I had grown too old for that sort of picture, and I remember that they hung up in its stead an engraving of "The Soul's Awakening!" Oh! How I hated that girl! I used often to turn the picture back to front. Well, I suppose that I gradually forgot about the whisky man; but several years later (I remember it was the night before Dr Benstead's funeral) I woke up in the dark to see him sitting in the chair at my bedside; not a flat four-inch figure as in the advertisement, but a real full-size man. Although everything else in the room was pitch-black, his face and body seemed to be in bright daylight.

'I could see the green of his coat and his chocolate breeches quite clearly; and somehow it all seemed quite right and natural. He was smiling at me. "Hullo Johnny," I said, for I always thought of him as Johnny, "How d'you do?" With that I held out a hand to shake his and then, as I did so, he began to fade and melt away; not abruptly but very very quickly, and the last thing to go was his smile. I thought afterwards of the cat's grin in the Alice book, but not at the time. All I was thinking of then was as to whether I had really been awake; but I knew that I must have, for I had heard a clock strike three while he was sitting there, and I never hear clocks strike when I'm asleep.'

'A projected dream-image, obviously,' murmured Miss Godwin-stowe.

'Well,' continued Mrs Ruthwell, 'I only saw him once again, and that was long afterwards; when I was married, I think. Why, yes, it must have been; because I remember little Paul was on his way, and my mother was so excited at the prospect of having a grandchild. I must have gone down to see her without you, Philip, as I was given my old little single-bedded room. Well, the whisky man came and sat and smiled and faded away, just as he did before. It was a Sunday night, I remember, because we had special prayers in church that morning for the dedication of a stained-glass window in memory of Dr Benstead; and mother had left her glasses behind, and put a lozenge into the plate in mistake for a threepenny bit. Well; there's nothing very excit-ing in what I've told you, I'm afraid, but that's all.'

'No, Susan,' said Miss Godwinstowe in her deep husky voice, 'that can't be all. Tell us now, did you ever know Dr Benstead personally?'

'Why yes, of course. He was our family doctor and such a dear man. It used to give me quite a thrill when he felt my pulse! It was a tragedy that he died so young, and unmarried too.'

Was he as good-looking as the whisky man, as you call him?'

'Well naturally he never dressed in a green velvet coat or chocolate breeches. He did wear an eyeglass, though, to look at one's tongue. In fact, though it's never occurred to me before, he *was* rather like the whisky man. I might almost say very like.'

'Exactly so, my dear Susan.'

'Why exactly so, Clara?'

'I'll explain to you tomorrow morning, dear, when we've got time to ourselves. The night of the funeral and the night of the memorial service; just what I would have expected! Very natural. And now let's hear what your husband may have to tell us in the way of a ghost story.'

3. LARGO

Mr Ruthwell cleared his throat. 'I was glad,' he said, 'to hear Miss Godwinstowe, with her long experience of *psychic phenomena,* use the word "natural" in regard to some point or points in my wife's narrative; for I most strongly disbelieve in anything supernatural. Than to use such a classification it is more honest to confess that our inability to explain, or even maybe to comprehend, certain phenomena is due to our imperfect cognition of the natural order. On the twin assumptions, which I predict that scientists will sooner or later verify and confirm, that personality survives physical dissolution, and that human perception is not limited to data furnished by the five physical senses, all that is ignorantly termed supernatural is natural. I cannot pretend to explain what I am about to tell you, but to future generations it might appear a very ordinary tale.'

His wife, his nephew and Miss Godwinstowe were restive under this prosy exordium; but they knew better than to bid Mr Ruthwell cut out the cackle and come to the horses; for, being of a disputatious bent, he would gladly have embarked on argument in preference to narrative. Finding a minute's pause unproductive of remark or question he cleared his throat once more and proceeded.

'As a boy I was brought up to regard talk of ghosts and their kind as taboo; my father called it silly and my mother sinful. Our Victorian *ménage* was certainly not such as to invite spectral visitation: everything and everybody were solid and substantial. Nevertheless, there arose one day a topic for conversation which necessitated removal of my young brother and sister to their playroom before it could be discussed. It started by the vicar asking my father whether he ever used the footpath through the churchyard and, if so, whether he had noticed a row of headstones to the left of it. My father had; four of them. The vicar nodded and made some remark about the quaintness of their design before passing on to other topics of parochial interest. He stayed to dinner; and, when he rose to take his leave, my father, always ready for a short walk, said that he and I would see him part of the way home.

'It was bright moonlight and, as we reached the graveyard, the vicar pointed with his stick at a row, of headstones and said "Five, you see; but I suggest that you count them again tomorrow morning." On our way back to the house my father was silent, which was unusual in him, and, what was still more unusual, said nothing to any of us at breakfast next morning; except to tell my mother that he had just been out for a stroll and would she mind coming into the study a moment to see about ordering flower seeds?

'Later the same morning my mother asked me to walk with her to the village. She chose the church path. As we passed through the lych gate, I saw her glance curiously to the left and then with her right forefinger touch in turn the four knuckles of her left hand. Whatever she was looking at seemed to puzzle her. Following the direction of her eyes I noticed, to my surprise, that where last night there had been five headstones there were now only four. The vicar had remarked upon the peculiarity of their design; and what he had meant by that was now, in the daylight, plain to see.

'At the top of each had been carved what presumably was meant to be an urn but unquestionably resembled a more familiar and less ornamental vessel. Beneath the urns, over dates of birth and death, were cut the names of Matthew Punnings, Mark Punnings, Luke Punnings and John Punnings. Like my father on the previous evening, my mother maintained an unwonted silence for the rest of our walk. She did not even answer me when I said that one of the headstones seemed to be missing.

'During the remainder of my Easter holidays my father made a nightly excursion to the graveyard, taking a lantern with him if there was no moon. He was a methodical man, and I noticed on his study table one day a time schedule, neatly ruled and lined, made out for these inspections. In the right-hand column a space was left for daily entries. When I went back to school for the summer term all entries up to that date consisted of the figure 5.

'My parents wrote nothing about this matter in their weekly letter to me; but on the second day of the summer holidays there was a sort of meeting in my father's study. The vicar was there, Mr Carrowlake from the Hall, my father and mother, old Tetteridge the sexton, and a man whom I did not recognise but who turned out later to be a monumental mason from Eaglebury. As a reward for having brought back with me from school a prize for English Essay I was told that I might sit in the window seat and try my hand at jotting down some account of what was said. My father announced his intention of correcting it afterwards; so I had to listen with particular attention. My opinion is that boys should be set to a task like that regularly in the course of their education; it stimulates their powers of attention and promotes accuracy.'

Mr Ruthwell paused here for a moment in the hope that one of his listeners might combat this opinion; but their silence remaining unbroken, he again cleared his throat and resumed his story.

'My father began proceedings by saying that their object in meeting together that morning was to elucidate certain points concerning the Punnings gravestones; and that, as Mr Smith (that was the monumental mason's name) wanted to get back to Eaglebury as soon as possible, they would seek his assistance first. Mr Punnings, they learned from him, had ordered stones for the graves of his five sons, who had predeceased him. Four of them, Mr Smith believed, had died of diphtheria or something to do with bad drains. The fifth had been a sailor and died a year or so later down Coastport way, the body being brought home for burial. By that time the other four stones were nearly ready for erection, and old Mr Punnings called in at their shop and altered his order from four to five. "I've outlived the whole bunch," he said. "They took after their mother, not me. You'd better put up all five stones at the same time, for I don't want to pay for extra cartage."

'Mr Smith remembered those words, for they had struck him as hard-spoken. He remembered, too, putting up the stones himself; for he was a young man then and sent by his father to do the outdoor jobs. The five graves were side by side, and he fixed a stone at the head of each in a straight row. They weren't bad stones but spoilt, he thought, by old Mr Punnings having insisted that the urns should have only one handle and not show any narrowing at the base. His father hadn't liked doing it; but an order was an order. That was all that Mr Smith could tell; he hadn't inspected the stones since and didn't want to, as he didn't consider them a good advertisement for his business; for which he ended by humbly soliciting the future patronage of all present.

'After Smith's departure old Tetteridge was interrogated, and I can give you what he told us in pretty well his own words; for, as you will remember, I was taking notes of what was said.

'"If I didn't know ole Punnings," he began, "I'd like to know who did! I "adn't the buryin' of 'im, though, because 'e died when visiting 'is brother up in Scotland and were put to earth there. What Mr Smith 'as told about them stones were true, but 'e told only 'alf. The fifth stone were the dead spit of t'other four 'cept for the name, which was Paul. But it 'adn't stood more'n a year afore Paul's widder come up out of Coastport and worrited ole Punnings for money what to buy winter clothes with. Now ole Punnings were never no mild-spoken man, and 'is boast 'ad always been to have got 'is five sons off 'is 'ands sooner than most, so 'e flares up proper at the widder, and 'you come with me,' 'e says, 'and I'll show you what I care for you and your dead 'un.'

'"So 'e takes 'er up to churchyard, with a crowbar in 'is 'and; and there I seed 'im, for I was a-diggin' Mrs Purves's grave close by, lay 'old on Paul's 'eadstone, wrench it sideways, push it over, and crack it in three pieces with 'is crowbar. 'Don't you go telling no tales to Parson,' 'e shouts to me, 'for I paid for this 'ere stone and that be what I choose to do with it.' Well I ain't a one to make trouble, so as soon as 'e were gone, with the widder cryin' shame on 'im and 'ollerin', I tidies up the grave; and no questions arst. The pieces of the stone what 'ole Punnings 'ad broke 'll be at the bottom of the churchyard well, where I dropped 'em. But I reckon that son Paul got even with 'is ole dad for what 'e'd done; 'cos most nights arter that I spied ole Punnings walking up the church path, and one night I follers him and sees what he seed.

'"But I ain't a one to make trouble and, 'cep' to say as the ten shillin' 'e offers me weren't enough, I says nothing; no, not to nobody 'cep' to young Mr Kirtle, what time 'e was a courtin' of Miss Apsney and 'imself see the fifth stone. ''Tain't no ghost, Tetteridge,' 'e says to me, 'for stones don't 'ave no sperrits. But there's a hinfluence 'ereabout,' 'e says, 'a powerful hinfluence as makes you see what you doesn't.' 'Same as gin and such like,' I answers: but 'No,' says 'e, 'for you needn't drink no gin but the hinfluence 'ereabout catches you unbeknownst, same as 'ooping-cough.'"'

'It was difficult to get Tetteridge to stop, now that he had got into his stride; but he was silenced at last by my father's mention of something awaiting him in a pint pot in the kitchen. What happened after he had gone is soon told, though there was lengthy discussion. At the joint expense of the rector, the squire and my father Mr Smith was commissioned to execute and erect a replica of the missing fifth stone; so that Paul's triumph over his father was rendered permanent and complete.'

'Interesting, very!' Miss Godwinstowe pronounced hastily in order to forestall any theorising on his tale by Mr Ruthwell, 'and I would much like to have had a word with Mr Kirtle. But now, Mr Vernon, it's your turn for a story.'

4. SCHERZO

'No, no; it's your turn, Miss Godwinstowe,' objected Vernon. 'Ladies first, you know, and *seniores priores.*'

'I always tell my stories last, selecting them with due reference to what has been previously told.'

'Oh! In that case I'll do what I'm told, but I'm afraid that my story's a pretty rotten one. In point of fact, it isn't mine at all, but one that was sent in anonymously to the *College Magazine.* We never publish anonymous contributions, though, so I just put it by. I can read it to you with the help of this desk lamp, for the writing's fairly legible. I warn you again that it's pretty rotten, but it's the best I can do, never having seen a ghost myself. It's got a silly title too: "*Not in these Trousers.*" Well, you've asked for it, you know; so here goes.

'Julian Markson was a piano tuner, whose job took him occasionally to out of the way places. He had never been to Angerthorpe before, and was surprised to find the Three Badgers Inn a good deal more comfortable than its size and remoteness would have led a visitor to expect. Food and service were excellent and charges moderate. He was sorry to be staying only one night; but he had two pianos to tune at Wallingstoke Hall next day. Wallingstoke was three stations further down the line towards Ladderbridge, where he had booked a room in the Commercial Hotel and had several pianos to attend to.

'As he undressed that evening, Mr Markson looked approvingly at the new suit which he was wearing for the first time. Nobody, he said to himself, would take it for a reach-me-down picked up at a cheap sale; it fitted him to a nicety. Finding no coat-hangers in the cupboard, and only one towel, the size of a dinner napkin, on the towel-horse, he

212

carefully arranged his suit on the latter; the trousers underneath, and the coat and waistcoat on top. Then, having brushed his teeth and said a prayer (thus reversing the proverbial precedence of godliness and cleanliness), he got into bed, blew out the candle and was soon asleep.

'Waking later in the small hours he noticed that a shaft of moonlight had fallen aslant the towel-horse. Even in this light, he thought, the trousers looked well-tailored and desirable. But what, he suddenly asked himself, had happened to the coat and waistcoat? The answer lay in a heap on the floor—oddly, because he had taken particular trouble over their disposition on the towel-horse. There was no wind or even draught, and he hoped that it wasn't rats. It must be, though, for there was now a slight movement in the trousers; a sort of twitching, as though they were being gradually inflated. Then to his surprise they jauntily vaulted off the towel-horse, stood erect for a moment, and then moved stealthily towards the door; which, he observed, had somehow come ajar.

'Reconstructing this scene from subsequent memory Markson used to say that his first feeling of intense uneasiness, almost of fear, suddenly gave way to a sharp realisation that they were the only trousers he had with him; and that, if they eloped, he would be a seminudist. He leaped therefore from his bed, caught them by the scruff of the seat as they were passing through the chink, hastily pressed them into a drawer and turned the key. In doing this he had felt nothing tangible inside them to account for their locomotion. Before getting back into bed he locked into two other drawers his coat, waistcoat, underwear, socks and shoes, in case they too should turn migratory. After that he tried to get to sleep again, but found it difficult because of an intermittent rustling noise from the chest of drawers. This at last seemed to cease with the faint flush of dawn, and he then enjoyed an hour or more of dreamless repose; for he was an enviably incurious and unimaginative man.

'There appeared nothing abnormal about his clothes when he came to dress. After shaving he sat down to breakfast and read the *Daily Scene*. Before the meal was finished, however, he had an uncomfortable feeling that his trousers were being shared. "I felt," he used to say afterwards, "as though a lump of frogspawn had somehow got between them and my shirt." Still, there was nothing that he could very well do but put up with it.

'A further annoyance awaited him at the railway station. He was standing on the down platform when a porter remarked that the train

213

had been delayed by fog up Pratford way. Even here at Angerthorpe one could hardly see the home signal. There was not a breath of wind; but, for all that, his trouser-legs kept fluttering out and in against his calves and shin bones. A mongrel dog began to bark at this from a few yards distance, and, to disengage himself from its attention, Markson took refuge in the general waiting-room. When at last the train arrived, and he was in the act of boarding it, a handful of coppers was whisked out of a trousers pocket, and fell tinkling between platform and footboard on to the permanent way below. "Lucky they were only coppers," Markson murmured. "This must be a *poltergeist.*"

'He had never believed in such things before; but his suspicion increased while he was tuning the Wallingstoke pianos. His work was rendered difficult by repeated applications of the loud and soft pedals by some agency other than his toe. The thing was getting really tiresome. On arrival at the Ladderbridge Commercial Hotel, as he was putting down his suitcase, the turn-up of his right trouser-leg got inexplicably caught in the tap of a radiator, and nearly had him over.

'It was there, however, in the hotel vestibule, that he saw a possible means of deliverance. The premises were in the course of redecoration. From a peg on the wall opposite the radiator hung a suit of painter's overalls. Before turning in that night, he took these down, and slipped them into his suitcase. Having carried it to his room, and unpacked it, he used his braces to make his trousers fast to the bar at the foot of the bed. At their side he placed, unsecured, the suit of overalls. After saying his prayers, perhaps more zealously than the night before, he set the door slightly ajar and turned off the gas. He lay awake, watching, for perhaps an hour. It was an incandescent gas lamp, and the tiny blue flame of its lighting jet enabled him at the end of that time to discern, though very dimly, an appearance of movement at the bed-foot. This was followed by two or three tugs at the bar; which he felt very distinctly. Thank heaven those braces were a strong pair! He next heard a rustling; then a scraping by the door. He lit a match. The overalls had gone!

'That, so far as Markson's personal experience was concerned, was the end. Some weeks later a friend, to whom he had described it, posted him a newspaper cutting, which may or may not be of relevance. It was from the *Ladderbridge Weekly Courier.*

'Nothing appears sacred to the professional clothes thief. The Marquis of Lynchester's bailiff, on unlocking the family vault at Haddle-combe on his annual inspection, was amazed recently to find it the repository of a large amount of stolen apparel; much of which has been since identified at Angerthorpe Police Station by the rightful owners. A peculiarity of this strange find lies in the uniformity of the purloined garments, all of which, but for a pair of overalls, consist of tweed trousers. Haddlecombe Court, the ancestral seat of the Wyk-evilles, is approached by a mile-long avenue of stalwart oaks on the south side of the main Angerthorpe-Ladderbridge road. It is of Tudor origin with additions in the Italianate style.

'It looks therefore as if Mr Markson's *poltergeist* may have been well connected.'

'You did perfectly right of course,' said Miss Godwinstowe, 'to re-ject that story for your *College Magazine*. It's typical fake-stuff; utterly fake.'

At this Mr Ruthwell cleared his throat ominously and was clearly about to stake a claim for haunted trousers in the field of future sci-entific investigation, when his wife restrained him with 'Tomorrow, Philip, tomorrow: it's Clara's turn now. Clara, will you begin, dear? We're all so anxious to hear one of your genuine experiences.'

5. *LENTO MA QUASI DRAMMATICO*

It was the dismal tradition of the Brindlestone Bellringers to knell the old year out by tolling each of the eight bells in succession during the quarter of an hour before midnight. This mournful process had begun just as Vernon Ruthwell was finishing the reading of his un-worthy tale. The manor house stood less than two hundred yards from the church; so that the clang of each bell-stroke resounded through it in uncomfortable volume. The company awaiting Miss Godwin-stowe's story reacted to this punctuating din in different ways. Mr Ruthwell rose and poked the log fire, which appeared to be dying with the old year. His wife at each bell-stroke struck the arm of her chair with a crochet hook, and Vernon did much the same by the ink-stand with his pencil. Only Mr Felworth was moved to words. 'That's not the way to ring bells!' he exclaimed. 'The vicar or churchwardens should stop it.'

The light from Vernon's reading-lamp lay in a small circle at its foot; the rest of the room no longer had the glow of the fire. Sit-ting next to Miss Godwinstowe, Mrs Ruthwell could barely see her friend's face, but just sufficiently to be sure that the eyes were focused on the chair which Vernon had vacated between herself and Mr Fel-worth. She wished that Clara would begin.

The remorseless tolling went on. The absence of any other sound was becoming intolerable to one whose nerves might have been steady enough under the smile of her 'whisky man', but were not proof against present suspense. Suddenly, almost savagely, she clutched at Miss Godwinstowe's arm and gasped 'For God's sake, Clara, do begin.' At this moment a flicker from a log, protesting against Mr Ruthwell's poker, shed a fleeting gleam on Miss Godwinstowe. She was gazing now, not at the vacant chair, but with a fixed intensity at Mr Felworth. Her response to her friend's appeal was, it seemed, deliberately belated. At least two tolls of a bell thudded on the room before she at last broke silence, in a low slow drawl very different from her accustomed incisive manner.

'This silence,' she droned; 'that bell; this surrounding gloom; those dying embers; you; I; the death of a year; all are part of my story.'

This intelligence was neither of much consolation to Mrs Ruthwell nor much of an antidote to the growing impatience of her other hearers; especially as it was followed by another lapse into only bell-broken silence. They noticed, however, with relief, that the tolling was now that of the eighth and last bell. Perhaps Miss Godwinstowe noticed it too; for, rising to her feet, she dramatically proclaimed in loud but deep and husky tones, 'There is no need to *tell* my story. It is here. Look at that chair!'

To which chair Miss Godwinstowe commanded their attention is doubtful; but all four fixed their eyes on the empty one, as if expecting someone or something to materialise in its vacuum. She, however, continued to stare unblinkingly at that in which Mr Felworth sat, or rather at the sitter himself.

It was on a party posed in these unusual attitudes that the bright light from the ceiling lamps fell when Vernon switched them on, on hearing the midnight chime. They remained thus, like some *tableau vivant,* while listening to the church clock boom twelve. Then, when the full peal fell jangling on the night, the spell was broken and Mr Felworth rose to take his leave.

'Well, I'm afraid I must be going now. Thank you so much, Mrs Ruthwell, for asking me round. Goodnight, and a happy new year to you all.'

As the door closed on him Miss Godwinstowe heaved a sigh. 'Poor man, poor man,' she said, 'I felt, I *knew,* that he saw what he will never, never, forget!'

'Oh, Clara dear,' half-sobbed Mrs Ruthwell, 'how wonderful you are. What can it be that he has seen?'

'If there had been anything visible,' Mr Ruthwell objected, 'we would have seen it too. We possess eyes, I believe. Our visitor appeared perfectly composed when he left us; rather sleepy in fact. Where has our nephew gone to?'

Vernon, who had seen Mr Felworth off from the front door, had gone to fetch something from his bedroom and now reappeared as if in answer to his uncle's question. Switching off the lights once more as he entered the room, he groped his way to his empty chair in the circle and from there to the desk where his notes lay beneath the reading-lamp.

'I was saying,' Miss Godwinstowe addressed him, 'that Mr Felworth saw something tonight that he will never, never forget.'

'Really? Where?'

Miss Godwinstowe's reply was delivered in her eeriest tone. 'There,' she droned. 'There in that chair—the one that you passed by just now. I have a feeling that something is hanging over it still!'

'I believe that Miss Godwinstowe speaks truly,' Vernon said with imitation of her Sibyllic manner. 'I have just brought my electric torch down and will flash it across the affected area. Maybe that she will see there what *she* will never, never forget.'

The next moment she did see; nor will she ever forget. Something did hang over the chair. A pair of trousers.

Authorship Disputed

1

Eustace Amberlake inherited money at an early age. Not a large fortune, but seven or eight hundred a year spelled independence and comfort for a young man of studious habit and inexpensive pursuits. The legacy was from a bachelor uncle who, impressed by Eustace's winning a scholarship at Ruggenham, and later at St Peter's, Oxford, hoped that the family name, hitherto undistinguished, might be writ by his nephew on some page of future history. Eustace was still at Oxbridge when his uncle died. He took first-class honours in history, but failed to take the Porthill prize, for which his tutors had backed him as a certain winner. It went to his college friend Terence Terrison. Amberlake was a year senior to 'Terrie, but from the day of their first meeting the two young men were inseparable. On moving out of college they shared lodgings; and, after leaving the university, set up house together in a London suburb. Terrison daily travelled thence to Fleet Street, where a minor post had been found for him on the staff of the *Recorder* through the influence of a large shareholder, a friend of his father's.

Content with his private means, Amberlake did not look for a job, but chose, as he put it, to round off his education. He attended concerts and lectures, and visited art galleries and exhibitions. At the Acropolis Club he made the acquaintance of a number of interesting people. They found in him a pleasant enough fellow, knowledgeable but unassertive. At the end of three years Terrison received an increase of salary sufficient to enable him, too, to join a club; so Amberlake put him tip for the Acropolis. The date of his election happened to be also that of the publication of his first novel, *Cain's Sacrifice*. It was well reviewed, and became widely read. Terrison was thus on the march, while his friend continued to mark time.

There was no sign in Amberlake of discontent with a life of doing

219

what he fancied when he chose, or of inclination to supplement his income by taking up work. 'A sensible chap,' said his friends. 'Why bother about getting a job if you haven't got to?' There was one thing about him, however, that began to bore. He was for ever talking of Terrie, and bragging about Terrie's success. So different from Terrison himself, who was modesty personified; never mentioning his articles or books, though they were frequently the subject of club discussion. One might almost have supposed that it was Amberlake who had written them! He resented Cliverton's criticism of the plot of Terrison's *Red Rage,* and, as a consequence of his perpetual harping upon Terrison's literary work, and touchiness if it were criticised, people began to avoid conversation with him. Most of his friends had soon become also Terrison's friends, and they were annoyed by his assumption of the role of a Boswell. They wondered indeed at Terrison's ability to continue living with such a monopolistic and proprietary bore. Many suspected that there must be some financial explanation of it. But there they were wrong. Terrison never borrowed from his friend, and scrupulously paid his full share of joint expenses.

The five novels written by Terrison, over as many years, show increasing powers of imagination and description. The style is distinctive, without being affected. The fourth, which has already gone through many editions, may perhaps find a permanent place in English fiction; but nobody can foretell the taste of posterity. After it there came *Amberlake,* with its laudatory dedication *'To my old friend Eustace'.* To everyone's surprise Amberlake appeared far from appreciative of the honour done him. 'Amberlake,' in the book, is the name of a moorland village, and Eustace was heard to complain that a liberty had been taken with, rather than honour paid to, his patronymic.

This complaint was not taken too seriously, for Amberlake at the time was a sick and nervy man. The doctors suspected a duodenal ulcer, or something worse. He had bouts of severe pain, slept badly, and found fault with everyone and everything. Placed on a strict diet, he was eventually ordered to the seaside by his doctor. Funtingham-on-sea was the chosen resort; and thither the faithful Terrison repaired every weekend to be with him. Then the quite unexpected happened. Amberlake began to recover with remarkable rapidity: Terrison to show signs of ill health. In spite of it, however, he persisted in his weekend visits to Funtingham, even during a January which the newspapers declared the bitterest for twenty years. Travelling back to London at the beginning of February, in an unheated railway carriage, he caught a chill; was in a high fever for five days; developed pneumonia; and died on the following Sunday. He was only thirty-four.

Amberlake, contrary to expectation, was well enough to attend the funeral. Arriving at the cemetery too late for the chapel part of the service, he found himself in the extreme rear of the procession to the grave. The few people who recognised him made way for him to pass, but to the majority he was unknown. Through them he elbowed his way, as though he were in a football crowd; they wondered how he could behave so at a funeral. Having reached the grave-side he attracted further attention, after the closing benediction, by picking up a clod of clay and shying, rather than dropping, it on top of the coffin. This done, he made off without greeting, or apparently recognising, any of his acquaintances. At the Acropolis next day, it was agreed that Amberlake's behaviour must have reflected some derangement of mind at his friend's death. Cliverton therefore felt it his duty to visit him and see whether he could be of any assistance. What Amberlake then told him was of so unusual a nature that, at Amberlake's own suggestion, he made notes of it. These notes, which were in dialogue form, are reproduced below with but few omissions.

2

Amberlake: The first time I set eyes on Terrison was at morning prayers in the college chapel. As a scholar, I sat in one of the stalls; and, happening to glance during the *Venite* at the stall immediately to my left, I saw him looking at me. He too was a scholar, but a year junior to me. I noticed at once his dark piercing eyes and full red lips. You must have noticed them too, for they never changed.

Cliverton: I can't say that I ever did. His looks struck me as rather ordinary, but quite pleasant.

A.: Ah! then he can never have looked at you like he used to look at me. The moment I saw those eyes fixed on me in chapel that morning I felt as though something were being drawn out of me; sucked out. I very nearly fainted during the psalms. Yet, after chapel, I found myself going up to him, asking his name, and inviting him to come round to my rooms for tea that afternoon. Somehow I felt that he had dragged something out of me that I must get back as soon as possible. I was a fool not to realise that I would be jumping from the frying-pan into the fire! He came to tea, of course; and, sitting opposite me, just sucked, and sucked, and sucked.

C.: Sucked what?'

A.: Me; what else? Sucked me like an orange.

C.: You talk as if he had been a sort of vampire.

A.: Precisely; so you have noticed his lips and eyes, though perhaps subconsciously. I felt sure that you must have. Well, I simply couldn't keep away from him. He drew me to him like a magnet—no, not a magnet, for a magnet doesn't suck—like a leech, or the tentacle of an octopus. Oh! it was horrible, day after day! And yet, somehow, I was fascinated by his attention, and did my utmost to invite it. I liked at first to imagine that he wasn't really getting anything out of me; but my eyes were rudely opened when he carried off the Porthill prize. Never thanked me either; not a word.

C.: Never thanked you for what?

A.: For all that he wrote in the exam. papers. All, that is, except for his beastly name at the top.

C.: You mean to tell me that he cribbed?

A.: No; nothing so honest and above-board as cribbing. There was nothing in my papers worth cribbing; he'd sucked my brains dry *before* the exam. If they set such and such a question, he used to ask me, what would be the right answer? Well, I would try to tell him; and so, when the exam. came, his brain was full and mine empty.

C.: But why empty? Talking over a subject doesn't empty one's brain of it.

A.: Not if you talk with an ordinary person; but it was a different matter talking with Terrison. After half an hour of his questions I would feel quite limp and sucked out. I just couldn't collect my thoughts, afterwards, about anything he had questioned me on.

C.: Did you ever tell him so?

A.: Good heavens, no! I had too much self-respect. Too much pride, if you will; for I liked having him come to me as the possessor of superior intellect. I wanted him to need me. Moreover, my disappointment at not winning the Porthill didn't last long, and I began to see my position in a new light. Terrison was dependent on *me*: he was no more than a marionette, or a ventriloquist's dummy. All his movements were *my* movements; his words *my* words. Reading his articles and books I began to recognise them as essentially mine. I started therefore to take a pride in my lay figure. I possessed and manipulated him to a degree never attained by parent over child, or teacher over student. In everything he wrote I caught the vivid reflection of something that I had said to him. He was just pen, ink and paper: I was the writer. Pretty good stuff, too, I was turning out through his agency. I loved to hear it discussed and appreciated at the Acropolis. Those first three novels were fine! I had no idea I could be so attractive and interesting. For two years, or more, I was a happy Narcissus.

C.: And then? What are you pausing for?

A.: Because I can hardly bring myself to tell of it. Terrie rebelled. He began not to reflect, but to distort me. It was horrible! It started over a very small matter. You may have noticed my fondness for proverbs: real proverbs, not these slick modern aphorisms and paradoxes. Well, Terrison was writing a fortnightly causerie in the *Parnassus,* and I told him to take some proverb as a headline, or text, for each instalment. He asked for some specimens, and I gave him half a dozen or so. Imagine then my disgust when I found that he had not cited, but parodied, them.

C.: Parodies of proverbs? How do you mean?

A.: I can remember only two: 'Imitation is the flattest form of sincerity' and 'Invention is the mother of necessities.' Both vulgar: and neither, I should say, original. I told him that they were utterly cheap.

C.: And what did he say to that?

A.: That to hear me talk anybody might suppose that I, not he, had been commissioned to write the articles. I didn't bother to argue the point with him, as I had no reason then to anticipate any further lapse. It came, though, and in a serious connection; for it had to do with religion. I had recently written a letter to the *Recorder,* about the objectionable practice of setting up images in professedly Anglican churches; and I was expecting an allusion to it in Terrison's *Parnassus* causerie. Instead of that, I was amazed to read some lines over his name that could only be interpreted as *in support of* images.

C.: Lines did you say? I didn't know that Terrison ever wrote verse.

A.: He couldn't. You see, I'm no poet. He never wrote anything worthwhile that wasn't really, if indirectly, mine. I've got the lines here and will read them. Mere doggerel, as you'll see.

Tell me, Madonna robed in blue,
What can these candles mean to you
Greasily guttering,
The shrine sill cluttering,
Winking up at you
From under your statue?
No less acceptable, better or worse
Is litten dip than written verse;

Orisons uttering,
Litanies muttering,
Why make men scandal
Of praying by candle?
Spirit need never be slave to tongue,
Muscle will pray when the bell is swung.
Gift-blossoms fluttering,
Votive wicks spluttering
Are prayers from the hand
That I well understand.

There! What do you think of that?

C.: A Protestant aesthete's apologia. No Catholic would have written it.

A.: I don't know about that. Silly popish stuff I call it, and said as much to Terrison. I let him have it absolutely straight. All his successful writing, I pointed out, had been really mine; and I rated him very little higher than my fountain pen. I didn't mince words.

C.: And what did he say?

A.: Made a pretence of thinking that I joked. Then, when I assured him that I was very far from it, he said something about his gratitude to me for various suggestions I had made; and that it was a source of inspiration to an author to live with a man of ideas. He proposed to dedicate his next novel to me, and to give it my name; all this in a patronising tone that made me wild. He seemed incapable of understanding that he was a mere tool. I came very near to hitting him; but somehow felt too weak. So that wretched book Amberlake came out; and I realised at once on reading it that the end was come. The vital juice in it had been sucked out of me; but dished up with futilities of his own or of somebody else's. I simply wasn't going to stand for it any further; and, by a stroke of good luck, I was taken seriously ill soon after Amberlake's publication.

C.: How was it good luck?

A.: Why, can't you see? He was for ever sucking at my thoughts and ideas, so I set my mind to dwell on nothing else but my illness; and on the fear of impending death. The result, naturally, was that I recovered and that he died. He sucked the mortality out of me into himself, and so came to his just end.

C.: My dear Amberlake, I don't believe one single word of what you say. I should consult a specialist, if I were you, or you'll end your days in an asylum.

A.: That's just where you're wrong. I shall end my days as a distinguished author. I intend in future to do my writing for myself. Just you wait and see.

3

Hildebrand Quarley, who reviewed books for the *Sunday Recorder,* was a member of the Acropolis and did the bulk of his reading in its library. A strict rule of silence obtained there; but on his way up or down the stairs to it he was continually buttonholed by Amberlake. There seemed no eluding him, and neither snub nor remonstrance kept him at bay. The purpose of his attentions was apparently to extract from the reviewer his opinions on a number of points in Terrison's novels. Would a posthumous novel prove a success?

'How can I possibly say?' Quarley exclaimed impatiently. 'It would depend on the novel. Terrison's authorship would undoubtedly predispose people favourably towards it.'

'But suppose it were published over another name?'

'Then it wouldn't be greeted as a posthumous novel by Terrison. It might not find a publisher.'

'Not even if it were by the man who wrote all Terrison?'

'I'm sorry, but I don't understand you; and I've got to catch a train. Good evening.'

The morning after this conversation Amberlake received, from somebody signing as 'Secretary', a letter informing him that Mr Quarley felt it incompatible with his position as a book-reviewer to enter into discussions concerning an author's work during his visits to the Acropolis Club. He would therefore be under the necessity of abstaining from further conversation with a member who, to his surprise and regret, had made repeated attempts to lead him into such discussion. The effect of this letter was to divert Amberlake's conversational gambits towards other members of the Acropolis. They understood him to say that he had found the typescript of an unfinished novel by Terrison; that he himself had been the real writer; and was now finishing it for publication under his own name. It seemed a queer project; but then there was no getting away from the fact that Amberlake had become queer. Nobody now paid much attention to him or his intentions.

Except Cliverton. That talk with Amberlake after Terrison's funeral had left Cliverton thoroughly uncomfortable. Ought he to tell anybody about it? Amberlake's obsession, he argued to himself, could have been of danger or injury only to Terrison. Terrison was dead; the obsession was therefore now harmless. Things could safely be left to run their course without interference by him.

It was in the evening of a day in mid June that Cliverton found himself in the same carriage as Amberlake on the Underground. 'Hullo! Been watching the cricket?' he asked.

'No, just coming back from my gloaming gloat.'

'Gloaming gloat?'

'Yes, I often run up to the cemetery of an evening; to enjoy a look at his grave.'

Cliverton's frown expressed incredulity and disgust.

'Really, Amberlake,' he said, 'you're indulging your morbid fancies too far. Anyhow, there's one thing I'm glad of. You can't really have believed in Terrison as a vampire, if you hang about his grave at sundown.'

'Vampire was your expression, not mine. What has it got to do with cemeteries? Blood-sucking bats, aren't they?'

'I suggest you look up vampire in any encyclopaedia, and you'll see. By Jove, this is my station! So goodnight; and do, for God's sake, put all this nonsense about Terrison out of your head.'

That was the last that Cliverton ever saw of Amberlake. Two evenings later he was dead of heart failure—at the foot of Terrison's grave.

An inquest was held. Cliverton, having time on his hands that day, attended it. There was only one other deponent besides the doctor. He was an assistant schoolmaster, and had been placing flowers on his mother's grave when he noticed the deceased jabbing, with a wooden stake, at the middle of a recently filled grave. It looked to him like wanton desecration. So, walking up to the deceased (who went on jabbing at the grave with his back to him), he shouted 'Hi! What do you think that you are doing there?' The deceased jerked his head round; glared at him with starting eyes; tottered backwards, and fell prostrate on the grave. Raising him he found the body quite lifeless; so, he propped it against a tombstone, and ran to the cemetery caretaker's lodge for assistance. From there they telephoned to the nearest doctor, who was round in less than fifteen minutes. That was all that the assistant master had to say.

Cliverton heard very little of it, for he was looking rather than listening. The witness's personal appearance had startled him. The eyes were dark and piercing, the lips red and full. Yes, and the features bore a distinct resemblance to those of the late Terence Terrison.

Final Touches

1

Mr Ridley Prandell's success as a barrister is of relevance to this story only to the extent that it enabled him to retire at sixty, and to buy the old mill-house at Boldrington. A childless widower, without near relations, he was considered unwise by his London friends to throw up work so early and bury himself in the country. He knew, however, what he wanted. Boldrington is but a mile or two from the Royal Southshire golf course, and less than five from Smallhaven, where he kept a small yacht on the Daven estuary. The house had a good garden, and there were trout in the mill-stream and pond. The mill barn he converted into a library, music room and workshop. Electric light and central heating were installed. The new home was, in short, a materialisation of his past dreaming.

Prandell soon made friends with the Kerringtons at Boldrington Hall. Sir Dudley, a man of much his own age, was the best shot in the neighbourhood, an authority on the culture of rhododendrons and a regular contributor to the journal of the Southshire Antiquarian Society. Lady Kerrington spent most mornings of her week in parochial good works, and most afternoons on golf. She played against Mr Prandell every Wednesday. After one of these encounters, in July 1913, she gave him a lift back in her car, and persuaded him to stay on at the Hall for an *alfresco* supper on the terrace. Sir Dudley had been reading and writing there, and by him on a garden seat lay a pile of journals and loose papers. The conversation at supper consequently took a turn towards matters of Southshire history.

'My husband,' Lady Kerrington explained, 'is doing some research into parish records and traditions. Quite a lot appears to have happened in Boldrington, though nobody has ever written about it.'

'Yes, I'm writing a little monograph for the vicar. He wants to place copies for sale in the church, in aid of the belfry repair fund. The pamphlet's going to be longer than I intended, I fear, for I've unearthed so many little items of interest. By the way, Prandell, were your forebears by any chance natives of Boldrington or Knapton?'

'Well, I rather fancy that they did belong to these parts: at least I've heard my father suggest so. Our ancestry isn't at all distinguished, and the family had never bothered about genealogy. That we have risen from the peasantry is certain, because an old fellow who married my grandfather's sister was ostracised by his relations for marrying beneath him. He too, I believe, lived somewhere on this side of the county. Bedsock; no, Ledsock; is that the name of a place?'

'Could his name have been Longbottom?'

'Why yes; however, did you know? Yes, of course it was, because the family always spoke of him as old—'

'What a lovely sunset sky!' exclaimed Lady Kerrington, rising from her seat; 'but this drought is getting serious. I must go and water those phloxes. So, I'll leave you two to your talk for a few minutes. You can tell me later, Dudley, what it's all about.'

'I have been looking through the church registers,' resumed Sir Dudley as his wife vanished behind the espaliers, 'and the two commonest names in them are Perrandale, Prandell, Prendall or Prandle, and Farribal, Farball, Farble or Fribble. As you know, people took liberties with the spelling of their surnames in time gone by. Well, one of the entries related to the marriage of Susanna Perrandale to John Jeremy Longbottom in 1841, their banns having been read in Boldrington and Ledsock churches. Can you remember your great-aunt's name.'

'Yes, that must have been Aunt Sue all right: and a vixenish old lady she was too, from all accounts. How strange my settling down in the old family haunt without knowing it!'

'Very strange. Your distant cousins here must be legion, for everybody seems connected with either the Perrandales or the Farribals. But never with both. I wonder whether you've yet come across the local superstition about people being touched, as they call it?'

Prandell looked at his host uncomprehendingly.

'No. I can see that you haven't. It's a silly idea to have got abroad and it's all mixed up with an old feud between those two families. No Perrandale has ever married a Farribal or *vice versa*. They never vote the same way at elections, or at village meetings. My wife is in despair about getting the people to pull together.'

'What reason is there for the feud?'

'Oh! each of the two families seems to have laid the other under a curse. No Perrandale will take the bridle-path to Knapton after nightfall, and no Farribal that footway to the north of the village green. They're frightened of being "touched", they say.'

'Touched by what?'

'Heaven only knows; I'm neither a P. nor an F., and not qualified therefore to find out. Perhaps you'll experience it one day! If you do, don't forget to give me particulars for mention in my monograph.'

'Certainly, I will: but I don't believe in that sort of thing.'

'Neither do I, yet one never knows!'

2

Mr Prandell had come to Boldrington with his mind made up to avoid participation in local affairs, as likely to encroach too much on the leisure of retirement. He was not therefore acquiescent when Stephen Perrandale, proprietor of the Boldrington Stores, called at the mill with a request that he would fill a place on the committee of the Recreation Club.

'Well, Sir, it seems as if you won't, and as Parson will; and he a Farribal on his mother's side. It'll be the first time that we Perrandales take second place at the club. I guess that Sir Dudley may have been mistaken in what he told me and that you're not of our old Perrandale stock. You can walk the path to Knapton without taking hurt, I reckon.'

Mr Prandell looked at him inquisitively.

'We never tell about the touching, not to strangers; but if you be really one of us, Sir, just you take a stroll there one evening and you'll need no telling.'

Mr Prandell, although loath to admit it even to himself, was curious. He had heard often enough of people seeing, hearing or sensing unaccountable things; but never before had he come across any suggestion of a tactual impact of the invisible on the mundane. It was a novel idea to him; and by tea-time, sceptic though he was, he had half made up his mind to submit it to experiment. The July day had been insufferably hot. He had spent the morning and afternoon reading in a deck-chair on the lawn; and a walk in the cool of the evening would afford him needful exercise. Though he had never yet been along the Knapton bridle-path, a full moon would enable him to find his way along it even towards midnight. That was the hour when, according to common report, immaterial agencies were most operative.

Between tea and dinner, he wrote letters; and at dinner dipped into a book, as usual, to prevent himself from eating too quickly. He had meant to pick his Pope out of the hall bookshelf; but, on propping the volume against a stand in front of his soup plate, he found that he had taken Poe's Tales by mistake. Never mind; he had not read Poe for a long time, and would refresh his memory of the *Fall of the House of Usher*. The meal was a light one, suitable to the sultry weather. With dessert he drank a glass of claret, and afterwards lit a cigar. Then, going into the study, he gave an hour and a half to the daily papers and a monthly review.

By now he was not somehow looking forward to his walk with much zest. Pope, he felt, would have been a pleasanter dinner companion than Edgar Allan Poe. However, what he had read, he had read: and he had better be starting off; for the clock said half-past ten, and it was three miles by the road to Knapton and two back by the bridle-path. So, he set out.

As he approached Knapton the daylight was failing rapidly. Who was it that wrote '*Layer on layer the night came on*'? He couldn't remember. It was a true description though. Ah, yes! Calverley. Moonlight reinforcing the western glow enabled him to read without difficulty the lettering on the finger post, BRIDLE-PATH TO BOLDINGTON. Something appeared to be scribbled beneath in black chalk or pencil; so, putting on his glasses, he went up closer to examine. '*Forbidden to Perrandales after sundown.*' That superstition, then, was well enough known in Knapton for some village wit to make joke of it!

He found nothing at all sinister about the path for the first half-mile. A warm scent of meadowsweet floated from the ditches on either side, and at one point he stood still for a few moments listening to a tawny owl. Had Shakespeare been truthful in describing that as 'a merry note'? He was not sure. It was merrier though than this silence in the leafy tunnel through Gravely Wood; so he began to hum and whistle. Here the moonlight, filtering through hazels, made a silver-black tapestry of the mould beneath; but did not illuminate the path sufficiently for him to see the tufts of grass or small bushes that kept scraping his ankles, or catching in the turn-ups of his trousers. Strange, he thought, that a well-trodden track between two villages should be so overgrown.

Further on there seemed to be roots or creepers as well as tufts and bushes. He tripped more than once. Ah! that last one nearly had him over! Well, he was out of the wood now, and traversing the narrow causeway through the Boldring water-meadows. From either side there rose to his ears a syncopated antiphon of frogs; but he was look ing rather than listening; looking, intently, at the moonlit surface of the causeway. It was level and almost grassless. Yet he still felt himself trudging through scrub and, here and there, brambles. His ankles were not merely brushed, but pricked. The loud hollow thud of his boots on the bridge over Boldring Brook showed that its planks were as bare as they looked; but in the middle of the bridge his feet caught an unevenness. He saved himself from a fall by grabbing and gripping the handrail.

Some thirty yards beyond the bridge there is a small brick culvert over a backwater. Just before he reached it, his walking-stick seemed to get entangled in some growth and was twisted out of his hand. He heard it splash into the side drain, but rapidly decided not to try to retrieve it in the dark. Over the culvert itself, where the path showed white and smooth in the moonshine, he hurried forward, only to bark his shin against what felt like a fallen branch. Starting aside, he must have misjudged his distance, for he fell knee-deep into the backwater. There was a burst of bubbles and a stench of mud and pondweed as he clambered up the bank. Then, suddenly, all his senses became fixed in one urgent sensation: that of dashing along the path as fast as leg and lung would take him. There had been no decision on his part to run. He just ran, lifting his knees as high as if his way led through heather or bracken. And so, to the junction with the main road, where he leaned against the sign-post, gathering breath and wits.

For the remainder of the walk, he reasoned with himself. Not very truthfully at first; for he began by taking credit for his good sense in running, after getting his feet wet. By the time, however, that he un-latched his front door he was in a mood to own himself a Perrandale, and to make his confession to Sir Dudley at the Hall next morning. He had been 'touched'.

3

On arrival at the Hall, Mr Prandell found himself not the only call-er. The vicar was there already, engaged in animated conversation with Sir Dudley, when the footman ushered him in. The Reverend Samuel Leslicote needed no introduction to him, for they had exchanged calls and met several times.

'You may remember, Prandell,' Sir Dudley began as they took their seats, 'my mentioning to you a local superstition about members of the Perrandale and Farribal families being liable to what is called "touching". You looked a bit incredulous, I thought, but the vicar here, whose mother was a Farribal, will tell you, as he has just been telling me, that he has been "touched"—and an unpleasant experience too, I gather! Perhaps you, being a lawyer, will want to cross-examine him before accepting his testimony.'

'Unnecessary, Sir Dudley. In point of fact, I've just called in to tell you that I myself have been touched.'

'What!' ejaculated the vicar and Sir Dudley in unison.

'Yes, and an unpleasant experience, too, as you have just remarked. Perhaps the vicar and I might exchange and compare notes of what it was like.'

'Yes, please do so,' Sir Dudley requested; 'I shall be a most interested listener.'

Prandell's experience has already been related. The vicar's had been of a more summary sort. He was at a meeting of the Recreation Club committee, when the new schoolmaster brought up a proposal about female membership. Argument ran high, and at a quarter before midnight the debate had to be adjourned until their next meeting. On his way home the vicar heard the church clock strike twelve as he strode along the gravel path on the north side of the village green. Just as he was passing the pink may tree, planted there when they removed the old stocks and whipping-post, he felt a sudden stinging lash across the shoulder blades, followed quickly by another on the buttocks. He did not wait for a third. He had been a sprinter, he said, at school, but never made a spurt equal to that with which he reached the vicarage gate. He was still feeling the smart of the two lashes, and quickly undressed that he might see what mark they had left. There was none. No weal, no redness, nothing at all. By the time he had read his compline, the smarting sensation had gone. That was all; but to his taste more than enough. He felt sorry now that he refused once to listen to what old Obadiah Farble had wanted to tell him. His reason had been that he thought it a parson's duty to turn a deaf ear to idle superstition.

Sir Dudley jotted down a few notes of both narrations.

'What you have both been describing,' he said, 'supports what was told me by Elihu Tampson up at the forge. He got it as a boy from his grandfather. Most of the story is still apparently current here, and in Knapton too, though more than a century and a half old. It happened, Tampson says, "in the year when many innocent people were robbed of their birthdays by Parliament". That of course makes it 1752, when the calendar was reformed and September the 3rd became September the 14th. History books, you will remember, tell us that the alteration led to complaints by the ignorant that they were being cheated out of eleven days of their mortal span. Well, in the summer of that year a quarrel arose about the rights over the Boldring water-meadows. They were unenclosed at that period, and the present channel hadn't yet been dug, the stream wandering about where all those stretches of backwater still lie. The dispute was over pasturage.

'One evening the Farribals of Knapton Surrey, and the Perrandales of Little Boldring turned their cattle simultaneously into the meadows. The cows got mixed up, ownership was contested, and next day there were all the makings of a free fight. The Perrandales stood on one side of the stream and the Farribals on the other. Stones and sticks began to be thrown; and at this juncture old Ebenezer Farribal, well on in his eighties, hobbled to the scene and urged his men to throw the trespassers out then and there. He was in the middle of his harangue when a great clod of mud and clay, hurled from the Perrandale side, caught him full on the forehead and laid him flat on his back. Being very old, I don't suppose that his heart was too good; anyhow he couldn't rise to his feet. Propped up by his men in a sitting position he proceeded to pronounce what he called his dying curse on the Perrandales.

'What the curse may have been no one knows. Tampson's grandfather told him that the Bible itself couldn't have said it stronger. It *was* a dying curse, too; for, although they got the old man on to a hurdle and carried him home, he never uttered again and died that night. The effect of his collapse had been to stay the fight, but feeling naturally ran high between the two sides. The Farribals indeed were not content to leave vengeance to the operation of a curse. Within a few weeks an information was laid against a Perrandale lad that he had stolen fowls. Whether the accusation was true or not, there were Farribal witnesses in plenty to support it; and the boy received twelve lashes at the whipping-post at Boldrington Green. His grandmother lay at that time on her deathbed, and once again dying words took the form of a curse, this time against the Farribals. The feud between the two families has persisted ever since; so too has a belief in the operation of both curses by what they call "touchings". That was what Elihu Tampson told me, and what you two have described this morning seems corroborative.'

'It's got to be stopped,' the vicar exclaimed.

'What has?'

'This rankling of a family feud. I shall do some plain speaking from the pulpit on Sunday; and on Monday, which is August bank holiday, you will both perhaps help me get up village sports on the green and a tea picnic afterwards on the water-meadows. You will? Thank you; that's settled then. I'll get busy with preliminary arrangements straight away. Josiah Farribal and Moses Perrandale will be in church on Sunday and, when they've heard what I'm going to say, they'll get busy too. People will probably think me a bit touched. Well, they'll be right; I have been!'

4

The vicar's address will be remembered. Its efficacy was attested by Josiah Farribal and Moses Perrandale shaking hands in the vestry after service.

Mr Leslicote began by giving a terse account of his and Mr Prandell's experiences. Whether real or imaginary, he said, they had the practical value of focusing attention on a state of affairs that must be put an end to. A house divided against itself could not stand. Boldrington must cease to be such a house. He therefore urged all his parishioners to meet together on the morrow's holiday at a sports meeting and picnic, which were being arranged. They could dissolve past rancour in present amity. At the beginning of the sports, and again at the picnic, he would ask all present to join in saying the Lord's Prayer. If they did that meaningly it would certainly destroy the potency of any curse that might still hang over place or people as a result of past discord.

Sports and picnic were both greatly enjoyed. Three Sundays later banns were published between Mark Horatio Perrandale, winner of the hundred yards, and Caroline Jane Farribal, second in the egg and spoon race. Immediately after the Amen to the Lord's Prayer at the picnic there had been cries of 'Snike! Snike!' and an adder was scotched at the side of the bridle-path culvert. 'There dies the curse,' everybody said.

There have indeed been no more touchings in Boldrington since; unless a literal meaning be attached to the vicar's remark that whenever he passes the pink may tree, he feels gently patted on the back.

What's in a Name?

1

'We must give him a name associated with the family; none of your fancy names!'

'Associated with *your* family, I suppose you mean. What about *mine?*'

'He can have two names, one from my family and one from yours. What's wrong with Ronald Austin?'

'Nothing, dear; but somehow I'd set my heart on Derek.'

'Derek be damned! He'll be Ronald Austin. He couldn't have had more respectable grandfathers to be named after.'

This conversation was between Mr and Mrs Transome, with the subject of the controversy sleeping in a cot beside them. The subject was not mentioned again until Uncle Charles, chosen to be godfather, counselled the dropping of one of the two names or the addition of a third. This he did not do until the eleventh hour, just before they were to set out for the christening.

'Nonsense!' retorted Mr Transome. 'One name's too few and three's too many. What's the matter with Ronald Austin, Charles?'

'He won't be Ronald Austin only; he'll be Ronald Austin Transome—R.A.T. He'll be nicknamed "Rat", sure as nuts.'

'I don't see why. Does he look like a rat?'

Uncle Charles looked down on the cot, and appeared uncomfortable. He was a truthful man.

Mrs Transome's entry into the room at this moment made it unnecessary for him to reply. 'It's time,' she said, 'we got off to church. The carriage has been waiting at the door for nearly ten minutes. Nanny, you go first and be careful to tuck the shawl well round Baby. Yes; that's right. There's quite a cold wind today.'

Uncle Charles's mind still dwelt on his talk with his brother-in-law, when the clergyman startled him with the command 'Name this child.' Horrified to hear himself mutter 'Rat', he hurriedly tacked on to the monosyllable a paroxysm of coughing before pronouncing a stentorian 'Ronald Austin'. Ronald Austin, therefore, the live part of the little bundle in the vicar's arms duly became. Nevertheless, the prelude to Uncle Charles's fit of coughing had been heard by two people. At tea that afternoon the vicar remarked to his wife that he had come perilously near to baptising a rat, and Nanny regaled the Transomes' domestic staff with a description of Mr Charles's *lapsus linguae*. Caroline, the cook, and Mrs Vicar were, at different social levels, notorious disseminators of gossip, so that within a fortnight from his christening Master Ronald Austin Transome was known throughout East and West Cattleton as the 'rat baby'. On his emergence from infancy this was changed to 'the little rat boy', and eventually abbreviated to 'the rat'.

Mr Transome did not come to hear of the appellation until his son was nearly four. The gardener had been showing Ronald how to bait a mousetrap; the little fingers got pinched in the process, but Ronald did not cry. He saw how to lift the spring and pulled them out. Mr Transome coming up at this moment heard old Haskins give vent to his admiration with 'Ah! the Rat be a rare young sport, and no mistake!'

'The rat, Haskins? Where is it? Why, that's only a mousetrap.'

'Beg pardon, Sir, for having said as I oughtn't. But we calls our young master 'ere the Rat, sort of affectionate-like; and I didn't mean no 'arm by it, for a rare young sport 'e be. Taking after 'is dad, Sir, I reckon.'

'Ah, well!' said Mr Transome, mollified by such reckoning; 'but Mrs Transome and myself prefer proper names to nicknames, Haskins, and please not to forget it. Rat, indeed!'

Ronald understood less than half of what was being said, but enough to catch its gist. '*Nice* people call me "Rat",' he said.

'Very well, Ronald: you can be "Rat" when you and I are alone; but not when your mother's about. Remember that.'

'But why, Daddy?'

'Because she wanted you to be Derek.'

'Ferret?'

'No, Derek. Now come along, and leave Haskins alone to get on with his work.'

Within a year or two Mrs Transome was also made aware of her boy's debased nomenclature. The vicar, a new one recently inducted, was paying her a call, and the parlour-maid had been sent to fetch Mr Transome from the garden. She found him hiding in the shrubbery; for he had seen the caller, to whom he had already taken a strong dislike, coming up the drive.

'Ronald is a dear little boy, Mrs Transome.'

'I'm so glad you think so, Vicar.'

'He needs your help, you know. Your influence.'

'My help and influence?'

'Yes, your help in acquiring something of great value and importance.'

'Of great value and importance? What can that be, Mr Grimledge?'

'A proper sense of reverence in God's house.'

'Good gracious! Has Ronnie been naughty during the children's service? His governess has told me nothing about it.'

'He made the other boys laugh at Catechism.'

'Laugh? But how?'

'When Miss Pemmity asked him "What is your name, N or M?" he answered, "Neither: it's Rat."'

Mr Transome, having heard this as he entered the room (with, it must be confessed, an uncharitable intention of making himself disagreeable), immediately took his cue.

'You would have Ronald grow up a little liar then?'

'My dear Transome, good afternoon! What can you mean?'

'I mean that his name isn't N or M and that everybody except his mother calls him "Rat".'

'But in church one uses only Christian names. The choir-boys naturally laughed when he said "Rat."'

'Well, Vicar, if you allow boys in your church to laugh at truth, Ronald had better attend services at East Cattleton in future. It's barely a quarter of a mile further from here, and the choir-boys there are better-behaved than yours.'

On the vicar's departure in dignified discomfiture, despite Mrs Transome's attempts at conciliation, there is no need here to enlarge. As soon as the front door was shut on him she dissolved into tears.

'You shouldn't have reproved him so rudely, Herbert,' she sobbed, 'but have left him to me. I shouldn't have spared him the least bit, but I would have been polite. Oh! just fancy him accusing Ronnie of irreverence; Ronnie who always says his prayers so nicely! He's not fit to be a clergyman; horrid man.'

Ronald's sudden irruption into the room at this juncture caused

Mrs Transome to smile through her tears.

'Hullo, Ronnie!' she called to him, 'Come along to Mummy, you dear little—Rat!'

2

The reader will have gathered that Ronnie was not fortunate in his parents: the father self-centred and irascible, the mother shallow and foolish. Happily, however, his character took its first impressions less from them than from an efficient and sensible nurse and, later, from a stalwart governess. From the former he learned to do as, from the latter to understand what, he was told. Miss Ethelstone was not merely a well-qualified teacher, but able, as the saying is, to draw her pupil out. But for her real companionship Ronald's early boyhood would have been lonely. There were few children of his own age in Cattleton, and of them not more than three or four were ever invited to the house, Mr Transome having outlawed the majority on grounds of social inferiority or of his dislike for their parents—a dislike which was widely reciprocated. Frequent conversation and voluntary jobs with old Haskins also helped to educate the Rat. Haskins was no 'scholard', but able to impart a knowledgeable love of countryside and garden which Ronald was never to lose.

About the time of his sixth birthday there was a plague of rats on the farms round Cattleton. Ferret, gun, trap and poison were used against the enemy, and on many barns and gates the tails of the slaughtered were nailed in competitive rows. One day Ronald happened on a small heap of them awaiting such a nailing-up. Picking two up he made a wristlet of them and, back home, showed it to Haskins.

'I shouldn't wear that if I were you, Master Ronald,' the old man objected; Miss Ethelstone won't like it nor your mother either. Rats be'ant exac'ly clean. Nor, I mind me, wouldn't my old grandad have liked it, considerin' 'is stories of girdlings and such like in them old times.'

'Girdling? What's girdling, Haskins?'

'Well, I don't rightly know, Master Ronald; but it was along of them witches what no longer troubles us nowadays. Though, mind ye, I've 'ad my doubts about my Aunt Jemima. She's dead and gone now, though, and I ain't a one to speak ill of them what's buried. Besides, she knit me good socks, did Aunt Jemima, what I wore for more'n three year afore Mrs Haskins chucked 'em into fire. It's for no use, she tole me, tacking one 'ole on to another 'ole; and there ain't nothin' else but 'oles, she says; 'oles and 'oles and 'oles.'

'But what's girdling, Haskins?'

'Ah! girdling. That was what my grandad called it—girdling.'

'Yes, but what *was* girdling;'

'Well, girdling weren't no more than makin' of a girdle and awearin' of it. Sure, there weren't no 'arm in that. But them witches, grandad says, or some on 'em anyway, wore girdles made of skins got from live animals, 'ares mostly, I believe. Then, come night-time, the witch'd turn same as 'er girdle and go abroad on 'er wickedness as an 'are. It don't sound like sense to me, Master Ronald; but grandad would tell as 'ow when Mrs Flintoff up at the 'all lay dyin' of spotty fever, and 'Annaway 'er butler shot and lamed a 'are as 'e see on 'er lawn, it were old Mrs Rushpen as were seen limpin' about next morning with 'er stocking all bloody; nor wouldn't show 'er leg neither to no one, not even 'er daughter. It were a fact, says grandad, as Mrs Flintoff 'ad given the Rushpens notice to quit for not payin' of their rent; and, as 'er coffin was bein' carried through the churchyard, hout crawls a lame 'are from be'ind a gravestone and makes off along toward their cottage. That, Master Ronald, was what come of Mrs Rushpen's girdling; and that she feared for what she'd done were clean proved by no girdle ever bein' seen on 'er and by 'er never ownin' to one. So just you take off them rat-tails, Master Ronald, or one night you'll find yourself a rat maybe, same as what you're called.'

Ronald did take off the tails; but stuffed them into a pocket and sought out Miss Ethelstone.

'You know that book,' he said to her, 'you used to read to me, about a girl going down a rabbit hole.'

'*Alice in Wonderland?*'

'Yes, that's the name. Do you suppose Alice had a rabbit-skin girdle, like a witch?'

'Whoever's been talking to you about witches, Ronald? Old Haskins, I expect. Witches are all nonsense, and one shouldn't listen to nonsense.'

'Why not, Miss Ethelstone?'

'Because it's easier to have nonsense put into one's head than to get it out again. No sensible boy or girl believes in witches or familiars.'

'What are familiars?'

'Animals that witches were supposed to exchange bodies with, or to send on errands. Such a stupid idea, isn't it? Fancy a person turning into an animal or an animal into a person! Alice's dream was far more sensible than that, though it was only a dream.'

'Could a rat be a familiar, Miss Ethelstone?'

'Well, Ronald; I know a rat, I think, who's being very familiar; asking his governess a lot of silly questions! Now come along, and let me see you help saddle the pony.'

That evening, after his parents had kissed him goodnight, Ronald extricated the tails from his coat pocket and wound them round his left wrist. His regular prayers had been said on his knees but, as he lay in bed, he added a special petition. 'Please, God,' he murmured tensely, 'let me dream myself into a rat-hole.'

3

The prayer was not answered: on that and many succeeding nights he slept a dreamless sleep. On his birthday, however, came more than compensation for this disappointment. On a chair in his schoolroom he found a large wooden box, with foil from biscuit tins tacked on to all sides but one. There there was a grating, made from an old bird-cage, and through it he saw a glimpse of something white. It moved! What could old Haskins have given him? He knelt down quickly to see. A white rat! With twitching fingers, he unloosed the little leather-hinged trap-door at the top for a nearer look. Yes: a white rat, a lovely white rat.

'I shall call him Snattajin,' Ronald cried jubilantly.

'Why Snattajin?' asked Miss Ethelstone, eyeing the new importation none too favourably.

''Cause he's as white as Mummy's tonic powder. Look! He's sneezing.'

'It must be from Haskins: it's a home-made box. Very rough work indeed; but strong, though, and not even rats can gnaw through tin foil. But we can't keep it here in the school-room. Rats smell, you know.'

'I'll put him on the shelf in the summer-house,' Ronald replied; 'he'll have a lovely view from there. Nobody ever uses the summer-house.'

Mr and Mrs Transome raised no objection, so Snattajin was duly installed in the summer-house, before lunch. In the course of a few weeks the lawn began to show a brown streak leading from the garden-door of the house to Snattajin's new abode; it was the track, worn bare of grass, of Ronald's feet hurrying to and from his new pet. That was what his parents and Miss Ethelstone called him— a pet. But, alone with Snattajin in the summer-house, Ronald addressed him by a less trite, more sonorous name, suggestive of deeper intimacy. He had not forgotten Miss Ethelstone's mention of familiars. Well, here was his! With his pocket money he bought a bottle of cheap lavender water at the village shop, with which Snattajin suffered chrism every morning.

A heap of superficially gnawed apples, potatoes and other comestibles in a corner of his box showed that his menu exceeded his appetite. He was neither lean nor fat, but just right. So sleek and clean, too. When at evening service in church they sang about saints being clothed in spotless white, Ronald made a mental reservation that they could not be whiter or more unspotted than Snattajin. In short, no present received by a boy of six has ever given greater pleasure and satisfaction than Snattajin brought to Ronald. Whether the pleasure and satisfaction were entirely wholesome is another matter.

The interval between the advent of Snattajin and Ronald's entry into a preparatory school was about two years. During them he made great educational progress under Miss Ethelstone. The headmaster of St. Olave's, Seaborough, wrote in his first report that he wished that all of his new boys had had an equally sound grounding. But Miss Ethelstone was not, after the birth of Ronald's little sister Lettice, any longer resident governess. Her room was required for a nursery; so, she went to live in lodgings at East Cattleton, coming after breakfast on weekdays to give Ronald his lessons and returning after tea. This left the boy much time to himself; for a baby is no playmate, and his parents had neither the psychology nor the inclination to join him in games or to interest themselves in his boyish pursuits. 'He's such a dear child.' Mrs Transome would say, 'always happy and occupying himself, and no bother to us at all.'

What Ronald most occupied himself with was Snattajin. Had the latter been a dog, this would have been all right. A dog has personality, shows affection and affords companionship. Not so a rat. What Ronald did was to clothe Snattajin with a whole wardrobe of bogus qualities, all woven from the fabric of his own imagination. He made of him an *alter ego* to console his loneliness. Nor had he forgotten the association of familiars with witches, but felt that his intimate communion with Snattajin was something for which, if he were to talk of it, he would be either reproved or laughed at. There was also a sermon one Sunday about King Nebuchadnezzar. Ronald listened attentively, for the idea of a king eating grass and letting his nails grow into claws was attractive.

He was, the preacher said, certainly like Ann Throppick, and Ronald began wondering who Ann Throppick might have been. The preacher then went on to say that there were two ways of being like Ann Throppick. One was to be mad, which of course you couldn't help. The other was to believe that you could turn yourself into an animal. This for people who wore God's image (Ronald wondered whereabouts it should be worn, and what size it would be) was very wicked indeed. Nevertheless, people had believed it in days gone by; people who were (he repeated the *were*) wolves or witches. Ronald was now all agog to hear something about girdlings, but the clergyman suddenly turned from Ann Throppick to another girl, Ally Goricle, who wasn't half so interesting. Ronald's thoughts therefore turned towards the prospect of his departure for school and consequent separation from Snattajin. Tears dimmed his eyes. It would be a terrible wrench.

So indeed, it was. Words are lacking to describe the poignancy of that final parting in the summer-house, with the fly waiting at the front-door. With difficulty he sobbed out an injunction to old Haskins to be careful to look after poor Snattajin. Mr and Mrs Transome saw in his too visible distress evidence of a right and proper filial affection. 'It is nice to feel,' said Mrs Transome, 'that we have made home so lovable to him. I must remember to tell Emily to give his room a thorough clearing out. I do hope that they'll teach him at St. Olave's to be tidier, and to wipe his boots. I doubt if we shall ever get those tar-marks off the stair carpet. Look, Herbert! How sweet of him to throw us a kiss out of the fly window!'

The kiss was thrown towards the summer-house. Miss Ethelstone, who was driving with him to the station, saw this. As he withdrew his hand from the window she patted it. 'Ronnie,' she said, 'I promise you I'll come every Sunday after church to make sure that Snattajin's all right.' Ronald's heart was too full for speech, but he smiled gratitude through his tears.

'And I'll write to you sometimes,' Miss Ethelstone added, 'to tell you how he's getting on.'

4

The big playroom in the basement of St. Olave's was known for some reason as the boot-room. On either side of it were ranged the wooden play-boxes of some forty boys. One of them was white and new; it bore the initials R..A.T. Inspecting it stood the head of the school, made responsible by the games-master for the orderliness of the boot-room.

'Whose box is this?' he asked.

'Mine.'

'You? You're a new boy, aren't you? What's your name?'

'Ronald Transome; but I like to be called "Rat".'

The head-boy looked at him quizzically, perhaps almost appreciatively.

'You'd have been called that anyhow,' he said, 'with R.A.T. on your box; so, it's lucky you like it.'

A number of boys were by now standing round, and Glayson (that was the head boy's name) addressed them.

'Hullo! you chaps,' he said, 'what was it Noah said when the ark ran aground?'

'I smell A-ra-RAT,' they yelled in reply.

It was a riddle from the last number of *The Olavian*.

'Well, come and smell this one, then. His name's Rat, he says; and his box says so, too. Look!'

A dozen boys clustered round Ronald and sniffed him all over.

'He doesn't stink so bad,' was the general verdict. 'Any fodder in that hutch, Rat? If so, open up.'

Yes, there was fodder in it. Five minutes later there was not. The rat, however, had been voted not a bad sort, for a rat. On going to bed that night he found between his sheets a coat-hanger with a large piece of cheese on the hook. Pulling it out he held it aloft, and began nibbling at the cheese. 'Well done, Rat,' said the dormitory captain. 'He knows his stuff all right. Now *I'll* eat the rest of it, thank you.'

Twice Ronald had done the right thing: done it because he was thinking all the time of Snattajin and what Snattajin would have him do. Snattajin the *alter ego,* the familiar!

It may be inserted at this point that, whatever his appearance in the cradle, Ronald had grown up not in the least like a rat. He was tall, blue-eyed and fair-haired; well-favoured enough by any aesthetic standard. Good looks undoubtedly added to the good opinion which other boys were forming of him. There was no virtue in liking to be called 'Rat' if you were like a rat; but, if you were quite a decent-looking chap, it was rather sporting, they thought.

The Rat's reputation was finally set on sure foundations when he fell a victim to the exceedingly unpopular 'Maths' master. While doing a sum in long division he chewed and gnawed the butt end of his pencil.

Transome,' Mr Stridwell hissed at him, 'stop gnawing your pencil. You're not a rat, are you?'

Ronald caught a sudden vision of Snattajin. He must be loyal and brave.

'Yes, Sir.'

There were gasps of surprise and expectation on all sides, for the boys knew their Mr Stridwell.

'Stand up, Transome. You heard what I said. I won't take cheek from you or any other boy. Are you a rat?'

Again, Ronald saw Snattajin. He was trembling a little, but managed to steady his voice.

'Yes, Sir.'

'Well, I've given you your chance, Transome, and you have repeated your impudence. Go down to the boot-room. I shall follow.'

There was a murmur of anticipation. How would the Rat take it? For the master's words had carried a fundamental significance. The boot-room was the place of execution. Mr Stridwell now left his desk to enact it. His class waited in grim expectancy.

Then from the boot-room below came the thwack of a cane, six times repeated. No other sound, though. Many eyes were turned on Ronald as he re-entered the room. He was white and tight-lipped; his hands were clenched. But there were no tears in his eyes.

'If any boy,' Mr Stridwell acidly announced, 'should have a taste for natural history, Transome can tell him where to find a rat with red streaks on its tail.'

Nobody laughed. They thought Stridwell a dirty swine and, after the lesson, the Rat found himself a hero. The games-master was known to detest his mathematical colleague, and several boys took care to let him know about the Rat's caning. As a result, Mr Tradger thereafter took a special interest in Ronald, coaching him at the nets and generally befriending him.

Back home for the holidays Ronald found Snattajin in good fettle, except for a few scabs on the tail. Haskins, he learned, had inadvertently banged the door of the box on it after feeding him one day.

'What day?' Ronald asked excitedly.

'Why, Master Ronald,' Haskins replied, 'I don't mind no dates; not for little things like that. But it were the first day of the fair; for that's how I come to be in a hurry and slam the door.'

The cook knew the date of the fair; for it had been that of her cousin Martha's birthday. The same also as that of Ronald's caning! He and his familiar had suffered simultaneously. Somehow, he had expected it. That was why he had asked.

In the course of his second term Ronald was bidden by Mr Tradger to try writing something for *The Olavian*. 'An ode to a rat', he suggested humorously with reference to Ronald's nickname, 'might liven up the pages.' Mr Tradger did not of course know of Snattajin's existence; but his request chanced to synchronise with Ronald's receipt of a letter from Miss Ethelstone reporting that a cat had tried, unsuccessfully, to get at Snattajin through the bars. From this news Ronald derived inspiration for a retaliatory anti-feline effort. He struggled with it for a fortnight, until Mr Tradger told him that it must be ready without fail for the typist next day. This is how his composition appeared in *The Olavian*:

> *Nick was a fine brave rat:*
> *He swore to kill the cat!*
> *Rats do not go to school,*
> *Yet Nick was not a fool.*
> *He watched and waited till*
> *He saw the cat was ill,*
> *So bad was her disease*
> *She could not scratch her fleas.*
> *The day came when Nick saw*
> *She couldn't lift a paw;*
> *So now he crept up close*
> *And bit her on the nose.*
> *He gnawed out both her eyes,*
> *Which caused her some surprise,*
> *Then nibbled through her hide*
> *And chewed the guts inside.*
> *It may be truly said*
> *That cat by now was dead;*
> *Yet not too proud was Nick,*
> *For why? She had been sick.*
> *His fate, if she'd been well,*
> *I do not care to tell.*
> *If Nick is still alive*
> *I hope that he will thrive.*

Mr Tradger declared that Transome might one day become poet

laureate; but the headmaster, on reading the lines, shook his head. 'Direct and monosyllabic,' he commented, 'and only one false rhyme. But I don't like the psychology. It's not quite boyish—it's ratty.' Next holidays Ronald recited the verses to Snattajin.

The headmaster may have written something about them in Ronald's school report; or possibly it was on his own initiative that Mr Transome informed his son one morning that he was getting too old to waste so much time on a white rat. 'Anyhow,' he went on, 'we can't keep that animal here any longer. Your little sister will be playing in the summer-house as the days get warmer, and she doesn't like rats. Besides, I can't have Haskins spending so much time on feeding it and cleaning out its hutch. It must be got rid of, Ronald, before you go back to school.'

Ronald went as pale as he had after his caning, but knew better than to argue with his father. 'All right; I'll give him away,' he managed to jerk out.

If his parents wouldn't keep his old friend for him, he knew someone who would. That same evening Snattajin was installed in an outhouse behind Miss Ethelstone's lodgings. 'I'll send you two penny stamps out of my pocket money each week,' Ronald told her, 'to pay for his food. I know he'll be happy with you, when I'm gone.'

5

Like many other schools that year, St. Olave's was smitten by an epidemic of measles. One by one the boys went down with it, and whole dormitories were turned into sick-rooms. Ronald, however, appeared immune; until one morning a letter arrived from Miss Ethelstone to say that Snattajin was off his feed and not looking too well. The same evening after tea Ronald was taken with violent shivers and a bad headache. The matron took his temperature and put a red query mark against his name on the call-over list. He was sent to bed in a small room by himself and, after the doctor's inspection next morning, moved to one of the dormitories being used as hospital wards. The matron altered the red query mark to a red cross.

All Ronald knew at this time was that he was feeling worse than the other chaps appeared to be. He was in fact in a very high fever. He was dimly conscious later, he could not tell how much later, of being moved back into a small room and of having somebody sitting by him in a nurse's uniform. He had a terrible ache in his ears. It was very dark in this dark narrow tunnel but his feet were freezing. Perhaps he had not got them properly into the tunnel yet. He struggled hard to pull them in, but could not do so without worming his body further along. This was difficult because the tunnel grew narrower and narrower; lower too, much lower; more like a rat-hole than a tunnel in fact. Ah! he remembered now; he had prayed for this long ago. But only for a dream-hole, not for a black suffocating reality like this.

He was being buried alive; powerless now even to wriggle. Sharp flints were pricking into his ears, it seemed, and into the brain. Something hot began to trickle from his nose; blood, he thought, for he was being crushed and squeezed like a tube of toothpaste. Suddenly the roof of the tunnel came crumbling against his face; he could feel the grit and dust of it against his eyelids. He could not open them. Now it was drifting up his nostrils and down into his throat: he choked violently. As he did so a great wind seemed to blow him further into the hole. In a book on the Indian Mutiny, he had seen a picture of men being blown from guns: was this happening to him? There was certainly a horrible roaring: it hurt his ears even worse than the flints.

There were voices in it too. 'Go down to the boot-room: I shall follow.' 'We can't keep that animal here any longer.' With a frantic convulsion he managed to cough out the one word 'Snattajin!' At that his eyes must have come open again, for there were vivid streaks of flickering green and purple flame on either side of him; and far away in front, facing him, two glowing red sparks. As he gazed, they grew smaller. They must be moving away; and he must follow, for he had recognised them—Snattajin's eyes! This was easier than he feared, for the tunnel seemed to have grown wider and higher; now he was crawling on his knees and, before long, walking. Mile after mile he walked, with that piercing roar of wind in his ears and his cheeks scorched by the green and purple flames. Mile after mile, with cramp in his legs, gulping for breath. Mile after mile.

But at last, the red eyes are stationary. Coming up to them he sees a great white rat crouched upon a green plush cushion. The eyes no longer shine, though: Snattajin must have fallen asleep. He thrusts forward an aching hand to stroke him. Hard, cold and smooth like marble. There is no hair! The eyes have changed again; they are open, but white—white as the body. He *is* marble; just like that dog at the feet of the recumbent statues in Cattleton church. Ronald tries to draw his hand away; but it too has become marble, frozen on to Snattajin. All of him was turning to marble; cold, stiff but aching, terribly aching. And then, suddenly, the rain began to fall; gentle, warm rain.

He felt a clamminess steal over him, and noticed that the green and purple flames had changed into great green and purple cushions. On the green one sat a nurse in uniform, and on the purple one his father. He heard the latter say 'Thank God', and then both cushions and sitters were blotted out by a pitch blackness. It seemed to cover him like a rug, and he knew no more.

One of the first visitors allowed to see Ronald during his convalescence was Miss Ethelstone. She was hoping he would not ask after Snattajin. Nor did he. His first question very much surprised her.

'Where have you buried him?' he asked.

'Under the mulberry tree,' she replied, 'and I've planted some snowdrops over him. He died quite peacefully; of old age, I think. I thought you would like a proper funeral, so I carried him on my best cushion.'

'The green plush one?'

'Yes; I didn't know you'd ever seen it.'

'He looked like white marble, didn't he?'

'Yes, dear; I suppose he did, now I come to think of it.'

Ronald lay still and silent for several minutes. Then he turned to her and said; 'He was my familiar, you know; I should have died too if the rain hadn't come. It did rain, didn't it?'

'Yes, dear; I got quite wet. But how could you know?'

Ronald appeared not to hear. 'Robinson tells me,' he said, 'that I've been given my second eleven colours.'

6

It is pleasant to be able to close this record with a *coda* in the major key. The Rat did great credit to St Olave's, winning a scholarship at Winchingham where he ended by being head of the school and captain of cricket. His career at Selham College, Oxbridge, was little less distinguished, though he just missed getting his blue. After considerable success at the Bar, he was appointed Chief Justice of a prosperous colony, where he now is. Mr Transome, now an octogenarian, is fond of repeating that 'all this comes of his having been brought up in a thoroughly happy home; no coddling or making too much of him.'

The chief justice's interests are wide. He is known to have read a paper before a Colonial Philosophical Society on '*Some survivals of a belief in Lycanthropy*'. His white bull-terrier's name is 'Snattajin'. The history of the first Snattajin used to interest his contemporaries at Winchingham and Oxbridge, also many friends of his later life. That is why it is here offered to a wider public. Names (except that of Snattajin himself) have of course been altered or disguised, but the text of the narrative was sent to the chief justice's private secretary for any alterations or amendments that His Honour might consider desirable in the interest of truth or accuracy. His Honour made none, but endorsed the manuscript with the one word: 'Ratified'.

Under the Mistletoe

1

Place-names have an interest and fascination not only for the ety-mologist. This ugly suburb has an attractive, that lovely hamlet an ugly, name. Origins are often forgotten; often, when traceable, found hidden under corruption, abbreviation, mispronunciation or vagaries of spelling. Romance and fancy weave legend round a name, erudition or ingenuity scaffold it with explanations. A dispute over derivation or pronunciation will strike sparks out of the dullest tea-party.

Kongean cartography was a fruitful field for such argument. The Director of Museums, with a profound knowledge of Kongahili, challenged the surveyor-general on his nomenclature of almost every place on the Colony's ordnance map. They quarrelled indeed over the scene of events here to be recorded, the Surveyor-General mapping it as Elland, and the director protesting that it should be L Land. It was a question of taste in spelling rather than of derivation; for the origin of the name was never in doubt. When the developmental road was constructed in 1908, old Hartingwell, the resident engineer, had had its milestones graven with Roman numerals. Why, nobody knew; perhaps not even he. If asked about it he would say that the only thing he studied year in and year out was the dial of his watch; so that Roman figures 'came natural'. 'Anyhow,' he would continue, 'what's good enough for a Bible chapter is good enough for a Kongean road.' Prospectors in search of land for rubber-planting, having found the first milestone on the new road marked with an 'L' and the area round and beyond it without any native name, dubbed it the L country or L Land; and the name stuck.

Elland, well-watered by the Gangra River and tributary streams, has a good soil. Pioneer planters, with insufficient capital, cleared only narrow strips of flat land on either side of the road; but in 1911 a Takeokuta syndicate (Elland Rubber Estates Limited) bought them out, and developed the whole area in five rectangular blocks of equal size. The road ran dead straight from west to east through the middle of each block, and some three hundred yards to the south of it, wound the Gangra in a steep rocky gorge. The bungalows of the five estate managers lay on its southern bank, each approached by a lane leading off the public road opposite a milestone.

The names given by the company to its estates were puns, so to speak, on the Roman numerals of each stone. From west to east, they were Elstone (L), Liston (LI), *Ellibis* (LII—somebody in the head office must have had some Latin!), *Elliter* (LIII) and Livingstone (LIV). Kongean labourers could of course neither understand nor assimilate such fanciful nomenclature; they talked simply of the fiftieth-mile estate, fifty-first-mile estate, and so on. It was indeed illustrative of the utter featurelessness of the terrain that, for European and Kongean alike, milestones alone could afford differentiation and identification of its component areas. At any spot along that seven miles of dull straight road a wayfarer could determine and describe his location only by its distance from the nearest milestone. Such was the scenic monotony of Elland.

The manager of Liston, Jim Wrightaway, was also general manager of the whole group. He had planted in Kongea for nearly twenty years, and spoke Kongahili like a native. A John Bull of a man, he was prone to express a contempt of the government, especially its labour department, and of the company's visiting agents. All daylight hours he gave to his job, and most evenings to a game of snooker at the Kilkurri club, three miles down the Takeokuta road. The Kongean natives liked and respected him, feeling his outlook on life to be almost as simple as their own, but his dealings far more straightforward.

Of the divisional managers the two Scots on Livingstone and Elliter found Wrightaway a plain-spoken but affable chief; but neither being of a social bent, they did not seek or desire terms of intimacy. The other two, considerably junior, managers took opposing views of him. Atterside of Ellibis admired his linguistic proficiency and management of native labour. 'The old man,' he would tell friends from Takeokuta, 'has little education but great practical capacity and common sense. A good sportsman too, and always well met in the club.' To Algernon Craigley, his neighbour on Elstone, Wrightaway was neither more nor less than a 'damned old Philistine'.

Craigley flattered himself on being a man of culture and breeding. Atterside thought him a pedant and a snob. The truth, as often, lay midway. The two young men (neither was much over thirty) had no affinities, Atterside being of an athletic type with mainly outdoor interests and Craigley of a studious disposition, fond, whenever he chanced on a kindred spirit, of bookish talk and argument. Unlike his neighbours Craigley was never to be seen at the Kilkurri club. He preferred, once or twice a week, to ride his motorcycle in the opposite direction and to argue an evening away with Barclay Tinkerwell on Elland End estate.

It is a common fault in anybody of but mediocre attainment in his profession to belittle its experts and grudge them their success. Such was the attitude of Craigley towards Wrightaway; especially when inspection disclosed something wrong on Elstone and he was told to put it right. After one such corrective visit he gave tongue to his resentment.

'As you've found fault with me again, Sir, perhaps you won't object to my reminding you of the visiting agent's order about those Tebanco trees?'

'I need no reminding, thank you, Craigley. So long as I remain here, so do those trees; and I've told you the reason.'

'Because you're afraid of ghosts or devils!'

'Because our labour force is afraid of ghosts or devils. You should know by now how superstitious they are about those mistletoe clumps. I'd sooner bring down a hornet's nest.'

'Well, the sooner all that nonsense is drummed out of them the better. Everyone who comes up here comments on the absurdity of leaving Tebancos standing in the middle of rubber. It makes me feel ashamed.'

'You mean,' said Wrightaway drily, 'that they give you the opportunity of telling them what an old fool you think me. Doubtless they agree; but better the wisdom of a fool than the folly of the wise. Those trees remain.'

For a reader unacquainted with Kongea the preceding conversation will need elucidation. The Tebanco is a large tropical species of *ficus,* the favourite host of a parasite resembling mistletoe. Viewed from below these parasitic clumps of leafage look like so many giant grey-green sponges; and in them, according to Kongean belief, roosts a sort of ghost or genie; harmless if uninterfered with but dangerously malignant if disturbed. Wrightaway in consequence had left all Tebancos standing when the rest of the jungle was felled and cleared for planting rubber. The visiting agent estimated that some ten acres of the Elland estates had been thus denied economic cultivation; for the Tebanco has extensive surface roots and a wide umbrella of branches. Nevertheless, Wrightaway swept aside his complaint, and defied a subsequent written order from the company's office in Takeokuta that the trees must be felled and uprooted. Of local shareholders many, like Craigley, thought him an obstinate old fool; others, mostly men of his own age, did not.

2

One morning towards the middle of 1922, Atterside discovered what looked like a leaf disease, *oidium* he suspected, in a field of ten-year-old rubber. Anxious to find out whether there were any sign of it on estates further along the road he bicycled after tea to enquire of his Scots colleagues on Elliter and Livingstone. Neither had noticed any withering of foliage, but promised to keep their eyes open for it. In order to render his enquiries complete Atterside rode on the further two miles to Elland's End and called on Tinkerwell. His answer also was in the negative; but he seemed eager for conversation and urged Atterside to stay for a drink.

'That's a dirty trick, I think, that Craigley's minded to play on your boss.'

'Trick?' Atterside frowned. 'What trick? He's said nothing to me about it.'

'Oh! Perhaps then I oughtn't to have mentioned it to you, and please don't let him know that I have. All the same I feel that you ought to be put wise, and to stop him if you can.'

Atterside frowned again. 'Craigley,' he said, 'likes me as little as he does Wrightaway. If I told him to stop anything he would take it as the signal to go on. But what's he up to, anyway?'

Tinkerwell poured out two whiskies and soda and handed one to his guest. Then, before resuming his chair, he lit a mosquito smudge and placed it on the floor between them.

'Craigley's a queer card,' he said, 'and he's got a fearful down on Wrightaway about those Tebanco trees. Personally, I think Wrightaway right to keep them standing, but Craigley sticks to it that he's actuated solely by personal funk of anything ghostly.'

'Wrightaway a funk!' Atterside exploded. 'I'd pity any ghost that got up against him!'

'Yes, I agree. But Craigley's got it into his head that big strong not over-brainy men are generally nervous about spooks; and that

Wrightaway's information about mistletoe spirits comes not from his chaps but from Collinson's *Kongea*, a copy of which Craigley saw on his bookshelf.

'Craigley's a bloody fool,' Atterside exclaimed angrily. 'He doesn't know enough Kongahili to understand a quarter of what a native says. They're for ever gassing about devils and ghosts.'

'Exactly what I tried to impress on him. I happen to be rather interested in things psychic and psychological; and I could tell him a thing or two about himself which might surprise him, if only he could understand. But he can't.'

'What are you getting at, Tinkerwell?'

'Well, Craigley's wrong of course about big strong simple-minded men being afraid of spooks. They haven't enough imagination or susceptivity. The vulnerable sort, so to speak, are people like himself; professed and militant rationalists, who subconsciously repress and hide from themselves inherited instincts of apprehensive belief. What Craigley predicates of Wrightaway is a reflection of his own, to him unknown, self. The desire to exploit Wrightaway's supposed superstition comes from the itch of his own subconscious fears.'

'I'm not sure that I follow you. But, tell me, what's the trick that Craigley proposes to play on Wrightaway?'

'Well, he's going to get Wrightaway down the lane to his bungalow next Saturday night.'

'He won't do that,' interrupted Atterside. 'The chief never visits any of us in the evening. Besides, there's a snooker tournament at the club that night, and he won't be home till late.'

'Exactly. That's why Craigley has chosen Saturday. It's always misty on the road after nine o'clock; and he's going to put that hurricane lamp, that he has placed every night under the fiftieth milestone, below the half-mile stone on the Kilkurri side. Wrightaway will then begin to slow down after passing the lamp, and he's pretty sure to turn down the Elstone lane at milestone fifty, mistaking it for fifty-one.

'In case he should take a glance at the stone Craigley's going to paint an "I" after the "L". It sounds like some silly prep-school plot; but unfortunately, it's very likely to succeed. We all know the sameness of that damned road; at night and in a mist it's always difficult to tell which turning is which. Wrightaway's thoughts too will still be on his snooker match; and, if he wins again this year, he will very probably have had a few.'

Atterside's look of annoyance and distaste at what was being told him suddenly changed to a smile.

'He's forgotten Sirono,' he said.

'Sirono?'

'Yes, Wrightaway's Kongean *syce*. When Wrightaway drives, Sirono's always behind in the dicky. He knows the feel of every yard of that road, and if Wrightaway takes the Elstone turning he'll shout out at once.'

'You've forgotten, Atterside, haven't you, that Saturday's the Kashtipuja holiday? Sirono will be at the temple.'

'By George, and so he will! Craigley thought of that too, I suppose. But what's his idea in getting Wrightaway down the Elstone lane? As soon as he reached the bridge over the Gangra he'd spot his mistake and turn back; for the Elstone and Liston bridges are quite different.'

'Another drink, I suggest, before I try to answer that!' Tinkerwell replied, and replenished both glasses. 'I put the same question to Craigley myself, and at once he became evasive and mysterious; muttering something about his being a good hand at decorating Christmas trees.'

'What on earth did you make of that?'

'Nothing at the time; but an idea has struck me since, that mayn't be far wrong.'

'Out with it then! Don't keep a man guessing.'

'Well, I feel—no, I'm certain—that Craigley's little game has something to do with his obsession about Wrightaway's being scared of mistletoe spirits. Christmas of course can have nothing to do with it, except that you may remember it was Craigley who rigged up those little electric bulbs on the Kilkurri children's Christmas tree. I've a hunch that he may be going to do something of the same sort on those mistletoe clumps in the Tebancos along the Elstone lane. A lot of little dim lights, switched on all at once, would certainly have an eerie effect on a misty night and startle anybody at the wheel of a car. I haven't a copy of Collinson here, but I believe the book says something about eyes in the mistletoe.'

Atterside took a long pull at his drink and grunted.

'You may have hit on it,' he said, 'though it sounds too damn' silly. Craigley, however, as I said just now, is a bloody fool, for all his brainy talk and swank.'

'Hadn't you better warn Wrightaway?'

'No, I don't want to put him against Craigley more than he already is. Besides, he's away in Takeokuta till Friday afternoon. I don't mind having a straight talk with Craigley, though.'

'No, no! You've promised not to let him know what I've been telling you. He's coming up to pot luck here tomorrow evening, and I shall do my best to put him off any nonsense with Wrightaway.'

Atterside put his empty glass down on the table and rose to go.

'Well, I must be trotting along. Many thanks for telling me about Craigley. I just can't understand the chap, and that's a fact. Yet you and he seem to find something in common. He's always coming up your way.'

'Yes, he's fond of argument, and his talk amuses me. Like me, he's interested in hypnotism and that sort of thing. Not that he knows much about it; precious little in fact. Still, the appeal that I am going to make to him to stop baiting Wrightaway can be wrapped up in palatable jargon.'

'Then I wish you luck. If I should manage to think of anything that I can do to prevent his making an ass of himself, I'll do it of course. Goodnight!'

Atterside's thoughts were so fixed on what Tinkerwell had told him, and the mist so thick, that he had to dismount twice on the ride home to see what milestone he had reached. He went on thinking as he ate his supper, instead of reading as usual, and afterwards thought on in a deck-chair on the veranda until past midnight. It was his habit from childhood to read a psalm, picked at random, before getting into bed. He did so tonight. It was *Psalm xxxv* and he reached the eighth verse:

Let a sudden destruction come upon him unawares and his net, that he hath laid privily, catch himself: that he may fall into his own mischief.

Shutting the prayer-book with a snap, he blew out the candle and, a few moments later, murmured aloud in the darkness, 'Thank you, David, for a good tip.'

3

Next morning for Atterside was one of usual routine, except that, Wrightaway being away at Takeokuta, he sat for an hour in the group office deputising for the general manager on a few matters that need not await his return. Having finished with these he took the opportunity of finding the copy of Collinson and turning up the passage about mistletoe spirits. It was not long.

The parasitic growths, resembling mistletoe, to be found on trees of the *Ficus* family (especially the Tebanco) are the reputed hives of demons called '*nyamika kunya*' or eye spirits. These are said to be invisible save for their eyes, which sparkle like moonstones amid the leaf-age or, if they are angry, like rubies. The clustering of fireflies on the clumps may have given rise to this myth.

That was all, but enough, it appeared, to set Atterside thinking again; for he sat on at the desk four or five minutes longer, staring blankly at the estate chart pinned on the blank wall above. Then, unlocking a drawer, he took from it a large key and walked, still meditatively, out of the office and across the paved yard to a large shed marked *Group Store*. Unfastening the padlock, he entered and took down the Stores Index.

Thence he passed to a stock book, and from it to rack J, Shelf 3, *Estate Cycle Accessories*. Item 23; yes, that was it—*Reflectors for Attachment to Rear Mudguard*. He took out two and dropped them into his coat pocket, but made no entry in the stock book, for he would replace them tomorrow. Ever since driving his car into young Koseni, the postal messenger, Wrightaway had insisted on all estate cycles and bullock carts bearing reflectors.

By lunch-time Atterside was no longer thoughtful. An onlooker (had there been one) might have detected signs of impatience in his manipulation of some little strands of wire which, having hurried his meal, he began attaching to the two reflectors. This done, he called his boy and told him to fill and trim a hurricane lantern, as he would be going up to the far field after tea and would not be back before dark.

The rest of the afternoon he spent in the factory and on an inspection of a new smoke-house, just completed by a local contractor. The daily paper from Takeokuta arrived at tea-time, but his reading of it was perfunctory, and he was soon pacing restlessly up and down the lawn. He had never felt an evening to be so long.

At last, the slow sun set and the *cicadas* began their crepuscular *whirr-whirr*, the same noise, he said to himself, as that made by a toy clockwork engine fallen off the rails wheels upwards. The twilight was already dimming fast when he heard the sound for which he had been waiting—the *chock-chock* of Craigley's motorcycle bound for Elland's End. In a moment he was back in the bungalow, stuffing two adhesive luggage labels into his pocket-book. Then, with the lantern in his hand and the reflectors in his pocket, he started off on foot through the rubber towards Liston.

It was dark by the time he came out of the rubber on to the Liston Lane. Here he turned right towards the Gangra River. Just short of the bridge stood a half-grown Tebanco; and on its lowest branch, not

258

more than four or five feet from the ground, a large clump of mistletoe. In front of this he stopped and lit the lantern. Then with great care and deliberation (for he knew that any pedestrian or cyclist going to or from Liston would take the short cut over a footbridge higher up and that he would not be disturbed) he fastened the reflectors on to the mistletoe, just two inches apart. Stepping back on to the lane he now walked back along it some twenty yards, turned round and let the light of the lantern fall on his work. Two red eyes shone in the mistletoe. They would shine yet more brightly, he told himself, in the beam of a motorcycle's headlamp. So far, so good.

He strode briskly, even jauntily, along the four hundred yards of lane that lay between river and road. Arrived at the latter he looked anxiously along it in the Kilkurri direction. The mist was only moderate tonight, but he noted to his satisfaction that it was sufficient to obscure Craigley's lamp below the fiftieth milestone. Setting down his own lantern at the base of milestone LI he took the adhesive labels from his pocket-book, licked them, and stuck them over the I. The milestone now read L; nor was the glimmer of the lantern sufficient to reveal the papering. Leaving it there Atterside strolled back to Ellibis and had dinner.

He ate and drank mechanically. The boy wondered at his master's omission to charge him with the usual threatening message to the cook; for the food looked to him more than ordinarily unappetising, as indeed it was. What Atterside was intensely considering was the probable reaction of Craigley to what awaited him. One possibility was that he might not see the reflectors but, finding himself on the wrong bridge, turn his machine round and regain the road.

If so, he would certainly dismount at the milestone to see whose lamp was there (for all the estate lamps bore numbers) and in so doing could hardly fail to see the paper stuck over the I. Such discovery might perhaps have the effect of aborting his design on Wrightaway, but would make future relations between himself and Craigley intolerable. The lantern and papering must, therefore, be removed as soon as they had served the purpose of deflecting Craigley down the Liston Lane.

The hour of Craigley's return from Elland's End would probably be late, but no risk must be taken. Atterside therefore set out again from the bungalow at nine o'clock, and on reaching the milestone satisfied himself that the gum-paper still adhered. He then sat down on a low bank in the rubber trees to await and watch events. It was a long and painful vigil. Never had he known mosquitoes so pestilent, or the steamy atmosphere of the rubber so oppressive. He had smoked the last of twenty cigarettes in his case before the distant throb of Craigley's motor-cycle punctuated the hot stillness. As the sound came nearer and nearer, Atterside became seized with a sudden misgiving about the part he was playing. He would give anything for the motor-cycle to flash by without Craigley noticing the decoy lantern. This, however, was not to be. He heard the machine slow down and, a few seconds later, the scrape of rubber tyres against grit and stone as it swung off the road into Liston Lane.

What would happen now? The throb of the exhaust was getting fainter, but with no deceleration yet for the Gangra bridge. Then, suddenly, it and all other noises were silenced by a mighty roll of distant thunder. Rain began to fall in sparse but heavy drops.

Atterside ran quickly to the milestone, ripped off the gum-paper with his pocket-knife and, picking up the lantern, turned it down and out. Retreating once more into the rubber he awaited Craigley's return. Minutes passed but he did not come. The claps of thunder were nearer now, the large raindrops more frequent. Craigley must have taken his machine along that path above the river, Atterside concluded; but he would find it bumpy.

There was one thing more that Atterside must do that night. The reflectors must be recovered; or they would be noticed, perhaps stolen, next morning. He walked hurriedly therefore down the Liston Lane; but never a sign of Craigley. Yes; he must certainly have taken the river path. By the time Atterside approached the Gangra bridge the storm had burst in full fury; the lightning was so incessant as to render easy unwiring of the reflectors. Putting them in his pocket he made off home as fast as he could; running every now and again, but soaked to the skin long before reaching the bungalow.

Though bodily tired he was long in getting to sleep. His brain felt branded with a huge question mark. How had Craigley taken his medicine? What might he be thinking of at that moment? What form had Tinkerwell's efforts at dissuasion taken? What expression would Craigley's face wear tomorrow? And so on, on and on, until question and imagined answer passed from fevered thought into fitful dreaming. Or perhaps nightmare is the right word; for twice during the small hours, he sat suddenly upright in his bed, straining to make sure that it was not really Craigley's face at the window; with red eyes in it.

After muster next morning Atterside bicycled to the group office and replaced the reflectors in store. He had difficulty in resisting a strong temptation to ride on to Elstone and satisfy his curiosity as to the effect of last night's experience on Craigley. His job lay, however, on his own estate, and he must carry on as usual. So back to Ellibis.

On returning from the field at noon he found an estate clerk from Elstone waiting to see him. Had he seen Mr Craigley anywhere about, the man asked. No; why? Because he had been absent from muster and was not to be found at the bungalow.

'Surely his boy must know where he is?' Atterside suggested, feigning an air of casual disinterest.

'The motorcycle is absenting itself also,' the clerk replied, 'and servant-boy is much wondering only.'

'Well, I heard his motorcycle pass here just before the storm last night; and that's as much as I can tell you.'

'But servant-boy says,' the clerk continued persistently, 'that master not utilising bed last night. We are all much fearing, Sir.'

'Fearing what?'

'Fearing evil things, Sir. Perhaps motorcycle running amuck. Servant-boy looks hither and thither for tyre marks, but big rain have made all wash-out.'

'Then you'd better get your Elstone natives on to a thorough search through the rubber.' Send a man, too, down to the Kilkurri police station to report.'

Atterside felt relieved when Wrightaway arrived back from Takeokuta at tea-time and assumed direction of various search operations. Once, as a small boy, Atterside had set a large stone rolling down a hill in Westshire, and had spent an afternoon of misery for fear that word might come at any minute of someone injured on the farm below. The memory had faded with the years, but returned to him now with an ugly vividness. As then, his plight was one of guilty apprehension. He slept not a wink that night: and again, he saw red eyes.

No one, except Atterside, knew that Craigley had taken the Liston Lane instead of that to his own estate. That was why Wrightaway and the Kilkurri police had the river dragged only near the Elstone bridge. The discovery of body and motor-cycle in the deep pool below the Liston bridge was due to an estate foreman's having noticed scratches on the moss and lichen of a rock at its side. The pool was jammed with branches and other debris of a recent flood, so that it took long to disentangle and extricate the corpse. A magisterial enquiry (they do not have coroners in Kongea) was held within a few hours, and the cleft and battered skull provided evidence enough of the cause of death. There was no need to summon the doctor from Kilkurri for a post-mortem. Craigley, instead of keeping to the roadway over the bridge, must have swerved into the side-drain where it plunges over a twenty-foot drop into the river gorge. At what point exactly he swerved or skidded nobody could tell, for the storm had washed away all wheel-marks. Death must have been instantaneous.

Atterside was white as a sheet as he testified to having heard the noise of Craigley's motorcycle returning from Elland's End. The magistrate asked him no questions, nor did Wrightaway when they conversed after the enquiry.

'Must have taken the wrong turning in the storm,' Wrightaway surmised, 'and then perhaps saw eyes in that Tebanco, I shouldn't wonder.'

Atterside started as if stung. 'Good God! What the hell do you mean?'

'The natives tell me that there's a big devil in the mistletoe there, and they know about such things.'

'But you don't mean to say that you believe all their nonsense?'

'I don't know about believing; but I take stock of all I see or am told. Maybe it's nothing but fireflies or glow-worms, but from all accounts what look like eyes are seen there. One night I fancied I saw something of the kind myself. If Craigley saw 'em he'd have had a nasty shock, for I shouldn't care myself to see anything I disbelieved in. Wouldn't seem natural, would it? But nothing's frightening to an open mind.'

Atterside heaved a sigh of relief. He was not suspected.

Tinkerwell called in at Ellibis that evening and conversation turned inevitably to the recent tragedy.

'I fear,' Tinkerwell said, 'that I may have been an unintentional murderer.'

'Really, whose?'

'Craigley's. He and I had been trying some experiments in hypnotism that night; and, before putting him out of a final trance, I thought of that dirty trick he wanted to play on Wrightaway and laid him under a post-hypnotic suggestion. "When you come to the Tebancos on your way home," I said to him, "you will see eyes in the mistletoe clumps; glaring red eyes."'

Atterside sat staring at the speaker, then at something beyond. The skin of his face was taut and grey. Suddenly he leaned forward and clutched Tinkerwell's arm.

'Look, Tinkerwell!' he gasped. 'Look behind you. Isn't that a face at the window?'

His Name was Legion

1

Who does not find it exhilarating to stand on a height and look down? For the Alpinist there is a measure of achievement in the pleasure; but the humble carefree hiker enjoys equally the sense of dominant aloofness that comes of viewing plain or valley from the hills. Such rapture is not for travellers by aeroplane: caged in a cabin, windowed but noisy. For the gliderman, yes; but for moments only. He may not relax control of his craft so long as to lose all sense in gaze. The unencumbered stroller alone can stand, out of time, yet robed with space, in silent impersonal unity with earth and sky.

There is, in Southshire, a place where the chalk downs protrude a northern knee of greensand on to the clayey levels of the weald. In spring there are waves of bluebell on its slope, foam-flaked with wood anemones. Here and there, too, are golden drifts of wild daffodil. Then, as summer comes, all is sunk in a green surge of bracken, turning with autumn to russet and ochre. It was summer now as Frank Lynton stood at the top, gazing abstractedly at the chessboard of field and copse below. He had stayed motionless for perhaps fifteen minutes, but could not have told you whether it had been a matter of seconds or a full hour. 'I like,' he said to his host, the Rev Vernon Vinetree, at dinner that night, 'occasionally to let the brain merely tick over so that my mind becomes absorptive, like blotting-paper.' The phrasing was neither clear nor happy; but the rector appeared to understand. It was he who had suggested that Frank should take that particular walk.

A clatter of twigs and the whirr of a cock pheasant rising from a clump of brambles woke Lynton from his reverie. Leaning forward, and pointing with his stick, he began identifying particular features of the panorama. He had studied the map which hung in the rectory hall before he started. The building half-hidden by elms in the left middle distance must be Affrington Court and the dumpy little spire

265

beyond it that of Westingly Church. And that group of buildings on the edge of the big wood clearly belonged to Eastover Farm. Save for these there was little evidence of human habitation. Wait a bit, though: what was that line of brown and grey against the oaks on the right? A stationary train? But surely the line ran down the Daven valley, not there? Lynton took out his field-glasses. Yes, they were certainly railway carriages; old ones used for fowl-houses, he surmised.

Replacing the glasses in their case he turned his eyes to the hill's apron of bracken just below him. Here and there the purple spike of a foxglove pierced the green fronds; and over them fluttered a few butterflies, common whites and meadow browns. The warm smell of bracken came floating to his nostrils, although there was no perceptible breeze. Loath to tear himself away from this loveliness he saw nevertheless from a glance at his wrist-watch that it was already four o'clock, and that he must be getting back to tea. It would be a good two miles back to the rectory. As he took a final look at the view a spiral of grey smoke rose above the middle railway carriage. It was not a fowl-house, then, but a kitchen; and the other two must be bedroom and living-room. He felt bitter that anybody should live so incongruously with his surroundings; there ought, he said to himself, to be some provision of law to prevent it.

2

There were visitors at the rectory for tea: one a lawyer from Thornychurch, the other the vicar of a neighbouring parish. They had left their wives shopping together at Thornychurch; for Mr Vinetree was unmarried and, from a feminine standpoint, prosy and unattractive. Lynton, slightly late, heard the trio in animated conversation. It hushed at his approach and during the necessary introductions: 'Mr Lynton—Mr Cowdle; the Reverend Silas Boringer—Mr Lynton.' Then they plunged into it once more, dragging him with them. He worked for a printing and publishing firm, didn't he? Yes: well, he would probably be interested in the problem they were discussing. Cowdle had been about to sum up the whole position just as he arrived, and would do so now.

'Our friend the rector,' Mr Cowdle began, thus invited, 'has for several years past issued monthly, at threepence a copy, a little newssheet entitled *Kidbury Parish Notes*. It's placed for sale in the Galilee porch of his church, and can also be had at the village grocer's. In addition to church notices and statistics it contains a leading article, and what are headed *"Pertinent Paragraphs"* from the rector's own pen; also excerpts, selected by him, from current newspapers and reviews. He received therefore a shock when, at a recent Diocesan *synod*, the Archdeacon called him aside and complained of the unorthodox tone of the *Kidbury Parish Magazine*. Asked what in particular he found at fault, the archdeacon pulled out a packet from his cassock pocket and replied "The whole of it". The packet being opened Vinetree saw with mixed surprise and relief that it contained not a copy of his *Parish Notes*, but a fair-sized magazine, bearing on its cover a picture of Kidbury Church and the title *Kidbury Notebook* (Quarterly).

'I haven't read any of the stuff inside it myself, but I'm told that it's not exactly of a sort to harmonise with the church on the cover. Now the question put to me by the rector is as to whether or not legal steps can be taken to prevent further issues of this magazine in a form that renders it mistakable for a parish magazine. He has consulted me as a friend, not as a lawyer (though I am one, Mr Lynton), and I have had no hesitation in replying "No". There is no impediment in law against reproduction on a magazine cover of a photograph of a place of public worship, and the title *Kidbury Notebook* constitutes no trespass on that of *Kidbury Parish Notes*. Perhaps, as a member of a printing and publishing firm, Mr Lynton has had experience of this sort of thing and will bear me out?'

'Yes, I agree. Still, if the publishers had been aware of *Kidbury Parish Notes* they would probably have suggested some other title than *Notebook. Scrapbook*, for instance. But what beats me is that a little out-of-the-way place like this should support two periodicals; one of them, you say, a fair-sized magazine. The Kidbury people must be great readers!'

Mr Vinetree tapped the tea-tray with his spoon. He had a way of tapping things when upset. On Sundays he would do it with his spectacle case to the reading-desk, whenever the choir sang out of tune. 'I'm happy to say, Frank,' he said, 'that our people do *not* read the *Notebook*. I've not come across a copy so far in a single cottage, and I've forbidden it in the village Reading-room.'

'Then where is its circulation? It takes the deuce of a lot of sold copies to make a magazine pay.'

'Ah! that's the annoying thing. It isn't meant to pay. It's financed by a crank named Tresdale, and he uses it for what he impertinently calls spiritual propaganda.'

'Spiritual propaganda?'

'Yes. When, after the archdeacon's mistake, I called to ask Tresdale to alter its title he told me that he couldn't, because it had been decided upon and communicated to him by directive spirits. Everything printed in it, he went on to say, had a spiritual authorship. He himself was no more than a human editorial agent, luckily possessed of enough money to fulfil his vocation. With that he pressed a copy into my hands and remarked that, by command of the spirits, he had some time back posted a copy to the Archdeacon. Every article, he assured me, appeared above the name of an author spirit. I had, however, already had a look through the archdeacon's copy, and knew that the names were all those of letters in the Greek alphabet. Of this fact Tresdale professed himself to be unaware: falsely, because I have since found out that he took a classical degree. The articles that most shocked the archdeacon, and indeed myself, were all subscribed *Upsilon*.'

Mr Cowdle had begun to fidget at the mention of Greek letters. Having no Greek himself he felt that the talk might pass out of his conversational depth. Looking down at his watch, and contriving a little start, he now jumped to his feet with 'Good gracious, rector! Half-past five and I've an appointment in Thornychurch at six! I must be off at once. Now don't forget that you've no ground whatever for legal action. I say that as a friend, but I've never given better advice for a fee. Mr Lynton's staying with you over the weekend, isn't he? Well, you might let him drop in at my place if he's in Thornychurch; and I'll introduce him to spirits of a decent potable sort that don't write stuff for dud magazines! So long.'

With this parting pleasantry Mr Cowdle hurried down the gravel path to his waiting car. So far, the other clergyman, Mr Boringer, had held his peace. Now, however, he broke silence.

'Cowdle's quite right, Vinetree,' he said, 'and between you and me I fancy that the Archdeacon may have been pulling your leg. Nobody who looks it through could possibly mistake Tresdale's quarterly *Notebook* for a church magazine! It's far too expensively got up for one thing. You say that none of your parishioners read it, so why worry about the thing? I confess to having glanced through a copy in the Thornychurch public library, and I rather enjoyed some semi-metrical stuff about an art cycle. That the articles are dictated by spirits I just don't believe. Some of them are not too bad, it seemed to me.'

'There's no accounting for tastes, of course,' the rector said disapprovingly, 'but I can only suppose that the articles signed "Upsilon" escaped your notice. They're thoroughly atheistic and unwholesome. I've been careful to excise them from both copies of the magazine now in my possession. I wouldn't have my servants read them for anything. If they weren't dictated, they were certainly prompted, by an evil spirit.'

'Satan's a clever journalist,' responded Mr Boringer, 'and doesn't confine his contributions to the *Kidbury Notebook*. His hand is visible enough in many of the daily papers. So don't you go giving Tresdale's publication advertisement by opposing it. Denunciation from the pulpit would make it a best-seller. When I worked in India for the C.M.S. I remember hearing a Tamil proverb to the effect that to prod excrement with a stick is to make it stink the more. Coarse but true. I should leave Tresdale well alone, if I were you. I must be off now, and will drop that parcel for you at Dawkin's cottage; no, no bother at all; I shall be taking the footpath in any case. Goodbye, Vinetree; goodbye, Mr Lynton.'

Left alone with his guest the rector expressed apology and regret that the conversation at tea should have been entirely taken up with discussion about Mr Tresdale's magazine.

'Oh! but I've been most interested,' Lynton replied, 'and am longing to have a look at it.'

'Very well, you shall—after dinner.'

3

Over soup at dinner his host hoped that Frank had enjoyed his walk to Farnley Edge. 'I often go up there myself,' he said, 'if I want to be alone and to get away from things. So much of this south country has been spoilt by the spilth of an electric train service; but the view from the Edge is still very much what it was when I was a boy, and the wild flowers no fewer.'

'The only pity,' Lynton replied, 'is that some Philistine has gone and stuck three railway carriages in that field by the oaks, and seems to be living in them.'

Mr Vinetree gave his now empty soup-plate a vicious rap with the spoon. 'Yes, even a bungalow would have been better than railway carriages. It's maddening that a fellow with money to spare, and all England to choose from, should elect to live in railway carriages and plunk them down just there, where there's no road, and where he had to dig thirty feet for good water. It must have cost him a pretty penny; and, as you say, he's polluted the landscape.'

'What on earth made him choose such a spot?'

'Nothing *on earth,* so he says.' Here the rector made another rap with a spoon, this time on the table. 'Spirits!'

'Good heavens! Spirits seem a bit too rampant in these parts. First, they engage a fellow to be their editor; and now another chap employs them as house agents!'

'No; not another chap. It's Tresdale again.'

'He must be a lunatic, I guess.'

'You wouldn't say so if you met him. He's quite interesting to talk to. Used to be in the Colonial Service, I believe, till he came in for money and threw his hand in. He's well read, paints in oil, and once had a picture in the Academy. It hangs now in one of the railway carriages. That makes it all the more deplorable that he should be spending all his time and energy on this spirit nonsense.'

'I suppose he's always attending *séances* and that sort of thing?'

'No, again. The people who call themselves spiritualists will have nothing to do with him or he with them. He has no need for mediums, he says, being clairvoyant and clairaudient. That's the mongrel word he uses, "clairaudient!" So he sits all day in front of a dummy wireless set and a dummy television screen, neither of them connected to anything or with any battery, imagining that he hears or reads the stuff that he jots down for publication in his magazine.'

'But how do *you* know all this?'

'Well, those railway carriages are just inside the parish boundary, and so I felt it my duty as rector to call on him. He comes to church, too, sometimes; and afterwards sends me on a postcard criticisms allegedly passed by his spirits on my sermons. No, don't laugh, Frank; it's a serious matter, for I'm perfectly certain that they are read at the village post office. Not that I mind my efforts being criticised, if in a proper way; but Tresdale, or his spirits, read impossible thoughts into my simplest utterance. It makes me quite nervous to see him sitting below me, all eyes and ears. So much so that one Sunday I twice misquoted my text! And yet somehow, I always feel forced to look at the pew by the second pillar to see whether he's there or not. He never sits anywhere else. Usually, he looks as white as a sheet, and the sockets of his eyes as dark as though he were wearing sun-glasses. I know that our doctor, Farrold, is worried about him, for he has told me so. Asked me in fact whether I couldn't do something about it! I only wish that I could. Tresdale would be a decent and useful enough fellow but for his infatuation about spirits.'

'I could never forgive him those railway carriages,' commented Lynton. 'No, no port, thank you: it makes me liverish. Now what about that magazine you promised to show me?'

'Ah, yes! I was forgetting. Come along with me into the study, will you? I keep it in a locked drawer. If you sit in the armchair by the window, you won't need a lamp yet awhile. The room faces west.'

They passed accordingly into the study. Finding difficulty with the lock Mr Vinetree discovered that he had inserted a wrong key. 'I've never done that before,' he murmured sarcastically. 'Tresdale's spirits at work again, perhaps! Yes, here's the right one; but the lock needs oiling: it shouldn't squeak like that. Well, here you are. Beautifully got up, you see: and that's an excellent view of the church.'

'Yes; and the magazine's printed on first-rate paper. But what are all those pencil crosses and underlinings?'

'Oh those! They're mine, I'm afraid. I've been checking up on a theory. No author's material, you'll agree, can be entirely of his own creation. It will be derived from history, acquired knowledge, observation of nature, experience of human society, and so on. Like a cook he can choose and mix, but cannot make, his ingredients. Like a cook, too, he will put them into a mould that will give the resultant pudding shape and form. That mould will be his personal style and structural arrangement. Now Tresdale claims to have either read or heard on his dummy apparatus the *ipsissima verba* of spirits, and to have reproduced them *verbatim* in his magazine. Nevertheless, you will see from my marginal crosses and underlines that a number of identical idiosyncrasies of style and vocabulary recur in all the prose articles. That satisfies me that these cannot have been in any literal sense dictated or visionally communicated. Tresdale has been the cook. I ought to tell you, though, that Tresdale's idiosyncrasies were not observable in the Upsilon articles, which I excised and burned. Those articles, however, were artificial stuff; all of them modelled on the pattern of apocalyptic scripture. Several passages indeed were recognisable reflections of the second book of Esdras.'

'What a queer bird Tresdale must be! I've never thought of dipping into Esdras II.'

'Well, you'd be better employed reading it than this magazine. Still, I would like your opinion on the dozen or so metrical items; they won't take you long to look through. "*Art Cycle*", which Boringer liked, is the first and longest. They aren't poetry of course, just versification; and a mere versifier has no style of his own, but writes to a

271

set form. So, although these items are dissimilar, I suspect them all to be of Tresdale's own manufacture. Probably you'll agree. Well; now I'll leave you to it. I always work at my bedroom desk before turning in, so will say goodnight now. Breakfast's at a quarter to nine. Sleep well, Frank, and don't get dreaming of Tresdale's spirits!'

4

As he sat back in the armchair, Lynton's first look at the *Kidbury Notebook* was to ascertain the name of its printers. Pyman & Pattercake, Limited. He knew the firm well, as one that throve on the publication of those exquisite brochures with which prosperous corporations celebrate their jubilees and centenaries. 'We are monumental printers,' old Mr Pyman would tell shareholders. 'We cater for boardrooms, not bookstalls.' The magazine now under Lynton's inspection had been turned out as elegantly as their other work, and Tresdale must have been footing a heavy bill for its quarterly production. Could he get any considerable return from its sales? Hardly, Lynton thought, for on the inside of the front cover was printed: 'Obtainable only at the Cloister Bookshop, Thornychurch; Price One shilling and sixpence.' Small wonder that the rector had come across no copy in a cottage: the Cloister Bookshop was not a haunt of the rank and file. And the price too! Hadn't the archdeacon noticed that?

Yet another notice appeared on the back cover: 'All items in this Number are contributed by Spirits. Direct communication may be had with the authors in the manner described on page 37 of the January issue, a few copies of which are (at the time of going to press) still available at the Cloister Bookshop, Thornychurch, price 2s. a copy.' Lynton smiled at the bait thus set for the curious in such matters; and, first lighting the lamp, for it was getting dark, plunged into the letterpress within.

For an hour and a half, he busied himself with a critical examination of the prose contents. Some of the stuff was well, none of it conspicuously ill, composed. He could not discern the significance of some of Mr Vinetree's crosses and underlines, but (though he could not agree that identity of draughtsmanship was positively deducible from internal evidence) he found nothing in the various articles to controvert the probability of their all being of Tresdale's composition, whatever his source of inspiration.

It was a pity, he felt, that the Upsilon items had all been excised, for he found nothing in the residue to account for the rector's grave censure. None of the contents would, it was true, be suitable for a church magazine; but then it didn't look in the least like a church magazine. The Archdeacon could have done no more than look at the cover and at Upsilon's scriptural style. The worst that could be predicated of the prose articles was that they seemed to Lynton complacently futile. Cynicism is spurious if self-satisfied, and the dressing of commonplaces in fancy costume is not originality. The resultant tone, despite the claim of spiritual origin, was spiritless. In bored distaste Lynton now turned to the verses, on which the rector had requested his opinion as to single or multiple authorship.

The eleven pieces fell, so Lynton decided after examination, into three categories: mere versification, perversification (his own term, that) and, in one instance only, sincere writing. A fair example of the first was entitled '*Love's Visit*', and ran as follows:

When Love looked in at breakfast
He drave morn's care away;
Her arms flung round his neck fast,
Jane begged the boy to stay:
And oh! the golden time we had
In frolic with the lusty lad.
We danced and sang till luncheon,
And Jane did roses pluck,
Whereof to lay a bunch on
Love's lap to bring him luck:
Then, with pretence to be a scold,
She chid the youth for growing old.
But Love laughed on and chatted
Till it was time for tea;
Jane's sleeve he gaily patted
And bade her brew for three.
The glance she threw him was not kind,
But went unheeded—Love is blind.
He lingered on to dinner
('Twas I besought him stay),
But laughter now was thinner,
His pleasantries less gay:
The talk, too, ran on times of yore
Until Jane voted Love a bore.
Not recking her sour faces,

I urged Love spend the night;
Told Jane to stop grimaces
And use our guest aright.
In vain! When dawn came chill and red
His bed was empty: Love had fled.
                    —Kappa

As typical of the second category, labelled by Lynton 'perversification', the short piece headed '*Whitsun Protest*' may be quoted:

Who stagger blindly on life's crumbling slope,
And in the gloom for hand or foothold grope,
What good to fling at us the loose unmadefast rope of Hope?
What good to prate of Faith, Reliance,
Trust To us who see the worm, the rot, the rust;
Whom observation teaches that the end of all things must be dust?
Doth charity, prime gift of Heaven's Dove,
Bid each of us with all live hand in glove?
Her score in life's rough game, whate'er the count above, is love.
                    —Lambda

Archdeacon and rector would rightly have taken objection to that!

The only piece to fall into the third category, of sincere writing, was '*Art Cycle*', for which Mr Boringer had expressed a liking after tea that afternoon. Here it is:

To her hairy lord cried the cave-woman
'What doest now
Pricking with flint thy wooden club-handle?'
Gave answer he:
'I mind the boar that I killed yesterday:
Thus was his head; his body thus;
And thus his legs—
Oh! but I had forgotten his tusks!
His tusks were so.'
'Fool!' frowned the woman, 'Fool!
Thy silly scratches shall not make a hog!
'Generations pass: their great-great-grandchildren
Cluster along the cave wall staring agape
At where a youth in charcoal, chalk and berry-stains
Has limned and daubed a story of the chase.
'See there, a boar!

And here a bear:
A fox, a polecat, and a badger!
Hounds too below.'
'Oh! wonderful,' they cry; 'wonderful!
He has caged all beasts of the forest on our wall!'
Millennia lapse into man-made history.
Great lives are lived;
Great deaths died; great names writ
By dint of music, letters, art, philosophy.
'Mark ye,' proclaims a painter's pupil,
'How the master never copies but creates:
His form robes essence;
Just like God in Genesis
He makes the light and sees that it is good:
And it is so.
The man who sat for yon portrait
Died of a quinsy yesteryear and lies
In an already unremembered grave.
Yet, new begotten of the master's brush,
Regenerate in paint and canvas,
He will live on, just as our master made him,
Through ages to attest the painter's power
E'en by his own anonymous nonentity!'
Noontide now turns to even; ripeness to rot;
Scions of giants grow pygmified
From grovelling under low roofs of convention,
Genuflecting to their idols of the past,
Breathing stale incense, nervous of open air,
Mumbling worn rules and musty shibboleths,
Followers all, spunkless to blaze new trails!
Critics, alas, abet.
'At the Dafton Gallery Mr Richard Doe, R.A.
Shows canvasses finely redolent of—and—.'
(Fill in the gaps with any old master's name;
You need not trouble to assess their affinity.)
What falser oracle?
As though a mill can grind with the water that has passed!
Revolt sets in; not with return to simpleness and truth,
But with much paraphernalia of isms and ologies
Pretentiously paraded by fists and ites;

Who, in their heresy of art for the artist's sake,
Mistake ingenious encipherment for creation
And puzzles for profundity,
Forcing the unled unfed multitude to pursue
Photography in Philistia.
Says Mr X:
'I'm glad we let young Harold study art:
He'll be a genius!
Just you look at this:
"The Boar Hunt".
Yet I can recognise nor boar nor hounds,
Nor anything resembling either,
Though it is possibly suggestive of a hunt breakfast.'
'How clever of him!' Mrs X replies:
But faint across the chasm of the years
Echoes the judgment of the cave-woman,
'Fool!' she frowns, fool!'
Thy silly scratches shall not make a hog!'

—Omicron

Having heard from the rector that Tresdale once had a picture of his hung in the academy, Lynton believed that the foregoing must represent some reflection of his true personality. That was what he would suggest to the rector at breakfast next morning.

It was now eleven o'clock and, tossing *Kidbury Notebook* on to a table, Lynton turned with relief to the last chapters of a detective novel that he had been reading in the train that morning. So engrossing was the plot that he read on to the end of the book; and, as he closed it, the chimes of midnight broke from the church belfry. Noticing that it was full moon he let himself out of the front door for a stroll down the drive before going to bed. The air was warm and close. Although the moon shone clear overhead, there were winks of sheet lightning from clouds to the eastward. On reaching the drive gate he leaned over it and lit a cigarette. Then, as he threw the dead match on to the road outside, he became aware of some belated traveller stepping briskly along it in his direction. As this figure drew level with the gate it halted; and, with the moonlight now full on its face, stood staring at him. It was speaking, too.

'So, what Upsilon told me an hour ago is true!' The voice was shaky, but clear. 'There is a guest at the rectory. I see him now at the gate, as Upsilon foretold. The spirits will have read his thoughts, and through him have discovered my interpolations. I wanted so badly to see myself in print! This they will never forgive. What will they do to me?'

At that the voice suddenly broke; and with a catch in his breath the speaker started to run—to run madly, as though he were hunted and a pursuer close at his heels.

Lynton too almost ran, so hurried were his paces back along the drive. At one point he jumped over the black shadow of a tree trunk. A dim light behind the blinds of an upper window showed that his host was still awake; and of this he was glad Climbing the stairs two steps at a time he knocked at the door, and was told to come in. 'rector,' he said, 'I have just seen, and heard, Tresdale!' With that beginning they talked for more than an hour.

<h1 style="text-align:center">5</h1>

All that has been told so far happened on a Thursday: we now skip to the following Sunday. First, however, an introduction is needed to Mrs Bruckett. If ever the words buxom and bonny adequately described a woman, that woman was Matilda Bruckett. You did not notice the colour of her hair or of her eyes, nor whether she were tall or short; only that she was bonny and buxom. To talk to her was to experience a sense of honesty, gaiety and contentment. 'Tilly' everybody called her, and 'Tilly' she liked to be called. She was, and owned herself with pride to be, a charwoman. In that capacity she would visit Mr Tresdale's railway carriages on three mornings in the week: Sundays, Tuesdays and Thursdays. 'I don't 'old with working on what some calls the Sabbath,' she confided to the rector, 'but, there, Mr Tresdale requires it, and I ain't a one to argify with a genelman as knows what he wants and pays accordin'. So that's why I comes to church these days of a hevening' 'stead of morning. I never could abide that Litany neither; beggin' your pardon, sir, for I knows as it wasn't you as wrote it.'

At the Lion and Unicorn of a Saturday evening Tilly Bruckett would eke out a half-pint of bitter with gossip about her *clientèle*. 'Mr Tresdale now were that strange,' she was heard to say; 'what with livin' in them railway carriages, and 'is goin's on with sperrits as only 'imself could see and 'ear. Sperrits be better than dogs though, for they doesn't make no mess about a place: which ain't surprisin' seein' as 'ow I don't believe there are no such things, 'spite of all 'is talk.'

It was a less philosophical Tilly that fidgeted impatiently in the church porch that Sunday, awaiting the termination of Mattins, and ready to pounce on Dr Farrold the moment that he emerged. "Ooever would want to marry 'is grandmother,' she muttered indignantly with a contemptuous glance at the Table of Kindred and Affinity, 'short of a loony! There; that's the last 'ymn, that be, and I 'ope as old Tasker won't loiter with the bag or the organ'll play twiddledy bits at the end. Ah! That's the Hamen all right, and now they'll be coming out.'

So, they did, to the strains of Handel's march from *Scipione;* and Dr Farrold found himself all of a sudden in the unceremonious clutches of Mrs Brackett.

'Come at once, Sir,' she said, 'and take me with you in the car as far as Gander's Green where we'll 'ave to cross the fields by the footpath. Mr Tresdale's been and taken a fit, and I left 'im lying on the floor as good as dead. Couldn't lift or move 'im', I couldn't, 'e's that 'eavy. Oh! Come along, Sir, or maybe 'e'll be gone.'

Lynton, coming out of the church door, found his way obstructed by Mrs Bruckett's seizure of the doctor, and to him the latter now turned.

'We haven't met yet,' Dr Farrold said, 'but I saw you in the rectory pew, and I may need assistance if Tresdale has to be got out across the fields. Could you come with me?'

'Why, certainly, of course. I'll just look in at the vestry and tell the rector that I may be late for lunch.'

'Right! I'll drive down to the surgery for a stretcher, and come back here for you in five minutes. The rector may like to come too. And you, Mrs Bruckett, please go at once and find the district nurse. If she's in, you can hire the Lion and Unicorn's car, and bring her down with you to Gander's Green and across to Mr Tresdale's. We may need her help too.'

Mrs Bruckett made off as directed, and Lynton found the rector very ready to accompany him. In a matter of minutes therefore they were driving down Hagland Hollow on their way to Gander's Green. There they alighted, climbed over the stile and hurried afoot over the fields.

On arrival at Tresdale's enclosure Mr Vinetree removed his hat, and, bowing reverently, said 'Peace be to—to these railway carriages.' The doctor, meanwhile, being several yards ahead, pushed eagerly into the middle carriage that had once been a saloon. There, still prostrate on the floor, lay Mr Tresdale, with one outstretched hand resting upon an open notebook. On a low table, and just above his head, stood the dummy wireless set and television screen.

'Take the table and other junk away, will you?' Dr Farrold requested, kicking the notebook to one side. 'I shall need more room here.'

Lynton and the rector were quick to do his bidding, and set the table (with the other articles upon it) on the pavement outside. While the doctor knelt to examine his patient, Mr Vinetree took up the notebook and began to read. His reaction to whatever he found written there seemed to Lynton unnecessarily theatrical: reminiscent of that once popular print in which Moses is depicted dashing to pieces on a rock the first edition of the decalogue. Lifting first the wireless case, and then the television screen, above his head with both hands he hurled them on to the brick pavement and smashed them utterly.

'Here, for God's sake stop making such a damned noise!' ejaculated the doctor, unmindful of to whom he spoke; and then, in a lower voice, 'By Jove, though, it seems to have woken him up! Hand me that brandy flask, will you, out of my bag.'

They did not need the stretcher. Tresdale, though dazed and speechless, managed to totter along through the fields, supported on either side by the doctor and Lynton. Mr Vinetree carried the doctor's bag, and the notebook. At the stile they met Mrs Bruckett and the district nurse. The latter was placed in charge of Tresdale in the back of the doctor's car; and, with the rector in the front seat beside him, Dr Farrold drove off to Thornychurch hospital. Lynton was left with Mrs Bruckett to go back and pack up Tresdale's night attire and sponges in a suitcase, to put the place generally in order, and then to lock up the railway carriages.

6

Dr Farrold had supper after evensong at the rectory. 'I must thank you both,' he said, 'for your help this morning. It's a queer case, and the hospital people can't make head or tail of it. Mental, they think, rather than physical; but the poor chap is half-starved after living alone there with nobody to cook for him. They're shifting him to that nursing-home at Funtingham tomorrow. By the way, Vinetree, that was a rum text you preached from this evening. *My name is Legion, for we are many.* Were you by any chance thinking of Tresdale?'

The rector nodded. 'I've thought of nothing else since we got back from Thornychurch. You see, I read what he had written in that notebook. You two had better have a look at it before I burn it, as I certainly shall. Here it is.'

The notes were in pencil and decreased sadly in legibility as they went on. These paragraphs were, however, more or less easily decipherable:

You will die from the toes upward. Tomorrow you will be ankle deep in death. Take off your socks and look at your feet. White! The blood will never. . .

Your shin and calves are numb: but, kneeling before us, you still feel the boards beneath your knees. For the last time.

You do not care to kneel today. You may lie on your belly and place the notebook on the floor. Take a needle and prick your thighs. They are dying.

It is difficult to write now for your fingers are dead. You broke that glass in your hand because you could not feel it. Take care of that cup of milk at your elbow. Drink it before you upset it, for it is your last.

You no longer hunger or thirst for your stomach is dead. We will respite brain, lung and heart and take only your eyes today. You are blind.

You still write what you hear, though the lines are crooked and your letters misshaped. That is well. We wish our punishment of you to be recorded.

Within an hour you will be deaf. There will thus be no more for you to write, and your arms now die. Your brain will alone survive to take your punishment; until you starve.

Tomorrow de. . .

'No, rector,' Dr Farrold emphatically objected, 'you must not burn this book. It may help in the treatment of the case. Thank you: I will take it with me.'

7

Did Mr Tresdale recover? After eight months' treatment under Professor Hasterton, the eminent psychiatrist, he did. He lives now, and paints all day, at a resort on the East Coast. Several more of his pictures have been hung in the Academy.

A year, almost to the day, after the events here narrated, Frank Lynton was again staying at Kidbury Rectory. He and the rector took a walk together to Farnley Edge, and stood gazing in silence at the steaming weald below. The rector was the first to speak. 'Those wretched railway carriages are still there,' he complained. 'I heard that they, and the field too, had been sold. So, I was hoping that they would have been removed by now.'

Lynton continued to gaze; unhearingly, it seemed. Then after a minute or two he remarked, still gazing, 'They wouldn't be seen from here if they were camouflaged green and brown. I can imagine no more delightful spot for a quiet weekend. In point of fact, I've bought them and the field myself.'

Note—It is probable that Mr Lynton did the archdeacon injustice in supposing that 'he could have done no more than look at the cover' of the magazine. It seems more likely indeed that Mr Lynton himself omitted to look through the pages headed '*Children's Corner*'; unless, which is possible, the rector had already excised them. Those pages included three sets of verses (each subscribed IOTA), none of which would appear wholesome meat for children. The reader, however, can judge for himself, for here they are:

LULLABY
Go to sleep, little one,
Shades of the night
Huddle around you
Gathering might:
Go to sleep, little one,
Till the daylight.

Go to sleep, little one,
Better to dream
Than know who enters
On the moonbeam:
So, to sleep, little one:
Eyes are agleam!

Quick to sleep, little one,
Lest you should see
What until cockcrow
Lurks in yon tree!
Safer, dear wee one, to
Sleep and let be.

FIVE-FINGER EXERCISE
The fire burns blue with caves of green,
A Hand amid the coals is seen,
A shrivelled hand with fingers charred:

The three who watch are breathing hard.
Did he who counselled this ordeal
Believe the Thing he spake of real?
How should they know, who breathe so hard
Watching that Hand, those fingers charred.
The fire burns bluer yet, they ween,
As something slips the bars between:
A cinder? No; it has no glow
Nor tinkled as it fell below.
As crab along a tidal edge
It sidles to the fender-ledge:
Each watcher tightly grips his chair,
The very silence screams 'Beware!'
Across the rug it flatly creeps,
Then, arched on five charred fingers, leaps!
Leaps to the rear of them that sit,
They have no longer sight of it.
But sounds they hear—a touch, a scrape:
They loathe but listen, mouths agape,
Cursing beneath held breath the Fate
That loosed this Terror from the grate.
Moments are frozen into years,
But comes no respite to their fears:
A reek of charnel taints the air,
But where the climber? Whose the chair?
At last a sob, a choke, a gasp,
A gurgling as burnt nails unclasp!
Blue sinks the fire, its caves dim green;
Within, once more, a Hand is seen.
A clock beneath the stair strikes one:
The Orders of the Night are done!
Two watchers rise to seek a bed;
The third still sits there silent—dead!
A grey dawn breaks on Fonterill;
White shroud of mist still wraps the hill,
When creaking fleshless shoulders bring
Another load to Kirsney Ring.

BED TALE
Burdened and wayworn up the drive
He limped, belated last guest to arrive,

When frost bit hard and snow lay deep on Hampden Clive.
Midnight had chimed an hour ago:
No gleam from any window lit the snow,
Only a narrow bar of light the door below.
A footman met him at the gate:
'The Master doesn't' old with sitting late,
'E told the other gents, what's staying, not to wait.
This 'ere's your candle, sir. Take care!
There ain't no carpet on the broken stair,
The whole place, if you asks me, badly needs repair.
Your room, sir! Fire don't seem alight;
Can't 'elp it, though; them logs is damp tonight.
I'll call you, sir, at eight: breakfast's at nine.
Goodnight!' The candles gutter: in the gloom
The guest now has remembrance of a room
In which 'twas said that old Sir Hubert met his doom.
There is no bottle in the bed,
And yet the sheets are warm! An ugly dread
Causes him seize the quilt and with it hide his head.
A bell tolls three. Still, still awake
He dares peep out—to see a curtain shake
And the red bell-cord sway and dangle like a snake.
How hot the sheets! Yet he how cold!
With what caress his body they enfold,
Too cold, too numb to rise and force them loose their hold.
Swathing of Death! The bed a tomb!
Ask not upon what warp or weft or loom
Were woven, by what hand, those living sheets of doom.

Tall Tales but True

'Telling a story' is in nursery parlance a euphemism for speaking untruth. Such use of the phrase is not unwarranted. No tale ever told or written has been wholly true. So much is missed in observation, omitted through forgetfulness, misinterpreted in judgment, misrepresented in verbal expression. History in consequence is never a full reflection, seldom a fair summary, too often a distortion, of events. Distortion is indeed inevitable when a record is handed down, not in writing or in memorised saga, but from mouth to ear, from ear to mouth, over a generation or more.

All this is prefatory to stating that each of the two tales that follow is what is commonly termed a true story. They are not, that is to say, of the narrator's invention, but a reproduction of what has been told him, in varying versions, about unusual occurrences which actually took place: the first in the late eighties or early nineties of last century, the second in the first decade of this.

1. A Phantom Butler

If the reader has found the foregoing introduction stilted and pretentious it will have served to prepare him for the presence of those qualities in the character of Tertius Holyoak Burnstable, British Officer-in-Charge of the small Malay state called Penyabong. To the few pioneer planters in that district, as well as to his colleagues in Government service, he was known as a generous, good-hearted fellow enough, but 'sticky'; confoundedly sticky. He was a tall, well-groomed, finely featured man of forty or so; very well pleased with himself in his role of virtual autocrat of a tiny territory recently brought under British protection. Riding, driving a tandem, and shooting were his main outdoor pursuits; billiards and whist his indoor recreations. He read novels, and had once written one.

Nobody who stayed at the Residency was allowed to leave without taking with him a presentation copy signed by the author. Such visitors were invariably persons of social distinction or of high official rank; for Burnstable was particular about his invitations, having admonished the central Secretariat that in their postings of public servants 'none but thoroughbreds' should be sent to Penyabong. It's blood,' he would say, 'that Malays and planters respect; not brains.' On one occasion he demanded the recall of a young surveyor on the ground that he had dropped an aitch in the course of official conversation.

Hospitality at the Residency was frequent and lavish. Unlike most Englishmen out East, Burnstable kept a large and choice cellar. His Chinese cook was no rough novice from Hainan, but the ex-chef of a well-known restaurant in Hong Kong. The table servants, however, were all Malays, attired, at their master's expense, in exquisite silk *sarongs* and *bajus*. Three of them, local recruits, had been drilled and trained to a fair level of proficiency by an admirable head-boy, or butler, from Penang. This was Ahmad, a Tamil strain in whose ancestry was evidenced by a darker skin than is usual for a Malay and a more nimble intelligence. The latter enabled him to imbue the local staff with a sense of their own inferiority, and to exact from Burnstable wages and pickings much in excess of the current standard. Ahmad in return rendered superlative service, with a cat-like contentment if not dog-like devotion. He was in fact *major-domo*.

That Lord Lettiswood, noblest of noble acquaintances, should have proposed himself for a weekend visit just when Ahmad was away on a fortnight's holiday in Malacca was most upsetting to Burnstable. There was no postponing the visit, however, for the ship in which his lordship was making a trip to China would not be in Malayan waters for more than five days. Burnstable therefore telegraphed to his Malacca friend Reddington (whose office *peon* was Ahmad's half-brother) requesting him to bid Ahmad cut short his holiday, and take the remainder of it later. To this telegram came the reply that Ahmad was down with malaria, and his immediate return out of the question. Burnstable swore.

He swore again when, on the very morning of Lord Lettiswood's arrival, the District Surveyor and the Public Works Engineer brought him a letter from the Secretariat requiring them to conduct a surprise survey of the district treasury. Such surveys were a periodically recurring nuisance, tying him to the office while cash and stamps were counted and ledgers inspected. Today he had intended absence from office in order to supervise preparations for the reception of his noble visitor by the Residency staff. Now he must leave them to their own devices.

Then, to cap all, Lord Lettiswood arrived a full hour before he was expected, and while Burnstable was still detained by the treasury inspection. When he at last got home, a few minutes before lunchtime, his guest was drinking a gin swizzle in a deckchair on the verandah.

'By Jove, Burnstable,' he said, 'your boys know how to mix a drink. The mint makes all the difference. Absinthe, too. I liked the way your old chap stood over the young 'un while he was concocting it. Nothing like training the young idea!'

Burnstable looked surprised. 'I was afraid that you mightn't find my staff quite up to scratch perhaps, because my head-boy is away in Malacca and down with fever. These local lads mean well enough, but they're young and raw.'

'Surely not that *old* chap? If he's your number two, number one must be a paragon.'

Conversation was interrupted at this point by the gong for tiffin, which was served far more deftly and expeditiously than Burnstable had dared to expect in Ahmad's absence. The real test, however, would come with dinner, to which he had invited six or seven guests to meet the noble visitor.

Afternoon and early evening were spent by host and guest in an expedition to the Ginting Merah waterfall, so that the Residency servants were again spared any fussy interference from their master. Lord Lettiswood was more impressed during their ride by the jungle scenery than by Burnstable's conversation, which was a long-winded reproduction of his last annual administration report. Matters of interest are often made uninteresting.

Despite an entire absence of ladies (the white population of the district being wholly male) the Residency dinner proceeded most decorously. Burnstable had warned Lord Lettiswood that he might find some of the guests rather rough diamonds, but the gentlemen so described found his lordship far less 'sticky' and much more interested in their daily doings than Burnstable had ever been. For the first time they felt at their ease in the Residency; for Lord Lettiswood was a good mixer and drew each of them out. Even dour old Sandy Matheson from Ulu Sibarau waxed conversational.

Burnstable, attributing the success of his party to good wine and a Lucullan menu, and finding that conversation needed no stimulus or reinforcement from himself, was able carefully to watch the waiting and attendance. The staff were certainly doing splendidly, just as if Ahmad were there. This passing thought of his head-boy caused him to turn his eyes towards a corner of the big Chinese blackwood screen behind the sideboard, from which point Ahmad had been wont to direct and supervise his assistants. Ah! so that was why everything was going so well and smoothly: Ahmad was there! He must have recovered quickly from the fever, and caught the afternoon mail *gharri* from Malacca. He was looking far from well, though, his cheeks wearing that clayey hue which on a brown skin corresponds to pallor. The nose was peaky and the eyes sunken. Burnstable regretted now that he had sent that telegram. Thirty-four miles in a mail *gharri* on top of a bout of malaria would be too much for any man; and Ahmad had never been robust. He must tell him to go to bed at once. That Ahmad saw him beckon he was sure, for the sunken eyes turned towards him. Ahmad, however, did not move.

The district surveyor was at this moment explaining to Lord Lettiswood a point of local matriarchal custom; and explaining it wrongly. Burnstable itched to interrupt and contradict, for he considered himself an authority on local custom. He found it impossible, though, to concentrate sufficiently on what was being said or to take his eyes or his thoughts off Ahmad. What could it be that so gripped and distracted him? He felt somehow, as he put this question to himself, that he would rather have it unanswered. This feeling arose from a consciousness of something being not quite right somewhere. For the first time in his life Burnstable was ill at ease at his own table. He hoped that nobody was noticing his stare.

He started violently when a fork or spoon dropped from the sideboard on to the floor at Ahmad's feet. One of the boys stooped and picked it up; but, as he did so, Burnstable noticed something that the boy apparently did not. The spoon had dropped, but not at Ahmad's feet. *For Ahmad had no feet!* The standing figure ended abruptly at the bottom hem of its *sarong*. For all its appearance of solidity, it must be floating on air. Then, just as Burnstable muttered to himself something about optical illusions, another boy coming with a dish from the kitchen walked straight through the figure.

Burnstable prided himself on his strong nerve. Subduing with a determined effort both fear and curiosity he plunged into the general conversation: so successfully that his guests on leaving remarked to each other that they had never known sticky old B. in such form. While talking, however, he darted frequent glances at the figure by the screen. It was still there when the company left the dining-room and passed out on to the verandah.

Burnstable knew better than to question his servants about what might arouse suspicions of the Residency being an 'unquiet' house. When, next morning, he complimented the second boy on the waiting at dinner he received the reply that they had all been careful to remember what Ahmad had taught them. So, *they* had seen nothing! Lord Lettiswood, however, before taking his leave handed a ten-dollar note to his host. 'I can't find your old chap about this morning,' he said, 'to give him this tip. So, you must do it for me. He's a marvel, isn't he? Such a quiet way of managing your other boys, and never a word audible. I should be careful of him, if I were you; for he doesn't look too fit.'

Ten days later Ahmad returned from Malacca. 'Never before have I taken the fever so badly,' he told Burnstable, 'On the day of your dinner party I was like a madman. I seemed to see you beckon to me and I strained every muscle to get up. My feet, however, felt embedded in the sand where I lay beneath the coconut tree outside my brother's house. I set myself to pull and drag them out; till, suddenly, they snapped off just above the ankle, and my body bobbed up like a bladder that has been held under water. Then there was a rushing of wind, and I seemed blown through the clouds and rain back here to Penyabong, where I found myself attending to Tuan's visitor. At dinner I saw that Sulong and the other servants were doing as I had taught them; so I felt very happy, except for having left my feet behind in Malacca. That was a strange dream, Tuan, was it not? But the fever was hot on me when I dreamed it.'

When Burnstable related what has here been told to the Malay Chief of Penyabong, the old man smiled and nodded. 'Shadows are sometimes thrown to a great distance,' he said.

2. DIPLOTOPIA

That the old fort house was said to be haunted is of importance to the extent that it was such hearsay that once prompted enquiry of a tenant as to whether he had ever seen or heard anything.

'Nothing,' came the reply, 'nor has my wife. All the same there's a queerness about the place that neither of us likes. We shall be glad to get into the hill bungalow when the Joneses go on leave.'

The speaker was Roland Belstrow, Assistant District Officer at Sialang from 1909 to 1911. A promising young Civil Servant, not yet thirty, he had recently married Diana Dowland, whose brother, Philip, was manager of Sialang Rubber Estate.

'What do I mean by queerness? Well, just queerness: there's no other name to it. Ever since we've lived here quite ordinary things seem to go a bit queer, and it makes us feel uncomfortable. For instance, there was that business with my brother-in-law. He had to consult Diana about some point in their father's will, and so—I'll give you his account first—he called in here one afternoon a little before tea-time. Sinnatambi, our Tamil boy, told him that we had gone away for the day up to Kuala Pasir, to do some shopping, and that we shouldn't be back until the seven o'clock train. Philip, however, said that he had just seen us walking up the short-cut from the station, and that we must have caught the four o'clock. Sinnatambi therefore went into the kitchen and prepared tea for the three of us. When (so Sinnatambi told us on our return) he came back ten minutes later with the tea things, he found Philip talking and laughing in a chair on the verandah as though he had company. He was, however, alone and Sinnatambi thought he must be tipsy. There seemed indeed to be no doubt about it when Sinnatambi came to clear away and wash-up; for Philip had drunk from all three cups and eaten from all three plates.

As Sinnatambi was telling us this at dinner-time, Diana and I concluded that it must have been *he* that had been drunk; and I will tell you why. We had run across Philip that afternoon at the Kuala Pasir club, and *he had had tea with us at the Orient Hotel*. Nevertheless, that Sinnatambi had not been drinking was soon obvious enough from the steady hand with which he poured out Diana's glass of sherry and my gin *pahit*. We discussed the matter over our dinner, and put a few questions to Sinnatambi; all of which he answered with composure and coherence. Alternative solutions seemed to be: either somebody had impersonated Philip (which appeared most unlikely), or Sinnatambi had been dreaming.

Both alternatives, however, were knocked on the head by what Philip told us after church next Sunday. He insisted that he had had tea with us *on the fort verandah* and, by way of evidence, produced a green pocket-book in which he had noted down what Diana and he had agreed to concerning their father's will. 'But,' said Diana, 'I saw you jot that down while we were sitting in the lounge of the Orient Hotel.' 'What nonsense,' Philip replied; 'I haven't been up to Kuala Pasir since Christmas.'

Well, there it was—and is; Diana's word and mine against that of

Philip and Sinnatambi; and no reason why any of us should be lying. That's what I meant by quite ordinary things going queer. As I said just now, we shall be damned glad when the Joneses go, and we get into the hill bungalow.'

A Book Entry

1

The Government House calling-book was of great size and weight: so big and heavy that nobody could walk off with it unnoticed. It was safe, therefore, to leave it unattended during daylight hours, laid open impressively on a shelf in the kiosk below the Flamboyant trees at the main gate.

Punctually every morning at nine o'clock it was deposited there, and as punctually every evening at half-past six removed, by two scarlet-hatted, scarlet-sashed *peons*. This function they performed with such evident satisfaction to their personal vanity as to make of it almost a ceremony. Indeed, the *aide-de-camp* referred to it in his Routine Orders as '*the Procession of the Book*'.

Before the governorship of Sir Oscar Sallerton, an unwritten law prevailed in Takeokuta as to who were, and who were not, to write their names in the book. On the official side Heads of Departments *must*, their deputies *should,* and other officers of more than ten years' seniority *might*, inscribe their signatures. Of unofficials, members of the Legislature *must*, Town Councillors *should*, heads of the mercantile houses and persons authorised to sign for them '*per pro*' *might* sign. All others might *not*. Such traditional limitation served a utilitarian purpose. It meant that every signatory could be invited to a formal luncheon or dinner party twice a year without overcrowding the dining-hall or over-taxing the gvernor's culinary staff.

Whether Sir Oscar found himself bored by the thus selected few, or overcome by a democratic conscience towards the thus excluded many, must be a matter for conjecture. All that is known for certain is that, in the third year of a not very popular reign, he instructed his A.D.C. to make it generally known that any loyal citizen was welcome to call at Government House. Every taxpayer, said His Excellency, contributed towards the governor's entertainment allowance; and was entitled to a *quid pro quo*. Though he couldn't ask more people to dinner than he was already doing, he proposed to give occasional garden-parties to which every Tom, Dick or Harry could be invited. It was unfortunate, perhaps, that Captain Preen should have repeated the use of this formula at the Takeokuta Club; for it inspired inscription in the calling-book next morning of the pseudonymous entries 'A. Thomas, A. Richard and A. Henry.'

If, as a consequence of Sir Oscar's revolutionary ruling, the calling-book lost significance as an index of people's social standing, it became on the other hand a treasury of Kongean autography. Aspiring minor chiefs wrote their titles in decorative curvilinear Kongahili script, and competitive merchants their business addresses in impeccable copy-book style. Here and there, in purposeful contrast, a resentful patrician would indulge a pride in illegibility; or a self-conscious aesthete eke out his signature with fanciful twirl or flourish. Yet the only eyes to feast on the inscribed pages were those of Mr Ariyasonu, the clerk whose business it was to copy entries from the calling-book into the Government House entertainment register.

These daily postings seldom presented any difficulty. Nevertheless, it was a standing instruction that, should doubt or question arise, immediate reference must be made to the private secretary. This was why Ariyasonu felt it his duty to invite Mr Lushmoor's attention to an apparent breach of etiquette on the part of a caller who signed his name as U. Nomi.

'This gentleman,' he explained, 'is signing the book after last three garden-parties, but is never answering invitations. That is surely wrongful, Your Honour; for the capital letters on invitation card say "Reply Soon, Very Pressing".'

Mr Lushmoor smiled. 'So that's *your* reading of R. S. V. P., is it? Not such a bad one, either! But tell me, Ariyasonu, who is this Mr U. Nomi, who doesn't answer invitations?'

'God alone is knowing, Sir. It is not a Kongean name.'

'Nor a European one either, by the sound of it. *You know me!* Well, apparently, that's just what we don't. A practical joker, perhaps.'

Mr Ariyasonu looked, and was, pained. The very suggestion of a jocular entry in The Book offended not only his sense of propriety but his feelings of loyalty. Were not the Crown and Royal Cipher deeply embossed in gold upon its red morocco cover? Nay, more; did not its pages enshrine the actual signature of one Royal Highness? Fortunately for his peace of mind he had copied without suspicion the fictitious signatures of A. Thomas, A. Richard and A. Henry, and had since wondered why the three gentlemen did not call again. So far as it is possible for a subordinate to show disapproval of his senior officer without disrespect, Ariyasonu now hinted it in his reply to Mr Lushmoor.

'Your Honour must excuse me,' he said, 'but nobody can dare to write wrongfully in the King's book. If this one or that one has written U. Nomi; then U. Nomi is surely this one or that one's true name. Indubittably.'

Mr Ariyasonu's fondness for long words outreached his knowledge of their pronunciation, and 'indubitably' is here spelt as he pronounced it. Indubitably,' he repeated with emphasis.

'Well, let's hope you may be right, Ariyasonu,' the private secretary replied, anxious to mollify. 'You might perhaps try and find out from the postal people whether they've got anybody named Nomi on their delivery lists. Captain Preen can also enquire of the police. Of one thing I'm absolutely certain, and that is that, if the fellow has ever attended a garden-party, he's never presented himself for introduction to His Excellency. Fancy having to announce "Mr You Know Me"! Captain Preen and I would certainly have remembered it.'

Enquiry of the Police proved fruitless. The post office was more informative. None of the three garden-party invitations had been delivered! As no address had been given beyond 'U. Nomi, Esq., Takeokuta', and as the addressee was unknown to any postal servant, the envelopes had been placed in the Poste Restante rack, and there they still lay. It could be inferred therefore that the coincidence of garden-party dates with those of Mr Nomi's calls had been purely fortuitous.

Indubitably,' agreed Mr Ariyasonu, relieved that there had been no breach of etiquette in the matter of answering invitations; 'no address was written in the book, and so I myself wrote "Takeokuta" in speculation only on the envelopes. Wherefore they have sat simply in postal waiting-box; but without my fault.'

'Yes, that's all right, Ariyasonu. But there still remains,' Lushmoor added, 'the question as to who wrote that name in the book. It's you who look through the entries every evening; so, if you come across Mr Nomi's name again, let me know at once; or, if I happen to be out, leave a note on my desk. Captain Preen has promised to inform the Police should the entry be repeated.'

At this point, for some two or three months, the matter rested.

2

It was about eight o'clock of a morning in early June that Toby Lushmoor dismounted at the stable gate and, leaving his horse to the *syce*, strolled over to the office to see whether the day's mail was light or heavy. A large and varied assortment of envelopes lay on the table; most of them, he saw with relief, of an unofficial sort that would be found to contain answers to invitations for the King's Birthday garden-party. Only a dozen or so bore the printed superscription 'On His Majesty's Service'. Placing these on one side he tossed the remainder into the clerk's tray. As he did so, he remembered that Ariyasonu had yesterday requested the issue of a new calling-book; but, before issuing it, he would see how many pages were left in the old one. Walking therefore to the table whereon it awaited the 'morning procession', he heaved it open, and, glancing at the latest entry, gave a little grunt of surprise. U. Nomi! Why on earth hadn't Ariyasonu told him last night, as he had promised to do? He must put him on the mat after breakfast.

Telling Preen, over their poached eggs, of his discovery and of Ariyasonu's default, Lushmoor added that, on seeing the signature, he had experienced a strange sense of familiarity with the handwriting. Would Preen come and have a look at it? While he was still speaking a *peon* hurried in with a memorandum form, to which a red 'Immediate Action' label had been pinned. It ran:

> To Private Secretary, from Chief Clerk. Your Honour, there is further autograph of U. Nomi in calling-book also, which is enigma only as book was without said autograph at 7.18 p.m. when I am leaving office. It will behove therefore to investigate.
> T. Ariyasonu.

'Well, that's a queer show,' Lushmoor commented, 'for the book's been lying in my office all night. Let's go and have a look at it, if you've finished your coffee.'

Three minutes later they stood before the book; Preen with a puzzled frown as he peered at the signature. 'Impossible!' he muttered.

'What's impossible?'

'Identification of handwriting from only two capital and three small letters. Still, I agree with you that there seems something reminiscent about it. I'll get on to the Police again this morning.' As soon as Preen had gone Lushmoor took another and longer look at the signature. He felt convinced that, when he muttered 'impossible', Preen had noticed what he himself had noticed; and had, like himself, written it off as impossible. What this was, and that it was not impossible, the following pages will make clear.

From this scrutiny and meditation Lushmoor was roused by a deferential cough. 'Your Honour has received my memorandum?' Ariyasonu began interrogatively; and at an affirmative nod, went on: 'It is greatly wrongful that anybody should sign in the night-times; and yet how not so? At seven eighteen I am leaving book here in accustomed location, and last name is Mr and Mrs Darley-Fernchurch. Next, when I come this early morning, I see the writing of U. Nomi. Wherefore it is done in the night-times and in this office also. I am asking myself many times who is culprit. The new *peon*, Your Honour. . .'

'Cannot write English,' interrupted Lushmoor, 'and so is out of it.'

'But, Sir, all others are long time tried and trustable; Your Honour will not be suspecting. . .'

'I suspect nobody, Ariyasonu; the thing's just unaccountable, and I doubt if the police'll be able to make anything of it. However, I mean to try a bit of sleuth stuff myself. I'm going to have my things moved to the downstairs bedroom across there; and, if in future you will place the book on the desk instead of the side-table, I shall be able to keep an eye on it even when in bed. The doors, you see, are opposite each other and both can be left open so long as I sleep there. Anybody signing the book must have a light to do it by, and I always wake up if there's a light. I shan't expect an early disturbance, though; for this Nomi fellow signs at pretty long intervals.'

Mr Ariyasonu appeared pleased at this plan of action. 'I am much grateful,' he replied, 'that Your Honour is believing my word that this writing was done in the night-times: for, if Your Honour not believing, where shall be my proof?'

'In the ink, Ariyasonu, in the ink: *you'll* never make a detective. The *peon* must have put some red ink into this black inkpot; for the stuff writes a dull purple. The signature, unlike the other signatures, is a dull purple. Therefore, it must have been written here, and the book is only here at night.'

'Ah! Sir, I never noticed that.'

Nor indeed had Lushmoor until a minute or two ago.

3

Lushmoor was right in his prognosis that weeks would pass without any repetition of the Nomi signature. They were not, however, in other respects uneventful for the inmates of Government House.

Dinners and luncheons had to be postponed more than once owing to Lady Sallerton's ill-health. She had been married to the governor during his last furlough, and was as generally popular in Kongea as he was not. The people contrasted her unaffected gladness to meet them with his standoffishness; her readiness to listen and sympathise with his indifference or cynicism. Over bridge tables at the Takeokuta Club, talk would sometimes dwell on the future prospects of what appeared a union of opposites, and the Colonial Secretary's wife maintain a rather too affirmative silence whenever it was hinted that all was not well between the governor and his lady. Later, when the wife of a public works department official charged with checking the Government House furniture inventory whispered that Lady Sallerton no longer slept in the same wing as His Excellency, her hearers shook their heads knowingly and smiled grimly at their cards.

The mirror of truth was by no means a permanent fixture in the ladies' bridge-room; but in this case their information was correct. Lady Sallerton *had* changed her room, and by doctor's order. She was suffering from disturbed nights and, under his cross-examination, had disclosed the fact that her husband not only snored but also chattered in his sleep, sometimes loudly, in a language that she did not understand. It was, she surmised, one of those spoken in Luganda, his first colony, where he had won a name, and consequent early promotion, by averting a threatened revolt among the Sasseni tribesmen.

On hearing this, Dr Thraplow counselled her to sleep out of earshot in future, and so informed Sir Oscar. 'Certainly,' he replied, 'you may move her away as far as you like. It's strange, isn't it, that she never appears to hear what I say when I'm awake!' It was perhaps well that, Dr Thraplow being unmarried, this rejoinder did not find its way to the ladies' bridge-room.

Before very long it became quite clear to members of his staff that Sir Oscar resented his wife's having told the doctor of his talking in his sleep. But for him, Lushmoor and Preen would never have heard of it at all; Lady Sallerton never alluded to it. He, however, talked of her before them as 'my nocturnal eavesdropper', and seemed to delight in making her uncomfortable. A grave deterioration in marital relations was obvious; and Preen and Lushmoor, in their turn, felt uncomfortable. Their efforts to make small talk at meals were laborious but unfruitful; Lady Sallerton would be listless and the governor snappily ironical. When, therefore, a cablegram arrived imploring her ladyship to sail home to see her mother, who lay dangerously ill, Lushmoor and

Preen heaved a sigh of relief. So also did the doctor, unable to arrest her neurasthenia. She left for England in the s.s. *Lithuania;* and, with her embarkation, passes out of our story. It was rumoured later that she found her mother in excellent fettle, and that the cablegram had been sent on receipt of letters reflecting inclement conjugal weather. But this was *only* rumour.

The governor showed no sign of regret at Lady Sallerton's departure, but informed Preen and Lushmoor that they need not bother to talk to him at meals, unless they should have anything official to communicate. They could conserve their conversational powers for parties; which, he sourly added, was what they were paid for. A Trappist discipline thus ensued, unless there was company, and food was digested over books or newspapers.

About a fortnight after Lady Sallerton's departure Lushmoor awoke in the small hours of a moonless night, and lay listening for a repetition of any noise that might have aroused him. He then suddenly realised that it had not been a noise but a light, or rather a reflection of light, in the office opposite. Someone, he saw, must have switched on the lamps at the head of the grand staircase. Jumping out of bed he slipped noiselessly into the office to investigate. Yes, the top staircase lamps were on, and slowly descending the stairs moved a figure in blue-striped pyjamas.

Lushmoor crept quickly behind the stationery cupboard, and had hardly done so before the figure entered the office and pressed down the light switch by its door. In the glare of the ceiling light he watched the governor, for it was he, walk straight to the calling-book, dip a pen in the inkstand at its side, and write an entry. There was something startlingly robot-like about these movements and, as the figure retreated towards the door, Lushmoor noticed that, although the eyes were wide open, they were expressionless and unreflecting. So, Sir Oscar was both sleep-talker and sleep-walker! His Excellency switched off the light as he left the office and also, on regaining the landing, the lamps above the stairhead.

After a minute or more of darkness Lushmoor flicked the office light on again and looked in the calling-book. Mr U. Nomi had signed once more and 'in the night-times'.

4

Lushmoor was natty with his fingers. Nobody inspecting the calling-book four hours after the events just narrated would have told that a whole page (at whose top Sir Oscar had written the name of U. Nomi) had been extracted. This Lushmoor had done after careful reasoning. Sleep-walking, according to Kongean belief, is the result of a soul other than the sleeper's own animating the dormant body—a usurping tenancy which reflected discreditably on the temporarily disowned possessor. To let Ariyasonu know of the governor's somnambulism would, therefore, never do. Yet there seemed no other way of accounting for the signature: so, it must be got rid of.

One other point Lushmoor had to decide. Should he tell Preen? Ever since Lady Sallerton's illness Preen had, Lushmoor thought, shown symptoms of antipathy towards Sir Oscar. If His Excellency had also noticed them, he probably interpreted them as reactions to his own sarcasms and mordant criticisms. Lushmoor, however, suspected a deeper source; for he knew that Preen, like himself, had felt the governor's treatment of his wife to be callous if not caddish. If Preen were now told of His Excellency's somnambulism, could he be relied upon in his present mood to keep the matter to himself? Or would he sooner or later retail it as a tit-bit of gossip in the club or at the police mess? The latter eventuality was certainly not impossible, so Lushmoor decided to run no chances and to keep his lips sealed.

In coming to this decision, he was quite unaware that the Police, in liaison with Preen, were still intermittently interested in the riddle of the Nomi signatures. The Detective Branch indeed, not unnaturally, suspected their authorship to be associated with that of the pseudonymous Tom, Dick and Harry entries. The two young men known to have been responsible for the latter admitted it without demur; but, asked whether they had ever taken any other liberties with the calling-book, they answered 'No'.

Although this reply was believed it was decided, with usual police thoroughness, to subject the two young men to a test. Two Assistant Superintendents were detailed to engage them in conversation at the next Government. House reception and to report their reactions when, by pre-arrangement, Preen should announce the name U. Nomi. The governor, so Preen assured the Commissioner, never paid attention to the announcements but shook hands mechanically with each guest as he walked by.

Preen intended, but forgot, to forewarn Lushmoor of this experiment. Consequently, when the day of the party arrived and Preen, amid several hundred other announcements, called out 'Mr U. Nomi,' Lushmoor gave a visible start. Knowing what he knew, his next reaction was to look at the governor. Others were looking at him too; for His Excellency, having ejaculated 'Give me a chair', had subsided into it in apparent collapse. Dr Thraplow hurried to his help, but was waved angrily aside and his place taken by Dr Strathless, the Principal Medical Officer. Supported by the latter and by Preen, Sir Oscar, grey and trembling, suffered himself to be led away to his private apartments. A buzz of conversation ensued, guest asking guest whether they should stay longer or take their leave.

This point was settled by the reappearance of Dr Strathless with a message from their host. His Excellency wished the party to proceed and his guests to enjoy it as though nothing had happened. The governor's condition, Dr Strathless added, afforded no cause for alarm or concern, though he would not be able to move among them as usual or to shake hands on their departure. So, the party went on.

A bulletin issued from Government House next morning stated that the governor had suffered from heat stroke. Subsequent bulletins, however, seemed to show that this had been a euphemism, and within the week it was announced that His Excellency, accompanied by a medical officer, would be leaving for England on recuperative leave by the s.s. *Lithuania*.

In after years Lushmoor would sometimes ask himself whether he ought not to have insisted upon telling the principal medical officer of Sir Oscar's somnambulism and of his having himself written the name of U. Nomi in the calling-book. He would certainly have done so had Dr Strathless been ordinarily human and approachable. Unfortunately, however, the doctor was not of the sort that invites or accepts the confidences of a young man. When Lushmoor began with 'I think I ought to tell you, Sir,' Dr Strathless cut him short with 'There is nothing, Mr Lushmoor, that you ought to tell me, or that I ought to hear from you. Remember that you are a *Private* Secretary. Sir Oscar's medical history is well known to me from his own lips. I enjoy his complete confidence and possess ample data for correct diagnosis. It is not a case for lay observation.' Thus, effectually snubbed, Lushmoor retreated to his office in silence.

The telegram reporting Sir Oscar Sallerton's death on board ship stated, without further detail, that it followed a severe heart attack. It was the following passages in a letter to Preen from the accompanying medical officer that worried Lushmoor's conscience.

. . .It was a very sudden attack. He seemed in good form and

301

was sitting on deck when the Purser handed him a typed list of entries for the ship's sports. He glanced at it, put his hand to his heart, and fell sideways off his chair—dead. The only other piece of news is that we appear to have a mystery man aboard. When the notice inviting entries for the sports was posted up a Mr U. Nomi wrote his name down for several events. The fellow has never turned up for his heats, and now it transpires that there is nobody of that name on the Passenger List!

5

Twenty years later Sir Tobias Lushmoor, K.C.M.G., now himself a Colonial Governor, found himself at a London dinner placed next to that lively octogenarian Sir Nathan Farmley, once Colonial Secretary of Luganda.

'I'm not a bit surprised,' Sir Nathan said, 'to hear that Sallerton wasn't popular in Kongea. We were damned glad, I remember, when he got promoted out of Luganda. None of us trusted him, and there was something fishy about his suppression of our first trouble in the Sasseni area. It flared up again seven years later, when the tribesmen complained that Sallerton had somehow managed to spirit away an itinerant medicine man. What was his name now? Ah! yes, I've got it—Umfalaga Nomi. The stories were so contradictory that nobody could make head or tail of them; but they left many of us with the suspicion that the fellow might have been disposed of—well, improperly.'

'Murdered, you mean?'

'I don't know about "murdered"; but some young spiritualists, messing about with their *ouija* board one night, professed to have got a message through from Nomi. It was for Sallerton, and the young idiots posted him a copy. He never acknowledged it though; it must have been about the time he first went to Kongea.'

'What sort of a message was it?'

'I can give it you word for word, I think. It stuck in my memory because it sounded like fake Bible stuff.

By thine own hand shall it be written in the book that I have called upon thee: my name shall be declared in the congregation. The waves of the sea shall cover thee; that thou mayest go down with me into the pit.

302

Seeds of Remembrance

1

A dead man's private account book, just a bare record of payments and payees, can arouse curiosity. What dealings, now, can Jack Robinson have had with Jones, Smith and Jones, Ltd.? Artists' colourmen, of course; a very-well-known firm. Yet Jack never cared for pictures; certainly, did not paint. A gift to a niece, perhaps, or accommodation for an artist friend? But had Robinson either? What a field for speculation, for imaginings! A rich quarry, such an account book, for the inventive novelist.

It was not, however, in any such generalised terms that Eustace Brayne was thinking, as he sat in the library of Sheldrake Hall, running through items in a ledger laid open on the writing-cabinet. He had already found out what he set out to find. The annual premium on Uncle Malcolm's fire policy had been duly paid before his death. Eustace's first anxiety as inheritor of Sheldrake Hall was thereby allayed. He had not liked the look of the electric wiring in his bedroom. The old-fashioned wooden strip-casing had in several places come away from the walls, and the flex of the bed-lamp had fused while he was reading last night. The whole installation clearly demanded immediate overhaul, even if he should have to sell the place for lack of means to live in it.

That was his second anxiety and the reason why, having set his mind at rest about the insurance, he was still delving into the ledger. He wanted to know what it had cost his uncle to live there in a comfortable but modest way. This should have been easily ascertainable from a smaller book, labelled '*Monthly Summaries, Sheldrake*', that lay beside the ledger. A difficulty, however, had arisen. The monthly totals shown in the summaries did not tally with those in the ledger. The latter were often much larger and must, Eustace inferred, include expenditure unconnected with Sheldrake.

The entries in both books covered a period of some seven years, beginning in April 1928, and ending with pencil postings made, probably in bed, for the writing was shaky, during Malcolm Brayne's last illness. It was in the course of examining the handwriting, out of curiosity to see whether the onset of illness was reflected in its deterioration, that Eustace noticed that the discrepancy between the totals first became considerable in the summer months of 1933. Until then they had corresponded more or less; but thereafter there appeared in the ledger large payments which Eustace was now marking with a cross against each, with a view to more particular scrutiny on the morrow. At first sight they appeared to fall, roughly, into two classes: handsome donations to charitable institutions, and presents—or loans, maybe—to individuals.

Closing the books and shutting the cabinet, for the daylight was fast failing, Eustace mixed himself a glass of whisky and water and sat down in an armchair to think things over. His uncle had been a bit of an enigma. Malcolm Brayne was a name still remembered in the city, although it was quite ten years since he sold his agency business, built up gradually over forty strenuous years, for incorporation in an older and larger firm of world-wide ramifications. After the sale he left London for good, bought Sheldrake Hall, and there lived the life almost of a recluse, seldom being seen outside its garden and park. Business acquaintances—he had no business friends—used to say of him that he listened but never told, got but never gave, ventured and never lost. A shrewd, severe, silent, secretive, successful man, he had never been known to overstep the tapes of commercial morality.

If it was never said of him that he was honourable, that may have been because he eschewed on principle any project or transaction that might possibly involve a point of honour; such was his conception of business. Trade for him must be strictly impersonal; quite outside the humanities. When his only brother and sister-in-law, Eustace's parents, lost their lives in the sinking of the *Pindaric,* Malcolm added without comment an orphan nephew to his schedule of assets and liabilities. Unmarried, and too old to look for a wife, he found himself thus furnished with a ready-made heir. It was not inconvenient, so he made provision for a suitable upbringing. Eustace went to Ruggenham and Oxbridge; his holidays and vacations were spent in reading-parties or on educative Mediterranean cruises. Only twice or three times a year would the youth be invited to stay at No. 18 Braxington Gardens for a few days, in order to undergo avuncular inspection.

How well he remembered quailing under the scrutiny of a clean-shaven Mr Dombey in that dark, austere dining-room! The first visit to Sheldrake had been less perturbing; and on later visits he found his uncle increasingly humanised, sometimes even companionable. During one such visit conversation turned towards the future. 'Eustace,' the old man said, 'I want to see you called to the Bar before I die. You won't need to practise, if you don't want to, for I shall leave you means to live as and where you choose. But it is better to be known as a young barrister that as *a jeune riche;* safer too. Do not therefore disappoint me.' Eustace didn't. In addition to his B.A., he took an honours degree in law, and duly ate his dinners. Shortly after being called, he was offered, as the result of an Oxbridge friendship, an assistant-secretaryship in the Omnibus Assurance Company and settled down unambitiously to that.

The reason for his uncle's retirement, Eustace reflected (helping himself to more whisky), must have been the doctor's warning about his heart. He had been given ten years more to live, and the prognosis was verified almost exactly by the event. He very nearly died, though, during his second winter at Sheldrake; and it was in the summer of his recovery that Eustace first noticed an improvement in his moods and sociability. He began to talk about, and to write to, friends of whom he had never before spoken; and several of them were asked to stay at Sheldrake. Those of them that Eustace met there seemed to have one point in common. Not one of them appeared to be aware that he or she had been a friend of Malcolm's! They gave the impression of liking him now all right, but spoke of him rather (so Eustace felt) as a missionary might speak of a converted and reformed head-hunter. So also did Mrs Appleton, whom he had installed as housekeeper after telling Eustace that she was the relict of an old friend.

The thought of Mrs Appleton switched the young man's attention from past to present, from Uncle Malcolm to himself. If he could afford to live at Sheldrake, would Mrs Appleton consent to stay on as housekeeper? It would not be so easy a job for her if, as he intended, there were to be weekend parties and frequent guests. He hoped that she might, however, for the comfort and cosiness of Sheldrake was mainly of her creation. She had transmuted a barrack into a home. Look at those flowers, now! They made all the difference to the library. What were they, by the way? Walking to the mantelpiece Eustace took a near look at them. Forget-me-nots. He had never seen them before of so dark a blue: more like anchusas. They smelt too: 'a

Chinesey smell,' he said to himself, as he walked back to his chair and his drink.

He took a sip or two but did not sit down, for he no longer felt restful. What a blamed idiot he had been just now ever to think of taking on Mrs Appleton as a fixture! There would be no need of, no place for, a lady housekeeper if—no! *when*...It was late now, past midnight, but he simply must write to Isobel at once. He dashed to the writing-cabinet and reopened it.

The envelope that Peddle, the garden boy, took to the early post next morning, contained the following letter:

Isobel Darling

For five whole days I have fooled myself in a pretence of trying to forget you—as you insisted I must. My darling, it's quite impossible. Your eyes have just gazed into mine out of a vase of blue, deep-blue, forget-me-nots: so, I knew at once that you were thinking of me. Yes, yes you were—and lovingly, too, for there was a tiny twinkle in them. I promised not to call round or ring up for a full week, but I never promised not to write. It's better than telephoning for I can kiss the notepaper and send it to you. There! see those smudges? Did I ever tell you, darling, that you have a large mouth? I hate women with little mouths, but yours is perfectly perfect—and I want it so. I just can't stick being without you, and you've simply got to come and see this place that I've come into. Telegraph that you'll come to lunch the day after tomorrow, and bring Vivian with you if you must. If you don't wire, I shall meet the 11 o'clock from London all the same, for you've got to come.

Yours and yours only,

Eustace

P.S. For God's sake telegraph, or I shall go mad.

Before getting into bed Eustace caught a glimpse of himself in the mirror above the wash-hand basin. He smiled wryly at the reflection, and addressed it. 'All the same, you had forgotten her, you know; for quite three hours!'

2

Eustace's letter must have reached London in time for the afternoon delivery next day; for a telegraph boy cycled up the Sheldrake drive just as Eustace was sitting down to tea. Tearing the envelope open he read:

I will catch and Vivian miss train you mention—Isobel

He tipped the boy a florin.

In spite of expectancy the morning and afternoon had passed not too slowly for Eustace, nor without consolation. None of the formidable items in the ledger proved on a careful survey to be annually recurrent. They could only represent lump-sum disbursements, final and complete. A copy of his uncle's will and a list of his investments arrived by the midday post. The former had not been read after the funeral, having to be recovered from a safe deposit; but the lawyers had previously told him the gist. Everything was left to him and unconditionally. The investments totalled considerably more than he had anticipated.

Even after deduction of death duties he would certainly have the wherewithal to live at Sheldrake. A third enclosure to the lawyers' letter was the copy of one received by them a few days before his uncle's death. It was in his handwriting, written in pencil, but without date or signature. The envelope, they said, had been addressed to them by some uneducated person, to judge by the spelling; probably a servant or nurse. The letter read strangely but seemed to call for no action either by him or them.

To Messrs. Lurgoyne and Bidmore
Gentlemen
Assisted by a horticultural phenomenon I have checked up on all invisible debts incidentally incurred by me in the course of my career. I have liquidated them in full; although none of them would receive cognizance from law or custom. If, after my demise, any claims should be lodged with you or my heir, you are to reject them out of hand. My audit has been exhaustive and final. Please to furnish a copy of this letter to my nephew: I am too weak to write myself.
Yours faithfully,

'So that,' muttered Eustace, 'accounts for those ledger entries. The old chap has been doling out conscience money; some fifteen thousand pounds in all, if I have totted them up right. I hope the recording angel has made equivalent postings to his credit! Anyhow I come in for a clean inheritance: not that I should have worried much where the splosh came from anyway. Why, who's that coming up the drive? Oh! the parson, damn it!'

The Rev James Forthwright promised not to stay long. He was calling to explain that he could not accede to the late Mr Brayne's request that a proverb should be engraved on his tombstone.

'A proverb?'

'Yes. "*It's never too late to mend.*" When I visited him during his first illness, three years ago, he said that he supposed I had come to expound to him the comforts of purgatory, and that he intended to leave instructions for that proverb to be engraved on his tombstone. I had of course to explain that whatever conception one may have of it, and our Articles of Religion do no more than repudiate the Romish one, Purgatory certainly cannot be comfortable. When Mr Brayne objected that he understood the word "purgatory" to be derived from a Latin expression meaning a "second chance" I realised that his knowledge of languages was as defective as his ideas of Church doctrine.'

'He never had any proper schooling,' Eustace interposed; 'he was an entirely self-made man. Rather wonderful, I think.'

'Very,' assented the vicar, 'but I wanted to warn you that he may have left instructions about that proverb; though I impressed upon him that amends must be made in this life so far as repentance, grace and opportunity may render them possible.'

'Well, I have proof here in my pocket that he took your counsel to heart, Vicar. Read this letter which the lawyers have sent me.'

Mr Forthwright read it slowly, and with a puzzled expression.

'H'm. Rather lacking in humility, I fear. Not exactly a troubled spirit or a broken and contrite heart.'

'What can he have meant by assistance from a horticultural phenomenon, I wonder?'

'I don't know, I'm sure; but he was always very proud of his garden here, and most generous in providing flowers for the altar. Regarded them as proxies perhaps,' added the vicar with a touch of bitterness, 'for he never came near it himself. Ah! and now I come to think of it, he made a most peculiar suggestion to me one day.'

'What was that?'

'He asked whether he should send a bunch of forget-me-nots for the confessional! I feared that he was being flippant; but his expression told me that the offer was made in all seriousness.'

'I never knew him anything else but serious,' Eustace commented, as Mr Forthwright rose to take his leave, 'but I quite agree with you about not putting that proverb on his tombstone. Many thanks for coming to tell me about it. Well, goodbye, Vicar, and I'll tell young

Peddle to continue taking down flowers to the church. You will see me there sometimes, though I'm afraid that I'm not too regular.'

After the parson's departure Eustace began a tour of the garden. He was not much of a gardener himself, but knew enough to appreciate that its condition and appearance reflected very creditably on Halden and young Peddle. It was while he was examining the timber supports of the fruit-cage, reported by Halden to be rotten, that he saw Mrs Appleton coming down the cinder-path, presumably in search of him.

'Oh, there you are, Mr Eustace. I've come to ask whether you'll let me have the key of the bookcase cupboard in the library. I placed your uncle's diary there until we should be lighting the hot-water stove; for I promised him to see it burnt. The sweep has been such a long time coming, but he's been this morning and the stove is already lit.'

Eustace hesitated a moment before replying. 'That's all right, Mrs Appleton,' he said, 'but I rather think that as executor and sole legatee I ought to have a glance through the diary first. I'll do so tonight; it'll keep me employed. And, by the way, Mrs Appleton, there'll be a lady coming to lunch tomorrow: so, will you please tell them to have the east room ready?'

'Certainly, I will, Mr Eustace—and, er, perhaps I ought to take this opportunity of saying that I shall have to leave you and Sheldrake this autumn. I shall be sad to do so, but I have to make a home for my mother and younger sister. It was so kind of your uncle to buy me an annuity. It will make our combined resources sufficient for us to live comfortably in a quiet way.'

'A due return for services rendered, Mrs Appleton. You certainly made my uncle very happy here. It's quite different now from when he first came.'

'Thank you, Mr Eustace, I've certainly tried to do my best; but I shan't be quite happy in my mind until that diary is burnt, as he told me.'

'Oh! You needn't worry about that. I promise to let you have it by Sunday, at latest.'

'Thank you; and now I'll go and give orders about the lady. I hope she'll like Sheldrake. It has great charm, hasn't it?'

The question was not intended for reply. Mrs Appleton turned down the grass path between the espaliers and was soon lost to sight. It annoyed Eustace to suspect that he may have blushed a little when telling her of Isobel's visit on the morrow.

On the way back to the house he noticed in one of the borders a clump of the dark-blue forget-me-nots. They did not look so attractive as in the vase last night, and were in fact beginning to go to seed. The blue was almost black in the dusk.

During dinner he read a detective story: a poor one, he thought, but it served to pass the time and keep him from eating too fast. He took coffee in the library and, while the cup was cooling, rummaged in the cupboard for the diary. He found it, a large and heavy volume, and sitting down in the armchair placed it on his knee, lit a cigar and began sipping his coffee. As he did so something fell from the book on to the floor at his side. He picked it up and replaced it: a pressed and dried dark-blue forget-me-not with leaves and stalk.

3

Although the word 'Diary' was embossed in gilt lettering on the cover the volume did not prove to be a diary in any proper sense. On the front page was written in capital letters '*NOTES OF FINAL AUDIT AND ADJUSTMENT*'; and on the second, at its top '*LEONARD AND DAPHNE DE HEAVILAND, £500*'.

Turning over the pages Eustace found a series of paragraphs or chapters, varying from one to fifteen pages long, each similarly headed by a name, or names, and a figure in pounds, shillings and pence. With considerable curiosity he set himself to read the first note or chapter, parts of which may be here reproduced.

Mrs Heaviland's letter (undated: Takeokuta postmark 7 Jan 1933) arrived 9.2.33, opened 3.3.33, *i.e.* after my recovery, which doctors thought improbable. Vicar's visit was about middle February. I never attend church, but he said it was his duty visit all sick persons. Read something from prayer-book about repentance and declaring debts: asked if I had made a will—no business of his, whatever's in book. Got on to future life. Argument. Doesn't know what life is: exercise of will, planning and achieving. Worms, weeds, etc., alive in sense only that they grow: they don't live. If no exercise of will after death it is extinction. (★★★★★) Agree strict man of business must make final audit, close his books before dying. Prayer-book right there. (★★★★★) Self-made man owes nobody nothing (*sic*); must liquidate obligations. Mrs Heaviland's letter clinches matter. Paste it in here:

Sir

My husband died in Takeokuta hospital yesterday of cerebral

malaria. You killed him by persuading him to come at his age to this hellish climate. He did good work for you: this was your return. He spoke loyally of you to the last, for he was blind to your callousness. On the last day but one he made me promise to send you enclosed packet of seeds to try in your greenhouse. The native name for them is 'seeds of remembrance', and they come from blue flowers on Mount Keriapalu. He told me to tell you this. For myself I hope that you may find in them the seeds of remorse.

Faithfully,

D. Heaviland

Language of hysteria. True, I got Josiah Pagworth offer him job with Cinchona Plantations. Was crocking up in my office and I wanted promote young Chidworth. (★★★★★) Many people older than Heaviland survive in Kongea. Mosquito, not me, responsible. Paste in my reply.

Madam

I regret your husband's death. Had he not left my service for better-paid employment you as his widow would have received a gratuity of £500 under my Scheme AQ for compassionate grants. I have decided to stretch a point in recognition of his past satisfactory work for me and enclose a draft for that amount on the General and Eastern Bank, Takeokuta Branch. Please sign and return enclosed receipt form. I thank you for the packet of seed; your late husband's wishes in regard to them will be respected.

Yours faithfully,

M. Brayne

Mrs Heaviland's reply says she will not touch tainted money: has endorsed draft to order of Medical Mission. No matter: her gift not mine. All square with Heavilands. Seeds came up. Flowers like forget-me-nots but darker. (★★★★★) Sneezed after smelling; effect like snuff. Brain cleared: memory too better. Hence perhaps native name; they know more about herbs than us. Specimen pressed and pasted on next page.

So much for the first entry. Eustace sat on reading others well into the small hours. It amazed him what things his uncle had remembered. Some recipients of his cheques or postal orders must have thought him crazy. A sixpenny stamp, for example, was sent to a Mr

Jones who had once lent him a pencil that he forgot to return. But among trivial items there occurred now and again entries that struck Eustace as sinister or even ugly. The cruelty to a dog, for instance, that was atoned for by a cheque of £100 to the R.S.P.C.A. At irregular intervals the succession of notes was broken by paragraphs headed 'PROGRESS REPORT'. One of the earlier ones ran as follows.

Halden has succeeded in raising more of the Heaviland seedlings. They flower better if planted out in the open. I find from the gazetteer that Keriapalu is nearly 10,000 ft. high, and night temperatures must be cold. The assistance lent by the flowers to my audit is most valuable. I had completely forgotten about that deal with Mabelson. He was a fool to accept my offer, but I was unable to treat his letter otherwise than as an acceptance. He died penniless, I believe, but without wife or dependants.

The clock striking two as he read this, Eustace decided to leave till tomorrow the remainder of the case-notes; but curiosity compelled him to find and peruse the other progress reports. They were easier to read than the notes, being free of contractions and abbreviations. The name of Greville Mabelson recurred in nearly all of them, but his case appeared to defy settlement. Here are some excerpts:

The flowers are helping Mabelson more than me. They make me remember his appearance too well. I had forgotten till now that he said to me 'Someday, Brayne, you will regret this. . .'

I shall have to give up smelling the flowers. They focus my attention only on Mabelson, and he has left no successors or representatives. . .

Mabelson keeps breaking in on me, even without the flowers. I seem to see and hear him in the room with me: a silly, senile illusion. Despite him I am completing all other settlements . . .

The final progress report may be quoted in full.

The settlement is complete. Happily; for my strength is giving out and the end is near. I have told Mrs Appleton to burn this book after my death. The final certificate at its end I will sign tomorrow. My will provides all necessary guidance for my executors. The settlements herein recorded are by me and for me alone. I meant to add a codicil to my will commanding that the book be placed with me in my coffin, but it is too late now. No matter; it can be cremated separately. It is ridiculous of Mabelson to say that he and I will meet tomorrow and that he forgives me. Forgiveness is no settlement, and I will not have it.

Before putting the book away and going to bed, Eustace looked for the 'final certificate'. It was there all right—but unsigned.

4

After breakfast next morning Eustace asked Mrs Appleton whether she had been present at his uncle's death.

'Probably,' she replied, 'but none of us could tell the exact moment of his passing. He went so peacefully. Oh! Mr Eustace, I was so surprised and thankful, for all the morning he had been so restless and strange.'

'Strange? In what way?'

'Well, he kept telling me to take the diary away after calling for it, and then bidding me bring it back again. Six or seven times this happened and all the while he seemed to be talking with someone, though his voice was so low as to be inaudible. Then at about midday he scribbled some capital letters in pencil on a page near the end of the book, and sank back exhausted. He never seemed to regain consciousness, and died during the afternoon. Just faded away.'

'What were the letters he wrote? Could you see?'

'Oh! just a jumble of two or three. They didn't spell anything.'

'Thank you, Mrs Appleton. I wonder if you'd mind coming into the library for a moment, and showing me whereabouts in the diary he wrote those letters?'

They walked across the hall and, as they did so, a strong scent of flowers was wafted in from the open door. In it Eustace sensed something Chinesey, like a faint smell of joss-stick. 'There,' said Mrs Appleton, pointing to a page near the end of the diary, 'it looks like "E. & O.E.", doesn't it?'

'Yes, a well-known commercial abbreviation: *Errors and Omissions Excepted*. You can take the book away now and burn it, Mrs Appleton. Many thanks.'

5

It remains only to record that Miss Isobel Paynton came, as arranged, to Sheldrake; saw, and was conquered. She and Eustace were married in October. As they sat, one December evening, over a log fire he told her about Uncle Malcolm's diary.

313

'You must tell Halden not to raise any more of those flowers,' she said.

'But why not?'

'Well, you see, darling, one always remembers the nice things that happen. But there are bound to be other things too. I shouldn't like to be married to a man, or you, darling, to a woman, who couldn't sometimes conveniently forget!'

Seated One Day at the Organ

1

While playing out the last hymn at evensong in the Abbey yesterday the organist was seen to collapse and fall forward over the console. A church warden and two choirmen hastened to his assistance; and, having announced that the collection would be taken at the doors, Canon Glenside closed the service forthwith by pronouncing the Benediction. Since his appointment to the organ last year Mr R. Fulstowe, F.R. C.O., has effected great improvement in the Abbey music, and we are happy to record that his condition last night was reported as one of rapid recovery.

Thus, the *Scarminster Mercury* of 15th October 1931. A dull enough paragraph! Little description and no story. Indeed, the canon had himself written and communicated it, in an anxiety to forestall the curiosity of reporters. For the happening had been ugly, and of a sort that none who were present can ever forget.

Hell had been loosed on their ears by a sprawling, immobile, surpliced body whose hands, elbows and forehead lay over, and at many points upon, the keys of three manuals. In its lunge forward a knuckle had knocked against the pneumatic piston that gives voice to the full organ, and the resultant blare was insufferable. A volume of Bach's fugues too had fallen on to the pedals and depressed half an octave of them. The whole church was aquake; the pews quivered. Many of their occupants pressed fingers into their ears; all of them glared protestingly towards the console, and at the inert sagging figure there huddled. The startled faces of the choristers resembled those of gargoyles. Although to sit still among such pandemonium was horrible, nobody stirred. Except for one man, and he, mercifully, with the sense and knowledge to act. Tearing apart the transept curtains verger Rustley pounced upon and turned the stopcock of the hydraulic bellows.

A second later the mad fury of sound wailed into thudding silence. Thudding, because every ear throbbed with a quickened and disordered heartbeat. Then it was that Canon Glenside stuttered out his notice about the offertory and gave the Benediction. The choir retreated to the vestry in distracted groups of three or four, forgetting to form file, while the congregation hurried to the doors without waiting for its recession. Never had the stately order of an Abbey service been so interrupted and truncated.

2

Canon Glenside called on his organist early next morning, 'But you *must* tell me, Fulstowe,' he was saying, 'what overtook you so suddenly. The doctor, you say, cannot account for it. Well, naturally I have to satisfy myself, and you, I suggest, yourself, that there is no possibility of another such exhibition; for I can call it no less. It was quite horrible; the worst sort of advertisement for our Abbey services. Hints are already abroad, no doubt unjustly, of a lapse from sobriety. Surely you must see, don't you, the necessity of a full understanding between us, whatever is said to or by the public?'

Fulstowe rose from his chair, walked to the fireplace and kicked a large lump of coal that lay in the grate. Then turning slowly round he faced the canon with an expression at once unhappy and quizzical. 'Why, of course, Canon, I want to explain; very much so. But the difficulty is that I can't explain the explanation. In point of fact, I saw and felt something that couldn't have been there!'

'H'm,' grunted the canon. 'Well, anyhow, you'd better tell me what you thought you saw and felt. Though, mind you, I don't at all like the idea of a person having hallucinations in a consecrated building.'

'Very well, I'll try. As it happens the source of my hallucinations—if you like to call them that, and I hope to goodness you're right—was something that has never been consecrated. I know that as a fact, for it wasn't in the Abbey until Saturday.'

'Do you mean that Sapstead memorial tablet? It's to be dedicated in the near future. I didn't realise that you could see it from the organ.'

'One can't. No, I was alluding to the mirror above the console. You will remember my telling you that the mercury was perishing at the back of the old one, and that you suggested my looking around for a cheap replacement. Walking down Raymond Street on Thursday I saw the very thing we needed in that second-hand furniture shop— Mortimer's, isn't it?—and I bought it for only eighteen-and-six. Rustley helped me to screw it up after lunch on Saturday. It fitted almost exactly: even Rustley approved, and you know what he is.'

'My wife has picked up a good thing or two at Mortimer's,' the canon remarked, 'but what has your purchase to do with your collapse yesterday?'

'I was just coming to that. At Mattins on Sunday I was at once struck by the clearness of the reflections in the glass; they seemed to me almost—what shall I say?—three-dimensional. My own image looked as though it were some actual person peering down at me through the frame. The face was rather unshaven too, but on touching my chin I found it as smooth as usual. As a matter of fact, I'd put a new blade in my safety razor that morning. Then during the prayer for the church militant, the reflection appeared to shake its head at me, although I felt myself to be sitting quite motionless. The thing had begun to get on my nerves, so I made up my mind not to look at the glass again. I didn't either, until the service was over and I was locking up the keyboard.'

'And what then?' the canon rapped out, for the organist had ceased speaking and appeared to be lost in thought.

'What then? Why, it smiled at me and—and it had a gold filling in one of the front teeth.' At this point Fulstowe jerked his head up and round with a forced laugh. 'Well, as you can see, Canon, I haven't! If you will excuse me a moment I will slip into the dining-room for a nip of brandy. I don't feel too good.'

The canon's face reddened at this interruption. He was a teetotaller. Would he have to look for a new organist? Most unfortunate, if so, for this one played well and got so much out of the choir. Still, if the fellow took to seeing things in the Abbey and to nips of brandy within half an hour of breakfast, it would become a plain duty to...

At this point the clerical conscience was relieved by the reappearance of its disturber and an immediate resumption of his tale.

'Sorry, Canon, but I never got a wink of sleep last night, and am all to pieces this morning. Well, at evensong I couldn't help throwing an occasional glance at the mirror while playing the first voluntary. It's my habit to do so. To begin with everything was as usual. Then gradually there seemed to be reflected in it a sort of view.'

'The choir-stalls, I presume,' the canon muttered impatiently, shuffling his feet on the rug.

'No; an outdoor view. The front of some country house with turrets at either end and a square tower in the middle. I saw the outline first during the Absolution, and it gained in distinctness every time I glanced at it. By the middle of the first lesson, it was as though I peeped through a small window on to a real scene. It was a terribly queer sensation, and during the second lesson a curious development took place. My own reflection which was in the forefront of what I saw began to recede; to be becoming part of the picture, as it were. I felt too as though I were being dragged forward. It was only by a great effort of concentration that I managed to accompany the anthem, and I dared not trust myself to look at the glass during the following prayers and hymn.

'When you began the sermon, however, I gave way to my curiosity and took another look. As I did so, the whole prospect seemed to move towards me; and as a result, the two end turrets passed out of view and the central tower grew larger and larger. At its middle first-floor window I could now see my own head and surpliced shoulders, small at first but returning to life-size as the window came nearer and nearer; so near at last that the top and bottom of the tower were out of sight and only the window remained. It was then that I became aware that the figure was no longer mine Surplices do not have collars and buttons; what it was wearing was an old-fashioned nightshirt.

'Nor was the face mine, or I hoped not. There were dark rings under the eyes, the cheeks were yellowish and the eyebrows grey: the chin was unshaven. Through the crack between the lips, I could just see the gold-stopped tooth that I had seen after Mattins. Its hands were now visible, the fingers clutching the window-sill with tips bent over it. Suddenly two things gripped my attention. First, that the finger-tips protruded not merely over the window-sill but over the frame of the mirror itself. They were nearer to me than the reflecting surface! Second, that the head which had usurped the place of mine was bleeding profusely from the neck. Before I had time to consider these developments, which nevertheless set me shivering, you were ending your sermon with the doxology and giving out the hymn.

'As I began playing it out, I noticed what looked like a splash of blood on the swell manual and in my surprise glanced upwards at the mirror. I saw there a throat slit from ear to ear and oozing great clots of blood. I gave a gasp and at that very moment the clawing hands shot forward from the mirror frame and downward to clutch my shoulders. It was then that I must have fainted; I felt an icy clamp round my neck and everything went black. Oh God! I must have another drink.'

The canon rose with a frown and stared aimlessly out of the window. He was thankful that Fulstowe had left the room, though disapproving his purpose. It afforded time to think of what to say. He must not be too sympathetic, for the possible necessity of the organist's dismissal pressed uncomfortably on his mind. On the other hand, he must not appear callous or offhand, for the man had obviously suffered a catastrophe of imagination for which he deserved pity. Really, a most difficult situation to find oneself in! What should, what *could* he say? In his quandary he grabbed and crushed with his right hand a frond of a fern that languished in a flower-pot on the window table. A knock at the hall door caused him to turn round with a start; he tore the leaf right off and dropped it, crumpled, onto the carpet.

The knock also brought Fulstowe back from the dining-room, apparently quite recomposed. 'Who's there?' he said. 'Come in.'

Verger Rustley did so; and, seeing the canon, addressed him obsequiously.

'I beg your pardon, Sir, but I didn't know as Your Reverence were here. I wanted a short word with Mr Fulstowe; but it can well wait, and I'll step in later when he's disengaged.'

'No, Rustley, don't go,' the canon smiled, grateful for the interruption; 'you'll be pleased, I'm sure, to find Mr Fulstowe so quickly recovered from his collapse yesterday evening.'

'Indeed, I am, Sir; especially as having been and had a collapse myself, a thing that's never happened before. Yes, Sir, this very morning. When I was opening up the abbey, it was. "Why you're looking as white as a corpse," said Mrs Rustley to me when I got back to breakfast. Couldn't eat much of it either.'

'I'm very sorry to hear it, Rustley,' the canon rejoined with some asperity. 'I had always regarded you as dependable. Faints and collapses denote a lack of self-control, you know. One has to keep a grip on things.'

'I'm far from boasting of it, your reverence; but anyone who saw what I saw—or what Mr Fulstowe saw yesterday, if I may make a guess—would come near to fainting. I feel sure of that.'

At this the organist broke in with eager interest; 'What did you see, Rustley? Nothing to do with the looking-glass we screwed up on Saturday, I hope?'

'Ah! Then you *did* see it. I thought as much and said so to Mrs Rustley. Yes, Sir, blood dripping from that glass and splashed all over the organ lid. Leastways that's what it looked like, but when I came to from my fainting—for I never could abear the sight of blood—it was all gone and no mess at all to clean up. Optical illusion is what Mrs Rustley calls it. Anyhow it wasn't that as I came to see Mr Fulstowe about, though it has to do with the mirror. Mortimer's have taken it back.'

'Taken it back?' exclaimed Fulstowe. 'Why, I paid them for it and have got the receipt.'

'Yes, Sir, but it appears that it wasn't theirs to sell. Young Mr Clarence Mortimer came along himself to explain, and asked me to hand you back the money. Here it is, Sir, seven half-crowns and two sixpences: that's right, I think? His men were taking it down as I came away, and they'll put the old one back till we get a better.'

'Thank God for that.' Fulstowe muttered under his breath, and then aloud: 'What explanation did young Mortimer give? It seems a funny way of doing business.'

'He said as it wasn't *their* fault but that of the auctioneer at the Curdlestone sale. He'd never had the glass removed from Sir Peregrine's dressing-room, though it was one of the pieces to be reserved. So, Mortimer's men took it away, thinking it part of the suite they'd bought. And a rare shindy Sir Peregrine kicked up, he said, when he found it gone. His favourite shaving-glass, as he'd used since at college and had given orders to be sent down to Rodneybury! That's the family seat in Northshire, as you know, Sir; where Sir Peregrine's now gone to.'

Canon Glenside, not relishing the role of listener and much annoyed that two of his staff should have been seeing things in the Abbey, had been restive throughout the preceding conversation and now seized the opportunity for interruption and contradiction. 'You are quite wrong, Rustley,' he said, 'in speaking of Rodneybury as the Randhams' family seat. The family was at Curdlestone long before Rodneybury was built. His ancestors would turn in their graves if they knew of the ruin which Sir Peregrine has brought on his inheritance. He will only have plunged deeper into disaster by selling the old estate and retaining such a big place as Rodneybury. However, that's no affair of ours; and I want you, Rustley, to come down with me to the abbey and point out the places where the south aisle roof is said to be leaking. It wouldn't be good for you and Mr Fulstowe to get talking together about your optical illusions. The sooner foolish things are forgotten the better. What do you keep looking at your wrists for?'

Mr Rustley appeared uneasy. 'I was afraid for a moment, Sir, that blood had got on to the cuffs.'

'Nonsense,' snapped the canon, now righteously indignant; 'come along with me at once. And as for you, Fulstowe, I advise you to put in some hard practice on Bach's fugues. You'll find them a wholesome antidote to hallucinations. Good morning.'

4

Seven years later Dr Richard Fulstowe, Mus.Doc., F.R.C.O., was appointed organist of Wintonbury Cathedral. In his rooms above the gateway to the cloisters we find him one morning sitting at breakfast, with the *Morning Courier* on the table beside his coffee-cup. Having helped himself to porridge he glanced at the pictures on the front page. There are two of them: one of a country mansion and the other of an elderly man. 'Good God!' he mutters; for he instantly recognises both, though he has known neither. The headline underneath is 'BANKRUPT BARONET DEAD', and the letterpress runs as follows:

"The inquest is being held today on the body of Sir Peregrine Randham, Bart., which was found yesterday morning on the floor of his dressing-room at Rodneybury Towers (pictured above), with the throat cut. It lay before his accustomed shaving-mirror and was clad only in a nightshirt. The deceased baronet (photo inset) had been involved in bankruptcy proceedings, as recently reported in these columns. Sir Peregrine will be remembered as a staunch patron of the Turf, and as owner of Red Blade, the winner of the Grinfield Plate in 1929."

It chanced that on the afternoon of the day when Dr Fulstowe read this at breakfast Canon Glenside was also in Wintonbury, attending a *synod*. Thus, it was that the two happened to meet at tea-time in the lounge of Caius Hotel. The canon having a *Morning Courier* in his hand, Dr Fulstowe's conversational gambit was inevitable.

'But, my dear Fulstowe,' the canon remonstrated after five minutes, 'surely you cannot ask me to believe that you saw the ghost of a man who had more than seven years yet to live?'

'Not exactly his ghost, perhaps.'

'Or that a mirror could reflect a place two hundred miles distant from it and an event seven years before its occurrence?'

'Well, canon, again not exactly.'

LEONAUR

ALSO FROM LEONAUR
AVAILABLE IN SOFTCOVER OR HARDCOVER WITH DUST JACKET

MR MUKERJI'S GHOSTS *by S. Mukerji*—Supernatural tales from the British Raj period by India's Ghost story collector.

KIPLINGS GHOSTS *by Rudyard Kipling*—Twelve stories of Ghosts, Hauntings, Curses, Werewolves & Magic.

THE COLLECTED SUPERNATURAL AND WEIRD FICTION OF WASHINGTON IRVING: VOLUME 1 *by Washington Irving*—Including one novel 'A History of New York', and nine short stories of the Strange and Unusual.

THE COLLECTED SUPERNATURAL AND WEIRD FICTION OF WASHINGTON IRVING: VOLUME 2 *by Washington Irving*—Including three novelettes 'The Legend of the Sleepy Hollow', 'Dolph Heyliger', 'The Adventure of the Black Fisherman' and thirty-two short stories of the Strange and Unusual.

THE COLLECTED SUPERNATURAL AND WEIRD FICTION OF JOHN KENDRICK BANGS: VOLUME 1 *by John Kendrick Bangs*—Including one novel 'Toppleton's Client or A Spirit in Exile', and ten short stories of the Strange and Unusual.

THE COLLECTED SUPERNATURAL AND WEIRD FICTION OF JOHN KENDRICK BANGS: VOLUME 2 *by John Kendrick Bangs*—Including four novellas 'A House-Boat on the Styx', 'The Pursuit of the House-Boat', 'The Enchanted Typewriter' and 'Mr. Munchausen' of the Strange and Unusual.

THE COLLECTED SUPERNATURAL AND WEIRD FICTION OF JOHN KENDRICK BANGS: VOLUME 3 *by John Kendrick Bangs*—Including twor novellas 'Olympian Nights', 'Roger Camerden: A Strange Story', and ten short stories of the Strange and Unusual.

THE COLLECTED SUPERNATURAL AND WEIRD FICTION OF MARY SHELLEY: VOLUME 1 *by Mary Shelley*—Including one novel 'Frankenstein or the Modern Prometheus', and fourteen short stories of the Strange and Unusual.

THE COLLECTED SUPERNATURAL AND WEIRD FICTION OF MARY SHELLEY: VOLUME 2 *by Mary Shelley*—Including one novel 'The Last Man', and three short stories of the Strange and Unusual.

THE COLLECTED SUPERNATURAL AND WEIRD FICTION OF AMELIA B. EDWARDS *by Amelia B. Edwards*—Contains two novelettes 'Monsieur Maurice', and 'The Discovery of the Treasure Isles', one ballad 'A Legend of Boisguilbert' and seventeen short stories to cill the blood.